SHANNON
SAGA

City of Angels

SHANNON
SAGA

City of Angels

TRACIE PETERSON
and
JAMES SCOTT BELL

BETHANYHOUSE
MINNEAPOLIS, MINNESOTA 55438

City of Angels
Copyright © 2001
Tracie Peterson and James Scott Bell

Cover by Koechel Peterson

Published by Bethany House Publishers
A Ministry of Bethany Fellowship International
11400 Hampshire Avenue South
Bloomington, Minnesota 55438
www.bethanyhouse.com

Printed in the United States of America by
Bethany Press International, Bloomington, Minnesota 55438

Library of Congress Cataloging-in-Publication Data

Peterson, Tracie.
    City of Angels / by Tracie Peterson and James Scott Bell.
        p.   cm. — (Shannon saga ; 1)
    ISBN 0-7642-2418-2
    1. Los Angeles (Calif.)—Fiction. 2. Women lawyers—Fiction 3. Young
women—Fiction. 4. Aunts—Fiction. I. Bell, James Scott. II. Title.
PS3566.E7717 C58   2001
813'.54—dc21
                                                          00-012017

TRACIE PETERSON is an award-winning speaker and writer who has authored over thirty-five books, both historical and contemporary fiction. Her latest book, *A Slender Thread*, is a compelling family saga. Tracie and her family make their home in Kansas.

Visit Tracie's Web site at: http://members.aol.com/tjpbooks

JAMES SCOTT BELL is a Los Angeles native and former trial lawyer who now writes full time. He is the author of several legal thrillers; his novel *Final Witness* won the 2000 Christy Award as the top suspense novel of the year. He and his family still reside in the City of Angels.

Books By James Scott Bell

Circumstantial Evidence
Final Witness
Blind Justice

Books By
Tracie Peterson & James Scott Bell

SHANNON SAGA
City of Angels

Books By Tracie Peterson

Controlling Interests
Entangled
Framed
The Long-Awaited Child
A Slender Thread
Tidings of Peace

WESTWARD CHRONICLES

A Shelter of Hope
Hidden in a Whisper
A Veiled Reflection

RIBBONS OF STEEL*

Distant Dreams
A Hope Beyond
A Promise for Tomorrow

RIBBONS WEST*

Westward the Dream
Separate Roads
Ties That Bind

YUKON QUEST

Treasures of the North

*with Judith Pella

Pride still is aiming at the bless'd abodes.
Men would be Angels, Angels would be Gods.
Aspiring to be Gods if Angels fell,
Aspiring to be Angels men rebel.

—ALEXANDER POPE
An Essay on Man

Prologue

BOSTON 1893

KIT SHANNON KNEW that the man seated on the platform held her life in his gnarled hands. Breathing in deeply, she
fought back tears.

Thirteen years old, frightened, and alone, Kit knew her only
hope was to keep her wits about her. Mama always said that a
person had to keep herself in one piece when everything around
her was falling apart. Oh, how she wanted Mama by her side now,
needed her, but that would never happen again.

Yesterday her mama had been buried in the cold rain in a
nameless graveyard. And now, without father or mother, Kit had
been thrust into this strange place they called a courtroom for what
they told her was a "resolution of her situation."

The judge who sat so regally above her had thick gray hair and
eyes as cold as the sleet pounding outside. Though his appearance
made her tremble, she reminded herself of something Papa once
told her. *"The law is a wonderful thing, daughter. This country was*

founded on the principle of justice for all, rich or poor, weak or pow-erful. And all justice comes from God."

So, Kit reasoned, this judge must represent justice, and in some way God himself. That was enough to give her the courage to hold back her tears. Surely this man would see to it that Kit was taken care of, that the small amount of property and belongings her mother owned would come to her and that the men—called law-yers—who had cheated her mother would be kept from doing the same thing to her.

It also comforted Kit to tightly clutch the Bible she had brought with her. Papa's Bible, the one from which he used to read to her and preach the Gospel to the unsaved. In a small but meaningful way, holding his Bible made her feel as though Papa was there with her.

"All right, then," the judge growled. His voice was deep and resonant, tinged with a strange anger that confused Kit. "I see this girl has been declared a ward of the court, is that right?"

What's a ward of the court? Kit thought. *Why am I that?*

"That's right, judge," the man with the sticky hair said. This was the man who, a few minutes before, had told Kit he would be her lawyer for this proceeding. She didn't like him. He would not look her in the eye, and he didn't ask her anything. She'd spent the previous night in a spare room in what seemed like a jail to her, even though they had called it a "house for girls." This afternoon she'd been whisked to the courtroom. The lawyer, named Smythe, had spent all of one minute talking to her before telling her to sit down and stay quiet.

"Well, then, let's hear it," the judge demanded, looking impa-tient.

"The family has recommended St. Catherine's," Smythe said.

St. Catherine's? What family?

"If that's the case, what are you wasting my time for?" said the judge. "That can all be done without me."

"There is just a little matter of the property," said Smythe.

"Well?"

"The girl's mother died intestate. Naturally a child . . ."

What is going on? Kit wanted to say, but held her tongue.

"Yes, yes," the judge said. "Is there a trust?"

"It's been done."

What's been done?

"Then there's no more to—"

"Please!" Kit heard herself shout.

The old judge seemed startled, then annoyed. "Young lady, you are not to speak."

"But I don't know what is happening to me, sir."

"You are being taken care of," the judge said. "Mr. Smythe, your attorney, will explain things to you."

But she did not want Mr. Smythe explaining anything to her. She didn't trust him. The judge was her only hope. If he did not help her now, if she was left with Smythe, she sensed it would be terrible, like falling into a dark pit with a hungry animal.

"Please help me," Kit said. If she asked politely, as her mother had taught her, surely this judge would . . .

"No more from you!" the judge snapped. "I don't see why I was dragged out here."

"We just need your signature on this document," Smythe said.

What document? Kit wondered as Smythe handed the judge a single piece of paper. What was on that paper, she did not know. What she did know was that it concerned her, and the judge—now dipping a quill pen into his inkwell and scratching his name on the paper—was not concerned about her in the least.

"That's that," the judge said. "I need a drink." And with that he stood and shambled out of the courtroom.

When he disappeared behind an austere oak door, Kit felt her hope leave with him. Smythe, a crooked smile on his face, turned to her and said, "That wasn't so bad now, was it?"

But it *was* bad, in ways she did not understand. In ways only this man and that judge, inhabiting a world that was beyond her reach or even voice, understood. Was this the great system of justice Papa had told her about?

"Better let me take that," Smythe said, reaching for her father's Bible.

"No!" Kit screamed, and without a thought of where or why, she ran as fast as she could toward the big doors that she had been led through only minutes before.

She ran as if the dark hand of death were reaching out behind her—and then she hit something big and blue.

"There, now, missy, that won't do." It was a policeman. And his hands were strong.

The realization of her fate washed over Kit in waves that threatened to take her breath. Her chest tightened. She then lifted her eyes to meet the stern expression of Mr. Smythe, who had followed. He did not look pleased with her actions.

That makes us even, Kit thought.

———

As the police carriage clacked through the streets of Boston, carrying her toward her uncertain future, Kit sat alone, the Bible still clutched to her chest. They may have taken everything else, but they would never take this from her.

Looking through the carriage window at the dark gray of the unrelenting clouds, Kit voiced a prayer. "O God," she said in a whisper, "Papa said praying is just talking, and we can talk about anything. I'm scared, God. I don't know where I'm going. I don't know what to do. Something bad has happened. . . ."

Her voice caught as she took in a deep breath and closed her eyes. "But Papa said you always make something good come out of bad. God, please do it now. Please make something good happen. Please show me what I should do now. You're all I have, God. Show me the way."

The sound of horse hooves on cobblestone streets mixed with the beat of the rain on the carriage. The wooden bench was hard underneath Kit, and the bumping of the carriage rattled her bones. *Hold fast,* she told herself. *Hold fast.*

It seemed like hours before the carriage pulled to a stop. Kit looked out the small window and saw high iron bars stretching on for what seemed like forever. In the dismal rain the place looked like a prison. Then Kit saw above the iron gate a sign that read, *ST. CATHERINE'S SCHOOL.*

"Out with you," the policeman said as he opened the carriage door. He was in a slicker and held an umbrella for her. Holding her Bible close, Kit stepped into the rain. Her feet landed in a puddle, wetting her cloth shoes.

The policeman put his hand on her shoulder and led her to the gate.

That's when she saw the angel of death.

Kit would always remember Sister Gertrude that way. In her nun's habit of blackest black and her face a mere shadow under her own umbrella, she looked like some malevolent spirit from the abyss. And as the iron gate creaked open, Kit did feel as if she were entering a tomb—her own.

"I take her from here," the nun said in a thick German accent.

The policeman said nothing as he turned away. For a moment Kit was between them, uncovered, rain pelting her relentlessly.

"Get here!" the dark nun said. She pulled Kit's arm so hard pain shot through her shoulder. "What is?" The pronunciation sounded like, *Vott iss?* Kit was momentarily confused, then felt the nun tugging at her father's Bible.

"No!" Kit shouted. She pulled the Bible closer to her breast.

The nun grabbed Kit's chin and cheeks in a viselike hand. "You vill not talk to me that vay again! I am Sister Gertrude. You vill obey me!"

Sister Gertrude let go of Kit's face and with one quick snatch took the Bible.

With a yelp and an anger she could not control, Kit reached out and grabbed the Bible with both her hands, pulling it free. She turned to run, not knowing where, but the nun caught her by the hair and pulled hard. Kit's head snapped back, fire shooting over her scalp. She felt herself falling backward, landing hard on the stones beneath her feet.

The impact jolted her arms, and the Bible flew from her hands. She sensed more than saw Sister Gertrude picking it up.

Rain blinded Kit as she looked up. Soaked and shivering, Kit heard Sister Gertrude say solemnly. "So vee haff trouble vit you. That vill end soon."

Kit heard the gates clang shut and some heavy lock click into place. Then she felt the nun grasping her hair again, pulling her to her feet. The pain was almost unbearable, but Kit was determined not to utter another sound.

In her mind, though, she was shouting, *Why, God? Why have you brought me here?*

Part One

Chapter One

"LOS ANGELEEEEZ!" the conductor yelled. "Next stop!"

Kit Shannon sat up with a start. Almost there! She reached up to force an errant strand of hair up under her straw hat and looked past her pale expression reflected in the train window to the scenery outside. More desert. It had been like this for hundreds of miles. The bustle of New York seemed but a distant memory.

I must be insane!

The words flashed into Kit's mind without warning, her heart pounding with the rhythm of the train. In just a few minutes she'd be turned loose in a world as unfamiliar to her as the tombs of Egypt.

I am crazy. *What do I know of Los Angeles? I should have stayed with Cousin Victoria and taken that teaching position in Manhattan. It was a good school and just right for an unmarried woman of twenty-three.*

Kit pushed aside her thoughts and squinted against the harsh sunlight. Was there really a city on the other side of all this dirt and sand? A city poised, as the eastern advertisements said, "to blossom in the sun"?

Would she blossom there as well? She glanced down at her simple traveling costume—a wrinkled serge suit of navy blue and a well-worn white shirtwaist—and thought she looked like anything but a blossom. Would her great aunt Freddy, whom she was to meet for the first time, be completely mortified at her appearance?

"Almost there, huh?"

Kit turned and saw a tall, leggy man standing by her seat. He looked young and dashing in his dark suit and jaunty straw hat.

"Mind if I . . . ?" He took the seat opposite her without waiting for her response and stretched out his legs. "Name's Phelps. Tom Phelps."

"How do you do?" Kit said guardedly.

"First rate. And your name?"

"Kit . . . Kathleen Shannon." She tried not to appear as nervous as she felt. Surely the man would be harmless here in such a public setting. She had heard that the western states were much more relaxed in their protocols.

"Sorry to be so forward, but that's how Tom Phelps is," he said. "First trip to Los Angeles?"

"Yes, it is."

"I could tell. Tom Phelps can always tell. It's how I make my living."

What did he want with her? Kit felt both intrigued and cautious at the same time. The man had a way of putting her at ease with his open friendliness, and yet it was this companionable spirit that also put her on guard. At least he was a momentary antidote for her anxiety over meeting Aunt Freddy and facing her new life in Los Angeles.

Without waiting for Kit to inquire, Phelps continued. "I'm a reporter for the *Los Angeles Examiner*. Ever heard of it?"

"I'm sorry, no."

"You will. It's new, owned by Mr. William Randolph Hearst. We'll give General Otis and the *Times* a run for their money."

She nodded, allowing herself to study his face as he spoke. His eyes seemed to take in everything at once.

"And what occasions your visit to our fair city, if I may ask?"

"I am coming to live with my great aunt."

"From?"

"New York."

"Quite a switch. You know, the City of Angels isn't as refined as your eastern hubbubs. We still have one boot in the Wild West."

"And where is the other boot, Mr. Phelps?"

He gave her a roguish grin. "Kicking at the new century, Miss Shannon. Do you realize it's already 1903? Doesn't it seem like yesterday that we turned the corner from the 1800s? Life moves fast these days, and people have to move fast with it or they'll find themselves run over."

"All I see out there is desolation," Kit said, glancing at the window. "I've literally watched the country change from cities and green farmlands to this dry and barren place."

"Looks can be deceiving, Miss Shannon. Remember that. There's plenty of life out there—you just need to know where to look. Me, I see plenty covering the law courts."

Kit sat up with sudden interest. "You know the courts of law?"

"Sure I do."

"What are they like?"

Phelps took a cigar from his pocket, bit off the tip, and spit it into the brass spittoon in the aisle. He took his time lighting it, then said, "Our courts are wide open, Miss Shannon. A far cry, I'd say, from what you have back East. Frontier justice, some say. But I'll tell you one little secret." He leaned forward, and Kit couldn't help but do likewise. "If you're rich," he said conspiratorially, "you can buy yourself a good lawyer. Money rides in our town, Miss Shannon. You ever murder anybody, make sure you got the money to get a good lawyer."

"I haven't any such plans, I assure you."

"Well, a word to the wise. If you ever do, hire Earl Rogers."

"Whom?"

"Best criminal lawyer in Los Angeles, Miss Shannon. Maybe the world. I've seen him perform more miracles than Moses."

Phelps took a puff on his cigar and regarded Kit closely. "Now, I've been sitting here revealing my charming self for a couple of minutes, and I haven't seen those eyes of yours light up once. Until just now, that is. Why is that, Miss Shannon?"

Kit hadn't realize how transparent she'd been. "Well . . ." she hesitated. What would he think if she told him the truth? Perhaps she would do better to completely change the subject, or better yet, close the conversation entirely.

"Come, now," he said, leaning ever closer. "Tell old Tom your secret."

She squared her shoulders and chided herself for acting like a silly schoolgirl. What did it matter if he knew the truth? Soon everyone would. "It's really no secret," she began. "I've come to Los Angeles to practice law."

His reaction couldn't have been stronger if she had revealed she was Theodore Roosevelt in a woman's dress. Phelps's mouth dropped open, and he nearly lost his cigar. His hand shot up quickly, and he saved the smoldering stogie with two fingers. The juggling act made Kit smile.

"Did you say practice law?"

"Yes, sir."

"Well, I'll be . . ." Phelps stuck the cigar back in his mouth, leaned back, and considered her as if she were a curio in a pawn shop. Finally he said, "You seem like a perfectly nice young woman, Miss Shannon. Might I give you a piece of advice?"

"Certainly," she answered.

"Go back to New York," he said.

"Go back? But why?"

"This city's no place for you. It's hard-edged, and so is the law here. You'll get eaten alive, like a purebred horse down in a field full of vultures."

"But I—"

He put a hand up. "I'm telling this to you for your own good."

Her own good? That was in the hands of God, not men.

"Thank you, Mr. Phelps, but I am going to practice law."

Phelps nodded, took another puff of his stubby cigar, then reached into his inner coat pocket and pulled out a folded piece of paper and a pencil. He started scribbling. "Kathleen Shannon, you said?"

"Yes . . ."

"With a *K* or a *C*?"

"*K*. What are you doing?"

He looked her squarely in the eye. "I want to keep your name handy, Miss Shannon, because if you ever do become a lawyer in Los Angeles, you'll be the story of the year."

Phelps put away the paper and pencil and got to his feet. Tipping his hat, he grinned. "We're almost there. I can feel the train slowing, and I still have some drinking . . . I mean, packing to do. Miss Shannon, it has been a pleasure." He offered his hand, and she took it. Then with a nod, he was gone.

The encounter had happened so fast, it almost seemed unreal. Was that how it was always going to be out here? She thought about what he had said, his warning about the city, his advice to go back. She breathed deeply, telling herself she would probably have lots of moments like this, where doubts might creep in. She would have to be ready. But was she?

Kit stepped off the train into a balmy breeze. The wind played havoc with her wide-brimmed hat while the sun seemed to shine right through any protection it might have offered. Everything, from sky to ground, seemed brighter than in New York.

The scene was not unlike any other depot she'd visited on this trip, and yet it was somehow completely different. The crowds teemed with all manner of customers, from the obviously poorer Indians and Mexicans to the wealthy and overdressed women of society to suit-clad men and roughhewn cowboys.

The depot itself was a strange dome-shaped creation that bore the placard, *La Grande Station*. The depot platform sprawled out alongside the track, making it clear that this was a highly trafficked station.

"Kathleen!"

Kit looked up to find a well-rounded matron furiously fanning herself with a lace handkerchief, looking rather like a humming-bird cooling itself with one wing. With her other wing she waved. Her face, while amply shaded by a fashionably large hat, gleamed with an overheated, ruddy glow. Her plump frame, clad in a teal-colored walking-out dress, was made even larger by rows of flouncing and a wide, bulky train.

Kit smiled and waved. "Aunt Freddy?"

"Goodness, child, come inside out of the sun," the woman chided and turned with her hired man for the protective shelter of the station.

Once inside, Kit found herself engulfed against an ample bosom. The embrace lasted only a moment before Aunt Freddy set her at arm's length.

"I knew it had to be you! I'm so glad I finally found you— you're more beautiful than I imagined. Almost remind me of myself when I was your age!" Her aunt surveyed her from head to toe before adding, "But word of mine, those rags will have to go. You can't mean to tell me you traveled from New York to Los Angeles wearing that!"

Kit tensed. "I'm afraid so, Aunt Freddy. It was the best I could do."

"Tut! We can always do better," Frederica Fairbank said, tipping her head back ever so slightly. "When I was your age, I couldn't have moved through the station for the crowd of young admirers who would gather. I'm telling you, fashion speaks for itself."

Kit could not suppress a smile. Frederica Stamper Fairbank had been, according to family legend, quite the coquette in her youth. She had married a wildcatter, Jasper Fairbank, even though everyone warned her he'd never amount to anything. But Freddy was a determined woman who always took matters into her own hands. Jasper wouldn't have dared to be anything but a success. He rose to oil prominence over the next forty years while Frederica took her place as a reigning queen of society, first in Texas and then in the budding metropolis that had once been known as *El pueblo de Nuestra Señora la Reina de Los Angeles*—The village of Our Lady the Queen of the Angels. Freddy inherited her husband's estate, worth over twenty million, about the time folks began calling it simply The City of Angels.

Now, according to her lengthy letters to Kit, Freddy spent her days doing charity work and her nights hosting bridge games, parties, and occasional seances. Kit could hardly imagine the latter, having no interest in Victorian *grimoire*. Apparently the practices of potion mixing and card, palm, and tea-leaf readings were as much the rage in certain circles of West Coast society as they had been back East.

"... and we'll simply put Mrs. Norris on it as soon as possible."

Kit quickly realized she'd missed her aunt's declaration. "I'm sorry. What did you say?"

Freddy looked at her with a momentary frown. "I have a seam- stress who will fit you for a more fashionable look. I'll have her come over with the latest copies of *The Delineator*. The fashions you'll find there will fit you nicely."

"That isn't necessary, Aunt Freddy. I can't afford—"

"Money is hardly the issue," Freddy proclaimed in a hushed tone. Looking at her hired man, she ordered him to find Kit's lug- gage. "Julio will see to your things." She waited until the man had gone to see to the task before leaning close to Kit. "Kathleen, we do not discuss the topic of money while in the presence of servants. Or anyone else for that matter. It simply isn't done. You are a part of my household now, and as such I will expect a certain decorum to be adhered to. No doubt you will need training along with new gowns, but I won't stand for any breech in etiquette once you are aware of the rules."

Kit felt duly chastened and looked down at her hands as a child might. By the time Julio had loaded the luggage into the one-horse surrey, however, Aunt Freddy seemed to have put the issue behind them. She now held an interest in laying out Kit's future.

It began with men.

"I know the finest eligible gentlemen in the city, my dear. We will discern those of good breeding and old eastern fortunes from those of new money and more ostentatious circumstances," Aunt Freddy said, as if the news were the most important since the tak- ing of San Juan Hill. "You shall meet them all. And I daresay, with your looks and my help, you shall have your pick."

"Aunt Freddy—"

"Marriage is the foundation of our civilization, and as pretty as you are, my dear, you're no spring chicken. A few more years of spinsterhood and you'd be expected to dress in black. What are you now, twenty-two?"

"Twenty-three," Kit replied flatly.

"Oh my. It's worse than I thought. Well, there's simply no time to waste. We'll get your wardrobe attended to, and I shall assign Corazón to you for your upkeep. She can work wonders with hair and accessories." She paused only long enough to rearrange the train of her gown before Julio started them for home.

"As soon as possible," she continued, "you must settle down and start having babies. Once you're married, with children, people will forget your delay in establishing matrimony."

Kit let out an exasperated sigh. How was she to get a word in? "Aunt Freddy—"

"I remember the day you were born. All that red hair! I knew we had a fire in the teapot, or a tempest, or whatever it is one finds in teapots. Now, one more thing, and I say this with all respect because you are an educated woman." Aunt Freddy dropped her voice, as if speaking about the dead. "You must disregard this fancy about the law."

"But, Aunt Freddy," Kit began slowly, "I thought I made clear in my letters—"

"My dear, I have only your best interests at heart."

"I know you do, but—"

"There are so many rich young men available here. It's like a field of gold nuggets. You'll never want for anything."

Kit couldn't stand it any longer. "I don't want gold, Aunt Freddy. I want to practice law!"

A small yelp squeezed out of Aunt Freddy's throat. "Scandalous! I won't have it!"

"Aunt Freddy, please try to understand."

Fanning herself furiously, Aunt Freddy replied, "I don't know what's happened to decorum. It's this age, this restless age! We can thank that cowboy in the White House, if you ask me. Getting everyone all fired up about progress, as if progress is always a good thing."

"But—"

"It isn't, let me tell you."

"Aunt Freddy, I—"

"No wonder the young have such crazy ideas. Oh! I can't imagine what your poor mother would think!"

An emotional spear pierced Kit's chest. She paused a moment before saying, "But I'm doing this for *her*, Aunt Freddy."

"My dear, your mother's death was a tragedy. I know it pains you, but—"

"My mother would be alive today if it weren't for—" The words caught in Kit's throat. She looked at her hands, which she noticed were balled into fists.

"Sweet Kathleen," Freddy sighed, patting Kit on the shoulder. "Can't you leave these things to others?"

Kit raised her head, emotion thick in her voice. "I believe this is God's will."

"And just how do you know what God's will is, young lady?"

Kit hadn't expected Aunt Freddy to be so blunt. How indeed did she know this was God's will? She had prayed, yes, and diligently. But there had never been any lightning bolt of realization. Scripture told her that God loves justice, and after what had happened to her mother, and then to Kit herself, the decision seemed inevitable.

"I'll have Madame Zindorf in for a reading," Aunt Freddy said. "You know, she can absolutely predict the future."

Kit shook her head. Her aunt was clearly a partaker in every sort of fad that promised health, beauty, or connection to the spirit world. Her stay here was going to be even more trying than she'd originally thought.

They rode in silence for several minutes. Kit wrestled against the voice of doubt her aunt had implanted in her. Thankfully, she soon found herself caught up in the sounds of the new city—horse and cow bells clanging, street vendors hawking to pedestrians, even an occasional motorcar. Buildings, a couple as tall as eight stories, rose magnificently from the street. Temples of modern commerce testified to the current economic boom—J. W. Robinson Co., The Broadway Department Store, Mullen & Bluett Fine Men's Clothiers. Kit took it all in like a child looking at pictures in an Edison Kinetoscope.

"This is so wonderful, Aunt Freddy!" Kit said. Pushing aside her lingering fears, she added with a sudden exultation, "Don't you worry about a thing. I'll clerk in a small, quiet office somewhere to start. Then I'll earn my own way, and the Fairbank fortune and name need not be affected by my actions."

Aunt Freddy's reaction remained the same. "It would be a scandal! I'd be ruined."

"Don't you worry, Auntie. If anyone tries to ruin you, I'll just take them to court!" Kit grinned broadly.

Her aunt seemed to consider her words only momentarily before rolling her eyes heavenward. "Oh, dear!"

 Chapter Two

HE MOVED THROUGH SHADOWS, unseen. Invincible.

Who would stop him? The impotent police? That was a laugh. Floating.

He had the sensation he was floating over the streets. Even as the rain fell, just as it had four nights ago, he was weightless above it.

Was he insane? No, merely on a higher plane of awareness than anyone else had ever known. And soon they would know about him. About his work. They would think him insane, but they were the ones out of touch with reality.

When he reached the doorway of the building, deserted now in the heart of the night, he rested. Like a jungle animal, attuned to every nuance and movement, every smell and flicker, he was coiled, ready.

Animal. That is what he was, after all. They all were. Everyone.

Animals in a long line of ascent. Animals with big brains.

And his was biggest of all. He would show them.

He calmed himself in the darkness, breathing rhythmically. He thought about the matter at hand.

Before it actually happened, he knew she would walk by. The same one he'd spotted three nights earlier, watched carefully two nights ago, and checked again last night. That was planning. No, more—it was ambition!

He would be like that fellow in England, the one they called Jack the Ripper. What a masterful animal he was! The world misunderstood that one—just as it misunderstood him.

A covered horse-drawn two-seater sauntered by, and a young couple laughed from within it. Revulsion gripped him. How could anyone dare to laugh? Laughter was a sign of frivolity, and that was loathsome to him. Life was a dark, brutish struggle to survive and thrive. He who laughed would never thrive.

Which is why he hated women who laughed.

They all did, the ones who sold themselves. Laughter, cloying laughter, painted faces that mocked you, hated you, even while they laughed.

His anger burned so hot it threatened to consume him. He felt faint for a moment, then hit himself in the face with his fist. A drop of blood slid over his lip and into his mouth. The taste of it calmed him.

And then she came, as he knew she would.

Singing.

He could see through the rain and darkness that she was swinging a purse with one hand and holding an umbrella with the other. Swinging her purse in time with the song she sang. It was a happy song. He could picture her laughing at it.

He stepped out of the doorway.

"Oh!" the girl said. "You frightened me!"

"So sorry."

"What are you doing, jumping out like that?"

"Couldn't wait to see you."

Her face twitched in momentary confusion. He liked that.

"Do I know you?" she asked.

"I know *you*."

"Who told you about me?" A coy smile twisted her face.

He clenched his teeth.

"Hey," she said, "your nose is bleeding."

"Help me, won't you?"

He motioned to her and backed into the doorway again, reaching behind him to open the door. She would be hesitant at first, but he knew she would follow.

"Listen, mister," she said as she moved forward, "I have a handkerchief. It's a little wet on account of the rain, but—"

"I want more than a handkerchief."

"Now, I don't just keep company freely, you know."

"I know," he said. "Come in."

"This a proposition, mister?"

"Come in."

She took another step. "You live here?"

"No. Work."

"What sort of work, then?"

"Come see."

She closed the umbrella and entered, as he knew she would. "It's dark. Why don't you put on a light?"

"No need for light."

"I can't help you if I can't see you."

"No, I'm going to help you."

"Me?"

"Deliver you."

"What?" she whispered.

"Deliver you from evil."

He slammed the door.

Chapter Three

THE RAINSTORM SEEMED out of place to Kit, but there it was, outside her window, casting a pall on what Aunt Freddy insisted on calling "her night."

Here only a week, and now the cream of society was gathering downstairs to receive Kit Shannon, the invader from the East. Kit felt like some sideshow attraction. Maybe it wasn't too late to run out into the storm and lose herself.

No, Aunt Freddy had done all this for her. She had brought her to this beautiful mansion atop Angeleno Heights, given her this palatial room as her own. Aunt Freddy had gone to a lot of trouble to make the room cheery. A huge bouquet of flowers was changed daily, set in a porcelain vase on a table in the center of the room. Kit loved the fragrance of the salmon-colored roses. The sweetness delighted her senses nearly as much as the visual treat. Kit had always been more readily affected by the visual. Colors and textures, angles and architectural designs . . . the wonders of sight always captured her attention and imagination. Perhaps that was why she loved the law. Some people would never have related it to a visual form, but it was to Kit. She saw stories in people's faces.

Yes, Aunt Freddy was sparing no expense. But her greatest gift had been Corazón. Aunt Freddy had assigned the pretty Mexican girl to be Kit's personal maid. Her name meant "heart" in her native tongue, and already she was becoming part of Kit's own heart—a true friend, though Aunt Freddy would not approve.

But the dark-eyed beauty made life bearable for Kit with her stories about the city and simple lessons in Spanish. They did their best to appear staid and proper in Aunt Freddy's company—Aunt Freddy had told Kit adamantly that non-white servants especially were to be kept in their place—but Corazón offered Kit a much-needed friendly ear. Her skin color did not matter in the slightest to Kit.

Now her friend and maid was helping her get ready for the big night. Corazón was dressed in her immaculate black-and-white uniform, reminiscent of the Harvey Girls Kit had seen in the food stops along the Santa Fe Railroad. Her starched white apron covered her like a jumpered gown, wrapping completely around her slender figure and falling from neck to toes. Only a black collar and sleeves revealed the shirtwaist she wore beneath. All of Freddy's maidservants dressed in such a manner.

Kit stared at her reflection in the mirror as Corazón put the finishing touches on her hair. The butterflies in her stomach had turned into a stampede of wild horses, and Kit seriously doubted she would ever make it through the evening without being sick. This, coupled with her painfully tight corset, was bound to make the evening's events difficult at best.

"I don't suppose I'm very knowledgeable about the latest fashions," Kit said. "But I don't want to embarrass Aunt Freddy."

Corazón continued to manipulate Kit's hair with quick, agile grace, and before Kit realized it, the maid had masterfully finished a stylish coiffure.

"How do you do that?" Kit said, putting up a hand to touch her hair. Corazón had created a look fit for a queen.

"I have been taught. It no hard if you know how."

Kit shook her head. "It's marvelous. Can you teach me to do that?"

"*Sí . . .*" Corazón looked at the floor.

"What is it?" Kit asked.

"I . . ."

Kit put her hand on the maid's arm. "It's all right."

"Can . . . would you teach to me the good English?"

"You speak it very well, Corazón."

"I wish to speak more . . . better."

"Of course I'll help. You show me how to do this magic with my hair and teach me Spanish, and I'll give you lessons in English. Deal?"

"Deal?" The maid's confused expression reminded Kit that she would have to take things slowly.

"A deal is an agreement. We will shake hands on it and promise to help one another. Understand?"

Corazón beamed a smile. "Yes. Deal." She reached out and tentatively shook Kit's hand.

Then she stepped back and looked at Kit admiringly. "You will have all of the gentlemen—how do you say it? Eating out of your hand, I think." She stepped forward and secured a diamond clasp in Kit's hair. The effect was stunning.

Suddenly Kit shook her head. "This is not who I am! I don't know why I ever agreed to this. There's no need to introduce me to society."

Corazón giggled and helped Kit up from the chair. "Madam has plans for you."

"Yes, but her plans are very different from my own. I feel . . . silly. Silly and foolish. I've been poked and prodded for so many dress fittings over the last few days that I feel like a pin cushion."

"Do you like the dress from Señora Norris?"

Kit smoothed down the silk skirt of the gown that had been completed that afternoon. She hesitated again at the low neckline. "I feel so exposed."

"This gown is modest, you will see."

Kit pulled a bit at the material, hoping to gain herself an extra inch of coverage. "It may be modest to some, but it is a far cry from the reserved fashion I'm used to."

"You would look good in anything, I think." Corazón gave Kit a smile.

Kit put a hand on Corazón's arm and said, "Thank you."

Aunt Freddy chose that moment to enter. She was clothed in a dark blue evening gown with a white feathered boa coiled around her neck. "And how is my niece faring?"

Kit felt her stomach fairly groan in protest against the tight corset. "I don't know how a woman is expected to breathe in this thing, Aunt Freddy. No wonder they faint left and right."

"My dear," Aunt Freddy said patiently, "the difference between the woman who always looks trim and smart and the luckless creature who is never well dressed, no matter what her garments cost or where she gets them, is chiefly a question of corsets."

Freddy approached Kit and ran her hand around the small of her back. "Ah, the very best," Aunt Freddy said. "For good reason. The best dressmaker in the world cannot make a well-fitting dress over an ill-fitting corset. I always say you cannot build a colonial mansion on the frame of a Gothic residence."

Kit shook her head. "But I feel like a condemned tenement. Does one inch matter so much?"

"Of course! For your height, the ideal waist is twenty-two

inches. No more, no less. And try to remember that the society woman should be as serene as a June day, with a golden leisure in her walk and calm confidence on her brow. Now, make me proud."

And with that, Freddy disappeared from the room in a swirl of feathers and satin.

Corazón handed Kit her elbow-length gloves. Kit pulled them on and allowed Corazón to fasten a band of diamonds and sapphires around her wrist. It all made Kit's head light. Aunt Freddy's money seemed to have no limits.

Finally Corazón took a step back and declared, "Beautiful."

Kit felt herself surprised at the assessment. *Am I pretty?* she wondered. It had been so long since anyone had told her so. Certainly the sisters at Leo House in New York, where Kit was sent from St. Catherine's after her seventeenth birthday, were not concerned about looks—theirs or anyone else's—with the exception of Sister Mary Monica, who had once told her in passing that she was becoming quite pretty indeed.

Should she should be more concerned with her looks? Was Aunt Freddy right about that? Perhaps, but all this fiddling with corsets and jewels, this overwhelming concern about just the right image, was too much.

Suddenly Kit felt alone and afraid, even with Corazón there. The maid couldn't possibly understand. Nor could anyone else she knew. In a world where men considered the female heart and soul to be much too delicate for such occupations as law and criminal disposal, Kit had become her own executioner. Was Aunt Freddy right? Was this just craziness—a scandal? Or was it truly God's will for her life?

She thought about her father. What would he have said about her dreams? The Reverend Harry E. Shannon had been a man of firm resolve and even firmer convictions. The former had sent him to America from his native Ireland in 1856. He was just fourteen years old, and with both parents dead, he had survived a treacherous sea crossing alone and an immediate lock-up after landing in Boston. Having been falsely accused of stealing tomatoes, the boy had fearfully made a jail-cell pact with God. "Get me out of here," he prayed, "and I'll spend the rest of my life in service to you. Even if I starve."

And he had kept his promise. Once freed, he moved through the ranks to become a noted preacher in the Irish section of town. Eventually he even went on to ride the circuit from Lowell to Philadelphia. He had told Kit over and over again, "If God tells you to do something, you do it. If God tells you to go, you go. Do those two things, and when you're finished in this life, your soul will be in heaven before the devil knows you're dead."

Kit smiled at the memory. Corazón finished smoothing Kit's dress and said, "There. Beautiful. May you have much fun!"

"I'll try," Kit assured her. "If I can breathe!" She walked out the door, feeling awkward in her long train and frippery. She would much rather be curled up with a good book.

Drawing as deep a breath as the corset would allow, Kit resolved to make the best of the evening. This was, after all, for Aunt Freddy's sake. She reached the stairs and began her descent feeling much like Daniel heading for the lions' den.

———

Aunt Freddy was in her element. She buzzed around the party like a dervish of delight, waving her ever-present handkerchief in front of her florid face. Nothing pleased her more than a social event in her home with all the right people. And they were all present, here to meet her great niece from the East.

A string quartet played softly near the grand fireplace in the ballroom. At least sixty people were in this room, Kit estimated as Aunt Freddy pulled her from person to person like a bee stopping at every flower in the field. At each introduction Kit smiled, answered questions about New York, and made polite conversation about the weather and the garden.

Freddy escorted her to a squat man standing near the piano. "Chief Orel Hoover," Freddy said, "I would like you to meet my niece, Kathleen Shannon. Kathleen, this is our city's Chief of Police."

The man gave a slight bow as he took hold of Kit's hand. "I'm charmed, Miss Shannon. It is always a delight to add another fair flower to our city."

"Thank you, Chief Hoover."

"And this is my son, William." He turned to a younger man beside him. The young man, unsmiling, nodded in Kit's direction. She noted that he kept his hands in his pockets, not offering to shake hers. Was this sort of sullenness common in Los Angeles? she wondered.

As they moved past, Freddy whispered, "They say the chief killed a man once over a gambling debt. Scandalous!"

"Then how did he become the Chief of Police?"

"Oh," Freddy snorted, "this is Los Angeles, dear."

They then approached an elegantly dressed couple. "This," Aunt Freddy said, "is Mr. and Mrs. Breckenridge, dear friends of mine. My niece, Kathleen Shannon."

The woman, somewhere in her fifties, gave Kit a cursory study before following with a slight nod. "Miss Shannon, I've heard much about you. You traveled to Los Angeles completely unaccompanied." She looked at Kit as if expecting her to deny the accusation.

"I did indeed," Kit said. "But I managed to make it here alive."

The man laughed. The woman did not. Kit immediately held out her hand to Mr. Breckenridge. "It is a pleasure to meet you, sir."

Freddy whispered as they moved along, "She drinks on the sly. Scandalous! Ah, and here we have . . ."

By the twentieth introduction Kit was exhausted, even though number twenty was a handsome young man by the name of Fante, or Fainte, or some such. All she knew was that he was a banker. Aunt Freddy had whispered that much in her ear, along with the advice that Kit breathe in to amplify her bust.

Kit breathed normally, however, and at the earliest opportunity stole away to the punch bowl. There she found relief, but only for a moment. The attendant had just filled her glass when she heard a voice behind her.

"Miss Shannon?"

Turning, Kit saw a man looking directly at her. He was almost fully bald and rather gaunt, but possessed a look of unmistakable prosperity. Kit guessed him to be about sixty.

"My name is Heath Sloate," he said, offering his hand.

"Enchanted, Mr. Sloate," Kit intoned, taking his hand. Even through her gloves she could feel his bony thinness as he held the grip a little too long.

"I know your great aunt very well. I've been able to help her on a number of occasions with her affairs."

"Thank you. I'm sure she appreciates it."

For a moment his deep-set eyes bobbed in their sockets, as if he were contemplating some secret vision. Kit felt her cheeks flush as his gaze dropped to her neckline. Glancing up again, his thin lips formed an appreciative smile. "I understand from your aunt that you have a certain, rather singular, ambition. Is that correct?"

"I suppose I do."

"Practicing law?"

"Yes, sir."

"Remarkable."

"Pardon me, sir?"

"When your aunt suggested your desire, I assumed you were most likely of a plain, perhaps even disfigured, appearance."

Kit frowned. "What does my appearance have to do with practicing law?"

"Why, everything. A fine specimen of womanhood such as yourself, undertaking to pass the bar. Not that it hasn't happened, you understand. But it's been mostly older women, widows with no hope of matrimony. Socialists. And suffragettes. Insufferable suffragettes."

Sloate laughed through his nose. Kit took a sip of punch, trying to control the anger welling within her.

"My dear," Sloate said, "if I may offer you a bit of advice. I've tramped the fields of the law for quite a number of years now, and if there is one thing I know, it is this. The law is not a place for women."

The deflation she felt must have shown on her face. Sloate said, "There, it's not all that bad. Let me tell you a story. A few years ago I was appointed special prosecutor in a case involving a particularly grisly murder. Man killed his own brother with an ax. Does that shock you?"

Swallowing, Kit said, "Evil is always shocking, Mr. Sloate."

"You have never come face-to-face with such evil, I'm sure. No one as lovely as you could have and still retained such natural, innocent beauty." He stole another glance at her bodice.

Kit suddenly felt uncomfortable. She looked around for a way of escape.

"The defendant hired a lawyer," Sloate continued blithely. "One skilled at spinning webs to ensnare juries. He tried every trick, both emotional and logical, twisting facts and soaring with high-flown oratory. The judge, an old friend of his, allowed him to get away with the most atrocious ploys. There was even a manufactured alibi. Through it all, as if juggling many balls at once, I persevered and gained the conviction. That could never have happened without a particular kind of legal mind. Do you know what I'm talking about?"

"I'm trying to follow, Mr. Sloate."

"What I'm talking about is, for want of a better word, the male mind. The practice of law requires the ability to consider facts, logic, and complexities all at the same time."

"I believe I can do that."

"I'm speaking from long experience, my dear. I have seen women try it. Believe me when I tell you this: You won't find happiness in the law."

Kit looked at the floor.

Sloate put a cold hand on her arm. "You're very young. The young always think they can sway the eternal verities. Believe me, Miss Shannon, women are the softer sex, the nurturers of our society. And you, my dear, seem eminently suited to that purpose."

Kit took a deep breath. "Mr. Sloate, I've read all of Blackstone and Greenleaf's *Treatise on Evidence*, and I do believe I have understood their . . . complexities, as you call them. I know the difference between incorporeal hereditaments and tangible gifts, and I understand covenants running with the land. I can read contracts and estate plans. I can help people who need help, especially the ones who usually don't get it."

The thin smile returned to Heath Sloate's face. "You have a certain spirit, I grant you. But Miss Shannon, spirit is one thing. A position is another. Without a position you'll never be able to begin. I know everyone in this city worth knowing, and I can tell you it will be impossible to find one. No, Miss Shannon, the law is not for you."

"With God all things are possible." The words popped out of her mouth, almost of their own accord. She met Heath Sloate's gaze full on. In it she could see a steely rebuke. But she did not look away.

At that moment Aunt Freddy flitted over to join them. "I see you have met each other," she said.

"Quite," said Heath Sloate.

"Did you have a chance to chat?"

"Oh yes," he replied.

"And?"

"Your niece is a charming girl, of stubborn stock, I'll wager."

"Stubborn?" Aunt Freddy said. "Didn't she listen?"

Kit said, "Listen?"

"Your aunt," said Sloate, "asked that I put a stop to your fantasies about practicing law."

"I most certainly did!" Aunt Freddy huffed.

"But it appears I have nothing more to say."

"Oh, dear!" Aunt Freddy took a step backward, tottering.

"Mr. Sloate," Kit said, "if I have offended you, I—"

Sloate silenced Kit with a hand in the air. She felt like crawling under the table. Sloate turned and gave Freddy the tiniest hint of a bow.

"This cannot work in your favor, Frederica. You'll be ruined if she insists on this course of action."

"That's hardly fair to say," Kit interjected. "What I've done— what I will do—has no bearing on my aunt."

Sloate's eyes narrowed to menacing slits. "For one so well educated, you truly know nothing." With that he took his leave and crossed the room to greet more companionable company.

Kit knew this display had wounded her aunt. She felt at a loss for words. What could she say? She could apologize—but for what? She wasn't sorry for speaking her mind, only for the pain it inadvertently caused her aunt.

"Aunt Freddy, I . . ."

Freddy held out a large drinking glass to the servant at the punch bowl. "Put some gin in there, too," she said. "And don't be stingy."

"Now, Aunt Freddy, you shouldn't," Kit said.

"Don't you tell me what I shouldn't do, young lady! I'll be ruined! I might as well not feel it." She took the drink from the servant and downed it heartily, then eyed Kit severely. "You should know better than to challenge a man like Mr. Sloate. He's only speaking on what he knows—on what is best."

"Best perhaps for him. But hardly the best for me. He knows nothing of me, Aunt Freddy." Kit tried to soften her voice. "You know very little of me yourself."

"Well!" Freddy declared, pushing the glass back to the servant. "We shall discuss this tomorrow. For now, I would ask that you comport yourself in a proper manner." She snatched the refilled drink from the servant, then left Kit to contemplate her words.

Kit nervously looked around the room. Although no one appeared to be staring, she felt every pair of eyes carefully considering her. Unable to remain at the party another moment, she fled through the rear door. In the refuge of the hallway she leaned against the wall and breathed deeply. Los Angeles suddenly felt like a stifling, overwhelming place.

"Bushed?"

Kit jumped at the sound of the voice. A man seated on the stairs a mere ten feet away looked at her and smiled. He was about her age, perhaps a little older, dressed in elegant evening clothes. Droplets of water stood out on his coat, as if he'd just come inside out of the rain. Kit couldn't recall seeing him at the party.

"Sorry I startled you," the man said, standing. As he walked toward Kit, she perceived brilliant blue eyes staring intently at her face.

"Here," he said, pulling out a handkerchief and reaching out to dab her chin. He held the handkerchief up for her to see. It revealed a dim red spot. "May have been a little punch or something," he said.

Powerless to stop the blush that rushed to her face, Kit muttered, "Thank you. I just came out for a moment."

"I'm with you," he said. "I'd rather be out here than in there. All that 'Oh, you must hear the latest!' talk gives me a pain."

Kit smiled. "I wouldn't have put it that way, but now that you mention it . . ."

"Ted Fox." He put out his hand.

"Kathleen Shannon."

"Ah, you're the one all this is for."

"My aunt insisted."

"Aunts are that way. I have one back home who delights in showing my photograph to everyone who comes to her house."

"I should think you would be flattered."

He leaned closer and whispered. "The photograph was taken when I was six months old, and I'm as naked as the truth on Sunday."

Kit laughed. It felt good. "I didn't notice you inside."

"Just got here."

"Were you going to spend the whole evening sitting on the stairs?"

"Maybe."

"Why?" Kit asked.

"Have my reasons."

"And you're not telling?"

He smiled in a way that lit up the hallway. "You're an inquisitive one."

"So I've been told."

"Tell me," he said, his face growing more serious. "Have you met a man named Sloate here?"

The name gave her a slight shudder. "You know him?"

"Unfortunately."

"Is that why you're not going in?"

"That and . . ."

"And what?" Kit could not contain her curiosity.

Ted smiled again, but this time his smile hid a mystery. "Do you think man was meant to fly?" he said.

Kit cocked her head and narrowed her gaze. "Fly? You mean with wings?"

"With wings that he builds with his hands."

"I think man has his hands full right here on the ground."

"Well, Miss Shannon, I don't believe man is glued to the earth. I think we were meant to soar!"

His enthusiasm was intoxicating. But fly? It seemed impossible, but then . . .

"I think it's a wonderful dream," Kit said.

"Ah, so you believe in big dreams, too?"

"Oh yes."

"What's yours?"

Before Kit could answer, a woman's voice rang out from down the hall. "Theodore Fox!"

A woman with golden hair, attired in an elegant gown of lavender crepe de chine, walked stiffly toward them. Her ears and neck dripped with diamonds.

Kit remembered her from the party. Her striking appearance— beautiful in a cool, assured way—was not to be missed. She obviously upheld all the social graces, making Kit feel rather lacking in her own skills. Coming of age in a Catholic orphanage was not exactly the pedigree of a polished socialite. And even with Aunt Freddy and Corazón's help, Kit knew she'd made more than her share of social errors that evening.

"Where on *earth* have you been?" the woman said, never taking her gaze from Kit.

"Getting to know the guest of honor," Fox said. "Elinor Wynn, Kathleen Shannon."

Elinor Wynn's look was caked with ice. "Charmed."

"How do you do, Miss Wynn?"

"My fiancé has, for some reason, refused to seek me out."

Fox glanced quickly at Kit, then back at Elinor. "I was talking to Miss Shannon about flying."

"Oh, not *that* again. Really, Theodore." She took his arm and looked at Kit. "You don't mind, do you?" It was not a question. It had the unmistakable tone of a dismissal and something more—a warning.

"Not at all," said Kit.

"See you," said Fox as he was being led away, looking for a moment like a condemned prisoner. And then, with a finger pointing toward the sky, he added, "Up there."

Kit watched until they disappeared around a corner. Suddenly she felt like the proverbial fish out of water. She was no polished socialite, like Elinor Wynn. And perhaps she was merely a wide-eyed dreamer for thinking that practicing law was something within her reach. What was she doing here?

She thought of running to her room and hiding, but her desire to please Aunt Freddy overruled such thoughts. Aunt Freddy had gone to a great deal of trouble. Kit owed it to her to see this matter to completion.

Walking to a large gilt-framed mirror in the hallway, Kit smoothed her dress and once again struggled to rearrange her neckline. Meeting her reflection she found green eyes, green like her father's, staring back at her. She could remember many nights by the fire, sitting on her father's knee, gazing into his eyes as he read to her from the Bible. How his eyes would sparkle when he told her the great stories of the Old Testament, and the greatest story of all—Jesus of Nazareth, facing the religious hypocrisy of His day with convictions born of His divine nature, going to the cross to atone for the sins of the whole world.

Her father had such convictions, too. And he had died for them.

Kit breathed in and knew she could easily face the benign tempest of a social fete. With a toss of her head, she strode back to the ballroom.

Chapter Four

IN THE DREAM a dark man held a hangman's noose. Kit didn't know if it was meant for her or for someone else. All she sensed, in this nightmare world, was that someone was going to die and she was powerless to do anything about it.

She tried to cry out, but no sound came forth. Nor could she run.

The dark man began to walk toward her. As he got closer, step by step, she found she could not move at all. His hands were bony, like the fingers of death. He advanced, and Kit could only watch in horror.

When he was within two strides of her, he stopped. Stared. She could not see the face in the darkness, but she could see the noose, upheld in his emaciated hand.

Then he pounced!

And she awoke.

Sitting up, breathing hard, Kit saw that her room was filled with the bright sunshine of a new day. The bed was soft and warm. She should have felt wonderfully refreshed, but the dread created by the bad dream—she had not had a nightmare in years—filled her with a grave sense of disquiet.

It was just a dream, she reasoned. Probably due to all the change and commotion in her life, culminating in the big party Aunt Freddy had given the night before. But no, there was something more. . . .

Rising, Kit went to the window and threw it open. The previous night's rain had seemingly refreshed all of creation. Warm morning air wafted in, along with the smell of laurel and sage and another smell, so sweet and pure, unlike anything she remembered from New York. It was intoxicating. She breathed in deeply and immediately forgot about the bad dream and her agitation.

A light knock sounded at the door. "Come in," Kit said.

Corazón entered. "Good morning, Miss."

The sight of Corazón brought Kit all the way back to normalcy. "Come here, Corazón," Kit said. "To the window. What is that smell?"

"Smell?"

"Yes. Breathe it in." Kit herself took another lingering breath.

"Ah, *las naranjas!*"

"What is that?"

"Oranges. From the grove."

"I've heard of oranges. I don't believe I have ever seen one. Are they good to eat?"

With a smile, Corazón said, "Very good, I think, but Madam, she does not like."

"Yet she grows them?"

"In Los Angeles, Miss, everyone grows las naranjas, I think."

"Can you get me one? On the sly?" Kit was enjoying this bit of girlish conspiracy.

"I will as you say," Corazón said. "Now would you like the bath?"

The warm water was a tonic. Corazón, despite Kit's protestations, insisted on dutifully washing her back.

"What time is it?" Kit asked.

Corazón poured a generous amount of rose-scented oil onto a cloth and began massaging Kit's back. "Seven-thirty, I think."

"Oh no! Why did no one wake me? I feel terrible! First I aggravate Aunt Freddy at the party and now I'm late for breakfast."

"Madam is the one to say not to wake you. She is thinking you need the rest."

"I'm sure she's thinking a whole lot more than that. My aunt Freddy is not at all pleased with me. Well, let's hurry the bath."

Corazón poured warm water down Kit's back, then stood up. "You would like me to wash more?"

"No," Kit replied. "You really didn't need to wash my back, but my, it did feel wonderful."

Kit took up the abandoned washcloth and began to lather it. The soap filled the air with yet another heady scent. She had no idea what it was. This foreign land was simply filled with pleasant aromas.

The maid smiled. "I am glad to please you."

Kit drew the cloth over her body in rapid strokes. "I'm far more pleased by our friendship. Friends are hard to find in this world."

"*Mi madre . . .*" Corazón paused, giving Kit an apologetic look. "My mother, she say a friend is a gift from God."

"Exactly so! I couldn't have said it better. You are like a gift from God to me. Moving from one end of the country to the other was like going to the moon." As Corazón's face scrunched into a puzzled expression, Kit immediately thought of Ted Fox. No doubt he had plans for flying there himself. The thought made her flush.

Thinking of Ted Fox at such a time would surely scandalize poor Aunt Freddy right out of her stockings.

"What I mean to say," Kit continued, "is that this is all so new and exciting. No one and no sight is familiar. I think that's why I cherish our friendship more than anything."

"Do you no have brothers and sisters, mother, father?"

"No. My mother and father died when I was young. What of your family?"

Corazón crossed the room to pick up a fluffy bath towel. "I am the oldest of six."

A feeling of longing came over Kit. What would life have been like had she been blessed with family to comfort her through the years? Would she have been driven to study the law? Would she already be married with little ones clinging to her knee?

"I'm sure they're wonderful," Kit murmured. She would not give herself over to sorrow for the things that could not be. She could not bring back the dead by dwelling on their memory, and neither could she find any real comfort in remembering what had been taken away from her.

With new determination, Kit finished her bath and allowed Corazón to help her towel off. Easing into yet another new silk wrapper, Kit sat down dutifully while Corazón worked on her hair.

"Today is a new day," Kit said. "I am going downtown to walk into the offices of the attorneys. I'll march right in with my certificate of law education and ask for a position. I might just start with a lawyer someone mentioned to me on the train. I think it was Rogers . . . Earl Rogers."

"I have heard that name," Corazón said as she pulled the brush through Kit's hair. "Yes, at a party here. Madam said he was a devil."

"Devil?" Kit said, intrigued. She remembered how that man, Tom Phelps, had looked when he mentioned Rogers' name. Perhaps he thought of Rogers as a devil, too.

"Yes," said Corazón, "because he takes the side of the bad man."

"A criminal defense lawyer?"

"I think that is right."

Kit had never even met a criminal lawyer before. Criminal law was an entirely different world from what she had envisioned for herself. A dark world indeed.

"I'll skip him, then. There must be a lot of other lawyers in town. What do you think?"

"I think," said Corazón, "you are very brave."

"What's so brave about entering a few offices?" Kit asked.

"That is not the brave part," said Corazón. "The brave part is to face Madam when she hear about it."

Laughing, Kit shrugged. *With God, all things are possible,* she thought. *Even facing Aunt Freddy!*

———

Breakfast in the Fairbank mansion was a sumptuous affair. Kit had been here over a week and still could not get over the silver serving bowls, the sizzling meats, the fluffy eggs, and the servants. Back at Leo House in New York, where Kit had earned her keep while attending college and then law school, she had been told that one egg each week was a luxury and she would have to prepare it herself.

Kit sat down, ready to discuss her future once and for all. But Aunt Freddy, sitting at the opposite end of the large table that could seat ten comfortably, began the conversation the moment Kit was seated.

"Well, my dear, you've had the night to think it over," Freddy began.

"Think what over?" Kit said, wondering what she might have

overlooked. The servants, Corazón included, began dishing out the meal, seeming to pay no mind. Kit wondered about that. How much did they listen?

"Men, of course," said Freddy. "I lost count of how many eligible men were putting out a scent."

Oh, that, Kit thought. It was a subject of little importance to her at the moment. "I had a lovely time," said Kit, mindful of her aunt's feelings and social concerns.

"I should say. Did any of the young men stand out for you?"

"Aunt Freddy, I—"

"I saw you in conversation with Mr. Frank Fante for quite some time. He's in the banking business, you know. A lot of money there."

"Aunt Freddy—"

"I know he's not the most handsome man this side of the Pecos, but that shouldn't be your first concern, my dear. Men can grow on you if they have the right social position. Was there anyone else?"

Sighing, Kit said, "Lots of nice men, Aunt Freddy, but I am not desperate to find a husband. I believe in God's timing, not my own."

"Stuff and nonsense! Catching a husband is the chief aim of a woman. It's a hunt, my dear, and you must bag a prize. Now, didn't you see any prizes in the bunch?"

Kit thought about it. Perhaps she owed it to her aunt to at least give the night a cursory assessment. She let her memory play back pictures of the party, looking for a face that stood out, but the pictures were fuzzy. It all seemed like a whirlwind, a maelstrom of featureless people, and then one face, in detail, became fully alive in her mind.

"Ah!" said Freddy. "I can see you've got one! Who was it?"

"Well, if you want to know . . ." Kit said coyly.

"Yes, yes! It was that Whitney fellow, wasn't it, the one with the cane?"

Kit smiled mischievously, playing a game. "No, not that one. He was a handsome fellow. . . ."

"Handsome? Let's see . . . was it the young man with the lisp?"

"No lisp, Aunt Freddy."

"I know!" Freddy said with a slap on the table. "It was young Fitch, the mayor's son!"

Kit vaguely remembered meeting this one. She had thought him handsome from afar but then, after looking into his eyes and sensing a certain oddness about him, recalled that saying about all that glitters not being gold.

"No," Kit said, "he wasn't the one, either."

"Well," Freddy said impatiently, "what was his name then? I hope it wasn't Mr. Hoover's son. William is a bit odd. Lacks ambition, yet acts rather aloof and superior. Besides, his father is only the Chief of Police. Although it is said he desires something more."

Kit could stand no more. "I believe he said his name was Fox."

Kit could see Aunt Freddy's face flush from clear across the table. "Theodore Fox!" she bellowed. "Of all the men!"

The reaction intrigued Kit. It was stronger than she had anticipated. The joke was supposed to be that Ted Fox was engaged. A subtle retort filled with social indignity would have been called for. But Aunt Freddy seemed almost angry.

"Why?" Kit prodded. "He seemed perfectly charming."

"You will have nothing to do with Theodore Fox, Kathleen Shannon! For one thing, he is spoken for. He is going to marry Elinor Wynn, who is from one of the finest families in the city. If you were ever to come between those two, it would be a scandal! I wouldn't be able to show my face anywhere in town!"

That much was no doubt true, Kit conceded. And she had no intention of breaking up that engagement. Ted Fox was not the object of her affections, only the most interesting man at the party. She merely wanted to know more about him.

"And another thing," Freddy said seriously. "Theodore Fox comes from a wealthy family, a fine Protestant family, but he has been trouble for them his whole life."

"How so?" Kit said, now uncontrollably interested.

"Well," said Freddy, appearing to slide into a social gossip mode, "his mother has told me that he's always been a bit on the dangerous side."

"Dangerous?" That was not a word Kit would have associated with Ted Fox.

"He was always getting into fights as a boy," Freddy continued, "and that hasn't stopped. He was expelled from Northwestern University for a fight, and then he ran off on a steamer ship. No one heard from him for a year. When he got back there was talk . . ." Aunt Freddy's voice dropped, ". . . that he had killed a man."

For some strange reason, Kit felt herself wanting to defend Ted Fox. It was absurd, she realized, for she hardly knew the man. Yet she had the odd feeling that Fox was being unjustly accused, and her lawyer's instinct was to wait until the evidence was in before reaching a verdict.

"If that is so," Kit said, "then why is a socialite like Elinor Wynn consenting to marry him?"

"Elinor Wynn is another matter," said Aunt Freddy. "She is rather spoiled, and she has decided that she is in love with Ted Fox. Perhaps it's that sense of danger that makes a woman lose her head sometimes. Regardless, she wants Ted Fox as her husband. And what Elinor Wynn wants, Elinor Wynn gets. It has always been so."

Kit decided to press the matter just a little further. "I wonder what he sees in Miss Wynn."

Squinting, Aunt Freddy said, "Don't you be getting jealous, young lady."

"I'm not!" Kit said indignantly. "I merely find it a puzzle."

"You keep your sights off of Ted Fox. There are many fish in our little ocean. Look to hook one that isn't already hooked."

Now was the time to strike. "Aunt Freddy, I am very grateful for all you've done for me. The party last night was wonderful and a lovely thing to do. But I have to confess that my concern is not to find a man to marry. That will come in time. I have come here to practice law. That is what I have been preparing myself for. I am not going to give that up."

The two women had not touched one morsel on their china plates, and Kit suddenly realized that the servants were standing at the sides, unsure of what to do. She caught the eye of Corazón, who gave her a quick smile and then, just as quickly, recaptured the stoic expression that was proper for her station.

Sighing heavily, Aunt Freddy said, "I thought Mr. Sloate made it abundantly clear—"

"Mr. Sloate attempted, at your insistence, to give me reasons not to pursue this dream. He did not make his case."

"Heath Sloate is the most powerful lawyer in all of Los Angeles, perhaps the entire West. He knows what he is talking about, child. You would be wise to listen to him."

"I must listen to God first, Aunt Freddy."

"All this talk of God! I won't have any more of it. Leave God to your religion, but leave your life to those who know best."

"Aunt Freddy, I cannot separate my life from God. I know you mean well, and you've already done so much for me." Kit touched the embroidered pleating of her stylish morning dress. "I don't want to seem ungrateful, but God must be my judge and guide in this."

"Society will be your judge," Freddy replied. "And it is a harsh mistress to serve. You must abide by the rules, and there are many, if you are to survive and be accepted. That is why you need not

God for a guide, but me. Do you have any idea of your inept social skills? Are you not aware of your mistakes and lack of understanding? These things are important."

"I never meant to embarrass you. As you might recall, I asked you not to show me off to your friends."

"That is not the point," the older woman replied. "The point of this matter is that you are educated for the wrong things. In this town, in my world, you need something more than book learning. Especially books on law. You need firm lessons in etiquette. I have a book for you to read. Corazón has taken it to your room. I suggest you study it, as you would those law books, so we can be better prepare to continue your introduction to society. High society rules this city—indeed, the very course of lives both rich and poor. You should know that from your life in New York. Was it not the mandates of the wealthy that directly affected the lives of those less fortunate? Was it not by the mercy of the rich that the poor were given provision?"

"No, it is by God's mercy that all are provided for—rich or poor. Society does not rule my life in any way, Aunt Freddy. Papa always said that Jesus must rule as king if He is to redeem as Savior."

"Stuff and nonsense. Jesus isn't here to tell you whether practicing law is good for you. But Heath Sloate is. He knows this town and he knows the law—probably better than anyone you've ever managed to keep company with. Heath Sloate is well respected and feared throughout the state. You would do well to heed what he has to say."

"I listened to what he had to say," Kit said, her anger rising to the occasion. "I simply do not agree with him. Please forgive my boldness, but Mr. Sloate's principles suggest women are incapable of reasoning and logic. But look at Madame Curie, for instance."

"I do not see Madame Curie gracing the tables of our select society."

"Perhaps she should," Kit fired back. "There are many more women like her, all of whom are making wonderful contributions to the world. You, as well as your friends, will no doubt benefit from their work."

"I will not argue what I know to be true," Freddy said, taking up her tea. "You have an obligation to me as your sponsor. You must trust me to know what is best. You must also trust that Mr. Sloate knows what is best, and he says—"

Aunt Freddy was interrupted by an entering butler holding a small silver tray. "A letter, Madam," he said.

"Letter?"

"For Miss Shannon."

Aunt Freddy's mouth dropped open, then quickly shut. She sat in frozen awe for a moment, then snapped, "Well, you'd better give it to her." Then a knowing smile spread across her face. "Perhaps you won't have to choose after all. Perhaps a young man has chosen you."

Kit frowned and lowered her gaze to her plate. This was all such nonsense. Pick a young man, read books of etiquette, build a wardrobe—ignore her heart!

The butler bowed and walked dutifully to Kit, holding the tray out to her. Kit took the letter gingerly. Her name was written on the front of the envelope. Nothing more. Puzzled, she turned the letter over.

"Hurry up, won't you?" Aunt Freddy said. "Perhaps it's an invitation for this afternoon, although that would be in poor taste."

Slipping the paper from its envelope, Kit unfolded the letter and read, in an immaculate hand:

Miss Shannon,

I request your presence at my offices at 321 South Spring Street tomorrow morning at eleven thirty o'clock. The purpose of this meeting is professional in nature. Until then, I remain,

Very truly yours,
Heath W. Sloate

"Well, what does it say?" Aunt Freddy demanded.

Kit read the letter out loud. Aunt Freddy let out a disconsolate sigh. "I can't understand that man," she said presently. "I'll call him on the telephone and give him a piece of my mind."

"Please don't, Aunt Freddy." Kit rose and went to her aunt, putting her arms around her. "Let me at least hear what his proposition is." She wondered what it might be. But he said *professional.* Had he seen something in her after all?

"I can't stand by while you throw away your life!" Aunt Freddy said, a whimpering tone to her voice. She frowned and looked away. "Still, if Heath believes the proposition to be worthy, perhaps I shouldn't fret. He always knows best."

Kit embraced her even more firmly. "It will be all right," she whispered. "You'll see."

———

" '*New Book of Etiquette,*' " Kit read aloud. She had found the book on her bedside table, just as Aunt Freddy had promised.

She opened the blue cloth-covered volume and read, *Men are not willing to have society ignore the establishment of rules. Judgement by appearance is not only properly acceptable, but demanded.*

Kit shook her head. "But God doesn't look on our outward appearance, but at the heart!" she said aloud. "Why should this book dictate my actions?"

Just then Corazón knocked and entered with a tray. "Madam sent this."

She positioned the tray on the table beside Kit's bed. Kit noticed the cup of tea, complete with slices of lemon. "Thank you."

"And I bring you this," Corazón said, reaching into her pocket. She held out an orange and gave a quick glance over her shoulder. "I show you how to eat?"

"Oh, yes," Kit said. She patted the bed and set the book aside. "I've been trying to read about ways to better my appearance and actions."

"Sí. Madam say this book is *muy importante*."

"Well, I'm not convinced. Already I'm reading things that prove false when held up to the light of Scripture. Judge people by appearance, for instance. I'm against that. The world trains us to see people in light of their circumstance, but that is hardly fair. We should not hold people in higher esteem simply because they've read this book of etiquette. Better they read the Bible. If I had money, I would go buy Aunt Freddy a copy. I'm nearly certain she does not have one in her possession."

Kit watched in fascination as Corazón peeled the orange, even as the memory of her previous conversation with Aunt Freddy weighed heavy on her heart. Corazón handed her a slice of the fruit and smiled.

"Be careful for the seeds."

Kit nodded and took a bite. Juice squirted out from the sweet fruit and ran down her chin. Laughing, she quickly took up the napkin beside her tea and wiped her mouth.

"Oh, it's wonderful. I've never tasted anything quite so grand," Kit laughed.

"It is good you like. We have many oranges here."

"It seems to be only one more thing that will put me at odds with Aunt Freddy. You said she didn't care for them."

Corazón nodded and shrugged. "It no matter. She no have to eat them."

Kit sobered. "That is so true. She doesn't have to eat oranges or practice law, but neither should she prevent others from doing so if they enjoy it." She took another bite of the orange, this time prepared for the juice.

Maybe that was what this entire matter of etiquette and oranges was all about. Preparation and careful handling could hold at bay the most difficult of circumstances. Kit would simply have to think things through and decide how to proceed best without ruffling Aunt Freddy's feathers. She would read the book of etiquette—all the better to understand the quirky thoughts of her aunt's world. But she wouldn't allow it to govern her life. Only God's Word would do that. Aunt Freddy would just have to get used to the idea.

Chapter Five

THE FOLLOWING MORNING Kathleen Shannon presented herself at the offices of Heath W. Sloate, Attorney-at-Law. A severe-looking woman positioned at an oak desk behind an ornate balustrade told Kit to sit and wait while she was announced.

A moment later Heath Sloate emerged from a large door with burgundy leather overlay and brass studs and strode to where Kit was sitting. He wore a dark vested suit with a flared collar shirt and black tie. On the middle of his nose sat pince-nez eyeglasses, which he removed with his left hand. He extended his right hand to Kit. His handshake was again bony, and he seemed aware of it, not lingering too long.

"Won't you come in?" he said and motioned toward his office. To the woman he said, "You may take your lunch, Miss Glendon. I will see you at one."

With a quick glance at Kit that seemed to ask how a woman so young had acquired a private consultation with the great Mr.

Sloate—and looking none too happy about it—Miss Glendon said, "Yes, sir." She turned her back swiftly, as if anxious to dismiss Kit from her thoughts as quickly as possible.

Heath Sloate's office was elegant and magisterial. An Oriental floor rug took up one half of the room, its muted reds and yellows a perfect complement to the browns of the leather and oak furniture. Behind Sloate's desk, a large window with slatted blinds let in perfect slices of sunlight, and to the side an entire wall was taken up by bookcases. One bookcase was filled with serried rows of tawny volumes. Kit knew these must be the official reports of California case law. The sight of them excited her, as if the endless grandeur of the law was beckoning to her then and there.

"Please sit down, Miss Shannon," Heath Sloate said, indicating a leather chair in front of his desk. Kit did so, placing her gloved hands on her lap, eager to find out what Sloate wanted to say. She had run through her first encounter with Sloate numerous times in her mind, convincing herself that she had been tired and entirely too harsh. Everyone deserved the benefit of the doubt when it came to important matters, and such was this meeting. She also admitted to herself that she was hopeful he would offer her a position, that he had been impressed enough by what he called her "certain spirit" to rethink his position on a woman practicing law.

She also thought, in the full light of day, that Sloate was not as objectionable, in look or manner, as she had earlier judged upon meeting him. Certainly, for whatever reason, being invited to a private meeting by Heath Sloate was a meaningful step.

"Thank you for coming today," Sloate said as he moved toward a small table with a clear glass carafe and several glasses on it. "May I offer you a drink of water?"

Kit's throat was dry from nervousness, but she said, "No, thank you." She didn't want him to think her in any way unsuited for discussions at the highest level. Such would be common in the practice of law. *I will show him how composed I can be,* she said to herself and straightened up a little in her chair.

Sloate tugged at his vest, from the pocket of which a gold watch chain looped downward and then back up to a middle button, ending in a fob the shape of a small gold nugget. "I imagine your great aunt was curious about the reason for this visit, eh?"

"Yes, Mr. Sloate, very much so. You know how she feels about my practicing law."

"Indeed, yes. It was at her behest I attempted to talk some sense into you at the party."

Kit's heart dropped. *Sense? Does this mean he still feels it is insensible for me to want to practice law? Then why am I here?*

"Or," he added, "what Freddy would call sense. I think there may be something to this idea."

A sudden rebound of her spirit brought Kit to full attention. "What idea, sir?"

Sloate smiled, the curvature of which was slightly asymmetrical, as if his lips and teeth had two different ideas about the enterprise. "Would you mind doing me a great favor and dispensing with addressing me as *sir*? I realize it is the polite thing to do, but it makes me feel more like a stranger than . . . someone of more intimate acquaintance."

"Of course, Mr. Sloate."

"That's better. And perhaps, when we are better acquainted, Heath will do."

Kit looked at her hands, slightly embarrassed. She hadn't anticipated such a familiar tone. Could it be that he wanted to talk to her about Aunt Freddy? Was that the real reason he had called her in, as part of his courtship? Oh, she hoped not.

"May I call you Kit?" he said.

"Yes, you may."

"How did that come to be your nickname?"

Kit said, "I was told by my mother that she called me Kat once when I was still a baby—short for Kathleen. But my father heard her and said something like, 'She's just a little thing. More like a kitten.' And that pleased my mother, too. It was Kit after that."

"Ah," said Sloate. "And now the Kit is all grown up." He looked at her admiringly. Kit wished he would change the subject from her to his purpose. Her hands suddenly felt hot in her lace gloves.

Looking out the window of his office, which was on the third floor and overlooked busy Spring Street, Sloate said, "I came to this city in 1883, when it was little more than a refuge for displaced Mexican revolutionaries. Electricity and telephones were mere curiosities then. The population was only twenty thousand. Then, after 1885, this little city began to grow."

Sloate peered more intently out the window, as if viewing the past. "People began to pour in when the Southern Pacific Railroad made Los Angeles its southern terminus from the San Francisco line and the Santa Fe chose it as its western terminus. In short, Kit, the railroads made this city what it is today."

He turned to face her, his hands clasped behind his back. "That is called progress. Inevitable, exciting. And it's happening all around us. We have electric cable cars everywhere now. The Yellow Line for the city, the Red Line for the county. Soon we won't see horses and carriages on our streets anymore. Everyone will be in gasoline-powered buggies, taking them wherever they want to go. What do you think of that?"

In all honesty, Kit didn't know what to think. Progress was inevitable, as Sloate said, but Kit was more interested in the progress of people than of industry. "It is certainly a most exciting time to be alive," she agreed.

"Quite. Progress happens whether we like it or not. And I mean progress in all areas, Miss Kit Shannon."

She looked at him, not knowing where he was heading next in

this colloquy. He sat down in the swivel chair behind his desk and then looked her straight in the eye.

"Forgive me for being something of a blind man," he said. "I know now, after giving it some thought, that women will have to be given a place at the bar that is of equal status with their male counterparts. It won't be easy, of course, but it will happen. And you, Kit, are going to be among the champions."

Her heart suddenly filled with hope. Was he really saying this? After all the doubts and discouragements, was one of the finest lawyers in all of Los Angeles on her side?

"You will need a sponsor," he said. "Someone to apprentice you, train you, then stand with you for the bar. And someone to make sure you meet the right people."

Kit knew what he would say next, and she was appreciative. She had misjudged him after all. He was going to help her!

"I will be that someone," he said. "How does that sound to you?"

"Wonderful!" said Kit, unable to mask her enthusiasm. "When shall I start?"

He leaned back in his chair and put a thin finger to his lips, tapping them gently, rhythmically, like a metronome. To Kit he looked as if he were thinking the whole thing over, perhaps collecting his thoughts as to the terms of her employment. She was prepared to take a fair wage and did not doubt her ability to provide a good return.

Sloate reached into his vest pocket and pulled out a gold watch. With a bony thumb he popped open the cap, peered at the timepiece, then shut it with a snap and slid it back into the pocket. "It's nearly twelve," he said.

"So it is," said Kit, missing the significance.

"What do you say to a nice lunch at The Imperial? It's the finest new restaurant in the city."

Kit shifted in her seat. "Thank you, but I promised to run some errands for my aunt."

"Frederica."

Kit didn't like the way he said her name, as if she was at once a social equal and an object of annoyance.

"We might have dinner, then," Sloate said. "You are still new to the city. I would be very happy to treat you to some of the brighter spots. Tomorrow night, shall we say?"

Kit said nothing. The conversation had shifted radically from professional prospects to a social direction. Maybe it was nothing more than a new employer showing kindness to his new hire. Maybe she should say yes, so as not to offend him. But something kept her from answering.

Sloate's scrawny eyebrows slid downward toward his aquiline nose. He stood up, walked again to the window, and looked out. Kit could hear the sputter of a motorcar passing below.

"Something you should know," Sloate said. "I've made the careers of more than a few lawyers and politicians. Powerful men who needed my help at one time or another. Without that help, I daresay they would never have reached certain positions. I have also, on occasion, had to do the very opposite. I have stopped certain men in their tracks and scuttled some promising careers."

Kit said nothing. The office, which had seemed so large when she entered, now suddenly had a claustrophobic feel.

"What you are seeking is something rather grand," Sloate said. "Something for the history books." He turned then, his dull gray eyes wide. "I am prepared to help you make history."

"I appreciate that very much, Mr. Sloate."

He removed his pince-nez from his vest pocket and placed them on his nose. He then considered her, almost as if she were a piece of art. Kit moved in her chair.

"Your hair is lovely," Sloate said.

"Thank you," Kit said.

"Red. Classically red. Not the color of carrots, but the red of a Titian. You know Titian?"

"The Renaissance painter?"

"Very good. Great passion in his work. You must see it sometime. Perhaps I'll show you."

How had they moved to a discussion of art? Kit took in a breath and boldly said, "About my position, Mr. Sloate—"

He silenced her with an upraised hand and removed his glasses with the other. "Yes, yes. As I was saying, I will give you the help you require. But as with everything in this life, my dear, there is something to be paid. A price, as it were."

Kit sensed from him a new hesitancy about her, perhaps about her willingness to pay such a cost, by which he no doubt meant hard work and sacrifice. "I'm prepared to do whatever it takes to be a success," she said.

"I'm very glad you said that, my dear. From time to time we shall have dinner together, not for business purposes but for the pleasure of social intercourse."

Kit frowned. This was not a prospect she looked on with even slight enthusiasm. Still, an older man of legal prominence might feel that being seen with a young woman on occasion was somehow good for business. If so, it would be a small price to pay.

"I suppose that would be acceptable, Mr. Sloate. When may I start?"

"And," Sloate said quickly, his fingers rubbing themselves rapidly now, "I will entertain you in my home on a regular basis." His smile showed crooked, yellow teeth.

It was the sight of those teeth that ushered in the sudden realization. Her face flushed hot. Waves of shock, anger, and mortification burst through her, dashing all her hopes on the rocks of Sloate's sordid intentions. Kit slowly stood up. Her voice shook as she spoke. "Mr. Sloate, I am not . . . I will not . . ." She shook her head vigorously.

"Don't be timid, my dear," said Sloate, his voice silky. "You are a woman of great ambition. You cannot think there is no price for that ambition, can you? To do what you are proposing will require a sacrifice on your part. What I am offering you is success guaranteed. And also something in return. I am an accomplished lover. Considerate, lavish in my spending."

He took a step toward her.

Kit stepped back. "You're mad if you think I would ever consider such a proposition."

Sloate's face suddenly tightened. "Now, you must think about this."

"I don't need to think about it!"

One more step from Sloate. "But you do. I am a very powerful man."

Sloate was between Kit and the door to his office. It would take physical contact to get by him, unless he allowed her to do so. And his look told her he wouldn't.

"You are so lovely," he said, advancing until he was a mere arm's length away. He smelled of sweat and the stale scent of cigars.

What should she do? Surely this man, as uncouth as he had turned out to be, was not going to put his hands on her.

Kit steadied her emotions by taking in a deep breath. "Mr. Sloate, please let me by."

"Don't go just yet," Sloate said.

"Please."

His eyes narrowed, becoming slits of gray. Suddenly his hands were on her shoulders, and he pulled her to himself. He found her mouth with his and then, unbelievably, engaged her in a forceful kiss.

Kit fought against his embrace, but he was stronger than he

appeared. She managed to turn her head.

"Stop!" Kit pushed away, but her back hit the wall with a hard thump. Sloate ran his hand upward from her waist. He squeezed her closer, his strong grasp taking the breath out of her. She tried once more to push him away, but he was imbued with a lustful intensity. He pressed his lips on her neck. She turned her head left, then right, her hat flying off in the process.

"No!" Kit managed to say, but it was muffled in another kiss as Sloate moved on relentlessly.

Kit felt along the wall with her hand, seeking anything that might serve as an anchor to pull herself away. She felt the corner of a small table and scoured its surface. Her hand closed around a small, heavy sculpture of some kind.

With a force that frightened her, Kit slammed the implement into the side of Sloate's face. He shrieked and crumbled to the floor.

Fighting for breath, Kit tossed the statuette on the table, seeing in passing that it was a small rendition of Michaelangelo's *David*. She ran for Sloate's door.

"If you breathe a word!" Sloate screamed after her. She raced down the wooden stairs that led to the front door of the building and burst out onto the street.

Chapter Six

HE HATED LIGHT. For as long as he could remember, light was his enemy. It shone brightly and exposed him, burned through him like a candle through a leaf.

Oh, he could walk in the light. He could go about his business and appear as normal and, yes, even as winsome as any other man. In fact, part of him desired to inhabit that aspect permanently.

But the greater part desired darkness.

He had known since he was a child that he was two people, two sides. One side was dutiful, even charming. It could live among people and thrive.

The other side, though, was the one that captured his imagination. This side told him there was no need to live a life of rules and regulations as everyone said, as everyone wanted to force on him. He had lived in that sort of world, with everyone telling him what to do, since he was a child, and they had put "the fear of God" into him.

As a boy he would sometimes go back and forth between his two aspects as his father laid the leather on his back. What he found was that the good side took the pain too much to heart. The other side, the side that showed contempt for God or any fear of Him, felt much better. He had learned early on to inhabit that side when his father was ready to beat him. He had learned early on to despise God.

He had also learned to fool everyone at his pleasure. He could be charming for as long as he wished, days even, and no one would be the wiser.

A few years ago he had read Stevenson's tale, *The Strange Case of Dr. Jekyll and Mr. Hyde*, and felt he was reading his own biography. It was true—two natures could co-exist in one body, both needing to breathe free. . . .

Now, as he walked the teeming streets in the light, he felt freer than he had in years. He had wondered what it would be like to shed blood finally, after thinking about it for so long. It had been good. It was liberating. The ultimate adventure. He was hungry to try it again.

Feeling that hunger rise within him, something he could not control, he also felt a slight pang of regret for what he knew he would soon do.

Why should he be this way? he asked himself. But the voice that asked was small in comparison to the rising vociferation of need.

It was now a matter of choice. Whom would he consume?

There was the unmistakable pull toward the dirty women who sold themselves to men. In that way he could purge not only their sin but his own, the sin his father so gladly reminded him of at every opportunity.

But there was another thought, one he had not had previously. There was also sin in the opposite world, the world of the beauties and socialites who flitted with such smugness across ballrooms and mansions throughout the city. The same ones he would charm and cajole when he was feeling, well, more like Jekyll.

One face came to his mind again, as it had done several times previously. The pretty, fresh face of the young girl from the East, the spirited one. Red hair, green eyes, lovely to look at.

Perhaps she should be the one. For he sensed she was not one of the smug ones now, but untainted. If he consumed her he could keep her from that sin, from being stained.

He had the day to think about it. His hunger always sought its final satisfaction at night.

Night . . .

———————

Almost swooning, Kit realized she had walked a city block with virtually no recall of her steps. Her head was ablaze with visions of Sloate's attack. Added to that was a volatile combination of indignity and outrage. That he had lured her to his office with a promise of a possible professional position and then turned so viciously on her, made her feel both soiled and livid. She didn't know whether to crawl under a rock or kick down a door.

The afternoon sun beat down on the city and Kit's bare head. Added to her indignation was the realization that her hat was still in the office of Heath Sloate. What would he do with it? Tear it to shreds or keep it as an object of scorn?

Her legs kept moving. Suddenly Kit heard a loud yell from a man seated on a buckboard being driven by a very large horse. "Watch out there!" he bellowed, and Kit found herself in the middle of the street as the man yanked at his horse just before it would have knocked her to the ground. It came so close she could feel the snorting breath of the animal, which seemed as angry as its master.

"Get outter the street!" the man bellowed, and Kit, her mind reeling, stumbled off the asphaltum strip and onto the cemented sidewalk.

Here she paused, finally, to catch her breath. She had no idea where she was. The street looked like others she had seen, and the passing parade of pedestrians paid her no mind. Though she had been told how the streets of downtown had been laid out in a grid, she had to admit that for the moment at least, she was lost.

Lost . . .

The feeling in the pit of her stomach was familiar. It was the same, she realized, as the day she'd been told her father—her anchor in the swirling world—had been killed in a local saloon.

As was told to her later, Harry Shannon had been riding through Lowell on his horse, having preached a Wednesday night sermon in the little village of Fawrhat. The locals knew her father by name and vocation, and more than a few of them didn't like him one bit. He preached temperance, and that was not what the liquor trade and barflies in Lowell wanted to hear.

This night as he rode by a saloon called the Blarney Cove—Irish in name and habitués—two of the town's loudmouths had shouted to him, calling him a coward for not coming in where all the "sinners" were.

Well, Harry Shannon was never one to run from a fight—with his fists when he was a pagan and with his words after he was saved. The two louts must have shuddered in wonder, Kit always believed, when the preacher took them up on their challenge.

Harry Shannon was a big man, too, and how Kit wished she could have witnessed that scene: Her daddy marching right into the pit with his Bible, slamming it on the bar, and announcing that he was going to preach a sermon right then and there.

She was told later that his text was from Proverbs 23, and that he kept returning to the verse, "Be not among winebibbers; among riotous eaters of flesh" when a drunken man shouted at her father to "shut his mug." Her father refused and kept right on with, "The drunkard and the glutton shall come to poverty, and drowsiness shall clothe a man with rags." At that point the drunk pulled a pistol from his coat and waved it around in the air.

Then things happened quickly. Another patron, this one more favorably disposed to her father's message, began urging the troublemaker to let things be. When the man refused and became even more insistent that Harry leave the bar, the other man tried to rush him.

The bystanders quickly ran away or ducked under tables, fearing gunfire.

Her father ran right toward the trouble. The two men were wrestling each other, the one man holding the wrist of the drunk with the gun, keeping the revolver at bay.

"Stop this, men!" her father was said to have shouted. Those were his last words. Just as he reached the combatants, the drunk freed himself, took one step backward, and the gun—depending on the account—was either fired deliberately or just went off.

A single bullet entered her father's heart. He fell to the floor and died almost immediately.

When Kit heard that her father was dead, all belief in the goodness of life rushed out of her eleven-year-old body. How could it be? She would never sit on his lap again, never smell his wonderful Papa smell and listen to his lilting Irish voice tell stories from the Bible. She still had her mother, of course, but Papa had been her lighthouse, her beacon in the darkness. She felt secure and right with him in her life. And she felt she could accomplish anything when he told her that she could, indeed, make her life account for something.

Without him she was lost. . . .

As she was now, standing in the heart of Los Angeles, suddenly as desolate a place as the farthest unexplored island.

Kit began to walk again, needing to move, not knowing or caring where she was going. Just to get as far away from Heath Sloate as she could.

At the crest of a hill, she came around a corner and stopped suddenly at the sight of a majestic rose-stone building. A proud clock tower dominated the front, winged by a tiled roof of copper, gold, and red. Kit was drawn to it as if hypnotized, as if a voice inside the place called out to her like a ghost in some Gothic novel.

She walked toward the building. When she reached the stone steps leading up to the large doors, she saw the brass-plated sign and knew why she had felt compelled. *County Courthouse*, it read.

That's when the tears came. The sting of humiliation was now coupled with a stark truth: She would never get inside that building. Not as a member of the bar, anyway. Maybe this was God's sign, His will that she forever be shut out of the inner court, a mere spectator.

Aware that people were near, she hid her face in her gloved hand and turned quickly to walk away.

She bumped hard into a man and fell backward. The jolt made her sorry she'd not allowed Mrs. Norris to sew padding into her petticoat.

"I am sorry!" the man said quickly. His voice was resonant, pleasant. Kit saw only his white pants and, of all things, spats. She felt his hands take hers and begin pulling her to her feet.

He would see her red eyes, no doubt. She attempted to look away even as she uttered her own apology.

"Now, then, what's the trouble?" the man said.

There was no hiding her distress. Kit turned to look at him. He was young, perhaps in his early thirties, and he had thick black eyebrows that almost met and arched upward at the temple. He was fine featured, his nose and mouth aqualine, with high cheekbones plainly marked. His eyes were a piercing blue. They reminded her of Ted Fox's eyes. But in these eyes was a coiled intensity as well as a sharpness of vision, as if he could see things others could not. A man, Kit thought, that could not be fooled.

"I'm sorry, sir. Please excuse my outburst," Kit said.

"Outbursts usually have a purpose," the man said, his tone friendly. In a resplendent white suit and straw hat, he looked like what her father might have called a "dandy." Yet there was nothing dandy about him. He seemed somehow tough even though he was, at the moment, tender. "Can you tell me why it should happen outside the courthouse?"

Should she tell him, a perfect stranger? Unburden herself to him, even though she didn't know him from Adam? Well, she had nothing to gain or lose at this point, so she heard herself say to him, "Sir, do you think it unseemly for a woman to practice law?"

The man smiled then, showing perfect white teeth. He seemed surprised and delighted. "That all depends," he said, "on the woman."

Who was he? she wondered.

"Would that woman be you?" he asked.

"I have a law certificate from the Women's Legal Education Society in New York," Kit said. "I thought in coming to Los Angeles I might find opportunity."

"I see. By your reaction, you fear there may be none?"

She didn't answer, knowing the look on her face was answer enough. The man took a gold watch from his vest pocket, looked at the time, then said, "Have you ever witnessed a trial?"

No, never. She had no thought of becoming a courtroom lawyer. Of all the women she had heard of who were admitted to the bar, none had been a trial lawyer. It just wasn't done.

"I have not, sir," she said.

"Tell you what. Come on inside. Spend a couple of hours watching."

Before she knew what was happening, he had taken her arm and was leading her up the steps toward the courthouse doors.

"I'm sorry, sir, but I don't know you," she said, feeling she should at least hold up a certain decorum for Aunt Freddy's sake.

"You do now," the man said. "My name's Earl Rogers. I practice law."

———

Heath Sloate pressed the wet handkerchief to his throbbing temple. He stopped the flow of blood, which hadn't been as much as he had feared. When that demon girl hit him he thought it was a deeper wound and feared blood would get all over his clothes and worse, his Oriental carpet. Luck had been with him there. The only sign of bleeding now was the red splotch on his linen handkerchief.

His head would hurt for days. How he hated physical pain! He loathed even a hint of imperfection in his physical or sartorial makeup. But much worse than all that—worse even than the pain and the bruise that would come—was the indignity. To have that strumpet turn down his proposition! A girl with no prospects at all, and he in a position to help her. He, Sloate, who could do more for her with a single wave of his arm than she could in one hundred years by herself. To have this little witch resist and then attack him! It was almost more than he could bear.

His first thoughts were violent, but he quickly reminded himself he would never have to stoop to that. After all, he had spent a lifetime learning to get his way without having to devolve to mere corporal measures.

Coming of age in a boarding school where he was the smallest in his class forced Sloate to learn all the tricks of mental survival.

He remembered how, when he was twelve, one of the "uppers," a sixteen-year-old, big and proud of his physical prowess, had pulled down Heath's pants in the open quad one day for no other reason than sport. In the midst of derisive laughter, unable to stop his humiliation, Heath Sloate felt his first real fire of lethal hate. But being at the top of his class academically, he knew that what he couldn't do with fists he could do with brains.

His tormentor, Wexell, was being groomed by his father for a career in politics, and Tomlin's School was considered the very best preparatory education for this. If one came out with a clean record there, one could pick and choose among a handful of eminent colleges—Harvard, Yale, Dartmouth, Princeton—and virtually ensure a jeweled career. The opposite was true as well. A black mark at this level would seriously hinder a climb up the rungs.

The plan Heath Sloate formed came to him all at once and involved the elegant silver snuffbox that sat regally on the desk of Headmaster James Mills, who also taught Latin. Mills had received it, he was fond of saying, from General Andy Jackson himself after the Battle of New Orleans where Mills, as a thirty-two-year-old officer, had distinguished himself.

The plan was simple because it was so inconceivable. No one would have dared to even touch the snuffbox. Old Mills, his bushy white mustache flecked with fine tobacco detritus, would have rapped with his knotty cane any hand that came close. However, it was not difficult in the least for Heath to purloin the box one day during the games.

Wexell and his roommate were, of course, involved in the races and throwing events, and the entire school was watching. So it was no great feat for Heath to enter Wexell's room and slip the silver box under Wexell's pine wardrobe, the one with the fancy New York clothes his daddy had purchased for him.

The next day the school was in an uproar, starting with Old

Mills waving his cane in the air like a saber, threatening to whack the entire student body unless the thief stepped forward. Heath felt exhilarated at the power he wielded. This pandemonium was all because of him! And no one knew, or would ever know, the source.

After letting the tempest play for a day, Heath enacted the final part of his scheme—he lied. He was pleased with his ability to lie because he saw it as the avenue of his rage. He knew from that moment onward he would be able to say whatever he wanted to say and people would believe him, whether it was based in truth or not.

He appeared in Old Mills' office sheepishly to report that he had heard a snippet of conversation, that it concerned the snuffbox, but that he was loathe to report it out of honor. He was even able to bring forth a tear as he asked the headmaster what he should do with his terrible secret.

The old man reacted just as Sloate had known he would. With a grandfatherly embrace, he told Heath that he was proud of him for coming forward and for feeling in his breast the tug of an ethical conundrum. "That is what makes men of boys," he said. "Now tell me who took my box."

Sloate asked if his identity would have to be revealed. Mills assured him it would not, for he was not *accusing* anyone but only reporting information. Assured of that, Heath let out that this was only a rumor based upon an overheard discourse, but that the name Wexell had come up and something about a hiding place right in his room.

Events happened quickly after that. Old Mills, with two seniors in tow, barged into Wexell's room and, in the face of Wexell's wailing and denials, proceeded to search the place. The box was found under the wardrobe.

Wexell was expelled, his reputation ruined. And Heath Sloate, upon his graduation from Tomlin's, was given one of the most glowing recommendations ever from the school, signed by James Mills himself.

And so Sloate discovered the pleasures of manipulation of humanity, of the elimination of competition. It wasn't too long afterward that he read Charles Darwin, and his philosophy of life was soon complete.

All of life is a struggle to survive and thrive. If you don't eliminate those who threaten you, you die. The world belongs to the strong.

Now, sitting in his office, Sloate knew he had come to another situation that would have to be dealt with. He knew the Shannon girl wouldn't say anything about the encounter. Women simply did not discuss such matters. It would be shameful.

Even if she did, no one would believe her. The word of a young snipe from back East against that of Heath Sloate, one of the most respected men in the community, indeed, the state? He was confident even Kit would know that would be no use.

He wondered if he should immediately report that *she* had attacked *him*. He could easily carry out the lie, but there would be questions raised. The biddies would begin to gossip and perhaps speculate about what Sloate *might* have done. In many ways, gossip was worse than a lawsuit. You could silence the law by a favorable verdict; not so the mouths of society busybodies.

He would have to get rid of Kit Shannon. Her independent streak was like a loose cannon, and if she stayed in the city and, worse, were ever to make it to the bar, she could become a true annoyance at best, a career-wrecker at worst. Once she gained professional credibility her accusations against him would become correspondingly believable.

She would have to be stopped now. At this stage, it wouldn't be difficult. And he had the perfect vehicle for it in the palm of his hand—Frederica Fairbank. In addition to getting his hands on her money, Sloate now envisioned another use for the old battle-ax. He would subtly poison her against her great-niece. She would withdraw her sponsorship of Miss Kit Shannon, and the girl would be forced to leave the city.

Simple, elegant, and as easy as snatching a snuffbox off a desk. The strong eliminating the weak. Sloate smiled and noticed that his head felt much better.

Chapter Seven

WHEN KIT ENTERED the courtroom, a buff-colored chamber with a high ceiling and a long row of deep-set windows with plush, brown curtains, she felt nearly breathless. The man leading her in was Earl Rogers himself, the one Corazón had called a devil. But he didn't seem devilish, at least not yet. And here she was, about to watch him conduct a murder trial! Kit could hear her aunt's voice: *The very idea!*

Rogers said, "I'll leave you here now, but let's talk afterward." And with that he headed up the center aisle.

Kit looked around the courtroom, which held rows of wooden seats, nearly all filled with spectators. Just past the front row, Kit saw the three-foot carved railing called the bar, with its swinging gate for the lawyers to pass through.

"There's a seat for you there, miss," a man in a blue uniform said, pointing to an empty chair in the back row. "You'll be set for an afternoon's entertainment."

"Thank you," Kit said, feeling at once completely out of place and immensely curious. The back row, all men, stood politely as she made her way to the chair. The looks on their faces told her she was a bit of an oddity, a young lady at a murder trial. She tried not to look nervous.

Kit took in everything in the room, from the judge's elevated bench to the somber jury box, now empty, with its twelve dark chairs. And then the counsel tables where an older gentleman, wearing a dark suit, stood chatting with some men in the first row. Rogers had headed to the other table and removed his hat, revealing black hair parted in the middle. Seated in a chair, with a policeman standing at the side, was a young man whom Rogers patted on the back.

"Well, I'll be hanged," a voice near her said.

Turning, Kit saw a familiar face seated at the other end of her row looking her way. It was the reporter, the one she'd met on the train. Phelps, wasn't it? In a second he was standing, requesting that the other men move so he could be seated next to her. They grumbled but complied. Kit noticed they all had pencils and papers.

"So you didn't take my advice," Tom Phelps said. "You're still here."

Kit smiled graciously. "I am."

"Fascinating. And now you're here to watch this shooting star, Earl Rogers, get his comeuppance?"

Her curiosity piqued even more, Kit said, "How is that?"

"Oh, we all thought he was unbeatable. That's all about to change, miss. You see that gentleman up there?" Phelps pointed to the older, stout man. "That's former Senator Stephen W. Garber. He's handling the prosecution of Mr. William Adair for the cold-blooded shooting of Mr. Jerome Hammon. And the evidence of guilt is overwhelming. There is no way out of this one. Adair's head is as good as in the noose."

Conflicting emotions charged through Kit. She found herself feeling sympathy for Rogers, who had been so charming to her, yet also a vague sense of repulsion. If the defendant was clearly guilty, then he should be found guilty. How would justice be served if Rogers prevailed?

Phelps seemed about to say something more when a back door opened and an older gentleman with a head of full white hair and an elegant mustache entered. "Remain seated and come to order," the clerk of the court said. "This court is once again in session."

The older gentleman sat down in the judge's chair and said, "Bring back the jury." The clerk left, and a few moments later twelve men entered the courtroom and took their places in the jury box.

The judge then addressed the prosecutor. "Senator Garber, you may continue with your examination of Dr. Khurtz."

"Thank you, Your Honor," Garber said, standing. His voice was resonant and full of confidence. He turned to a man in the front row. "Dr. Khurtz, will you please resume the stand?"

The man walked through the gate and took a seat on the witness chair. He was around forty and looked composed and alert.

Kit leaned forward in her chair, mesmerized.

"Now, Doctor," Garber began as he strutted up and down in front of the jury, "when we broke you were describing the entry wound of the victim, Jerome Hammon."

"Yes, sir."

"And you have determined that he died from a bullet wound, is that correct?"

"Yes, sir."

"And can you describe for the gentlemen of the jury the direction from which the bullet entered Mr. Hammon?"

"It would have been a downward direction."

"I see. So the shot that killed Jerome Hammon was fired from a man standing in front of him, firing downward into his stomach. Is that right?" Garber questioned.

"Yes, sir."

Garber, a smug look across his face, whirled toward Earl Rogers and said, "Take the witness!"

Phelps leaned over toward Kit and whispered, "They've already established Adair shot the gun. He's done for."

Kit watched as Earl Rogers stood up. In order to move past his table, he turned slightly toward the gallery, and for a quick moment glanced her way. Kit thought she saw the hint of a smile on his lips, as if signaling to her that he knew something no one else did.

Rogers strode toward the witness and then stopped. From a vest pocket he withdrew a gold lorgnette tethered to his vest by a black ribbon. He put the eyeglasses to his face and peered at the witness as if studying him. The entire courtroom held a collective breath.

Suddenly he shoved the lorgnette back into his pocket and said, ever so politely, "Good afternoon, Dr. Khurtz."

"Good afternoon, sir."

"We have heard you this morning, and just now, describe the wounds of Jerome Hammon. But we haven't heard you describe the wounds to my client, Mr. Adair."

"No one has asked me."

"May I be so bold?" Rogers bowed slightly.

"Of course."

Kit cast a quick glance at Stephen Garber. The prosecutor shifted slightly in his chair, poised to catch every word.

"You also made an examination of Mr. Adair after the shooting, did you not?"

"I did."

"And you made a written description for the police?"

"Yes," the doctor said.

"Mr. Adair suffered several wounds to his head and face, is that right?"

"Yes."

Rogers turned from the witness and strode to the prosecution's table. His grace was elegant, Kit thought. Rogers reached under the table and withdrew a cane with a thick gold knob and returned to the witness.

"This is Mr. Hammon's cane," Rogers said. "According to your written report to the police, the wounds inflicted upon Mr. Adair are consistent with being struck with a cane."

"Yes, sir."

Handing the cane to the witness, Rogers said, "And what part of the cane was that."

"Objection!" Garber shouted. "It has not been established that the defendant was struck with that particular cane."

The judge nodded. "Sustained."

"Let me rephrase," said Rogers. "If, hypothetically speaking, a cane hypothetically similar to this one were used on Mr. Adair, which hypothetical part of the cane would that have been?"

Most of the jury and spectators began to laugh. Kit felt a broad smile on her face, as well. Garber looked as if he might object again but held back.

The witness held up the cane and pointed to the shaft near the tip. "It would have been around here," he said.

"In other words," said Rogers, "not the handle."

"Correct."

"The wounds would have been inflicted by someone striking Mr. Adair several times while holding it like a weapon, correct?"

"Yes, sir."

Rogers took the cane and turned to Garber. "Hypothetically speaking, of course."

Once more, laughter filled the courtroom. This time the judge gaveled for order.

To Kit it was clear that Rogers had scored several points, though she wasn't sure of the significance. At the very least he was holding the entire courtroom in the palm of his hand. It was almost like a revival preacher captivating a tent full of rustic sinners.

"Your Honor," said Earl Rogers, "at this time the defense would like to present an exhibit for the doctor to examine."

As if this were simple routine, the judge said, "You may present."

Earl Rogers looked toward the back of the courtroom and motioned someone to come forward. Kit turned, with everyone else, toward the doors. A rough-looking man, obviously uncomfortable in his gabardine suit, entered the courtroom carrying something covered by burlap. It was the approximate size of a loaf of bread.

"My associate, Mr. Jory," Rogers told the court.

The judge seemed as fascinated with the mysterious package as everyone else. The only face that showed any animosity belonged to Stephen Garber.

The man Jory, at Rogers' direction, placed the exhibit in the middle of the counsel table.

"And now, if I may question the good doctor," said Rogers, "on his very own findings."

With that, Rogers reached down and dramatically snatched the burlap cover from the object on his table. Kit strained to see, but her vision was obscured by two men in front of her.

She did hear a shriek from a woman in the front row and a collective gasp from just about everyone else. The faces of the twelve jurors were pictures of wide-eyed incredulity.

Immediately Stephen Garber was on his feet, shouting at the

top of his lungs. "Your Honor, I protest! This is outrageous!"

Not able to stand it any longer, Kit jumped to her feet so she could see the object of so much commotion. And see it she did, though she had never seen anything like it before.

It was a large jar filled with clear liquid and stuffed with what looked like dead snakes.

Immediately the judge banged his gavel and shouted, "I will have order here!" The room became immediately silent. And then Kit realized the judge was staring directly at her. "Young woman, you will please take your seat!"

Earl Rogers turned and looked at her. She felt her cheeks catch fire as the debonair attorney, blue eyes glistening, smiled.

She dropped back in her seat, wishing it were in a ten-foot hole.

"Now explain yourself, Mr. Rogers," the judge said.

"Why, of course, Your Honor," said Rogers. "In this jar are the intestines of the deceased, Mr. Jerome Hammon."

Another gasp from the spectators. Garber slammed his hand on his table with a loud *thwack*. "This is unholy, Your Honor!"

Rogers smiled at Garber. "Say, Steve, you're not trying to keep evidence from the jury, are you?"

Wagging his finger at Rogers, Garber shouted, "Grave robber! Ghoul!"

"I claim no such honorifics, Judge!" Rogers said sharply. "Chief Autopsy Surgeon Khurtz has testified that the bullet from my client's gun ranged downward, that it must have been fired from above to penetrate the intestines as he found them. I propose now, by this medical exhibit, to prove beyond a reasonable doubt that the bullet didn't go down at all. It ranged *up*!"

In the stunned silence that followed, Steve Garber could only whisper, "You're out of your mind."

"Your Honor, the prosecution's entire case rests on the surmise that the bullet could not have been fired by Mr. Adair as he lay on the floor being attacked by Hammon. I propose to prove to the jury that it couldn't have been fired from anywhere else. My client's life depends on my ability to prove what I just said. I'm offering the best possible evidence, the bullet's actual path through the actual intestines of the deceased, which I have had delivered here by court order from the coroner."

"Your Honor," Garber said weakly, "if you please!"

The judge ran one finger across his mustache as he scowled at Earl Rogers. He repeated that gesture several times over the next minute, which seemed to stretch out endlessly. Then quickly he said, "Mr. Rogers, you may proceed."

"I object!" Garber shouted, "I object with the utmost vehemence, Your Honor!"

"Your vehemence will be noted by the reporter," said the judge. "Go ahead, Mr. Rogers."

Bowing to the judge and then to Garber, Earl Rogers once again approached Dr. Khurtz.

"Dr. Khurtz, you were present at the autopsy of the deceased, were you not?"

The obviously flustered witness said, "Yes, sir."

Rogers took the jar from his table and carried it to the witness. "I show you now the defense exhibit, containing the intestines of Jerome Hammon. Doctor, do you see an entry wound in what is commonly called the bowels?"

The doctor, along with the jurors, leaned forward. "Yes, I do."

Rogers turned the jar and held it up higher. "And do you see the exit wound?"

"Yes, sir."

"And you have testified that the only way to explain the relationship between these two wounds is that the bullet ranged downward, correct?"

"That is correct."

"Sir," Rogers said, "will you please come stand next to me?"

The confused witness looked toward Stephen Garber. The prosecutor waved his hand. "Go along with Mr. Rogers' circus," he said disdainfully.

"Thanks, Steve," Rogers said as Dr. Khurtz joined him. "Now, Doctor, please face the jury."

Khurtz obeyed, albeit slowly.

"I will hold the jar in front of my body, in the position where the intestines would normally be. With your finger please show the jury the approximate path of the bullet as it entered Mr. Hammon."

Using his right index finger, Khurtz pointed to the jar of intestines at a forty-five degree angle from above, tracing the air until he touched the glass where the bullet wound showed.

"Now, Doctor, will you please trace the path of the bullet again." And before Khurtz could react, Rogers turned the jar upside down. The contents moved slightly, causing a woman in the front row to squeal.

Khurtz shook his head. "But I can't."

"Of course you can. Holding them this way, the bullet would have traveled what direction?"

"Up, but—"

Suddenly Rogers reached into Khurtz's pocket and removed a fountain pen. He placed in on the floor in front of Khurtz's feet. "Would you be so kind as to pick up your pen, Doctor?"

Khurtz hesitated, shrugged, and then leaned over. Just as his fingers reached the pen, Rogers shouted, "Stop!" Khurtz froze in his position, and before anyone could react, including Garber, Rogers continued. "In this position, Dr. Khurtz, as you are bending over with your shoulders below your waist, the position of your intestines is precisely as appears in this overturned jar. Is that not correct?"

Slowly, the light of realization across his face, Khurtz stood up. His fountain pen remained at his feet.

"I object to this sideshow!" Garber cried. But it was too late. The expression on the judge's face showed that the trap had already been sprung.

"Overruled," the judge said.

Rogers did not hesitate. "And so, if Mr. Hammon was leaning over the prostrate body of Mr. Adair, beating him about the head, and Mr. Adair fired up, the trajectory of the bullet would be exactly as it is, in fact, represented right here!"

He held the jar aloft like a trophy.

"That is correct," Khurtz said quietly.

"No further questions," said Rogers triumphantly. As he returned to his chair he paused to face the gallery, like an actor at a curtain call. And then he smiled at Kit—and winked!

Kit realized her heart was racing as if she'd just run up a hill.

"Well, I'll be hanged," she heard Phelps say.

Chapter Eight

EVENTS AFTER THE THRILLING afternoon in court followed quickly. After adjournment, the gathered reporters rushed to Earl Rogers, seeking comment. It was as if the *Maine* had blown up right in this courtroom, and Rogers was holding the dynamite.

Then Rogers, asking for patience, strode to the back row to ask Kit if she would join him for dinner, and said she really had no choice because he would not take no for an answer, and she had found herself saying yes.

She knew why, too. What she had just experienced was an epiphany, and it felt to her like a pillar of cloud, a sign from God. Everyone in that courtroom, including herself, had assumed the defendant was guilty. Public comment and opinion made it a foregone conclusion.

Then Earl Rogers had struck. With cunning cross-examination and a ploy more outrageous than she could have imagined—the dead man's insides!—he had turned the entire matter on its head.

That is *it*! Kit thought. The skill of the lawyer to see justice done in the face of seemingly insurmountable obstacles! It moved her as nothing had before in her life. She never thought criminal law could make her feel this way. But she had not known Earl Rogers.

And when she found herself seated at a table for two in an exquisite restaurant, across from this legal miracle worker, it had seemed like a continuation of God's mighty hand.

She had a million questions for him, and he had a few for her. As they dined he elicited from Kit her desire to practice law, her education, and a bit of her background. He seemed most interested. Then Kit asked about the cross-examination he had conducted, and his eyes flashed with passion.

"Cross-examination is the greatest engine of truth ever invented," he said. "But it is an art as well as a science. The witness, especially the lying witness, will do everything in his power to protect his story. The trial lawyer must know how to pry the truth loose."

"How?" Kit asked anxiously.

Rogers chuckled. "A number of ways. In every cross-examination there should be one major aim. Like a magician, the lawyer must misdirect the witness from that aim, lest he hide behind some prevarication. At precisely the right moment, the lawyer can change his course, leave an innocuous line of questioning, and suddenly thrust home."

"But how does he know when that moment occurs?"

Rogers tapped his head. "Instinct, mostly. Also knowing what the witness will likely say. Like the good doctor."

"How did you know what he would say?"

"Because I was more prepared than he was. That's the key."

There was that word again. *Preparation.* Hardly pausing for a breath, Kit said, "Will the jury believe your version?"

"Yes," said Rogers without hesitation.

"How can you know that?"

Rogers smiled as a teacher would at an eager student. "Because of the Rule of Human Probabilities."

Kit frowned. "What is that?"

"It's really very simple. Everyone judges events against a standard of human experience. They ask themselves, how would I act under similar circumstances? If the action seems in line with common sense or experience, it is likely to be accepted as true."

Rogers leaned forward and placed the elegant salt and pepper shakers together. "Now, when two people get together, they combine that experience of observation, and it becomes sharper. But put twelve good and true men in the jury box, and you have the Rule of Human Probabilities in its greatest force. I merely try to anticipate what is probable human action, and then undertake to show the jury why they should believe one or the other."

Then Rogers pointed a finger at Kit's head. "Just remember this," he said. "You have an instinct, right up there, that will help you find the truth. You can size people up and determine what they probably did or did not do. That's what it takes to become a great trial lawyer."

Those last words were the ones that quickened her heart. Was he really saying *she* might become a trial lawyer, too? Like him? But how?

Then he asked, "How would you like to work for me?"

Kit thought for a moment she might faint—fall right off her chair and lie there on the floor in front of a dozen aghast patrons. Some of them would grumble before turning back to their brandy or beef Bourguignon, while others would snap for the maître d' and order the baggage removed.

How could this cream of society possibly understand that the course of her life had just taken a hairpin turn?

Rogers must have seen the color leave her face, for he quickly offered her a glass of water. Laughing, he said, "Did I upset you?"

Waving a hand in front of her face, Kit said, "I don't know what to say." And in truth, she didn't. On the one hand, this seemed to be an offer God had dropped in her lap. On the other, though, was the thought of what had happened when she was offered a position by Heath Sloate. That memory made her shiver.

At that precise moment, Rogers said, "I determine, from the Rule of Human Probabilities, that you are concerned about my intentions."

Amazing! she thought. *Like a reader of minds!*

"Let me assure you," said Rogers, "that this offer is strictly professional. My wife's name is Hazel, and I have a daughter, Adela. And mind, I am only asking for you to help with research and working up cases. I can't pay you much. You'll have to prove yourself. But if you do, I promise you this. I'll train you and then stand with you for the bar."

Kit hesitated. How could she be sure this was right? Would she be acting merely on her own feelings and desires? She could almost hear her father's deep voice, paraphrasing Scripture: *"Do not be wise in your own eyes."*

"What were you thinking just then?" Rogers asked.

Smiling sheepishly, Kit said, "Just of my father."

"Where is he?"

She looked down at the table. "He was killed when I was eleven."

"I'm sorry," Rogers said.

"He was a preacher. I miss him terribly." When she looked up, wondering if she had said too much, she was surprised to see a look of sadness etched across Rogers' face. At first she was afraid she'd offended him somehow, bringing ruin to what had been a lovely dinner.

Then he said, "That's quite a coincidence. My father was also a preacher. He also died, and I also miss him terribly."

There was in that moment such a vulnerability in Rogers that Kit knew she could trust him. The fact that they had this much in common seemed like a sign.

Kit said, "I would be honored to work for you, Mr. Rogers. When can I begin?"

"Would next week be too soon?"

"No, sir."

"Then next week it is."

The meal thus became a celebration, and Kit took in all she could from Rogers about Los Angeles, the courts, and the practice of law in the new century.

When they stepped outside, Rogers ordered her a cab. The night air was warm and inviting. As the horse-drawn carriage clopped up to them, Kit heard a young voice breaking through. "Extra! Extra!" cried the newsboy.

"Breaking news," Rogers commented, and he waved to the newsy. A lad no older than twelve, wearing a cap on his head and a grin on his dirty face, bounded over holding a stack of newspapers. Rogers fished out a dime, told the boy to keep the change, and took a paper.

Kit saw that it was an *Examiner*.

"Hmm," said Rogers, perusing it. "Another prostitute murdered."

The thought filled Kit with dread. "Another?"

"Second one," Rogers said. "It could be unrelated, or it could be the same killer."

A killer of unfortunate women at large in the city? This wasn't what she had thought Los Angeles would be like. On the lower east side of Manhattan she'd come across her share of criminality. But out here?

Then she thought, *Why wouldn't it be? People are the same everywhere. Sinful, fallen. There is no place free from the darkness of evil intentions.* Hadn't she experienced that truth firsthand in Sloate's office?

Rogers put her in a cab and waved her off. The look on his face told Kit that in spite of this darker news, he was pleased. Pleased with himself—maybe even pleased with her and the challenge she represented.

This was her first step toward her dream and, in a way, vindication for her mother. A more generous and loving woman had never existed on the earth. Molly Morgan had married a handsome Irishman named Harry Shannon. Together they had given life to their love in the form of a baby girl.

Kit had been spoiled by their love, lavished with encouragement and praise the way society children were with toys and sweets.

"You can do anything you put your mind to, Kit," her mother was fond of saying.

Of course, that had been prior to her husband's death. After his passing, her mother was never the same. She strived to be supportive of Kit, to keep her spirits high and her focus on the knowledge that they would all see Harry again in heaven. But Kit knew her mother's heart was broken.

And that broken heart was only tormented by the knowledge that a supposed family friend had robbed them blind. Posing as trusted legal counsel, shoving papers at her mother she did not understand, the man had systematically taken what little they had left of value.

That had been the final straw.

Molly eventually succumbed to her broken heart and the weight of worrying over how she would provide for her young daughter.

"Oh, Mother," Kit whispered in a sigh. "I want so much to make you proud of me—to keep others from facing what you had to go through."

She thought of the murdered prostitutes then and shivered. There was an ugliness in the world that she would have to fight against over and over so long as she worked with Earl Rogers. Was she up to it? Could she master what would be necessary to face such evil and yet remain untainted by it? Would her mother—her father—have approved of her choice?

The cab drew her upward toward Angeleno Heights and Aunt Freddy's estate. The bittersweet memory of her mother faded as the Fairbank mansion came into view. Kit sat up a little straighter and squared her shoulders. The time for looking back was past. Through obstacles big or small, Kit pledged her commitment toward the future.

Her future.

Her dream.

Frederica always rose early to greet the day. It was a habit of many years, one her dear Jasper had thrust upon her. *"The oil won't come to you,"* he had loved to say, springing from his bed just before dawn. *"You've got to go to the oil!"*

She loved that about him most, his vigor and enterprise. Another of his favorite sayings was "Jump first, and grow wings later." That was the life of a wildcatter, and it is undoubtedly what led to his wealth. If there was one thing she could have changed about him, however, it would have been his manners. Jasper was not one for the niceties of the social graces.

That, in fact, had been what had driven a wedge between Frederica Stamper and her family. Proper Bostonians, they were aghast when Freddy had fallen under the charms of a dashing wildcatter from the South. Jasper Fairbank was rugged and handsome, but he hadn't been within miles of any proper school. And he had no patience for those who, he would say, "drank with their pinkies in the air." That immediately set the Stamper clan against him.

They put tremendous pressure on Freddy. Worst of the bunch was her older sister, Dabne, who almost single-handedly created a whispering campaign in the upper crust of Boston society. Freddy was forced into a choice, and she chose Jasper. Together they fled the East and the comforts of culture for an uncertain future of digging in the ground.

But Jasper had a sixth sense about oil and struck it rich just before the Civil War. He lost his fortune in the post-war depression, then gained it all back in Texas and later added to it in California.

And Freddy was finally able to reclaim a position in the upper echelons of society, this time in Los Angeles, where she knew she belonged.

Now, as she moved through the dim light of her Angeleno Heights mansion, she realized she was facing another choice, much like the one she'd had to make all those years ago.

Kit would have to go back to New York. If she stayed in Los Angeles, it was clear that there would be no avoiding scandal and, for Freddy, personal hurt.

Freddy reached into her morning coat for the letter she'd received yesterday. Maybe, if she read it again, there would be something in it she hadn't seen the first time, some small ray of hope beaming out from between the lines. Something that would allow her to keep Kit here, after all the effort she had gone through to find her.

Her mind flashed to her sister Dabne's face, screwed up tightly in that malevolent scowl she'd inherited from Mother, and her promise that Freddy would never have contact with the family "as long as I live." Well, that had been true, and Freddy had been completely cut off until word of Dabne's death in 1891.

From there, bits of news and pictures had come Freddy's way. Her other sister, Esther, had married and given birth to several children, who in turn had blessed her with grandchildren. One of these was a girl named Kathleen, but there had been some "bad business" in that family Freddy didn't fully understand. She decided she was *going* to understand, if for nothing else than to put to rest the memory of Dabne. Regaining family contact would be her revenge.

That had led to the hiring of a Pinkerton man and the eventual unfolding of the story of Kit's years in a Catholic orphanage in Boston and her life in a poor section of New York.

Now, after all that and her determination to bring Kit to Los Angeles to become the sort of woman Freddy knew she could forge—yes, a project, she would admit, but a socially acceptable one—her great-niece's presence was threatening everything Freddy had worked so hard to gain.

Freddy sat on the window bench in the library, gazed again at the letter in the impeccable hand of Heath Sloate, and read.

My Dear Frederica,

It is with deep regret and profound sorrow that I write to you. My heartfelt concern, however, and my own pervading feelings of affection for you, prompt me to do so.

Since I have known you these last several, wonderful years, I have perceived that you have always been one who wishes to know the truth, unadorned, even when it is a truth that affects you directly. It is my unhappy duty, then, to tell you the truth.

Your niece is a social danger, and I would advise that you send her back to New York. She will bring you nothing but grief in the months to come.

Today, as you know, I had an interview with her in my office.

The purpose was to see if I might, in some small way, help your niece to find a position that would make use of her education without involving her in the masculine pursuit of a legal career. It was as a friendly uncle that I made this gesture, out of respect for you, dear Freddy.

My hopes to be of service, however, were dashed the moment she set foot in my office. She was unmannered and insulting. She questioned my integrity and competence, relating to the brief conversation we'd had at your party. I will not tell you the name she called me, but it is one that I had thought reserved for the waterfront and never one I expected to be mouthed by any feminine creature.

When I attempted to interrupt her tirade, your niece struck me on the side of the head.

I thought for a moment of notifying the police and issuing a complaint against her for battery. For your sake, Freddy, I did not. In the cool light of reflection, I have come to believe that your niece may be unstable, perhaps owing to her years of confinement as a young girl.

Whatever the reason, Freddy, it is imperative that you send your niece back to New York. It would be of no consequence then if you sent her an occasional sum of money, conditioned upon her seeking treatment from medical authorities and seeking a job.

If she stays, it will be a social disaster for you. Already I have heard from two women of high station. I shan't give you their names as they have sought my advice in confidence. Suffice to say that your niece's continuing to live under your roof will result, inevitably, in painful ostracism. I will be in no position to help you.

Finally, I cannot see our own social intercourse continuing so long as your niece remains here. That would be grievous to me, as I am growing to love you more each day. Dare I think that matrimony might be our shared destiny? I dare not, unless our shared malady, your niece, is dealt with, and decisively.

Freddy, it is imperative that you keep all this to yourself. Only tell your niece she must go, and do not back down. Do not listen to anything she might say in her defense. I am afraid that, in view of her recklessness, she is not above lying.

You know my reputation, Freddy. You know that I have a stainless record of integrity. You must also know that my heart is heavy in writing this. However, I cannot in good conscience keep from telling you the truth.

For the good of all concerned, including your niece, send her forthwith whence she came.

Assured of your good sense and firm resolve, I remain,

Yours very truly,

Heath W. Sloate

Hot tears stung Freddy's eyes. It was all so complicated now and so, so tragic. There was no equivocating in the letter. As hard as it was to accept, Freddy knew Heath's way was the only way.

"He loves me," she reasoned aloud. Perhaps it was that love that drove him to such demands. He feared for her. He only wanted the best for her, and obviously the best wasn't keeping Kit in Los Angeles.

But what of her family obligations? She had already grown fond of Kit, but fondness alone was not enough to allow her to stay. And, in a way, it would be for Kit's own good. Forcing her back to New York would disabuse her of her fantasy about practicing law. Kit would have to learn practicality, something that Los Angeles was apparently not teaching her.

Freddy folded the letter, put it back in her pocket, and began to rehearse what she would say to Kit.

It may have been an hour—Freddy lost track of the time—but when she heard Kit calling her name, her body jolted to attention.

"In the library," Freddy said.

Kit entered, looking fresh as a magnolia in a flowing gown of layered white muslin. How very innocent she appeared. So unspoiled—so sweet. A perfect blossom. For a moment Freddy thought of relenting, of throwing her arms around Kit and squeezing her until she forgot about everything. But she reminded herself that this was a flower that held a social poison. Pretty, but ultimately deadly. Freddy did not want to crush her, only see her transplanted in another soil far away.

When Kit kissed her on the cheek, Freddy sensed she had something to say. Rather than immediately proceeding to the business at hand, Freddy said, "You seem invigorated this morning."

"I am!" Kit said, her green eyes dancing. Could such eyes hold a hidden malice? Freddy had seen Kit's Irish temper flare. And after living seventy years, she knew that things often were not as they seemed. Still, the girl seemed so gentle and sincere. Perhaps there were reasons for her actions with Heath. Perhaps they were misunderstood actions.

Her niece continued. "I did not see you last night."

Freddy snapped to attention. "Yes, I am well aware of that. You had me worried. A young lady of quality cannot parade around the city unaccompanied—especially after dark. It simply isn't prudent."

Kit nodded. "I know and I'm sorry. I never meant to be gone so long, but it was quite an eventful day. I was so excited that I nearly woke you up. I just had to tell you what had happened."

Flushing a bit, knowing that part of Kit's day had been spent in Sloate's office, Freddy forced herself to be calm and merely said, "Oh?"

"Yes. I don't want to bore you with everything, but I was offered a position. A real, honest-to-goodness legal position!"

"Heath offered you a position?"

Kit's expression grew sullen. "No, Aunt Freddy."

"Then why did he want you to—"

"Please, let me tell you my news."

Freddy considered her niece carefully. She seemed to be hiding something, or maybe it was just youthful confusion. "Well?"

Kit put a hand on her aunt's shoulder. "I know you have reservations about me, Aunt Freddy. But please let's wait and see. I am going to be an assistant to an attorney. He's a wonderful man. I actually was allowed to watch him at work. He invited me to observe him in the middle of a case. It was wonderful! He was wonderful!"

"What is the name of the paragon?" Freddy demanded.

She saw Kit look down at the floor, as if afraid to speak. Her red hair, which had not yet been pinned up, fell forward over her shoulders. Freddy momentarily envied the youthful image. It seemed only yesterday that she had been that age. Kit looked as though she were a young girl about to receive her comeuppance for some naughty deed. Perhaps a cookie taken without permission or a china cup accidentally broken.

For a moment, Freddy forgot herself all together. The ache in her knees reminded her that time had taken its toll. The young beauty before her, so full of guarded excitement, reminded her that the years ahead would be given over to other, more capable, hands. Freddy's reign would not last forever.

Kit finally found her voice. "He really is a very nice man." She looked up to meet Freddy's stern gaze. The action brought Freddy back to the matter at hand.

"Come now, child!" Freddy said. "Who is he?"

"Aunt Freddy," Kit said softly, "it's Mr. Earl Rogers."

The shock could not have been greater if the name had been Satan. In an instant, Freddy knew it would have to be as Heath said. Having Kit work for that man, alone, would be enough to ruin them both socially.

Gathering her thoughts, Freddy said, "Sit, my dear." She guided

Kit to the window bench and gently urged her down.

"What is it?" Kit said, her voice revealing concern.

"I regret very much what I have to say," Freddy began. "But you must believe I have only your best interests at heart. I have thought all this through, and my decision is firm. I must send you back to New York." There. She'd said the words—there was no turning back.

Kit looked up at her, a dumbfounded expression on her face. When she opened her mouth, Freddy put up a hand. "I must tell you the signs are very clear."

"What signs?"

"Many. I consulted with Madame Zindorf yesterday—"

"You *what*?"

"Now watch your tone of voice, girl!"

Her niece's cheeks flushed. "You spoke to a fraud about me?"

"Madame Zindorf is not a fraud, young lady. She is one of the finest mystics in this city!"

"Oh, Aunt Freddy." Now Kit's voice was tinged with disappointment. "We can't have someone read tea leaves or palms in order to tell us what the future holds. Those things are of the devil, and you mustn't toy with them."

Freddy reddened. How dare Kit presume to preach to her elders! "You are a child and you speak as a child. I have known the benefit of Madame Zindorf for years. Why, she once even contacted my departed husband. Jasper himself told me to continue to consult with her."

"But don't you see?" Kit protested. "She would say such a thing because she stands to benefit. She makes money on keeping you tied to her."

Freddy's mind was made up. "I am firm on this. I cannot allow you to keep on pursuing a legal career and live under this roof. Especially working for the likes of Mr. Earl Rogers! No, never. I will not continue to provide you with home and income here in Los Angeles. I will send you a monthly stipend if you will return to New York and take a teaching position there, as you once had opportunity."

"But, Aunt Freddy—"

"No, child," Freddy said quickly. Fearing she might hesitate if she allowed Kit to speak, she went on, "That is my decision in this matter. I will not have any further discussion."

She watched her niece's face change from incredulity to wretchedness. Her heart ached but she remained steadfast, even as Kit stood, her eyes brimming with tears.

When Kit spoke, it was as if her voice came from a deep, abandoned well. "If that is your desire," she said, and quickly fled the room.

Freddy took a step toward her, then stopped. She noticed her hand was raised toward the door of the library. Slowly, she put it down.

Chapter Nine

KIT THREW HERSELF on the bed, burying her head in a pillow. She pounded the mattress with her fist.

Oh, dear God, why is this happening? Am I a plaything to be thrown between people? I'm sorry, God, I just don't understand!

She felt a gentle hand on her shoulder and turned to see Corazón.

"What is it, Miss Shannon?" she said softly.

"Oh, Corazón," Kit said, and without thinking anything of it, she hugged her maid. There was no social distinction now, only the warmth of a friend, her only friend. Kit did not speak for a long time, and Corazón did not once move or ask what the matter was. It was as if they understood each other without any words.

Kit finally pulled away. "I tried to reason with Aunt Freddy, but she has that Madame Zindorf taking her money and telling her to send me away. Of course she wants me to go. She probably fears

I'll see how she's taking advantage of poor Aunt Freddy. How can I not speak my mind?"

"Sí, Madame Zindorf, she is bad for your aunt. I no like her," Corazón said, lowering her face. "She frighten me with her ways."

Kit squeezed the younger woman's hand. "I'm sure I would not like her either, but God wouldn't have us be afraid of her." Kit sighed and shook her head. "I just don't know what to do. Aunt Freddy is insisting I go back to New York and be a teacher, but things are just now starting to work out. Mr. Rogers has offered me a job in his law office."

"I no want you to go," Corazón admitted. "I like very much that we are friends."

"As do I. I've had so few friends in my life," Kit admitted. "I just hate feeling confused. I don't know what to do about this." She didn't know why she was bothering to tell Corazón, for there was nothing her maid could do. It was one thing to share a burden, but Kit knew Corazón didn't have influence with Aunt Freddy or anyone else that could help. But she did offer a reminder.

"Our heavenly Father will help you," Corazón said. "And I will light for you a candle."

Kit held Corazon's hand tightly. "Yes, thank you." Corazón was right. Times of distress were not times to give up praying. "Will you pray with me now?" she said.

"Oh," Corazón said, "I only pray the rosary."

"I know," Kit said, remembering her training at the hands of the nuns, "but my papa taught me that prayer is a conversation with God, just like we're doing now."

"*Es verdad?* I mean, this is true?"

"Quite true," said Kit. "Just close your eyes and I'll show you how it is done."

Bowing her head, Kit began to pray. "I'm completely spent, Lord. I've tried to work this out in my own strength. I know you will fight for me. I know you will give me the strength to face my future and the wisdom needed to make choices for that future. Please guide me, Father. I wish only to do your will. Amen."

Kit opened her eyes and met Corazon's hesitant glance. The maid shook her head. "It is not my way. It seems very strange."

"I know, but that's all right. Maybe in time you'll feel more comfortable with praying on your own. God is there all the time, no matter what. That's a lesson I often fail to remember. But God always makes a way. I remember times when there was no food in the cupboard and my papa was off preaching. Mama would tell me to pray for provision, and lo and behold, Papa would come riding home with saddlebags full of supplies given to him by people along the way."

"I did not know you were poor. I thought you always live like this."

"Oh no. There were some very lean times, even when my parents were alive."

Corazón seemed to fully understand. "My family is very poor. This job is important to me. I make money to give my mother, and it helps because my father, he no make good money. He work at whatever he can do with his hands. It never pay so good. But Mama, she is smart. She care for the children and make food that seems to come out of nowhere. She trade for things, and we always have clothes and blankets."

Corazón spoke with such love that Kit's heart ached. "You must be very loved. Your parents sound wonderful."

"Oh sí. They are."

It was then Kit heard a distant noise, something oddly mechanical, with a loud bang every now and then. She wondered if someone was shooting a gun. Then it stopped.

A few minutes later, however, there was a thumping sound at her window. The two women turned to each other with shrugs.

"I will see," Corazón said, going to the window. She pulled back the curtain and gazed out. "For you, I think."

Curious, Kit joined her and looked down.

There below in the yard stood a smiling Ted Fox. He waved at her to come down. He was dressed in a huge tan jacket that came down past his knees, heavy gloves, and strange goggles perched on top of his head. But it was the smile that intrigued her most of all. It started on his lips but seemed to light up his entire face.

"But what—" she began, then stopped when Ted put a finger to his lips. He waved at her again, conspiratorially.

Why was this? Kit wondered. And then she remembered Aunt Freddy's warnings about him. Well, despite that, she was intensely interested in Ted Fox. Though he was engaged to another woman and apparently had a less than honorable past, Kit had thought about him frequently since she'd made his brief acquaintance. Of all of the men she had met in what Freddy called "polite society," he was the only one who stood out. There was something different about him, something that made him seem out of place among the elite of the city. Just as she was out of place. Her one snippet of conversation with him had given her the impression of a man looking for something *more* than what was accepted. And she could certainly relate to that.

She nodded at Ted, grabbed a hat, and told Corazón, "I'm going out."

———

"Mr. Fox," she said. "This is a surprise."

He smiled, and Kit felt something stir inside her. She stifled it quickly and reminded herself again that he was engaged to the icy Miss Wynn. She had no desire to disturb that young woman's arrangements. No doubt heads would roll if Miss Wynn failed to get what she wanted. Hadn't Aunt Freddy said so? In view of this thought, Kit resolved to be strong. She would not allow any feelings for him to take root. That would only ensure further disaster, and Kit's social status, which already hung by a thread, would definitely be ruined.

Ted said, "I was sitting at home, noticing the sun coming out bright and clear, and said to myself, it's too nice a day to go sit in a stuffy bank. It's a day to look at the ocean. Have you been to the shore yet, Miss Shannon?"

"No, I—"

"And that's what I said to myself, too. Here is a visitor from the East, and I'll just wager she hasn't seen the Pacific up close. Tell me, Miss Shannon, have you ridden in a horseless carriage?"

"Why, no."

He leaned toward her and whispered, "I happen to have one down the road. Would you like to take a ride?"

The timing of the request seemed perfect. She had to get out, away from this house, away from Aunt Freddy. She needed time to think.

But this was Ted Fox, and she felt compelled to ask, "What about Miss Wynn?"

His face turned somber. "Ah, the lovely Elinor is in San Francisco with her mother, shopping for the latest trinkets from the Far East." He smiled again and added, "She won't mind."

Kit heard herself say, "Why not?" Something inside her warned that this was not the best choice she'd made since arriving in Los Angeles. The air of danger built as Ted took her arm and guided her down a path toward a buggy that looked like it had everything except a horse. It was painted a stately green with large spoked wheels at the back and smaller ones in the front. It was not the first time Kit had seen a gas-powered auto, but it would be her first time to ride in one.

Ted reached onto the seat and removed another riding jacket, holding it up for her. "You'll look lovely," he said.

She laughed as she slipped her arms inside the heavy coat, which reached down to her ankles and covered her entire dress.

"Charming," she said.

"Now beekeeper netting," Ted said. He pulled a length of fine mesh from the seat and laid it over her hat, tying it under her chin. "To protect your hair from dust," he explained.

At last he produced a pair of goggles like his own. He placed the lenses over her eyes and fastened the straps for her. The world was suddenly tinted orange. The goggle straps also helped secure the beekeeper get-up to her head.

"I feel like a mummy," she said.

"Ah, but there's life in you, Miss Kit Shannon," Ted answered.

"And I'd like to keep it. You sure this thing is safe?"

Ted laughed, took her arm, and helped her up onto the seat. "She's a Duryea," he said proudly. "Safe and secure. Isn't she a beaut?"

"She's something all right," Kit said as she avoided the metal shaft sticking straight up off of the floor, culminating in a circular wheel with a knob. The steering mechanism, Kit decided. Could that control this entire contrivance? At least the seat was comfortable.

Ted was in the rear, turning something or another, and then she heard an explosion, like a gunshot. The entire carriage began to vibrate and expel a chugging noise that was loud and insistent.

In a second Ted hopped up next to her, placed his goggles over his face, and shouted, "Are you ready?"

"Shall I pray?"

"No need! You're with Ted Fox, master of the machine!"

Another gunshot-like pop issued from the rear of the auto.

"I'll pray," Kit said.

Ted pushed and pulled a gear next to his leg, and the clamorous vehicle began to move.

It was a bumpy, loud, dusty, exhilarating ride. The sputtering contraption moved along at a rapid clip—about the speed of a cantering horse, Kit thought—and Ted seemed perfectly at home, his white teeth smiling through an increasingly dirty face. What must she look like? Kit wondered. But it was such wonderful fun she didn't care. The earlier hurt of the morning was, at least momentarily, relieved.

They couldn't talk above the noise, so Kit contented herself to take in the scenery. Spreading pepper trees and blossoming magnolias, which lined the streets of the city's outskirts, soon gave way to fields of scrubby brush interrupted by orchards and a few agricultural enterprises. So much food grown here! Kit thought. Nothing like that back in New York City. Would she really have to return East? The thought was simply unbearable. *How could I have come all this way, only to give up now?* She thought of something she'd read—something Teddy Roosevelt had said. "It is hard to fail, but it is worse never to have tried to succeed."

Is that what I'm doing? Am I failing to try?

But what other alternative was there? Kit could hardly go out and find proper quarters for herself. She might have a job, but Rogers himself said the pay would be minimal. How could she hope to pay rent and buy food? The situation wasn't a matter of not trying to succeed. It was a matter of the odds being stacked against her before she'd even gotten started.

The air had a distinctive smell to it, drawing Kit away from her mournful thoughts. This wasn't the smoky industrial odor of her youth or the redolence of crowded tenements—laundry, garbage, horses, sweat—but a clean, fresh, bracing smell. Even with dust and dirt flying around the automobile, Kit felt the air was somehow pristine.

Then the ground around her became a mix of dirt and sand. The air took on a salty essence, and then she saw it as Ted drove over a ridge—the expansive blueness of the Pacific Ocean, its tiny caps glistening in the sun like jewels. It took her breath away. She had never seen anything so majestically beautiful.

Ted brought the car to a stop on a rise overlooking the sea. The sudden cessation of noise from the gas buggy gave way to the sound of ocean waves rushing to the shore.

"It's incredible!" Kit shouted, leaping from the auto. She removed her goggles, wondering if she looked like a raccoon, and emerged from the coat. She took in a deep breath of sea air.

"The view, yes," said Ted Fox. He knelt and picked up a handful of the sandy dirt, looked at it, then threw it to the wind. "Not the ground." His voice was bitter.

"What's wrong with the ground?"

"You can't grow anything here. But my mother thinks you can. She's been sold a bill of goods. She won't listen to me, only to . . ." He paused.

"Someone trying to take advantage of her?"

There was a sudden flash in his eyes that chilled Kit. He seemed in that instant a man truly capable of doing something dreadful. Deadly? Aunt Freddy had said there was a rumor about his killing a man. Was that mere idle gossip? Kit began to wonder, but then he smiled and she could not deny the spark that flared within her.

"Let's talk about something else, shall we?" Ted said.

"Like what?"

"Like you."

"Oh, then the conversation will be quite short."

"I doubt that sincerely. The word is that you have a crazy notion to practice law."

Kit stiffened. "What's so crazy about it?"

"It isn't done, is it?"

"You mean by a woman?"

"Especially one as attractive as you."

This time his smile failed to move her. "You can drop the blarney, Mr. Fox. Women may have been denied this privilege once, but no more."

"Truly?"

"It may interest you to know that most state codes limit bar admission to 'any white male citizen.' That is changing. Here in California a woman named Clara Shortridge Foltz fought for a woman's lawyer bill, and in 1878 the code was changed to allow any citizen to pass the bar."

"I had no idea."

"Now you do. But women in the law are still rare. And they are not exactly being welcomed with open arms." Kit looked out at the ocean. "It's a fight," she said quietly. When she turned back she noticed Ted staring at her with an intensity she felt all through her body.

He said, "Then you fight, Miss Shannon. You fight for your dreams, and I'll fight for mine."

A bracing gust of sea air blew past them. "And what are your dreams, Mr. Fox?"

He smiled and spread his arms out wide. "A glider!"

Oh yes! At the party he had talked about "soaring." Did he really mean to fly? It was a dazzling thought.

"They've got gas-powered buggies," he said, "and so I'm going to build a gas-powered glider. I want to launch from here."

Kit felt a strong kinship with Ted Fox then, as if they were the only two people in the world who understood each other.

"You know," he said, "those of us who dream about doing what hasn't been done are bound to ruffle feathers. Well, let 'em ruffle. We make our own way in this world, Miss Shannon."

Mesmerized by the way the breeze blew Ted's hair across his

forehead, Kit said, "But not alone."

"What do you mean?"

"God is on our side."

"If it were only that simple." There was a glimmer of sadness in his eyes. But then the look passed, immediately replaced by a sparkling aliveness. "Tell you what," he said. "As soon as I get my flying machine up, I'll take you for another ride."

"That," Kit said with a smile, "is a pleasure I think I will forego."

He smiled widely and stepped toward her, as if drawn to her. Kit suddenly wanted something—his touch. She wanted to feel his arms around her, and she was frightened. He belonged to another woman! She barely knew him anyhow. And her heart was not set for love, not yet, not with so much to accomplish in her career.

Thoughts jumbled around in her mind as Ted took one more step and was nearly touching her. His blue eyes seemed as deep as the ocean itself, full of the same mystery and power.

She was sure he would kiss her now. She was frozen, wanting to turn away and yet not wanting to.

An agonizing moment labored past, then Ted drew back. "Come along," he said. "Let's ride a little further."

They did. At various points along the way Ted would stop and tell her something about the sights. He was a perfect gentleman. But Kit could not shake the feeling that he held something in reserve, something secret and deep. And she wondered if she would ever truly know him.

Chapter Ten

BACK AT HOME, still managing to avoid Aunt Freddy, Kit took a long bath to remove the dirt of the day's adventure. She bathed alone, with Corazón away on some errand or other. But it gave Kit the opportunity to think and to pray. She knew she had a decision to make. For some reason, Aunt Freddy had turned against her. She wasn't sure why, but remaining under her roof was apparently not an option. Should she simply return to New York? She had a teaching job waiting for her, a safe and secure position with a future.

But one thing Ted had told her—about fighting for her dreams—resonated inside her. It sounded much like her father. He had been a fighter his whole life, too. He'd faced tough opposition in his quest to preach the Word of God, persevering under conditions that might have crushed a lesser man.

Thinking of him, Kit reached under the bed and pulled out her father's Bible. The rich, brown leather was starting to fade a bit, but it still felt solid in her hands. She began reverently flipping pages.

How she loved the notations in Papa's Bible! Papa had heard the great D. L. Moody speak once and adopted his method of Bible marking—red ink underlining passages about the blood of Christ and symbols to mark important doctrines.

Now she was reading for devotion and direction. Papa had taught her that Scripture always came first when seeking God's will.

Kit suddenly thought back on the dark time at St. Catherine's when she had to read her father's Bible in secret. They had taken it from her when she first arrived. "No one can understand Scripture without the infallible Church to guide us," one of the nuns had told her. Thirteen-year-old Kit had cried when they took it, but a rap across her bottom put a stop to any hope of getting it back.

Hope, in fact, was in short supply at St. Catherine's. Her memories of the place always began with a vision of Sister Gertrude, the severe nun with a German accent and narrow eyes—eyes that seemed always to be watching.

After her arrival in the pounding rain, when Sister Gertrude had taken away her father's Bible, things only got worse. She was issued a uniform, housed in a room with four other girls, and assigned work. Her life suddenly became regulated, routine, and difficult. The only times she felt hopeful at all were in her classes. She found she had an insatiable love of learning, and she couldn't get enough.

The only exception was in Sister Gertrude's language class. It was clear Sister Gertrude had singled Kit out for her particular brand of torment. If Kit made even a single mistake, the entire class would know about it as a "warning" of what "dull minds" do. The other girls seemed to enjoy the sideshow, with one exception—a girl named Martha. While not overtly friendly, Martha at least never raised her voice in ridicule against Kit, nor laughed when the other children did.

Kit had determined not to crack under Sister Gertrude's heavy hand. In her mind, the sister was no different from the lawyers who had cheated her mother. She wore a habit, but it was power she wielded unjustly, just like the lawyers. That was what steeled Kit against the sister and everything she represented. There was nothing she could do about it except remain strong.

It wasn't easy. Kit's hands bore ugly welts and bruises from the canings she received from her tormentor. Still, she refused to give the sister more excuses to beat her.

Then one day the full force of her Irish temper and righteous indignation poured out like the bursting forth of a dam. Sister Gertrude had been leading the class in grammar and pronunciation exercises when Kit felt a sting on the back of her neck. She looked behind her, knowing that someone had thrown something at her— a bean? a pebble?—with the intent to get her to commit some breach of classroom decorum.

"Kat'leen!" she heard Sister Gertrude say. "Eyes front!"

Turning back, her cheeks red, Kit felt a smoldering in her that was both frightening and, in a small way, exhilarating. She remembered how her father's eyes sometimes burned when he spoke of an injustice or of an insult to God. There was a time for anger.

As Sister Gertrude droned on, turning her head toward the blackboard, Kit felt another sharp pain on her neck. And the dam broke.

"Stop it!" Kit screamed, hot tears suddenly rushing to her eyes. "Stop it, stop it, stop it!"

"Kat'leen Shannon!" the Germanic bellow came. "You vill step here!" Sister Gertrude pointed a bony finger at the floor in front of her.

There was only one thing that meant—another caning. In Sister Gertrude's class there was no jury, no judge, no appeal. As the nun reached behind her for the cane, Kit screamed, "No!"

A hush fell over the class as ominous as the silence of a graveyard. Even Kit, her head pounding, knew she had stepped over a boundary that none of the girls had ever dared come close to.

Sister Gertrude's eyes widened more than Kit had ever seen them. Raising the cane she slammed it on her desk, sending a loud *crack* echoing off the walls. "Now!" she screamed.

"No," Kit repeated, but this time in a trembling voice that matched the scattered stream of tears on her cheeks.

Sister Gertrude seemed to swell then, becoming somehow twice her size, like the gathering of storm clouds before the issuing of thunder. Kit saw a hatred in the eyes of the sister, something for which there was no explanation. It was simply . . . *unjust*! That was the word. There was no justice here and never would be.

Suddenly from one side of the room, a voice said, "She didn't do anything, Sister!"

Kit, as if awakened from a dream, looked over and saw Martha, her angelic face now serious, sitting bravely in her seat.

For a moment Sister Gertrude's wrath was diverted. "Martha Milligan, you vill be quiet!"

"But, Sister—"

"No!" This was accompanied by another loud *whap* on the desk with the cane.

Martha stopped then and looked at Kit. Kit saw a look of apology in her face, and in that instant Kit loved Martha Milligan more than any other person in the world.

"Kat'leen Shannon! This is last varning!"

Knowing that the awful sentence could not be avoided, Kit slowly stood. Her legs wouldn't move for a long moment, then finally they began taking her forward. It was as if she had a ball and chain on her ankles.

And then she was in front of Sister Gertrude.

"Hands!" the nun demanded.

As if trained to act by themselves, Kit's arms raised in front of her, her palms upward. Her thoughts screamed that this wasn't right, wasn't fair, but fairness was no consideration here. And then Kit saw again the hatred in Sister Gertrude's eyes as the nun raised her cane in the air, a hatred that chilled Kit but also confirmed her thoughts of injustice. No one should be punished for hatred. No one!

The cane swished downward . . .

Kit pulled back her hands. "No!" she cried.

Sister Gertrude's cane hit the floor with such force that it flew from her hand. The nun yelped in surprise and what must have been pain, for she grabbed her right shoulder with her left hand.

"You Protestant devil!" Sister Gertrude screamed.

And then she slapped Kit across the face.

Kit grabbed her cheek, now stinging hot, too stunned even to cry. Sister Gertrude grabbed the cane off the floor and began to rain blows all over Kit—legs, head, shoulders—shouting all the while "Devil! Devil! Devil!"

Crumbling to the floor, Kit put her hands over her head. The pain became unbearable and Kit prepared herself for death. Surely God would use death to take her away from this terrible place!

Then suddenly the blows stopped and Kit, a heap on the floor, heard another voice shouting, "Sister, no!"

Kit recognized the voice of Sister Agatha, the overseer of schooling. Kit had always thought of her as a distant observer, not fully involved in the daily operations of the school. But she was here now, and Kit felt a comfort and a hope that soon everything would be all right.

The caning incident resulted in a series of events that Kit, now looking back with the benefit of time, could only conclude had come from the hand of God.

Sister Gertrude was transferred to another convent. It was all done in silence—Sister Gertrude was not seen by any of the girls before news of her departure was disseminated. Rumors spread that she was actually going to a convent where sisters were "looked after" for various reasons. There was also a rumor that Sister Gertrude had once been assaulted by an Irishman who was a convert from Catholicism. That explained, for Kit, the irrational hatred the sister had for her, the daughter of an Irish Protestant.

Another benefit that occurred was a friendship with Martha Milligan. The girl with dark blond hair, worn always in twin braids, proved a godsend. She had been at St. Catherine's for ten years and knew things about the place. She also had influence among the other girls, and life became more bearable for Kit.

One night she was awakened by Martha. "Do you want to see something secret?" she said. They sneaked out of the rooms, and Martha took Kit to a stairway that Kit had never seen before. It was dark and mysterious, but also exciting.

Martha guided them through another door and hallway, and then through a door into a chamber lit only by moonlight. In the silvery glow Kit could see what it was—a library! A wonderful library with shelves filled with books, just waiting to be read. "It's Sister Agatha's private study," Martha explained.

To Kit, it was wonderful. Then Martha showed her a cabinet that was filled with still more books, these seemingly discarded or stored. "Sometimes I take one," said Martha. "Then put it back later. Want to?"

Kit had trembled at the thought of being caught. Canings weren't restricted to Sister Gertrude for violations of the rules. "No," Kit said, "but I'd like to feel them."

It was like a treasure chest for Kit, and she pulled out books and held them, opened them, ran her hands along the smooth pages. If only she could read them all, if only they'd let her, if only . . .

Kit stopped suddenly at the touch of the book in her hands. She knew instantly what it was. Her father's Bible! This is where they had put it!

"This one," Kit whispered to Martha. "This one I'll keep."

And she did. Martha took her to a secret place to hide it, under some loose floorboards in a classroom for the younger girls. No one apparently missed it, and Kit would read it sometimes in secret. It was a balm to her soul through the dark days at St. Catherine's.

It was perhaps a year after the beating by Sister Gertrude when Kit got the impression that Sister Agatha knew all along what Martha and Kit sometimes did at night, and even about her father's Bible. But for some reason, the nun said nothing. Instead, one day when Kit was fourteen, Sister Agatha asked Kit if she'd like to be in charge of cleaning her study. In return, she could read any of the books in it, so long as her work was done.

It was the one ray of light in this otherwise drab world where Kit lived. From that point onward, Kit was never without a book.

But first and always was the Bible, even though she had to read it in secret. One verse she returned to over and over was one that her father had underlined: Psalm 32, verse 8. *I will instruct thee and teach thee in the way which thou shalt go: I will guide thee with mine eye.*

It was to that verse Kit, sitting in her bedroom in Aunt Freddy's mansion, now turned. She read it again and prayed.

Lord, I ask you to show me the way. I will trust in you, wherever you lead. I ask you for a sign, Lord, a sign of your will. Show me!

Chapter Eleven

THE SIGN POINTED BACK to New York.

Aunt Freddy was a rock of resistance the next morning. Kit couldn't help but wonder about the influences on her aunt—Sloate, Madam Zindorf, and who knew what else. But one thing was clear: Aunt Freddy controlled her destiny in the form of sponsorship. And that was to be withdrawn.

Now too many things were against her. Aunt Freddy insisted Kit be on the afternoon train. And so the morning was spent packing and engaging in tearful good-byes with Aunt Freddy and, in secret, with Corazón. Oh, how Kit would miss the sweet friendship they had shared, though their time together had been so short.

Then, with a heart split in two—her desire to stay against her perception of God's will—Kit had Julio drive her to Earl Rogers' office before taking her to the depot.

With a sigh, Kit entered the building. With each step up the narrow wooden staircase, Kit tried to reassure herself that there really was no choice in the matter. God had spoken. Hadn't He?

Gripping the banister in one gloved hand and holding tightly to her linen skirt with the other, Kit topped the flight of stairs and drew a deep breath. She looked down the hallway of glass-paneled doors, one of which had gilt-and-black lettering stating: *EARL ROGERS*. Nothing else, not even a designation of "attorney-at-law." It was as if Rogers were saying that his name alone would be enough in the years to come.

Kit forced her steps forward. She put her hand to the brass doorknob. There was still time to change her mind. Perhaps Mr. Rogers would have something to tell her. Some way to make it all work out. But remembering the trunks of clothes already packed and ready for her departure, Kit knew it would take a miracle to alter her course.

Inside the door was a large waiting room. The room seemed to suit Earl Rogers' character. The furniture consisted of two leather divans and a half dozen wooden chairs, all painted dark green. Brass spittoons were placed in every conceivable location, and two oak hat racks stood sentry near the door. It seemed very serviceable and businesslike. A reception desk sat by a door on the opposite side of the room.

Oddly, the room was empty, giving Kit the chance to peruse the many framed photographs on the wall. One she recognized as former President Grover Cleveland. Another was of a dashing young boxer in pose. She saw writing on this one. It was autographed by someone named James J. Corbett.

On the back wall was a beautiful painting of a cowboy on a bucking bronco. It seemed to sum up perfectly the aura of Los Angeles. The artist's signature simply said *Remington*.

"Miss Kathleen Shannon," a voice boomed out.

Looking up, Kit found Earl Rogers beaming her a smile from

the doorway. "What do you think of it all? Would you mind working in such an environment?"

Kit smiled but felt no enthusiasm for the question. "It looks just as it should."

This reply made Rogers laugh. "Spoken neutrally enough. Come into my office. Let's get down to business."

"Well, I suppose that is why I'm here," Kit replied. Her heart raced as she forced herself to continue. "I needn't bother you by taking up time in your office. I can't stay."

Rogers' eyes narrowed, and he studied her as he might a witness in one of his trials. "What are you saying?"

"I'm saying I can't accept the position. I am returning to New York."

"May I ask what has brought this about?" He folded his arms across his chest and waited for her response.

Kit had wrestled with the idea of whether to give Rogers the full truth as she knew it or to make up some flimsy excuse. Standing in front of him now, she knew she would level with him. He had a way of drawing it out of her with nothing more than a glance. Was that how witnesses felt upon his cross-examination?

"My aunt is far from pleased with my desire to practice law. She is my sponsor and as such, she is exercising her right to withdraw her support."

"I see. So society has reared its ugly head, and the grand dame is dismissing you from view. Is that it?"

"I suppose you could say that."

"And you're giving up?" He snapped his fingers. "Just like that? Bah!"

He stepped back into his office as if to dismiss her. Kit, without even thinking, followed him inside.

"She's withdrawn her support, sir. She's putting me from her home, and I have no other place to live."

Rogers sat at his desk and raised his gaze to Kit. "It doesn't seem likely to me that a young woman who has constantly stood up in the face of proper decorum and regulated society should so easily give up on her dream. What is this really about?" He motioned her to a chair. "Sit down and tell me the truth."

Kit did as he suggested. Her face grew hot. "I'm not wanted here. My aunt is facing social upheaval if I stay. I have no money with which to secure a place of my own, and even if I did, it would hardly be an acceptable solution. My aunt would still face a great deal of discomfort."

"Frederica Fairbank does not have a reputation for concerning herself too much with what folks think."

"You know my aunt?"

He laughed. "Most of Los Angeles knows your aunt. Or at least knows *of* her. Besides, I did a little checking on you. Wouldn't be prudent to do less than that."

"I don't want to be the cause of hurting her," Kit said seriously. "She's been good to me."

"The decision is up to you, but if it's just about a place to live, well, you can stay here. We have a spare office."

It was hardly an offering of residential comfort. But glancing around the room at the walls lined with floor-to-ceiling law books in light calf bindings, Kit knew she wanted this job more than ever. From the impressive windows behind Earl Rogers' desk, Kit saw the austere, gray-granite *Times* building. It appeared to be watching them, just waiting for some news to be made by Earl Rogers. Perhaps waiting for the news of his latest folly—the hiring of a woman assistant.

God, what are you saying to me?

"You'll work hard and get paid horribly," Rogers continued. "You'll lose sleep and pace the floors. But if you stick to it, if you listen and learn, I'll give you this guarantee: Someday you'll be a lawyer."

Her heart raced and her breath seemed strangled in her throat.

"The building isn't the Nadeau Hotel," Rogers continued, "but it'll do. There are washroom facilities in the building, a small cooking facility, and an icebox. I have a small quarters in the back of this office. I'd designed it for myself, but since I rarely use it—you might as well. There's a bed there, and we could probably make some arrangement for your clothes. If you keep up the office and give it a cleaning once in a while, you can live here until you find more a more desirable situation."

Kit's hands were trembling. She remembered the inappropriate proposition of Heath Sloate. "I don't know that it would be a good idea. What would people say?"

Rogers raised a brow and leaned forward. "What are they going to say about you anyway—and do you really care?"

Kit shook her head. "I do care about Aunt Freddy."

He leaned back and shrugged. "The choice is up to you. I'm offering you a solution, a place, and wages as my assistant."

Kit swallowed. Could God be working through Earl Rogers? Was this her answer? Her heart cried out within her.

"What do you say?" asked the lawyer.

She had come all this way, hadn't she? Surely another few weeks wouldn't make a difference—certainly it would give her time to see God's hand more clearly. Hadn't that been exactly how her own father had led his life? How many times had he told her that faith was a risk, but one that required us to walk anyway?

Kit found herself saying, "All right."

"You mean we're agreed?"

"Yes, Mr. Rogers."

"Fantastic!" Rogers slapped his desk, pleased. "And you will start calling me Earl."

"I'll try, sir."

"And you won't call me sir."

Kit shook her head. "It's just so unconventional."

Rogers laughed heartily. "But then, so are you."

Kit couldn't argue the point there. The famed lawyer had turned on his considerable advocacy skills and given her answers to her arguments. She was unconventional. The arrangement was unconventional. But it would allow her to pursue her dream. She smiled and looked her benefactor in the eye.

"All right, Earl."

"That's the ticket."

Ticket! She had a train ticket waiting for her and Julio downstairs!

"Something the matter?" Rogers asked.

"There is something I have to attend to."

"By all means. Take your time. You have your whole future ahead of you!"

Kit went back down to the street, where Julio was waiting for her. "A change of plans," she said to him.

"Sí?"

"Have my things brought back here."

"Here?" Julio frowned.

"Here. I'm staying."

A look of fear—for *her*—swept across Julio's face. "Señora Fairbank, she no will be happy."

How well I know that! Kit thought.

What had she gotten herself into?

Chapter Twelve

"WHY DIDN'T YOU insist that she return?" Heath Sloate demanded.

Frederica Fairbank wrung her hands, hopelessly twisting her lace handkerchief. What she had hoped would be a nice tea in her home had suddenly turned to an argument. "I tried to make her go," she said. "I purchased the ticket and even had her things delivered to the station."

Sloate gave her a look of disbelief. "So what detained her?"

"Apparently... well, that is to say..." Freddy stammered, knowing Heath would never be happy with her lack of information. "I don't really know. She left here, I thought, to take the train back to New York. Her things were loaded, I'd given her some money..."

"You gave her money? I thought I told you... Oh, never mind. What happened after that? Where did she go?"

"She had my man leave her at the station, and he returned with this note." Freddy stopped wringing her hands long enough to reach into the pocket of her dove-gray morning dress. She produced a folded piece of paper and handed it to Heath.

He opened it and read aloud in a clipped tone. " 'Aunt Freddy, I am grateful for your generosity and help. Please do not worry about my decision or choice in this matter, but I cannot return to New York. I will be working for Mr. Earl Rogers. I will make my way here and in doing so, make you proud. Love, Kit.' " He growled out her name as if it were something spoiled and rotten in his mouth.

"Rogers! That addlepated woman will be the ruination of you, Frederica! Mark my words." He threw the note onto the floor. "I'll get to the bottom of this."

"She has a will of her own," Freddy replied, then turned away in shame. *I used to have a will of my own. Oh, Jasper, I'm not half the woman I used to be.*

She squared her shoulders. "What will you do?" she asked without bothering to face Sloate.

"I'll do what I have to," he said in a menacing tone. "Just as I always have."

He started for the door.

"Where are you going, dear?" Freddy said.

"I have an appointment," Sloate snapped. "It may surprise you, but in spite of your travails with your niece, I have other matters to attend to."

And with that he left the room.

Freddy sat down, her heart heavy. *Oh, Kit. What's to become of you?*

———

"Now, listen," Earl Rogers said, meshing his fingers and putting his hands behind his head. "One cannot practice law without remuneration. In criminal law, you'll be coming across numerous cases involving the lower order of society. These are not your upper-crust citizens, and the management of money is a foreign thing to them. So the number-one rule in criminal law is not finding out who did what to whom. It is this: Get the money up front. Understood?"

Kit understood, but she wasn't comfortable with it. But she was working for Rogers now, not the other way around. "Yes."

"Good. You can use Jory's room for the interview."

"What interview?"

"Your first interview."

"When?"

"Now."

Rogers stepped to his office door, opened it, and called for Bill. A moment later a rough-looking man came in.

"This is my chief investigator, Bill Jory," Rogers said.

"Pleased to meet you, ma'am," said Jory. His smile was amiable and his handshake sure.

"Thank you," Kit said.

"A man named Ryan has come in to see us," Rogers said. "He is asking us to represent him in some sort of matter involving his daughter. He wasn't clear. I want you to interview him, find out what his case is, and most important, how much he can afford to pay."

Kit cleared her throat. "All right."

"Bill, let her use your office for this."

"Right. This way, Miss Shannon."

Jory showed Kit to his office. It was tidy and reeked of cigar smoke.

"You sure you know what you're getting yourself into, working for Earl?" Jory asked.

"No, Mr. Jory, not in the slightest."

"That's what makes our line of work so interesting. Have a seat."

He offered her the chair behind his desk, and Kit sat. She suddenly felt official, like the real lawyer she hoped she would be someday.

"I'll send in the client," Jory said, "and leave you alone. It's good to have you with us, Miss Shannon."

"Thank you, Mr. Jory."

Jory stepped out for a moment, then returned with a smallish man, perhaps in his middle forties, looking scared. He was dressed in what must have been his best suit of clothes, but which was starting to fray at the elbows and shoulders. His brown hair was unkempt with shafts of gray streaking through it. His eyes were red-rimmed, as if he had been crying before coming up the stairs to Rogers' office. His hands were trembling slightly as he held his hat.

"Mr. Thomas Ryan," Jory said. "This is Miss Kathleen Shannon. She'll be conducting your interview."

Ryan looked momentarily confused, perhaps at the sight of a woman doing official legal business, but he nodded and took a chair. Jory excused himself and shut the door.

"Good day, Mr. Ryan," Kit said.

"Day, miss," he said. Kit noted a slight Irish brogue. It gave her a sense of familiarity and set her more at ease.

"I'm here to assess what sort of case it is you have, and I will report to Mr. Rogers."

"I understand, miss."

"May we begin?"

"Surely," he agreed.

"Let me begin by asking where you live."

"I have a shanty about five miles from here."

"And are you employed?"

"I'm an orderly at the San Fernando asylum."

The word brought a chill to Kit. "Insane asylum?"

"Yes, miss. By the mission, run by the Franciscans."

A flash of memories came to Kit, taking her back to her own incarceration. She wondered how different an asylum overseen by priests would be from an orphanage where a Sister Gertrude could rule. She redirected her thoughts to the man before her and said, "And what is it you're being charged with?"

"It's not me, miss," said Ryan, his face anxious. "It's me daughter."

Kit began to take notes. "What is her name?"

"Millie."

"How old is she?"

Ryan's hands twisted in his lap. "She is just twenty. Still a little . . ." His voice broke off. He seemed to be holding back more tears.

Kit shifted in her chair, conflicting emotions inside her. She had a natural sympathy for someone who was obviously suffering, but she reminded herself of a rule her teacher, Melle Stanleyetta Titus, had told her back in law school. A lawyer must learn to separate emotion from analysis. Too much emotion never serves the client well.

"I realize this must be difficult, Mr. Ryan," said Kit. "But please try to tell me the story as best you can."

"I'm sorry, miss, I am. It's just that Millie is me only child, her mother long since dead. I tried to raise her right, to teach her right. I tried to teach her the Bible and how to please God."

Kit felt an immediate connection with the man. He had tried to do what her own father had done. She found herself wanting to help him even more.

"But I guess I don't know about girls and all," Ryan finished. "I didn't know what to say when that man, Uland, stepped in."

"Who is Uland?"

"Ace Uland, he calls himself. A gambler and a . . ." Ryan stopped himself.

"And a what, Mr. Ryan?"

"A man who sells women."

Goosebumps broke out on Kit's neck. The whole picture was starting to form in her mind. She had seen it happen to young women in the Lower East Side.

"He took her away from me," Ryan said, his voice cracking. "She fancied herself in love with him. I tried to tell her . . . there was nothing I could say. And then he led her into sin. . . ."

Ryan choked. "Me own daughter . . ." He couldn't finish, but broke into sobs, his head in his hands. Kit poured a glass of water from a pitcher on the credenza and slid it toward Ryan.

"I'm sorry," he said. "I don't know what to do."

"That's why you're here," said Kit. "Tell me what trouble Millie is in. Has she been arrested for prostitution?"

"Oh no," said Ryan, sniffing and rubbing a sleeve under his nose. "The cops don't care about that. They're saying attempted murder."

"Of whom?"

Ryan's raw eyes now burned with anger. "They wouldn't tell me. I tried to see her. They wouldn't let me. Me own daughter!"

"How did you hear about it?"

"One of the other girls. She thought I should know. She said Millie was too ashamed. Oh, please, miss. I've got to do something! They say Mr. Rogers is the best there is. Can he help us?"

The mention of Rogers' name brought Kit back to a stark reality. She realized that for the last few minutes she had been completely caught up in Ryan's plight. Now came the part she dreaded.

"Mr. Ryan," she said slowly, "Mr. Rogers is much in demand as a lawyer, as you must know."

Ryan nodded, his expression without any indication that he knew where she was leading.

"His fee for legal service reflects that. He would require his fee in full before starting his representation."

Ryan looked down at his hands.

"I'm sure you understand, Mr. Ryan." Kit knew from his downcast head that he did not—or, rather, that he did only too well. The words were as hard for her to say as for him to hear.

"I wish I didn't have to discuss fees," said Kit, "but Mr. Rogers cannot . . ."

"I know, miss. I'm not a rich man, I work me land mostly. I get a pittance from the church for me duties at the asylum, but I fetch what I can from the crops. It's not the season now, though. I do have a horse. She's me only animal, but I could sell her. . . . She ain't worth much, but maybe I could get fifty dollars."

Kit closed her eyes, knowing fifty dollars would not come close to Rogers' fee. Besides, she couldn't bear the thought of this poor man selling his only horse.

What to do now? She couldn't give Ryan any hope that Rogers would take the case. And what good would it do to recommend he seek other legal counsel? She knew the poor had little recourse in matters of criminal justice. It wouldn't take long for him to fall into the hands of a less than honest attorney—one who would not only take his horse, but title to his land as well. And Ryan would no doubt sign it over for the sake of his daughter.

"Not enough, is it?" Ryan said.

Kit swallowed. "As I said, Mr. Ryan, Mr. Rogers is much in demand. . . ."

"I thought as much. It was just a hope." Ryan stood and extended his hand. "You've been very nice, miss. I'll try me luck somewhere else."

There would be no luck, Kit knew. She saw the future for him in her mind—bad lawyer, quick verdict, daughter sent away to the women's prison where, if she survived, she'd come out worse than she went in, unable to make a living except by selling her own body over and over again.

Kit stood up quickly and without a moment's reflection said, "I'll see your daughter, Mr. Ryan."

He frowned in seeming confusion. "You, miss?"

"I have a legal education, Mr. Ryan. I work as Mr. Rogers' legal assistant."

"Well, I'll be," he said, scratching his head. Then he smiled hopefully and said, "I would be much obliged to you, miss! And I'll sell me horse as soon as—"

"No," Kit said. "You keep your horse. I am not representing your daughter, nor is this office. Not yet, anyway. But I'll see what I can find out, and maybe there's a way to settle this matter without Millie going to court."

"Oh, thank you, thank you!" Ryan said, pumping Kit's hand. His face was now so full of optimism Kit felt, suddenly, as if she'd stepped into quicksand. And on her first day!

Chapter Thirteen

KIT SHOULD HAVE TOLD Earl Rogers. She knew that. She also knew, if she had, that he would have forbidden her to have anything to do with Millie Ryan's case. Kit hadn't lied to him. She never would have done that. She'd only waited for Rogers to leave his office for court. There was no sin in waiting, was there?

Nor was there anything wrong with her walking into a jail of the county of Los Angeles and asking to see Millie Ryan, right? She did notice, however, that her step was lively.

Dressed in a simple plum walking-out dress, Kit had taken care with her hair, styling it just as Corazón had taught her. She topped her head with a matching hat concocted of straw and feathers and ribbon. Corazón said the creation looked like a bird at rest—its head all tucked down into a nest. The very memory made Kit smile.

How she missed her friend. She thought of paying the maid a visit, but Kit knew that she would probably have to come face-to-face with Aunt Freddy as well, and frankly, she simply wasn't ready for that scene.

The jail for women was located behind the police station itself. The uniformed officer at the jailhouse desk—a portly, ruddy-faced man—had snorted at her, as if the request was as ridiculous as asking him to unlock all the cells. But then Kit mentioned that she worked for Earl Rogers, and the officer's look had changed immediately.

"That mouthpiece is trouble," the officer had said.

Kit had immediately snapped back, "And you don't want that trouble to rain down on you, now, do you?" She was astonished at herself for saying it, but there was something exhilirating about standing up and being able to use the name Rogers to get results.

The guard grumbled and took her to the back of the station, through a large wooden door with a barred window to a row of dark green cages in a dimly lit corridor. In a few of the cages sat women—some young, some old—but all seeming to be under a pall of darkness.

Kit quickly scanned the occupants of the cells. One woman who caught her eye grinned toothlessly at Kit and screeched, "Well, ain't she the fine one, all gussied up? Come to give us ladylike lessons, have you?"

"Quiet there," the guard said. He shook a billy club at her.

"Aw," the woman said, "don't you love me no more?"

Kit found herself wondering about the woman, what she might have done to get here, if anyone could have helped her in some way in the past. Would she be able to help Millie Ryan now?

The guard stopped at a cell holding two women. One sat on a stool near the back wall. The other was lying on a cot. "Millie Ryan," he said. "You got a visitor."

The one on the stool looked up. Her face, Kit thought, had a natural prettiness. But it was obscured by streaks of dirt and an ugly, blue-black bruise that covered most of one cheek. But most chilling of all were her eyes—they seemed almost lifeless.

"Who is it?" Millie said in a quiet, abject voice.

"My name is Kit Shannon. I'm here at the request of your father."

"Papa?" Millie said, as if surprised. Kit felt an affinity at Millie's use of the name Kit had used for her own father.

"Yes," said Kit.

Millie let her head hang down again. "Go away," she said.

"There you are," the guard said quickly, taking Kit's arm. "She don't want to see you."

"Wait," said Kit, pulling her arm back. "Millie, let me talk to you."

"What good will it do?" she said.

The guard raised his billy to indicate the way. "Come along, now."

"Wait," Millie said. She stood and walked to the bars. "How is Papa?"

"Let's talk," said Kit.

With a heavy sigh, the guard growled, "I'll give you fifteen minutes."

"Twenty," Kit said. "And in a private room."

———

The room was only semi-private. A police officer stood guard just inside the door as Kit sat across a table from Millie Ryan. This poor creature—just twenty, Kit reminded herself—looked as if her life was over. There was no spirit in her voice when she spoke, only a slight tinge of concern for her father.

"But don't let him see me," she added. "He can't." She pulled a chain from under her blouse. Revealing a gold locket with a cross, she showed Kit the photos enclosed. "My papa and mama," she explained. "It's all I have left of them now. I couldn't bear to see Papa face-to-face. Not after this."

"He loves you," Kit said. "He wants to help you."

"Too late."

Was it too late? Kit suddenly felt as if she were clinging to a buoy at sea. Would she be able to do anyone, let alone Millie, any good? She had legal training in her mind, but this was suddenly real-world experience staring her in the face. But she had come to investigate, and that's what she would do.

"It's not too late for anything, Millie," Kit said. "Now, why don't you start by telling me what happened, what led to your arrest."

Millie looked at Kit with those lifeless eyes. The bruise on the side of her face was like a stain. "What good will it do?" she said.

"I'm here to help you."

"Who *are* you? How can the likes of you help the likes of me?"

"I work for an attorney."

Millie let out a derisive laugh. "Attorneys can't help me. I got no money. Papa's got no money. Just leave me alone." She started to get up.

"No," Kit said forcefully. "I'm here. We don't have much time. I want you to talk to me."

Millie sat back down and shook her head. "I'm not worth it."

Reaching across the table, Kit grabbed Millie's hand and squeezed. "I say you are. Give me a chance. Please."

Millie looked at their entwined hands, almost as if she couldn't believe anyone would touch her. Then a small, almost invisible light seemed to flicker in the back of her eyes, like someone holding up a match in the depths of a dark cavern. "You really want me to?"

"Yes," Kit said.

With a quick glance at the policeman by the door, Millie lowered her voice and said, "You know about me, right? I'm not a good girl. I take money from men."

Kit's heart nearly broke for the girl. "I know."

"It's not the way I wanted it to be. Never planned to end up like this—especially here." She looked away, and her voice took on a tone that suggested Millie was lost in regret. "I didn't want to shame my family, it just happened that way. I know my papa is disappointed in me—probably hates me. Oh, I'd give anything to do it all over." She buried her face in her hands.

"I'm sure you would," Kit said sympathetically. She wasn't at all sure what to do or say. She certainly couldn't condone what the woman did for a living, but neither could she turn away. This woman was a human being, a creation of God. She had a heart and a soul just like anyone else.

Kit waited a moment as Millie straightened and seemed to regain control. "Can you tell me what happened?" Kit asked.

"Sometimes," Millie began with a slight stammer, "the men who come are well off. One of them, who took a liking to me, is a man named Thorn Wilson. Heard of him?"

Kit shook her head.

"He's rich," Millie said. "From making buggies, I think. Has a wife and family. He's the one that did this." Millie pointed to her bruised face.

"When did he do that?"

"About a week ago. He likes to do things like that. Hit me, you know."

For an instant Kit felt like crying, for Millie Ryan and all the other Millies in the world. "Go on," she said.

"Well, two nights ago he comes to see me," Millie said. "But I tell him no. Not after what he did. He can go find somebody else. Then he says he don't want nobody else, he wants me, and he wants me the same as always. Then—" her voice broke off.

"Then what, Millie?"

Through a choked sob, Millie said, "He hit me . . . he hit me. . . ."

The policeman at the door took a step toward them. Kit saw it and put up her hand and, amazingly, the officer stepped back.

To Millie she said, "What did you do next, Millie?"

A single teardrop coursed jaggedly down Millie's cheek. "He grabbed me and put his hands around my neck. I couldn't breathe . . . I scratched his face, and he screamed. He called me a bad name and said he was going to kill me."

Kit patted Millie's hand, waiting.

"I grabbed my shears . . . and then I did it."

"Did what, Millie?"

"I stabbed him."

"Where?"

"In the side." Millie pointed to her right rib. "And then I screamed. And he ran away."

"This was in your room?"

"Yes, ma'am."

"And then what happened?"

"The police came a few hours later. They broke down my door and woke me up, took me away. I've been in here ever since. They won't tell me anything except I tried to murder him and I'm going away for a long, long time."

And then, as if retelling the events had taken a huge emotional toll, Millie added, "Maybe it's where I belong."

"No, Millie," Kit said, taking her hand once more. "I won't let you think that."

But Millie shook her head. Her expression was one of complete resignation. "I've done too many bad things. I should die."

Without hesitation, Kit said, "Your papa told me he taught you from the Bible."

"Yes," said Millie. "I've sinned against God, against Papa..." Her sobs began again.

"Millie, look at me," Kit said. "You know the Bible says the Good Shepherd will leave the ninety-nine sheep to find the one that is lost. Your Good Shepherd is looking for you now."

"But I've sinned..."

"And the price for your sin was paid on the cross! Do you believe that?"

Millie looked confused. "I know about the cross. I know about Jesus. When I was a little girl I was baptized in the ocean. Papa gave me this locket to remind me of the cross and him and Mama...." Her voice trailed off. "To remind me that Jesus loves me."

A glimmer of hope was born. "He does love you, Millie."

"I want to believe that."

"Return to Him, then. You can do that right now." Kit's grip was firm on Millie's hand.

Then, from the darkness of her face came a look of deep yearning. "I want to," Millie said. "Oh, I want to come back."

"Then do it now," Kit said. She reached out and took the young girl's hands in her own. "Close your eyes, Millie, and tell God you want to come back to Him. Now, Millie."

"Yes."

Millie closed her eyes and began to pray.

Chapter Fourteen

THE DESK SERGEANT looked at Kit as though she were standing there with a gun. "You what?" he said.

"I want to speak to the officer in charge of the case," Kit said.

"That's what I thought you said. You must be bats."

"No. I'm a legal representative." This was at least true in a general sense.

The sergeant scratched his head, no doubt mulling over the fact that she worked for Earl Rogers. He did not look pleased. "Wait," he said brusquely.

Kit, aware of the stares of other police officers walking to and fro, stood frozen at the desk. She knew instantly what it must feel like to be a suspect. They were watching, looking for clues, sizing her up. The only difference was she hadn't done anything wrong. Not from her perspective, at least. But what about the police? What was she doing, making demands?

A few moments later the sergeant returned, flanked by a stocky man in a brown suit. His nose was large and flat, like an ex-pugilist she had met once in New York. He had a cold stub of a cigar plugged into one side of his mouth.

"This the one causing all the trouble?" the stocky man said.

"She's the one," replied the sergeant.

"My name's McGinty," the man in the brown suit said. "Detective McGinty. You work for Rogers?"

Swallowing, Kit managed to say, "Yes."

"Uh-huh." McGinty looked her up and down, reminding her of Sloate's leer. "I got to say I like his taste in secretaries."

"I'm not a secretary, sir," said Kit. "I am a legal representative here on behalf of Millie Ryan. Are you the investigating officer?"

"Now, look, miss, I—"

"Are you?"

"Water your horses, miss. Yeah, I am." McGinty looked like he was withholding something. Was he just playing with her? Was this all a joke to him and everyone else?

"Then I want to ask you some questions," said Kit.

McGinty glared at her, working the cigar from one corner of his mouth to the other. "Why?" he said finally.

"To determine what evidence you have against Millie Ryan."

At that McGinty laughed and looked at the sergeant, who also laughed. "Maybe Earl hasn't told you this," McGinty said, "but we don't have to tell you anything."

No, Rogers hadn't told her that. She had only heard secondhand accounts of lawyers being able to talk informally to cops. But that was if you were a real lawyer, which she wasn't, and if you had a working relationship with them, which she didn't. Still, she had played her card and was determined to see out the hand.

"I know that's formally true, Detective," said Kit. "But surely if it becomes apparent your case is thin, you may not want to file the charges. You may want to see that justice is done. Unless, of course—" Kit paused for effect—"you're not confident in what you have."

"Confident!" McGinty almost lost his cigar. "Miss, your client, if that's what she is, tried to kill a man. In this state that's attempted murder."

"Are you so sure?"

"Sure as I'm standing here."

"How can you be?"

McGinty now took the cigar out of his mouth. "Because I got the complaining witness here, with his lawyer, and I just took his statement."

The complaining witness? Here? "Then let's talk to him," Kit said, shocked at her own audacity.

McGinty squinted at her. At first he looked as though he would physically eject her from the station. But then a glint flashed in his eyes. He looked suddenly amused. "Oh, you want to talk to him, do you?"

Too late to back down now. "I do," said Kit.

"Well, then, missy, why don't you follow me?"

The desk sergeant looked thunderstruck as Kit followed McGinty through a side door.

Entering a large green room, Kit observed a row of wooden desks. A haze of smoke hung like a canopy below the ceiling. McGinty strode toward a desk where a man with three ugly scratches on his left cheek was seated. Thorn Wilson, Kit thought. He looked up from a newspaper on his lap. He had a thick black mustache and cold, dark eyes.

Kit locked on those eyes immediately, seeing an animosity in them that she had not earned. It was just part of Wilson, she concluded. This is a man who would lie.

A tall, angular man had his back to Kit and McGinty. He was stooping over the desk, apparently reading something. As he heard them approach, he stood up and turned.

And Kit lost all breath.

Heath Sloate's face whitened when he saw her. His eyes widened behind his pince-nez glasses, appearing to fill both lenses. For a brief moment, Kit thought he might cry out like a crazed soldier, pointing out a spy in the camp. But he seemed to regain control quickly, his eyes scanning the room, as if knowing they were being watched.

Her own knees buckled slightly, but she fought for balance. Heath Sloate! Now what would she do?

"Mr. Sloate," McGinty said, "this here lady works for Mr. Earl Rogers. What was your name again, miss?"

Kit took in a breath and tried not to let her voice tremble. "Kathleen Shannon," she said.

McGinty said, "She doesn't think we have much of a case against that poor murdering slut sitting in our jail. She wanted to talk about it, if you can believe that. I thought you could set her straight."

Every eye in the squad room seemed to be trained on her. "There's nothing to set straight," Sloate said. "This woman is not a lawyer. She has no right to be here. Have her removed."

McGinty paused, raised his eyebrows, then took a step toward her.

Kit said, "Wait. I do have a right to be here."

"How?" Sloate said.

"Law of agency."

"Law of what?" McGinty asked around his cigar.

"Agency." Kit quoted from memory, "Every relation in which one person acts for or represents another by the latter's authority. Isn't that right, Mr. Sloate?"

Sloate's thin lips tightened.

"What should I do?" McGinty asked.

"You're going to charge attempted murder," Sloate said. Then he looked at Kit. "And there's nothing this... pretender can do about it."

From some deep wellspring came a rush of anger in Kit so strong she thought it might burst out in a scream. Her body burned with indignation, but she held her voice in check and suddenly felt her mind click into a slot that almost seemed pre-chosen for her. She followed her thoughts without hesitation, confident.

"The evidence," Kit said, "is that this man engaged my client in a criminal transaction, prostitution, and then attempted to do her physical harm. Millie Ryan acted in self-defense. And we will prove it."

Thorn Wilson wrapped his big hands around the arms of his chair, squeezing so hard his knuckles turned white. "I did no such thing! I was walking along the street, on my way to a prayer meeting, when she jumped out at me! She wanted to rob me!"

"Then how did you leave evidence of being in her room?"

McGinty suddenly snapped to attention. "What evidence?"

"He knows," said Kit. She knew the only evidence was Millie's own testimony, but something about his look told her that Wilson was a man who would crack easily.

Wilson shifted again and looked at Sloate. "You said there wouldn't be any—"

"Quiet," Sloate admonished.

"But you said no one would take her case!"

"Quiet, I said!"

Kit looked at the tense interplay of the two men and added, "Not only that, but my client is going to bring an action for assault and battery against Mr. Wilson. She will be seeking an award of money to compensate her for her injuries."

Wilson shot to his feet, looking at Sloate. "Wait just a minute here. You didn't tell me this would happen!"

"She's bluffing," Sloate said. Then he focused his steely eyes on Kit. "She knows that no one will believe the story of a pitiable woman against a man of standing."

Kit felt the full brunt of Sloate's contempt. How many people had he looked at in just this way? How many people had capitulated, as he was expecting her to do now?

Then she realized—Heath Sloate was Sister Gertrude! He ruled this roost, holding the long cane of his influence over her inexperienced palms. She was not going to let him strike.

She looked at Wilson. "This will be a fine story for the Hearst paper, Mr. Wilson. It loves a scandal. I know a reporter who will appreciate this scoop."

A thin layer of sweat made Wilson's forehead glisten. "Heath, I want to stop this."

"Don't listen to her," Sloate said.

"I mean it," said Wilson, his eyes reflecting such guilt Kit was sure McGinty would not be able to ignore it. "I won't swear out a complaint, and I won't testify."

"You're beside yourself," Sloate said.

"No, no," said Wilson. "I can't have this in the paper." He turned to Kit. "If I drop the complaint, will you promise not to bring suit against me?"

A slow moan, almost like the wail of a wounded animal, issued from Sloate's mouth. Kit said to Wilson, "I think my client can be convinced, provided she is released immediately and you send her the sum of five hundred dollars for the trauma she has faced. Then I can assure you the story will go no further."

"This is blackmail!" Sloate shouted.

McGinty, taking the stub of cigar and tossing it into a spittoon, said, "Nope, it's trading. I think she's got you, Sloate."

Suddenly a few titters arose around them, and Kit remembered they were all being observed by policemen.

"Done!" said Wilson, extending his hand.

Sloate quickly said, "You're making a big—"

But before he could finish Kit grabbed Wilson's hand and shook. "Done," she said.

"I'll send a check to Rogers' office in the morning," said Wilson. "Come on, Heath, let's get out of here." Wilson grabbed his coat from the wooden chair and started walking, looking as if he couldn't wait to get out.

Kit, her head whirling, smelled Sloate's sour breath by her ear. "This isn't over," he whispered with palpable malevolence. Then he followed his client.

For a moment the world was silent around her. She felt her entire body buzzing, as if it couldn't quite believe what its owner had just done. To Heath Sloate!

McGinty stared at her. And then, suddenly, he slapped her on the shoulder. "Now that was worth seein'!" He laughed then, and a few others in the room laughed, too.

"Yep," McGinty said, "I got to hand it to you. I've never seen Sloate so flustered!"

Kit was speechless.

"I'll tell you," McGinty whispered, "I don't like him much. Seeing what you just did was a tonic."

"Thank you," was all Kit could think of to say.

"You tell Rogers something for me, will you?"

"Of course."

"Tell him to hang on to *you*."

Kit couldn't help smiling.

"And one more thing," said McGinty.

"Yes?"

"Watch your back. Sloate isn't a man to forget something like this."

Kit nodded solemnly.

"Now come on," said McGinty. "Let's go bounce your client."

Chapter Fifteen

HEATH SLOATE WALKED SLOWLY, almost automatically, into his Adams Street home. Set well back from the street, it was surrounded by large date and fan palms, grevillas, and magnolias, as well as orange and pepper trees casting their shade upon a parklike lawn of brilliant green.

This neighborhood had been called the most beautiful in the entire city. To Sloate, that mattered not at all, especially now.

Inside, the large Victorian home was dark. The heavy brocade drapes were drawn as always. Sloate rarely opened them, even when guests came—which wasn't often. He preferred his isolation. No one had ever lived in this home but he.

Walking straight through toward the kitchen, then out the kitchen door toward the lush backyard, Sloate did not notice any of the beauty of the roses, jasmine, and heliotrope covering the porch. Instead, his eyes immediately fixated on a hand ax lying in its spot by the back steps.

He picked up the ax, intending to chop some kindling for a fire, then stopped. He looked at the ax and, with a sudden, blinding flash of white inside his head, he gave a primal, guttural cry and lashed out with it. The blade embedded itself deeply into an ornate wooden post.

His rage was both shocking and familiar to him. He hadn't felt such hatred for a woman since just after the war. That was when he'd learned about the twisted heart and soul of women, and why he would never allow them power over him again.

Margaret Chenson was a southern belle, raised in the embrace of pre-war Charleston. She had beauty, yes, and also all the social graces. She was ripe for marrying, just seventeen to his twenty-five. He had selected her from a set of prospects for which he'd drawn up columns listing attributes both positive and negative. Of all of them, Margaret had the most to offer an ambitious young lawyer who would reach the top of his profession. Her beauty unequalled, her intellect surprisingly keen for a woman, Margaret Chenson stood out as a rose among lesser flowers. And, he finally had to admit to himself, despite all his efforts to remain cool toward the transaction of matrimony, he had fallen in love.

He had followed the laws of southern courtship, even in the swirl of Reconstruction, and had invested nearly a year in the often uncomfortable rituals before he actually proposed. Despite all that time, he was somewhat surprised when she said yes. He knew he was not a woman's ideal in looks, but he was sensible and would provide security. Margaret, who held a passionate and romantic streak that Sloate could not fully understand, seemed to accept the sober reasons without qualm.

That was before she met the Union soldier, part of the post-war security forces. It had all happened in secret. Sloate was too stupid or blind to see the signs. But one month before the wedding Margaret ran away with the soldier—away from her family, her roots, and Heath Sloate. In her note she confessed she had never loved him and that she had no choice but to follow her heart.

Her family had been horrified—completely devastated to learn of their daughter's treasonous action. They had disowned her and settled a huge sum of money on Sloate, encouraging him to go quietly and make little noise about this in Charleston's most fickle society.

Sloate was not mollified and allowed the full intensity of his hatred to burn all emotion to the ground, like Atlanta under Sherman's torch. The money, while appealing, would not quench his rage. She had made him the laughingstock of the town. Despite his willingness to keep the matter hushed, most everyone seemed to know the details practically overnight.

"That's Heath Sloate," they said in conspiratorial whispers. "He's the one Margaret Chenson threw over for a Yankee!"

Their disdain was obvious. How could any woman prefer the enemy to one of their own people—unless, of course, something was horribly wrong with the man in question. It didn't take long for that assumption to circulate, and before he knew it, people were avoiding him altogether.

Sloate had been livid. That this mere slip of a woman should have the power to put suspicion and doubt on his shoulders was more than he could accept. The thought only gave fuel to the conflagration in his soul. It was then he made an unalterable decision. Never again would he allow a woman to deceive him. Never would he give his heart away. Never would he let a woman get the better of him.

But now one had.

Kit Shannon! She was a curse, a cancer. It wasn't enough that she should deny him her companionship when to do so made perfect business sense. No, she had come in under his very nose and humiliated him in front of Thorn Wilson, a valued client, and most of the police squad as well.

Sloate removed the ax from the wood and hefted it to his shoulder. So she was going on with this pretense of practicing law, was she? Well, now was the time to cut her off. Like a sapling before its roots became strong.

Earl Rogers howled with laughter. It was the last thing Kit expected. She thought Rogers would be outraged that she had gone behind his back to visit a penniless client. But there he was, filling his office with such a guffaw that Bill Jory and Rose, the office secretary, rushed in to see if anything was wrong.

"She's won her first case already," Rogers explained, "without even passing the bar!"

Bill Jory slapped her on the back so hard it stung. But it also felt wonderful, like an official acceptance of her presence.

"The best part, though," Rogers continued, "is that Heath Sloate was on the other side! That snake has been slithering around this town too long. He needed to get stepped on."

Kit remembered the look in Sloate's eyes. He did not like getting stepped on one bit. That made two times she had gotten the upper hand on him. The thought of him exacting retribution made her shiver.

"This calls for a celebration," Rogers announced, standing and grabbing his coat. "We're closing the office and having a dinner party. Rose—" he turned to his secretary. "See if you can get young Barrymore. I think these two should meet."

"But ... wait ..." Kit stared at Rogers in disbelief. She didn't have the money for dinner parties. She stood up, straightening her hat as she got to her feet. "I can hardly afford—"

"Nonsense!" Rogers bellowed. "I'm buying. You can't afford

not to. This is a monumental moment. One I intend to savor. I'll not take no for an answer."

Kit caught his enthusiasm and smiled. "Very well. You're the one with the purse."

They ended up at The Imperial, apparently the place to be seen. The maître d' knew Rogers and Bill Jory and had a large table waiting for them. A string quartet played softly as couples took turns dancing around a hardwood floor. They were also joined by Luther Brown, another Rogers assistant, lean and smart. The only one missing was the young actor Rogers had referred to. Kit wondered why an actor would be part of this circle.

Rogers ordered champagne and when it came, poured drinks all around. When he proposed a toast, Kit lifted only her water glass.

"What," Rogers said. "No wine?"

"No," Kit said.

"Ever?"

"I'm sorry."

"Not even champagne? Why not?"

"My father was killed by a drunkard," Kit said.

The last comment seemed to cause a strange reaction in everyone, Kit noticed. Rogers seemed embarrassed, the others possessed of some hidden knowledge. The silence was uncomfortable until Rogers looked up and said, "Ah!"

Kit looked up, too, and inhaled with a quick burst. Standing in front of her was the most incredibly handsome man she had ever seen—a perfectly chiseled face rounded out by dancing brown eyes that seemed to hold both mischief and merriment. Dressed in evening garb, his broad shoulders and chest tapered downward in a faultless V shape. Kit suddenly felt underdressed.

"Greetings!" the man said with a theatrical trill. "I trust I'm not late."

"Not at all. We've only popped the cork on the first bottle," Rogers said. "May I present to you Miss Kathleen Shannon, new to my office? Miss Shannon, John Barrymore."

Barrymore's eyes sparkled as he bowed and extended his hand. "Jack to my friends," he said. His handshake generated something like a current of electricity up Kit's arm. She felt such a flush in her face that she wished she could crawl under the table.

As Barrymore pulled up a chair, Rogers said, "Jack is making his West Coast debut as Mercutio down at the Morosco. But you'll find him in the courtroom much of the time."

"Earl Rogers is the greatest actor of them all," Barrymore announced. "I watch him to learn." He pounded the table twice. "A drink!"

Rogers poured Barrymore a glass of champagne. As the glass filled, Barrymore looked at Kit. His gaze was mesmerizing. "May I ask what a fair young flower is doing planted in the arid climes of a criminal law enterprise?"

His voice was so magnificent! It flowed like honey. "I . . ." Kit stammered, "I'm hoping to practice law."

Rogers beamed. "Hope nothing! Won her first case already."

John Barrymore said, "A maiden among scoundrels! This is the stuff of drama." He tossed back his head and downed the entire glass of champagne. "More!"

Rogers poured another glass for Barrymore and for himself. It was a pattern that would repeat over the course of the next hour, as three bottles of champagne came to the table and disappeared. It was a strange, almost otherworldly experience. Kit continued, sipping only water in the midst of an increasingly boisterous group of hard-drinking men.

Barrymore and Rogers soon began reciting Shakespeare to each other. Amazingly, to Kit at least, Rogers held his own. She thought if she were ever in need of a lawyer, either one of these men would do!

Suddenly Barrymore stood, walked around the table, and offered his hand to Kit. As if hypnotized, she took it. As he helped her up from the chair he said, "This dance is mine."

Panic, like a jungle cat, leaped into her body. She had no idea how to dance. That was something the sisters of the Catholic church did not have high on their list of items to teach! And now she was walking toward a dance floor swirling with finely dressed and ever-so-graceful couples with an impossibly handsome and charming man.

She looked heavenward. *Don't let me step on his feet! Oh, please, not that!*

Barrymore noticed her hesitation as he pulled out a handkerchief before putting his hand on her back. "There is the slightest hint in your expression that suggests to me disdain. But surely not. Surely I cannot have put you off already." He smiled devilishly and tightened his hold on Kit's hand.

Her inadequacy on the dance floor was the last thing she had hoped to discuss. Still, the truth might well be her salvation. Perhaps he would quietly lead her back to the table before she could make a fool of herself.

"I can't dance." She admitted the fact softly, almost as if it were something to be ashamed of.

Barrymore studied her for a moment as if ascertaining the truth in her words, then shrugged. "Neither can I, but I walk quite gracefully to the music. Care to give it a try?"

Kit smiled in spite of her fears. "I could probably manage walking."

"Then let us be about our business." They began, Barrymore proving to be a gentle and patient teacher. He guided her with his arms and smiled—what a smile!—to comfort her unease.

For a few moments Kit thought she was in a dream. Back in New York, scrubbing floors to earn her keep and studying law the rest of the time, she never envisioned herself in a setting like this, dancing of all things. And certainly not with the most beautiful man she'd ever seen.

I have to stop thinking that! Get hold of your senses, Kit Shannon!

"You dance like an angel," Barrymore said softly.

"You lie like a devil," Kit rejoined. At which Barrymore laughed heartily. If he was not truly charmed by her, he was a great actor indeed.

For several more minutes they danced, Kit ever aware of her partner's toes. Yet she began to feel more and more free, perhaps finding opportunity to let go of all the things that had seemingly gone wrong since she'd arrived—Aunt Freddy, Heath Sloate, the police. Let all that go, at least for this night.

She suddenly took a more exuberant step in response to the swelling music—and caught the hem of her dress. Next thing she knew she was hitting the hardwood floor, face reddening with the awful realization that she was surrounded by aghast patrons.

"Will you look at that!" one woman whispered indignantly. "No doubt she is drunk."

Kit was instantly reminded of her father's teaching from the Bible. What was that about living a life above reproach? Dazed momentarily, but wishing the floor would open up and consume her, she felt two people lifting her, one on each side. One was surely Barrymore, but who was the other?

Once on her feet she saw it was Ted Fox. "Hello, Miss Shannon," he said.

Kit saw Barrymore's right eyebrow lift. "A friend of yours?" he said.

"Y-Yes," Kit stammered. "Mr. Ted Fox, Mr. John Barrymore."

"How do you do?" Ted said.

"Very well," replied Barrymore, "especially with so charming a partner." Then, in a louder voice so all around them could hear, Barrymore apologized. "My dearest Miss Shannon, I cannot tell you how sorry I am for tripping you. You must forgive me. My heart will be sorrowed, nay, broken in two, should you withhold your forgiveness," Barrymore finished with great aplomb.

That was when Kit heard a hard voice behind her say, "Well . . ."

It was Elinor Wynn, holding a fan almost like a weapon, her face as hard as the floor. "I certainly didn't expect to see you here," she said to Kit.

Kit felt her cheeks grow hotter still. She wasn't sure how to respond, so said nothing. But John Barrymore did. "That, madam, is an uncouth thing to say."

Elinor Wynn looked like she'd been slapped. Kit, in spite of herself, couldn't help feeling slightly pleased. And she thought, out of the corner of her eye, she saw a slight smile from Ted Fox.

Barrymore stood there, his eyebrow raised even higher, his body teetering slightly. Elinor Wynn gave him a quick, dismissive look. "You, sir, are drunk," she said.

"All right, that's enough," Ted said, stepping closer to Barrymore. Dutifully, if unwillingly, rescuing his lady, Kit thought.

"Let's forget the whole thing," Barrymore said grandly. "Come to our table and we'll order more champagne."

"No," Elinor said. "I'd like to have a word with Miss Shannon."

"Come on, sport," Ted said to Barrymore, taking his arm and leading him away. Indeed, it looked to Kit as if Barrymore might stumble without the help.

Elinor Wynn swept off the dance floor, and Kit followed. When they reached the women's lounge, Elinor turned around and looked at Kit with obvious disdain, though Kit thought she sensed something else at work. Fear, perhaps, as if Kit's presence in the city was somehow threatening to Elinor Wynn.

"I know what you did," Elinor said.

Kit shook her head. "I don't know what you're referring to."

"Don't play dumb with me."

"I assure you, I'm not."

"I believe you are," said Elinor. "But if we must play games, then I'll tell you that I am referring to my fiancé's and your little tryst the other day."

"Tryst? It was nothing of the kind."

"I really don't care to discuss what kind it was. Ted can be a little headstrong, even to the point of doing terribly unsound things."

"Like taking me for a ride in his buggy?" Kit said, her anger attempting to claw its way into her voice.

"Exactly. I want you to know it won't happen again."

Was that because Ted had said so, or because Elinor was threatening her? Kit studied her face and saw two things there. First, an impetuous will to have her own way. Elinor Wynn was from the privileged class and not used to being defied. But there was also a vulnerability there, a certain weakness that came from the same social privileges. Elinor Wynn, Kit was sure, had never had to fight too hard or suffer too dreadfully. In a pinch, with enough force against her, she would probably be as delicate and resistant as the powder on her face.

But Kit was not going to fight Elinor Wynn. There was no need. Ted Fox, as attractive as he was, was pledged to her, and Kit would respect that.

Kit said, "You have no need to—"

"You don't have to tell me my needs," Elinor interrupted. "I am telling you that if you even hint at showing your face around Ted, I shall see to it you are made miserable. And don't doubt that I can do it."

No doubt at all, thought Kit. This was a woman who would go through life making many people miserable. She felt sorry for Ted. His would be a tough road.

Kit said, "I understand."

"I knew you would," said Elinor.

Kit nodded, turned, and walked out of the lounge, her heart throwing punches against her chest.

Ted Fox approached her immediately. "Been talking to El?"

"She's in there," Kit said.

"What did she say to you?"

"She'll tell you, I'm sure." Kit took a step, but Ted put his hands on her shoulders.

"I want you to tell me," he said.

"Ted!" It was Elinor, appearing like a ghost at the mouth of a cave.

"What is this all about?" Ted demanded.

"Not here," rebuked Elinor.

"I want to know."

"Not here," Elinor said again in a tone that suggested she would brook no disagreement.

Ted looked into Kit's face for a moment, and she saw there a deep, penetrating darkness. And danger. But also a pleading, something calling to her.

Elinor grabbed Ted by the arm and led him away. He gave Kit a glance, just as he had at the party where they had first met. But this time his expression resembled that of a lost child—no, more than that. A lost soul.

Kit had only a vague recollection of getting back to the table where Rogers, Barrymore, and the others were well into their drinks. Feeling out of place, Kit made her good-byes. Barrymore tried to charm her into staying, but she was no longer in any mood for celebration. She suddenly felt rootless and abandoned, as if she hadn't a friend in the world—as if Los Angeles had become an abyss of despair instead of a city of hope.

Rogers insisted on paying for her cab home, and for once, Kit didn't argue about it. She had no desire to walk the streets alone. Lost in her thoughts, Kit wondered if she should have stood up more to Elinor Wynn. The woman was impossibly haughty and needed to be taken down a few pegs. But, on the other hand, she had reason to be upset with Kit. Kit had gone out with Ted, unchaperoned. It didn't look good. No doubt, if Ted had have been engaged to Kit instead of Elinor, Kit wouldn't have liked his doing such a thing with that icy but beautiful woman.

The driver stopped only long enough to help Kit down from the carriage. He then tipped his hat and was gone. Kit stood outside the building for several moments. The streets were surprisingly void of activity.

Suddenly the back of Kit's neck tingled. She felt as though someone were watching her. She took hold of her skirts, ready to run if need be, but her feet seemed frozen in place.

In the distance a dog barked, then whined miserably as though someone had kicked it. Behind her a rustling sound caused Kit to whirl around, ready to greet her adversary face-to-face. It proved to be nothing more than a crumpled bit of newspaper.

Her movements were enough to break the spell, however, and without further ado, Kit bolted for the door and raced up the narrow stairs. Her heart pounded as she imagined hearing footsteps on the floor behind her. Surely her thoughts were simply running away with her.

She fumbled the key into the lock and threw the door open with such enthusiasm that it rattled the glass. Ignoring the possibility of breaking the window, Kit slammed the door shut, locked it, and pulled down the shade. For just a moment she leaned back against the door without bothering even to turn on the light. She was panting, more afraid than she'd been since her encounter with Sloate. She realized then how vulnerable she was. Living in an office? With a killer loose on the streets? She must be mad!

It was while standing there, gathering her thoughts and calming her heart, that Kit caught the unmistakable sound of footsteps in the hall. Her breath caught in her throat. She put a hand to her mouth to keep from crying out as the steps stopped just outside her door.

She waited, hearing nothing.

Then a knock sounded! What should she do?

"Miss Shannon?" a familiar voice said.

Corazón! Kit opened the door and threw her arms around her friend. "You scared me to death!"

"I am so sorry," Corazón said.

"Come in!" Kit's heart was filled to bursting at the sight of her dear friend. "I've missed you so!"

"I am having to sneak out to see you."

"I'm glad you did!" Kit lit an oil lamp and said, "What do you think?"

"Where do you sleep?" Corazón said, looking around the room. "You no sleep here?"

Kit laughed. "Mr. Rogers created a little bedroom off the back of this office. I don't have much space there, but it is enough. I've even managed to bring in a little washbasin. Oh, you've no idea how I long for a real bath."

Corazón smiled. "There are places for such things. Near my home, there are people who charge for hot bath and hair cutting."

"Yes, but those places are generally more appealing to men. Perhaps I could find an establishment devoted to the needs of women. I'll check into it." Kit walked to a shelf and pulled down a small bakery sack. "How about a treat? Imagine me playing hostess here!"

Kit pulled two shortbread cookies from the sack. "One for you and one for me. Sorry I don't have any plates."

"No plates? Where do you eat?"

Kit shrugged and handed Corazón the cookie. "Mostly I pick up fruit or bread at the market. Sometimes I splurge and eat at the little café around the corner."

Corazón frowned. "That is no good. You will grow too thin."

Kit reached out and patted her arm. Smiling, she said, "I don't mind. Honestly. I'm doing what I love. The sacrifice is worth it. Come, sit."

The two sat on wooden chairs and began to munch cookies. It didn't matter to Kit that the fare was modest and the setting dim. She was just so glad to see Corazón.

"Tell me how Aunt Freddy is faring," Kit said. "I worry about her, and I've longed to contact her. I wanted to give her time to get used to the idea of having me remain here in Los Angeles, and I certainly didn't want to discuss my living here in Earl Rogers' office."

"She is sad, mostly. I think she misses you much."

"Does she talk about me?"

"No, she no talk, but her eyes, they are sad, and her heart is no feeling good."

Kit frowned. "What do you mean? Is she ill?"

"I think she is afraid of what to do. Mr. Sloate, he come to tell her things sometimes. He put on such, how you say, the charm?"

The thought repelled Kit. "Poor Aunt Freddy."

"She want to marry him bad, I think."

"I can't let that happen," Kit said with intensity.

"You would try to stop her?"

"If she would listen to me. But I fear she won't now. He must be after her money. Why doesn't she see that?"

"He has promised to help."

"Help? How?"

"Sally, she tell me Madam want to have a park in the city for the memory of her husband."

"Jasper?"

"Sí. Mr. Sloate, he has the pol . . ."

"Political?"

"Sí, political ways to make this thing to happen. Madam, she wants it bad, I think."

Kit nodded. He was using charm *and* influence on Aunt Freddy. But he appeared to be making Aunt Freddy *happy*. Who was she to come between her aunt's happiness and harsh reality?

However, she knew Sloate better than Aunt Freddy did. If only she could find a way to reveal his true character.

"Corazón," Kit said, "can you stay with me tonight?"

"I no go home?"

"Only if you want to. But I have extra blankets and the couch here. We could stay up talking and be like schoolgirls."

"Oh sí! I would like that!"

"Then it's done."

They did talk into the night, giving each other lessons in their own languages and laughing together over secrets only friends share. But Kit could not help feeling a sense of dread at it all, as if this were merely a short dream that would end soon. More than once she felt as if the shadow of Heath Sloate hovered outside her door, listening.

Chapter Sixteen

"YOUR COMPASSION IS GOING TO get you into trouble," Earl Rogers said.

Kit was sitting in his office, where he had summoned her. Earlier in the day she had pleaded with him to take the case of yet another indigent client.

"The first rule in criminal work is what?" he asked.

Remembering, Kit muttered, "Get the money first." But it left a terrible taste in her mouth as she said it.

"Right."

"And what about innocence? Doesn't that matter?"

"No."

Kit felt like she had been jolted by a punch. How could innocence, actual or apparent, not be relevant in a criminal proceeding?

"You want me to explain?" Rogers said.

"By all means."

"A career in criminal law is based upon winning. I don't care if my client is innocent or guilty. If he's innocent, that just makes the task a little easier. But you don't build a reputation on losing cases."

"Isn't there more to law than reputation?"

"If you want to practice law, you need clients. If you want clients, you need reputation. If you want clients who can pay you in sterling silver, you need a sterling reputation. And if you want gold, well, you just don't lose. I don't lose."

"I don't know if I can accept that," she said. "That's not why I chose to study law."

"And why did you?" Rogers looked genuinely interested.

"I'll tell you," Kit said. "When I was fourteen I made the most important discovery of my life. A thick, leather-bound book tucked away in the far corner of the library. It was obscured somewhat by the end of the bookcase, which overlapped the shelves slightly, and also by a carelessly deposited volume of sixteenth-century church doctrine."

Rogers watched her but said nothing.

"I saw the title on the spine—*Commentaries on the Laws of England* by Sir William Blackstone—and, I don't know, I was drawn to it." She remembered the moment as if it had been yesterday. She had never seen a law book before. Indeed, had not been aware they existed. She thought all the laws were written in the heads of lawyers and judges and shared among them like some secret language.

She had slipped the book out, opened it, and read upon the first page, *When the supreme being formed the universe, and created matter out of nothing, he impressed certain principles upon that matter, from which it can never depart, and without which it would cease to be.*

For as God, when he created matter, and endued it with a principle of mobility, established certain rules for the perpetual direction of that motion; so, when he created man, and endued him with free

will to conduct himself in all parts of life, he laid down certain im-
mutable laws of human nature, whereby that free will is in some
degree regulated and restrained, and gave him also the faculty of rea-
son to discover the purport of those laws.

"I thought it made so much sense," she told Rogers. "The law flows from God, to nature, to man. That is why it is binding. And He gave us reason to discover it all."

Still Rogers said nothing.

"And I thought of my mother. I thought of what was done to her by men who twist the law. I knew that law, even from God, could be made something wicked. I decided at once I would learn the law, and with God on my side I would fight for just outcomes. I read the entire volume in two months. And when I was finished, I knew that the law was about the will of God. And that's what I've always believed. I won't go back now or think any less."

Rogers had grown quiet and now looked as if some inner wound had suddenly been opened, causing pain. Kit thought she must have said something to offend him. He looked past her, not at anything specific, it seemed to Kit, but into some amorphous yet palpable darkness. She dared not speak, feeling he wanted to be alone with his thoughts.

"You can go now," Rogers said finally, quietly, in the voice of someone who had given up a fight. That shocked Kit most of all. Never had she heard that voice come from Earl Rogers. Not the great trial lawyer, the supremely confident advocate who prided himself on winning at all costs.

Without another word Kit stood and turned. Just before stepping out the door she glanced back. Rogers, seemingly unconcerned with her presence, was lifting a bottle out of a drawer.

Kit met Bill Jory in the hallway.

"Hey, what is it, gal?" Jory said, putting his huge hands on her shoulders the way a big brother might have.

"What?" said Kit, as if being called out of a daydream.

"You look like trouble's been callin'."

"I'm sorry, Bill."

"You been with Earl?"

"Yes."

"And?"

She looked into Jory's eyes and saw a soft concern there, as well as understanding. "He suddenly got very sad."

"Anything else?"

Kit didn't answer. It seemed Jory already knew.

"Is he drinking?" the investigator asked.

Kit nodded.

"Come with me," said Jory. She followed him down the hall to the new office he had taken—*Jory Investigations* it said on the door. It was a small office with one desk, two chairs, and not much else.

Jory sat Kit down. "Tell me exactly what happened."

Kit recounted her conversation, all the way up to her story of finding inspiration in Blackstone. When she told him that, Jory nodded.

"I get it now," he said.

"What is it?" Kit asked.

Jory sighed, then said, "You need to know something about Earl. You know he drinks more than he should. What you don't know is why."

Kit waited, intensely curious.

"Earl's father was a minister," Jory explained. "He wanted his son to follow in his footsteps. Earl idolized him but didn't have the same fire in his belly about religion. I think that tortured Earl. He wanted to believe, wanted to please his father, but couldn't. It got worse when he went into law."

"His father didn't approve?"

"He didn't approve of what Earl has come to believe, that the job of the lawyer is to win. Rev. Rogers didn't think God was pleased with that. So when you started talking about that fella . . ."

"Blackstone?"

"And that talk about God and the law, it brought all that back to Earl."

"He told me his father died. How long ago?"

"A year. It was bad for Earl. When he heard, first person he told was his daughter, Adela. He woke her up to tell her, and Adela told me what he said."

Kit leaned forward, attuned to every word.

"He said, 'What kind of God would take him away from me now, when I need him most?' "

The scene was painted in her mind, and Kit almost shed tears.

"So my advice," Jory said, "is not to bring this up again. He ain't spoke of his father since, and he don't want to. It only makes him drink more."

"Is there nothing I can do?"

"You can do good work," Jory said. He put a comforting hand on her shoulder. Kit nodded.

Suddenly they were interrupted by the pounding of steps up the wooden stairs. In a second the door flew open, and a breathless Luther Brown stuck his head in. "They found another one," he said.

"Another what?" demanded Jory.

"Prostitute. Murdered."

Kit put a hand to her chest. "No . . ."

Brown directed his large eyes toward her. "And not only that, Kit."

"What do you mean?"

"It's Millie Ryan."

Chapter Seventeen

OREL HOOVER, Chief of Police, was a fireplug of a man—or so Heath Sloate thought. With thinning white hair over a mottle-cheeked face and an ample stomach, Hoover had long since abandoned any pretense of appearing as a man of action. He had become just another politician. And Heath Sloate thought of politicians as his "meat."

So when he entered Hoover's office that afternoon, Sloate was quite sure he would have no trouble with this politico-policeman. If he met resistance, Sloate would find a way to put a little pressure on him, devise a plan to destroy him if need be. Just as he'd fixed old Wexell back at school.

Sloate had come to embrace a favorite saying of President Roosevelt's: "Speak softly and carry a big stick." The president had used that as a rallying cry when threatening to send in federal troops during the Pennsylvania coal miners' strike a year before. The coal mine owners backed down. Now "Rough and Ready Teddy" was using it in foreign policy as well, applying it to the situation in Panama.

Sloate realized that he had applied the big stick over and over again his dealings with people. It worked, and he was confident it would work again now.

Sloate had done his homework on Chief Orel Hoover—just in case things got difficult down the line. There was the matter of Hoover's odd son, a potential embarrassment for a man who had visions—illusions, Sloate thought—of someday becoming mayor. There was also Mrs. Hoover, an unrelentingly obnoxious woman who could, merely by opening her mouth, scuttle any future political plans Hoover might entertain. Such information was putty in his hands, Sloate thought. From it he could fashion a veritable work of art in blackmail.

"Ah, Chief," Sloate greeted. Though he thought Hoover's face seemed redder than usual, he added, "You're looking well."

"Sit down," Hoover said.

Sloate complied. Hoover didn't seem happy to see him. No doubt he thought this visit an imposition.

"Now, what is this urgent matter?" Hoover asked.

Sloate did not answer immediately. One did not reel in a fish right away. Instead, he glanced at the walls of Hoover's office, noticing framed letters displayed prominently. Commendations, no doubt, from Hoover's days as a beat cop. Or cloying missives from politicians who might someday need a favor.

"Quite a career you've had," Sloate said.

"Had? You make it sound like it's in the past." There was a snappishness in Hoover's voice that Sloate understood. Sloate had, after all, all but forced this meeting. But there was something else, too, a deeper layer under the cop's brusque exterior. He was troubled about something, Sloate was certain of it.

"Did I?" Sloate said. "I'm sorry. I understand full well you have future plans. Mayor Hoover, that has a nice sound to it."

Hoover eyed Sloate directly for a moment. "I think so," he said.

"And our fair city is growing at a rapid clip. The mayor of this hamlet might go on to even greater things. Governor. Senator, perhaps."

This time Hoover said nothing. Sloate now knew he had pegged him perfectly.

"The life of a United States senator," Sloate continued, "now that's what I call living. Maybe I should consider it."

"Mr. Sloate, I'm sure if you considered it, nothing would stand in your way. I've heard that about you."

"Heard what, sir?"

"That nothing—and nobody—ever gets between you and what you decide to get."

Sloate smiled, letting the fish take out a little more line. "I have a certain way of doing things that has proved successful, yes."

Hoover cleared his throat, and Sloate thought he saw again the shadows of a dark secret. Well, if it was there, he would find it. And use it, if need be.

"Why was it so important for you to see me?" Hoover asked.

"How would you rank our police force, Chief? I mean, over the years of your oversight?"

Pulling himself up a little higher in his chair, Hoover said, "It's good. No, great. We have a great force."

"Effective?"

"Very."

"Skilled?"

"Yes."

"Well off?"

Hoover narrowed his eyes. "What do you mean by that?"

"Come now, Chief," Sloate said smoothly, "we all know about

the take. I bet the brothels on New High Street bring in a pretty penny, eh?"

Hoover's face turned the color of beets.

"I pass no judgment," Sloate said. "It's the way business is done. And that, Chief Hoover, brings me to the reason for my visit. I propose a little business transaction, one that does not involve money, but potentially involves something of even greater value."

"Such as?"

"Your political future."

Hoover seemed poised between two reactions—outrage and interest. To relieve him of the difficulty of making a choice, Sloate added, "Don't fool yourself into believing I can't make good on my..."

"Threats?"

"Promises."

"I know you, Sloate. Know your reputation. You're a snake," Hoover stated.

"Is that the best you can do?"

"A low-down snake."

"That's better. And it's true. I do bite, and that bite can be very, very deadly. Shall I make my proposition?"

Hoover snorted air out his nose in a sound of contempt. But he said, "I'm listening."

———

Kit, feeling as if her mind were a thousand miles away, sat still in the darkness of her room. She couldn't focus on work, on anything. Millie dead! Murdered the night before by some animal who was still on the loose. It was too horrible!

Kit had been this close to murder before. Back in New York, when one of the boys who worked for the sisters at Leo House went walking home one night and never arrived. A bootblack found the poor boy's body in an alley, his neck broken. There was no motive—who would kill a penniless boy?—and no one was ever brought to justice for the crime. For weeks Kit brooded about it. She liked the boy, Mickey O'Sullivan, a mere ten-year-old. She wondered how something so senseless could happen under God's watchful eye.

Those same feelings had come flooding back to her earlier this day, when she had ventured to Thomas Ryan's pitiful shanty. His shack was full of lit candles. His way, he explained, of praying for his daughter's soul. Kit had offered him what comfort she could, though words were small solace. But he did tell her he believed Millie was in heaven because of Kit.

"She was a changed girl," he told Kit, "sure as I'm still alive. Told me she was going to leave her life of sin and come back to live with me. She wanted to find a way to serve God, she said. That means God's accepted her, doesn't it?"

Of course, Kit thought now in the silence of her room and office. *That's the kind of God I serve.*

A pounding on the door ripped her from her reverie. Heart beating, Kit realized just how dark it was now. Only thin slivers of moonlight entered through the window.

Pounding again.

Kit didn't move. Who would be here at this time of night? This wasn't the soft knock of Corazón.

The pounding became more insistent. Then a voice. "Kit! Are you in there?"

It sounded like . . . Ted Fox! What would he be doing here now?

Kit practically leaped from her chair. When she opened the door, Ted shot into the room and closed the door himself. "It's dark in here," he said, breathless. "Good."

"Ted, what is it?"

"I need help."

He raced to the window, opened the wooden slats with his hand, and looked out. Then he turned to her, his face barely visible in the dim moonlight that seeped into the office. His eyes were dark pools. "Tell me, if somebody does something, not knowing . . ."

"Not knowing what?"

"What he's doing. Not of sound mind."

"Yes?"

"Does the law say he's guilty?"

"Why, are you—"

"Just tell me!"

Kit took in a deep breath. "Sometimes not. There's *mens rea.*"

"What's that?"

"Guilty mind. For crimes requiring intent. Please tell me—"

"So if somebody doesn't know what he's doing, the law won't make him pay, right?"

"Sometimes. But the facts . . . Ted, what are you telling me?"

He didn't answer immediately, looking toward the window again. "Do you hear something?"

Kit strained to listen. At first she did not hear anything, but then got a sense that there was someone else in the building, perhaps more than one person. Whoever—or whatever it was—meant trouble. Of that she was sure.

And Ted, from the look of him, was the object of it.

She wanted to help him. But he was not giving her anything to work with. On the contrary, he seemed to be hiding something from her. But why?

Then came an insistent knocking on her door.

"They're here," Ted whispered.

A voice outside the door said, "Police!"

"Don't say anything!" Ted urged.

"I have to answer," Kit said.

"No!"

Suddenly the door flew open, slamming against the wall. Light from the single gas lamp in the hall backlit two figures in police uniforms. One of them was so enormous he almost obscured the other.

"Stop!" Kit said. "You can't break in here!"

"Who says?" the big one snapped, moving toward her.

Before she could answer, Ted made an attempt to run out the door. With grunts and curses, the two cops apprehended him.

"What's this about?" Kit said.

"Look out," the big cop said.

"I demand an answer!"

"You do, eh?" the cop said with barely veiled derision. "Well, if it's any of yer business, this guy's under arrest for murder."

Kit's heart jumped into her throat. "Murder?"

"Oh, yeah," the cop said. "He's been a bad boy, this one. A very bad boy."

~~~

Part Two

Chapter Eighteen

NOW HER CASTLE was a prison.

Frederica Stamper Fairbank gazed out the large, leaded windows of her home and could not catch her breath. Her face was flushed, her head felt light. She could not venture out into the city, she could not! What if she should luncheon at the Women's Club and faint dead away at the first titters of gossip? What of furtive looks? The whispers behind fans and gloved hands?

Gossip there would be, gossip there was—she was sure! She could almost hear it now, as if it came up from the city below and echoed through Angeleno Heights like some scandalous yodel.

Did you hear? Freddy's great-niece, the wild one from back East? Do tell!

Working for that common lawyer, Rogers, and defending a killer!

Oh my, yes . . . and Ted Fox, too. Weren't they seen together before this? Poor Elinor.

Do you think they were lovers?

*I've always had my doubts about Mr. Ted Fox! And now this fast
girl comes in. . . . Poor Freddy! How she ever overcome it?*

Freddy shook her head. Oh, why wouldn't Kit listen to her in
the first place?

Perhaps she could go to her. Take her back in. Maybe now she
was ready to listen to her, to withdraw from this ugly position she
was in. Surely enough time had elapsed.

But what would Heath say? That was why she had summoned
him. How she needed him now!

She then noted his carriage coming up the drive. Black as a
hearse—even the horse was the color of coal—but oh, he was her
only light. He would tell her what to do.

When he was announced and came into the morning room,
Freddy thought he looked annoyed with her, as if her desperate
plea—she had tried to be moderate in her note, but could not, for
this was all so confusing and hurtful—was more an imposition
than the duty of a suitor.

"Heath!" Her voice escaped before she could stop it. She went
quickly to him, her silk day dress sounding a desperate swish, then
all but threw herself into his embrace, which seemed stiff yet efficient. "Thank you, dear, for coming," Freddy said. "Oh, I am in
such a state."

"There, there," Sloate said. "Let's sit, shall we? You can tell me
all about it."

With his arm he guided her to one of the chairs near the fireplace, which lay cold. Why hadn't she ordered a fire? Heath would
have appreciated it, but it was too late now. Freddy took a lace
handkerchief from her dress, preparing for the tears she knew
would come.

Sloate sat opposite her on the settee. Freddy noticed he gave a
quick look at his pocket watch before he crossed his legs and said,
"Now, what is this terrible situation, my dear?"

"Heath, have you heard the news?"

"There is much news, Freddy. That young Italian tenor Enrico Caruso is getting rave notices in *Rigoletto*."

"Please, Heath, don't play with me. I mean about my niece, about those horrid murders!"

"Ah," he said, but it was as if he knew this was her concern all along. "Of course I've heard, Freddy. It's the most sensational and sordid crime story this city has ever seen."

"My point exactly! And Kit in the middle of it!" The first of her tears began to fall.

"Yes, Fox has retained the services of Rogers."

"You mean his mother has, poor thing. Dorothea has always been, shall we say, a trifle giddy, but this must have absolutely taken her to the limit," Freddy continued. "What shall I do, Heath? I can't stand to think that Kit will be involved in all this!"

"You mean you can't stand the talk that will be going around, eh?"

"That's mean, Heath. Please don't hurt me so."

"But isn't it the truth?"

Freddy knew it was, yet somewhere deep inside she knew also that she had an affection for her niece, a love that was equally strong.

"I don't want her to go down this path of life," Freddy said. "Shouldn't I reconcile with her? Bring her back under my roof where I might be of some influence?"

"That would be foolish," said Sloate.

"But why?"

"You must remain firm."

Nodding, Freddy said, "I suppose I must."

"Of course you must. You will understand when I tell you *my* news."

"Oh, please do, dear!"

"I have been busy these last few days. First, I want you to know that I have talked to a well-placed city councilman regarding the lovely greenbelt in memory of Jasper's accomplishments. I can assure you, without reservation, that you will see Jasper properly honored for all posterity."

"Oh, Heath! Thank you, thank you!" Tears of joy sprang to her eyes.

"It is my pleasure, dear one. I know what that means to you, and while I cannot entertain the notion that I should replace Jasper in your affections, I can at least hope that I should attain one small measure of fondness within your heart."

Freddy could not contain herself any longer. She rose from her chair, went to him, and embraced the only part of him she could encircle—his head. "Don't you worry, Heath, my darling. You have found that place in my heart already. Now and forevermore."

She realized at once she might be suffocating him and stepped back. Indeed, he took in a deep breath. "I am giddy with delight," he said flatly.

"And what other news do you have?"

He rose, walked to the mantel, and leaned upon it. "I have been to see the District Attorney."

"Whatever for?"

"I know one thing about our D.A. for certain, and that is that he is tired of losing to Earl Rogers. So I asked him to appoint me as special prosecutorial counsel for this case."

Freddy's heart began to beat faster. "You don't mean . . . Kit . . ."

"I do, Freddy. For all concerned, it is best that Rogers be stopped dead in his tracks, and your niece along with him. Then she may see the light."

It sounded so hard to Freddy, yet somehow unavoidable. Yes, Heath was right, as usual. She would have to stay the course.

"I hope it won't break her spirit," Freddy sighed.

"I hope it will do just that," said Sloate. "Without that, there can be no correction. And giving her aid and comfort, my dear, would be the worst thing you could do. Besides..." He leaned toward her. "I wouldn't want your niece to come between us."

Freddy put her hand on her chest. "But why would she?"

"We would be at cross-purposes, and that would be intolerable. Freddy, let us be adult about this. It is fast becoming time to solemnize our companionship. In fact, I thought as I drove up here that after the trial is completed, it might be a fitting way to celebrate my victory. What would you say to that, Freddy dear?"

He was asking her to marry him! At last!

"Oh, Heath..."

"But let us keep it a secret until then, eh?"

"Yes, Heath, yes. Whatever you say, dear, I shall do."

———

"And so we go to war," Earl Rogers said.

They were all gathered in his office—Kit, Bill Jory, Luther Brown—and for the first time in her life, Kit was going to be part of a criminal trial team.

Or was she?

Even before being summoned into Rogers' chamber, Kit knew he was expecting her to play a pivotal role in the preparation of the defense of Ted Fox. Now she faced the question she had been trying to avoid—could she undertake defense of someone she believed could be guilty?

That was what she had been contemplating ever since the arrest. It all made sense, fit into a pattern. Ted had a darkness somewhere inside him, and Kit had been warned about it. His odd behavior the night he came to the office. His unwillingness to share information. Though Kit believed in the presumption of innocence, a standard for the jury, she was under no such compulsion as a lawyer or a person. She could not deny her own mind.

It tore at her, this belief. Because inside her was that part that had been drawn to Ted Fox, that had seen something in him that was strong and visionary. She did not want him to be guilty, but she could not deny the circumstances.

One of those was his admission that he had done something when "not of sound mind." What did he mean by that? Was it possible he was really insane?

Kit remembered her class in criminal law and the so-called M'Naghton Rule. In 1843, in England, a man named Daniel M'Naghton shot and killed one Edward Drummond, private secretary to Sir Robert Peel. M'Naghton thought Peel was heading a conspiracy to kill him, and shot Drummond because he mistakenly thought him to be Peel. M'Naghton claimed at his trial that he was delusional, and the jury found him not guilty by reason of insanity.

There was outrage over the verdict, and the House of Lords eventually enacted a rule, named for the M'Naghton case, for a defense based on insanity. That rule stated that the defendant must suffer a diseased mind so that at the time of the act he did not know the nature of the act or that the act was wrong.

Did Ted suffer from a diseased mind? It certainly didn't seem so. He was lucid, aware, and able to get along with people. Though there seemed to be much talk these days about "split personalities," as in the Jekyll and Hyde story, Kit knew this could not yet be proven in open court.

Nor did it seem possible that Ted didn't know that what he was doing was wrong. His behavior at her office indicated he knew he was in trouble. That awareness cut against a claim of moral unawareness. So insanity was probably not going to fly as a defense, which meant that Ted Fox was probably guilty and . . .

Rogers' voice broke through her thoughts. "Kit, where are you?"

"I'm sorry."

"Well, listen. This is crucial."

"Yes, sir."

"So far we know the cops have an eyewitness who is going to say he or she saw Fox leaving Millie Ryan's room the night she was murdered. We have to find out who that witness is. I have a feeling it's one of the crib girls."

Kit knew he meant another prostitute. That would make sense. They were always on the street, in doorways. They saw things in the night.

"We have to find out," Rogers continued, "because that's going to be half the case. We have to prepare to take that witness apart."

Almost involuntarily, Kit said, "What if she's telling the truth?"

Silence. Jory, Brown, and Rogers exchanged glances. "That doesn't matter," Rogers said finally.

"How can the truth not matter?" Kit said.

"The truth is for the jury. Our job is to defeat the prosecution."

"But—"

"Do you have an objection to that?" Rogers' voice was cold and hard as steel.

Did she? Yes, somewhere inside, she did have that problem.

"Well?" Rogers said.

Kit felt the eyes of the three men boring holes in her. "I want to know what really happened," she said. And then she stood up. "If that's not good enough, Mr. Rogers, then I shall take my leave."

For a long moment it seemed to Kit that Rogers would dismiss her then and there. His hands were balled into fists and resting on his desk. His blue eyes were intense. Then he stood.

"Don't be rash," he said. "Tell you what. You want to know what really happened? You want the truth?"

"Yes."

"Then you go down to the jail. See if you can get any more out of Fox than I've been able to. Maybe you're the one to do it. Go over the sequence of events with him. Look into his eyes. Then report back to me."

Suddenly her throat felt dry. Face Ted Fox? Take a statement? Yes, that is what he was challenging her to do. She had dared Rogers, and he had thrown it back at her. If she was really interested in the truth, as she had said, then now was the time to prove it. That, or quit right now and get her ticket back to New York.

"I'll see him," Kit said.

———

The Los Angeles County Jail was a stern, four-story building of gray granite blocks with barred windows set in narrow recesses. It sat on Temple Street near Broadway, across the street from the courthouse. It was a short walk from the offices of Earl Rogers.

Kit trembled slightly as she entered the front doors, drawing looks from uniformed sheriff's deputies, who no doubt wondered about her business here. She approached the deputy who sat at the duty desk. He was casually reading a newspaper and did not look up when she reached him.

"Excuse me?" she said.

With what seemed like some annoyance, the deputy raised his head. He was an older man with a bushy gray mustache sprouting under a bulbous, pink nose. "Visitors through that door," he said, then returned to his paper.

"I am not a visitor," Kit said.

"What's that?"

"I am here to see a client."

He looked up again. "You're a woman," he said.

"I work for Earl Rogers."

A slight flush came to his face, his cheeks now matching his nose in coloration. "I don't believe it," he said.

"You may believe it," she said and handed him the letter Rogers had given her just before she left his office. It was his written assurance of her employment.

The deputy read it and shook his head. "Don't know what this world is coming to," he muttered. "Women coming in here to conduct business!"

"May I see Theodore Fox, please?"

The deputy was still muttering when he led Kit to a small room at the end of a hall. She entered and sat on a hard wooden chair at a spare table. Ten minutes later the same deputy let Ted Fox into the room and said, "I'll give you thirty minutes."

Kit said, "I'll notify you when I am finished."

That brought a grumble this time, and then the door slammed.

Ted Fox, steel shackles on his hands, garbed in the colorless coveralls of the jail, stood before her. "Why are you here?" he said.

"Why don't you sit down, Mr. Fox?" Kit did not like the way her voice sounded. Official. Unfriendly. But she couldn't be familiar with him, not now.

"I prefer to stand."

"I am here to ask you some questions."

"Why?"

"Because that's my job."

"How much is my mother paying Rogers?"

"I don't know."

"Got to be ten thousand at least."

"Ted . . . Mr. Fox, I have to ask you—"

"How do you like it?"

Kit looked at him quizzically.

Ted said, "The ugly side of life."

Why was he saying this? He seemed aloof, even angry at her

presence. "I'm here to help," she said.

"You shouldn't be here at all. This is not the place for you."

"Well, I *am* here. And I'm not going until I get some answers."

For a brief moment Ted's face softened, and she saw in his eyes the illumination she had seen the night she first met him. But then the flickering light faded as if doused by a bucket of water. "All right," he said softly. "Do what you have to do and then leave."

Kit set paper in front of her and took up the pencil. She noticed her hand was shaking and put it down firmly on the wooden table to steady it. "You are being charged with the murder of Millie Ryan," she said. She summoned her courage and looked him in the eye. What unspoken clues would she find there?

None immediately. He merely nodded, waiting for her to ask a question.

And what question would that be? Should she come right out and ask if he did it? That was her instinct, but Rogers told her before she left that was the one question she should *not* ask a client. Focus on the evidence, Rogers told her. Their job was to defeat the state's case, nothing else.

But she wanted to ask, felt the words forming in her mouth. What came out was, "Can you account for your whereabouts on the night of August tenth?"

"Let's see. Was that Saturday?"

"Yes."

"What time?"

"All the time."

Now Ted sat on the wooden stool that was the only other piece of furniture in the room. "You want to know if I did it, don't you?"

Kit's pulse throbbed in her neck. "I want to know where you were on August tenth."

"I did not," he said.

She looked into his eyes. Did she believe him? She knew she wanted to.

"Have the police questioned you?" she asked.

"Sure."

"What did you tell them?"

"Nothing. They want me to confess."

"Can you tell me where you were, then, on the night of August tenth?"

Ted looked at his manacled hands. "I don't remember."

"Try. You must try," she urged.

"I don't remember everything."

"Start with what you do remember," Kit said. She would have to be firm to get him to open up, to help if she could—and to determine for herself if he was telling the truth.

"I think I had dinner in the Chinese quarter."

"Do you remember where?"

"Not the name."

"What time was it?"

Ted sighed. "I didn't notice."

"Was it dark? Light?"

"Getting dark."

"But still some light outside?"

"Yes."

Kit paused to write some notes. Millie Ryan had been killed in the dead of night. The only thing Rogers knew about the eyewitness was that she, if it was a she, had claimed Ted was seen fleeing around midnight.

"Where did you go after dinner?" Kit asked.

"I walked."

"Where did you walk?"

"Toward the center of town."

"What street?"

"I don't know. Broadway maybe. Maybe New High."

Kit wrote all this down. "Was it dark then?" she asked.

"Yes. By then it was."

"Where did you end up?"

"At the Plaza."

"Where is that?"

"Olvera Street. There was a band playing. I listened for a while."

"Did you talk to anyone?"

"I don't speak Spanish."

"How long did you stay there?"

"I wasn't keeping track of time."

Kit put the pencil down. "Mr. Fox, these are the sorts of questions you are going to be asked by the prosecutor. A jury of twelve men is going to be looking at you when you answer. You have to try to be precise."

"I didn't do it, Kit," he said. "Isn't that precise enough?"

She wanted it to be. But she knew it wasn't. "Millie Ryan had a room on Alameda Street near Oro. I don't know the city well enough yet. Do you know where that is?"

Ted hesitated before answering. "Yes."

"Where?"

He looked at her. "Not far from the Plaza."

Kit felt a jolt. Ted had placed himself near the murder scene at night. "Mr. Fox, is there—"

"Call me Ted, will you? You did once."

Kit looked at her hands. "All right."

"I'm sorry. Finish your question."

Raising her head, Kit asked him the most important question. "Is there anyone who can say they saw you on the night of August tenth, at any time?"

There flashed across his face a look of remembrance. It was

unmistakable. There was someone. Kit was sure of it. She leaned forward a little.

"No one," Ted said.

"But are you—"

"No one, I tell you. I suppose that's it." He stood up, the chain between his manacles jangling. He crossed the room and banged on the door with both fists.

"Wait," said Kit.

"Tell Rogers to come himself next time," Ted said.

"Ted," Kit said, "you told me you did something when not of sound mind. What was it?"

The door swung open, and a guard stepped into the room.

"We're finished," Ted said.

The guard cast a quick glance at Kit, shrugged his shoulders, and held the door for Ted. He walked through it without looking back.

Chapter Nineteen

ON HER WAY OUT, Kit saw a man at the front desk wagging his finger in the face of the unimpressed desk deputy. Something about him was familiar. He was wearing a straw hat, cocked to one side, a light-colored suit, and a high-collared shirt.

"You can't hold out on me!" the man said. "I have a right to see him."

The deputy snorted and lifted a billy club. "You want me to explain your rights?"

"You don't know who you're dealing with! You ever heard of William Randolph Hearst?"

She recognized him now. It was that reporter, Tom Phelps. He turned in exasperation and spotted her. "Well, I'll be hanged!" he said.

"Hello," Kit said.

"This is a pleasant surprise. What on earth are you doing here at the jailhouse?"

"Business," Kit said.

Phelps looked momentarily stunned. The deputy said, "Now, her I don't mind giving rights to."

"Will you step into my office please?" Phelps said, taking Kit by the arm. "It's clear I'm not wanted here."

The deputy huffed as Phelps led Kit out the doors to the front steps. "I got that big ape's name," Phelps said. "He'll be seeing his name in print soon."

"Make sure you don't get arrested."

"Can't promise that! Now, newspaper man that I am, might I inquire as to your business here?"

"As I said, I'm working."

"For whom?"

"Earl Rogers."

Phelps's jaw dropped open slightly. "Well, make a tamale out of me." He reached into his coat and pulled out a pad of paper and a pencil. "You're working on the Fox case!"

Kit nodded.

Phelps looked almost giddy. "Were you just with him? Fox?"

"Yes . . ." Kit hesitated as Phelps started scribbling.

"What did he tell you?"

His directness took her aback. Though she had no reason to distrust him, she knew she couldn't let on about the case without Rogers' permission. Besides, Rogers was the star. He would be the one to talk to the newspapers.

"Mr. Phelps, I—"

"Oh no," he said. "Don't tell me you're gonna hold out?"

"I can't give out any information on the case without—"

"Shh!" Phelps took her by the arm and led her down the stone steps toward the street. His conduct seemed conspiratorial. A big policeman gave them a mean look as he walked past them.

"This is the biggest scoop of my life," Phelps said in a low tone.

"You can't hold out on me now." His grip on her arm tightened.

"Mr. Phelps, please," Kit urged.

"Tom, call me Tom."

"Let go of my arm, Mr. Phelps."

His face betrayed shock. He let go of her arm.

"I am not at liberty to discuss this case with you," Kit said.

"All right, all right," said Phelps. He put the pad and pencil back into his coat pocket and held up his hands to show nothing was in them. "Then off the record. What you tell me stays with me."

"Not even off the record, Mr. Phelps."

"Tom, please. You can trust me."

Could she? Perhaps, but still, the information was not hers to give.

Then, as if sensing her thoughts, Phelps added, "I'm in a position to help you."

"Help me? How so?"

Phelps pushed his skimmer higher up on his head. "You've got a client who may have murdered some ladies of, shall we say, questionable character?"

"Yes."

"And you, a young lady of breeding from the East, have little knowledge of the . . . profession as practiced in our fair city."

There was no question of that. She had wondered what her next step would be in this investigation.

"Well, I have," Phelps said. "From a purely journalistic point of view, of course. I might be able to get you access to the right people."

She had no doubt then he could do that very thing. He had the right profession, and his attitude was one of firm assuredness. She knew Rogers' own Bill Jory probably had the same connections and would do some investigating. But he was a man, and she sensed this case would require a woman's angle. He was speaking of a class of women who might firmly distrust men.

"I would appreciate any help you might offer," Kit said.

"That's just fine. Now you tell me something. Did he do it?"

Kit blinked back her surprise. "I . . . that is, he denies it."

"But did he? You talked to him. You looked at him. What do you think?"

Recovering, Kit said, "What I think isn't important."

"Ah, spoken like a true mouthpiece! But I'm asking you as a fellow human being."

Actually wondering what she thought about Ted's guilt, Kit said nothing.

"I see," Phelps said, nodding.

"See what?" Kit said quickly, wondering what he had perceived.

"Doubts. Which is why I'm here. How can I help you? What do you need to know?"

"The police have an eyewitness, someone who claims to have seen Ted leaving Millie Ryan's room on the night of the murder."

Phelps let out a snort through a half smile. "The cops have a way of coming up with eyewitnesses when necessary."

Kit's eyes widened. "You don't mean they would . . ."

"That's exactly what I mean, little lady. You're not dealing with angels here."

A sudden chill coursed through Kit's body. "Whom can I talk to?" Kit said. "Is there anyone?"

"Tom Phelps will help you, Miss Shannon. And you will help me."

"How?"

"Come along."

Kit puzzled over what Phelps might consider help, but she kept her questions to herself. Tom Phelps was giving her something she never could have gotten on her own: access. Specifically, access to a world she scarcely knew about.

In her New York days, living at Leo House with the sisters, she had met two women who were, as the nuns put it, "fallen." They had come to Leo House out of desperation and need of protection. Kit knew what they had been, but was never quite sure why they needed protection, and they never volunteered an explanation. All she knew was they were from a world that was so foreign to her own experience she prayed she would never go there. And the sisters of Leo House were vigilant in keeping her from it.

Now she had to descend into that world for the sake of Ted Fox—and her own determination to find out if he was innocent. And Tom Phelps was her guide.

The cab Phelps hired took them down Main Street and through the El Pueblo Plaza—a circular park with stately rubber trees on the outskirts of downtown. Phelps mentioned that this had been the center of Los Angeles back in the '60s, when the city was little more than a collection of *ranchos*.

And here is where Ted was the night of Millie's murder, Kit thought. Or said he was. Would she ever know the truth?

The horse-drawn cab turned left at the corner of the Plaza, where a red-plastered Catholic church stood sentry. A Mexican man wearing a large sombrero scuffed at the hard ground in front of the church with a hoe.

Almost immediately, the cab turned right. "New High Street," Phelps said, as if that term had significance.

Kit saw the cab driver, a roughhewn man, turn and wink at Phelps.

Presently, Phelps told the cabbie to pull up at a white two-story building with an ornately designed door. After telling the driver to wait, Phelps led Kit to the door and knocked.

A moment later a small eye-level window opened, filled with an angry-looking face.

"Hello, Clancy," Phelps said.

The window slammed shut, and the door slowly opened. Kit followed Phelps in.

The angry face belonged to one of the largest men Kit had ever seen. He had a barrel chest and massive arms, all packed into a suit that barely fit. He had a huge black mustache that was curled upward with wax. Kit judged him to be in his forties.

"Miss Shannon," Phelps said. "May I present Clancy Muldoon."

The mean face suddenly squinted into a smile as Clancy bowed slightly.

"Clancy here fought the great John L. Sullivan once," Phelps explained.

"Would have whipped 'im, too," Clancy added with a singsong Irish lilt, "if I had not broken me right knuckle. See?" He held his right hand to Kit, who thought she noticed an enlarged knuckle in the middle.

"Tell Pearl I'd like to see her," Phelps said.

"At your service," Clancy said. "And very pleased to meet you I am, Miss Shannon." He strode through a bead curtain, leaving Kit and Phelps alone in a foyer that Kit now noticed was done up in plush scarlet tones.

"Is this . . ." Kit began.

"A house of ill repute," Phelps finished. "But if it means anything to you, it's the finest in the city."

Kit's heart began a drumbeat. She became immediately aware of her womanhood and the fact that she was standing with a man inside a place she'd never, in her wildest imaginings, thought she'd ever have occasion to enter.

Clancy returned and said, "This way, if it please you."

Phelps and Kit passed through the beads and into a muted pink hallway with several doors on either side. Ferns and flowering potted plants lined the walls, and a spiral staircase led up to another floor. Kit looked up and saw two women in sheer décolletage, with more rouge and eye shadow than Kit had ever seen on any face, looking down at her as if observing a zoo exhibit.

There was a faint scent of gardenia in the air as Clancy led them to a large door at the end of the hallway. He rapped on the door with his large knuckle. A deep woman's voice said, "Enter."

The room looked like some sort of paradise for an Arabian sheik. There were diaphanous curtains that seemed almost suspended in midair, huge soft pillows covered with silk and tassels on the floor, and against the wall an enormous bed that seemed fashioned from a cloud. On the opposite side of the room, in seeming contrast, was a single rolltop desk and chair, such as any businessman might use.

And rising from the chair was a woman who took Kit's breath away.

She wore a suit of plum-colored silk. Her waist was tightly corseted, accentuating her ample bust and hips. *A perfect hourglass,* Kit thought. Her hair was an intense russet color—the color of Kit's own hair if it had been illuminated by some inner light. She almost floated toward them, so elegant was her walk. She extended her hand to Phelps.

"So nice to see you, Tom," she said. Her smile was friendly and sensuous at the same time. Kit couldn't help staring.

"Pearl," Phelps said, "may I present Kit Shannon? Kit, this is Pearl Morton."

Pearl turned to Kit and smiled even more broadly. "It is my pleasure to meet you, Miss Shannon." Her handshake was strong. A distinct odor of perfume greeted Kit—hearty but not unpleasant.

"Thank you," Kit said, her voice squeaking at the end.

"Clancy, some coffee, please," Pearl Morton said. Clancy bowed and retreated from the room. Pearl motioned for the three of them to sit at a small table topped with red felt.

"This young lady works for Earl," Phelps said.

Pearl's face lit up. "Really? Well, Earl is a good friend of ours. He's helped a number of my girls. Especially with the new administration." Pearl leaned forward. "The mayor doesn't like us too well. Or I should say the mayor's wife."

Phelps laughed and Pearl joined him. Kit forced a smile.

"Now, what can I do for you, Miss Shannon?"

"Earl's got the Fox case," Phelps said.

"Why don't you let Miss Shannon answer for herself?" Pearl said. Then, looking at Kit, "Newspapermen don't know when to shut up."

Kit felt a warmth coming from this woman and marveled at the way she handled Tom Phelps. She seemed so at ease in doing so, as if she had some innate power. Certainly a power that Phelps respected, for he fell silent.

"Go on, dear," Pearl said.

Gathering her thoughts quickly, Kit said, "The police have an eyewitness. Mr. Rogers thinks it is a . . . prostitute." Kit struggled to say the word, feeling suddenly shy.

Pearl Morton patted her hand. "That's all right. I prefer the word courtesan, but I'm sure Tom here uses quite another." She winked at Phelps, who grunted.

"I brought her to you," Phelps said, "because if anybody would know who the . . . *courtesan* might be, you'd be the one."

There was a knock at the door, and Clancy entered with a coffee service on a silver tray. Even Aunt Freddy would have approved, Kit thought. Whatever Pearl Morton was, she certainly had good taste.

After Clancy left and Pearl poured coffee for them, she said, "The girls down in the cribs are unfortunates. They don't have someone like me to look after them. But I do hear things."

"What things?" Kit asked.

Pearl Morton took a sip of coffee from a beautiful china cup. "Things that a girl of your pedigree might find a bit jarring."

It was a clear warning. Pearl was asking Kit if she wanted to venture down this path. "Please," Kit said.

"It's a rather dark world down on Alameda Street. The clientele is not the sort that frequents my establishment. They're drunks, gamblers, cattlemen in from Arizona and Nevada with mean dispositions. It's a wonder more girls don't end up like those three. Don't you like your coffee?"

Kit had not taken a sip, indeed did not even drink coffee. But she wanted Pearl Morton to keep talking, and being sociable seemed the proper thing to do. She lifted her cup and took in some of the hot liquid. It tasted bitter.

"You might wonder how I manage to keep open my own establishment," Pearl continued. "It's because we take care that certain interests are satisfied." She cast a knowing look at Phelps.

"What she means, Kit," Phelps said, "is that some of the money goes to the police."

"Tom," Pearl said, "you're so discreet."

"Discreet don't get stories."

"Your command of the language is inspiring," Pearl said. Kit couldn't stop a laugh from escaping her mouth.

Turning again to Kit, Pearl said, "But the girls in the cribs don't have that opportunity. So they do not get the protection they most desperately need. Some, however, get more than others."

She paused again for a sip of coffee. Kit saw from the glances exchanged between Pearl and Phelps that they both knew exactly what they were talking about.

"Cards on the table, dear," Pearl said. "Certain beat cops offer the girls a little more time and attention, seeing to it they aren't taken advantage of by those they entertain and the like. In return, the girls may provide information about a crime, or sometimes an evening's diversion."

Now Kit understood perfectly. She had heard about the corruption within the police department here, but now it had a specific face. An ugly one.

"Dear," said Pearl, putting down her cup and placing a warm hand on Kit's own. "Do you think your man did it?"

It was the same question Phelps had asked her, and which she had refused to answer directly. But this was different. Somehow she felt she could be open with Pearl Morton and that it would ultimately help solve the question that plagued her.

"It seems that way," Kit said, dropping her head a little.

"Ah," Pearl said. "I see."

Kit looked up. "See?"

"He's more than just a client."

Amazed at her insight, Kit could only nod. She saw Phelps turn his head away.

"You listen to me," Pearl said. "Don't give up on this until you've turned over every rock. You might find a cop underneath one. If there's a girl down there who has said anything to anyone, I'd put my money on Rita Alonzo. She's a bad one, she is, and you'll need to keep your wits about you. Start with her."

"Thank you, Miss Morton."

"It's Pearl."

"Thank you. You were most kind to help me."

"Nothing of it. I like you, Miss Shannon. And any friend of Earl's is a friend of mine. Come see me anytime."

Kit swallowed, wondering if she would ever again venture into such a place.

Clancy showed them to the front door, giving Tom a playful jab on the shoulder. It was evident from Tom's wince that Clancy Muldoon still packed a punch.

Outside, the sun was blazing and bright, in stark contrast to the interior of Pearl Morton's establishment. The cab was waiting.

"Shall I see you home?" Phelps asked.

"No," said Kit. "I want to find that Rita Alonzo. Would you like to come along?"

"Are you joking? I can't miss this."

Kit put up her hand. "May I remind you, Mr. Phelps, that this is all to be confidential?"

The reporter's expression was blank. "Let's say, then, that I have a personal interest." He helped Kit into the cab and to the driver said, "Alameda and Oro."

What sort of personal interest? Kit wondered.

Chapter Twenty

THE SO-CALLED "CRIBS" were rows of tight rooms set in nondescript brick buildings. First built for quick rooming for transients, they were now used almost exclusively by women for transactions in flesh—so explained Tom Phelps to Kit as the cab brought them to the neighborhood where Millie Ryan had met her killer.

In the daylight, the street was oddly quiet. Kit saw little traffic, cab or foot, as if the area were waiting for a signal to come to life. That would come when darkness fell, Kit suspected.

Phelps ordered the cab to stop at one of the squat edifices. Alighting, Kit noticed a woman sitting on the front steps of a crib. She was young, Kit sensed, but her face looked much older than her years. Her dress was wrinkled, and the petticoat lace that showed beneath the hem was dirty and slightly frayed. She glanced at Kit, who was suddenly aware of her own clean dress, and looked surprised.

Immediately Phelps spoke to the girl. "I'm looking for Rita Alonzo," he said. Kit was glad he was here. She would not have felt so confident alone.

"You a copper?" the girl said with a scratchy voice.

"That'll be the day," said Phelps.

"What do you want her for? With your lady friend along, I don't think it's the usual."

"I just want to talk to her, that's all."

"Supposing she don't want to talk to you?" the girl asked.

Without a moment's hesitation Phelps plucked a bill from his pocket and held it in front of the girl. "Suppose I make it worth your while?"

Without a moment's pause, the girl snatched the bill and shoved it into the top of her dress. "Two doors down," said the girl. "But don't tell her I told you."

Phelps turned to Kit. "Let's go."

"Come back anytime," the girl said to Phelps. "Without your lady friend."

Kit felt her look of contempt and it jarred her with its intensity. She issued a silent prayer for the girl, and then for herself.

Phelps stopped at the door—light wood, unpainted—and knocked. No answer. He knocked again, louder.

"Go away!" shouted a voice from within.

Once more Phelps pounded.

"I strangle you!" the voice said. Then the door swung open. A brown-skinned woman glared outward, a robe thrown carelessly around her, her black hair a tangled mess. Her eyes were flashing with anger.

"What is this?" she said.

"You are Rita Alonzo?"

"You are who?"

"My name's Phelps. And this is Miss Shannon."

The woman squinted at Kit. "So?"

"We'd like to talk to you."

"I no talk to nobody."

"You will talk to us."

A look of fear flashed in Rita's eyes. *The eyes of someone who has known beatings at the hands of men,* Kit thought immediately.

"Go," she said.

"No," said Phelps, and he immediately pushed his way inside. Kit, feeling awkward, followed.

"Hey!" Rita shouted. She slammed the door shut.

The small, windowless room was without decoration. A four-legged table with some dingy dishware on it stood by one wall next to two plain wooden chairs. Against the opposite wall was a bed that was too big for a room of this size, with mussed linens on top of it.

"You can no come in!" Rita cried.

"We're in," said Phelps. "You want to call a cop?"

"I may might do that! You will be surprise!" The moment she said it her expression changed, as if she had let something slip out she wished she could have back.

"Now listen," Phelps said. "We know you're the witness."

Kit tried to keep her face passive. They knew nothing of the kind. But Phelps was obviously playing a bluff.

Rita didn't answer at first, her dark eyes studying Phelps. "You know nothing," she said finally.

"No?" said Phelps. "Miss Shannon here works for Earl Rogers."

The name meant something to Rita, who looked Kit up and down. "So?"

"He can play pretty rough if he wants to," Phelps said. "It's easy now or hard later. Your choice."

For a long moment she thought about it. "What you want?"

"Just a few questions from Miss Shannon."

She looked at Kit. "What question?"

Kit cleared her throat. "What did you tell the police you saw on the night of August tenth?"

"I already tell police," she said.

"Tell me."

"I see him, that man. I see him good."

"What man?"

Rita laughed. "You know."

"Can you describe the man you saw?"

"Sí."

Kit waited for her to do so. Rita only stared at her.

"Now, look . . ." Phelps said, taking a step toward Rita.

Kit put her hand up and stopped him. "It's all right," Kit said. "Let me go on."

With a shrug, Phelps stepped back. Kit said to Rita, "Where were you when you saw him?"

Rita inclined her head toward the door. "Out. There."

"Show me."

Looking more confident now, Rita turned and opened her door. She pointed to the front step. "There."

"And where was the man you saw?"

Rita pointed across the dirt street to a door that might have been a mirror image of hers.

"Did he run away?" Kit asked.

Rita nodded.

"Which direction?"

The woman pointed up the street, toward the Los Angeles River.

"If he ran," said Kit, "then you wouldn't have seen him for very long, right?"

"He stop at first, look right at me."

"For how long?"

"Long enough."

Kit noticed Phelps writing something on his pad. Then to Rita: "What time was it?"

"I no know. I no have clock. Night."

"Well, then, it was dark, wasn't it?"

With a slight smile, as if this was something of a game, Rita said, "No. The moon, it was full."

"You sure of that?"

"You say I lie?"

Kit put her hand in the air. "No. I just want you to tell me if you are absolutely sure about the moon."

Suddenly Rita whirled on Kit. "I no talk to you no more. Get out."

"You listen," Phelps said.

"No," Kit said quickly. "We'll go now."

The reporter considered Kit with a stunned expression. "But—"

"Let's go," Kit said. Then to Rita, "We're sorry to have disturbed you. Thank you for your time."

Rita's expression softened slightly, but she said nothing.

Kit grabbed Phelps' arm and led him back to their cab. As soon as they were in and on their way, Phelps said, "What did you do that for? We had her. I could have strong-armed her into more."

"That's just it," Kit said. "I got what Mr. Rogers needed. There's no need to antagonize her. We won't want her angry when she testifies."

"Why not? Seems fine to me."

"You catch more flies with honey than with vinegar, Mr. Phelps."

He looked at her. "You are some woman." The way he said the words should have alerted Kit, but it was too late. His arms were suddenly around her, strong arms, and he pressed his mouth on

225

hers. At first she was too stunned to move, but when he kept his lips on her mouth, she turned her head away and pushed with her arms. His grip loosened only a little.

"No," she said.

"Come on, now," Phelps said. "You need me." Once more he kissed her. This time Kit slapped at his face, landing a glancing blow.

"Stop!" she cried.

The cabbie slowed the horse and looked back at them.

"Not you, you idiot!" Phelps shouted.

"Yes, you!" Kit said. "Stop this cab!"

The cabbie stopped. Kit was about to open the door when Phelps grabbed her arm. "Hey," he said. "What gives? I helped you!"

"Let go of me, Mr. Phelps," Kit said.

He paused, his grip tightening for a moment, then released her. She quickly exited the cab. She wasn't angry. She liked Phelps, but not that way. She turned to him. "I'm sorry," she said.

"Forget about it," Phelps said, then he ordered the cabbie to move. The wheels kicked up a cloud of dust into Kit's face.

Chapter Twenty-one

THE LATE AFTERNOON CROWD at The Imperial was settling in to early dinner conversations. Kit noticed again that the place carried the atmosphere of a premiere social scene. She thought of Aunt Freddy then, wanting to be here with her, to hear her laugh again—even if it was at Kit's own foibles.

Instead, she was here with Earl Rogers, who had called this an official meeting. He wanted a complete briefing on her interview of Rita Alonzo. She was gratified at his trust in her, but then he did two things that made her uncomfortable.

The first was that he said nothing to her about what she had done. He merely grunted as he wrote notes on a paper.

The second thing was that he had the waiter bring him a full bottle of whiskey from the bar and leave it with a glass.

She had noticed—it was hard not to—that as the Fox trial drew closer, Rogers seemed to drink more. Was it because of some insecurity? Bill Jory had told her Rogers was terrified of losing, that he would do anything to win.

Jory told her of one of Rogers' early cases, when he was young and unknown and was up against a wily old prosecutor named C. C. McComas. McComas was good, and Rogers thought he might be losing the case. But he noticed something interesting. McComas would often come late to court for the afternoon session, smelling of liquor.

With a little investigating, Jory found out McComas liked to take an afternoon slug or two in a nearby watering hole, then repair to his office for a short nap.

So when the day for closing arguments arrived, Earl Rogers accidentally-on-purpose showed up at the same saloon, told McComas how much he admired his trial work (this was sincere) and kept buying him drinks. McComas reveled in telling Rogers some war stories, then realized he needed to get to his office before the afternoon session began.

But McComas didn't show up at one o'clock. At one-fifteen the impatient judge ordered the prosecution to argue to the jury. A young, nervous deputy district attorney had to stand and try to make a convincing address. He failed.

Rogers' closing was masterful. And short. Just after the judge ordered the jury to their deliberations, McComas stormed into the courtroom. It took him only a moment to see what had happened. He went immediately to Earl Rogers.

"That was a dirty trick, Earl," he said.

"But C. C.," Earl replied, "you tell some good stories."

Rogers' client was acquitted.

Now, as Rogers scribbled notes in the restaurant, Kit wondered what he might pull during the upcoming trial.

Suddenly Earl looked up, poured himself some whiskey, drank

it down, and said, "If you want to be a trial lawyer, it's time you learned a few things."

Now he was the teacher. It was exactly what Kit wanted, but what would he teach? Not how to pump opponents with drink, she hoped.

"What is the most important part of a trial?" Rogers asked, as if it were a test.

Kit thought a moment. "I should think the cross-examination of witnesses."

"It's good that you think that," Rogers answered, pouring himself more whiskey. "Your answer is not correct, but it is close."

Kit watched as he took the drink, longing to say something to him.

"Then what is the correct answer?" said Kit.

"It is the selection of the jury. Even the most brilliant courtroom attorney cannot overcome the prejudices of the wrong men sitting in the box."

"How does one prevent that from happening?"

"As the poet said, 'The proper study of mankind is man.' The more the trial lawyer knows of human nature, the better equipped he'll be to select jurymen. To the ordinary observer, a man is just a man. But to the student of life and human beings, every pose and movement and opinion is another clue as to who they really are."

Kit was silent as Rogers finished his whiskey. *Please stop*, she thought.

Roger set down the empty glass. "When representing an accused, you want jurors who will side with the underdog. I always keep Irishmen."

"And well you should," said Kit.

"Irishmen are emotional, kindly, sympathetic. An Englishman is not so good as an Irishman, but he has come through a long tradition of individual rights. The German is not so keen about individual rights except where they concern his own way of life. Still, he wants to do what is right and is not afraid."

"Fascinating."

"It gets better." Rogers poured another drink. "Catholics are generally emotional. They love music and art. Keep them. But if a Presbyterian enters the jury box, get rid of him as soon as possible. He's as cold as the grave. He believes in John Calvin and eternal punishment."

"I see."

"Baptists are more hopeless than Presbyterians. They think that the real home of all outsiders is Sheol, and you do not want them on the jury. The sooner they leave the better."

Rogers had lost some of his jocularity and was now drinking almost furiously.

"The Methodists are worth considering. They are nearer the soil. They are not half bad, even though they will not take a drink." Rogers laughed sardonically, then took a hearty gulp.

"Beware of Lutherans," he continued. "They are almost always sure to convict. Your Lutheran learns about sinning and punishment from the preacher and dares not doubt. A person who disobeys must be sent to hell."

Rogers paused at the last word and poured still more drink for himself.

"As to Unitarians, Universalists, and agnostics, don't ask them too many questions. Keep them. Especially agnostics. And never ever pick a temperance man. He knows your client would not have been indicted unless he were a drinker, and anyone who drinks is guilty of something."

Rogers drank and fell silent. He looked for a long time into his empty glass.

Finally Kit could stand it no longer. "Earl," she said, surprising herself by using his first name. He looked up at her, his eyes glassy. "May I speak plainly?"

"Sure," he said quietly.

"I know how it hurt me inside when I lost my father. I know how it must have hurt you when you lost yours. And I know there are times in our lives when we face crossroads. And we choose one way or another. . . ." She paused.

"Go ahead, Kit. You have my permission."

Kit breathed in deeply. She recalled what Bill Jory had told her about Rogers' reaction to his father's death. "When your father died, you lost an anchor. Perhaps you felt that God was to blame."

"And so?"

"You turned to drink."

His eyes widened, revealing more redness and perhaps a flash of anger—Kit could not tell. How dare she talk to her employer this way! But she couldn't deny the urge she felt to do so.

Rogers relaxed his expression. "You have what it takes, kid."

"What, sir?"

"That insight we were talking about. You pegged me. You've got a gift." Ironically, he raised his glass and drank to her.

"Have you ever thought of stopping?" Kit asked.

Rogers looked down at the table, a lost expression on his face. Then he slowly shook his head. "It's too late for me. I've made a pact with John Barleycorn."

"It's not too late!" Kit said. "With God all things are possible."

With a slight smile—at her temerity, Kit thought—Rogers said, "I've lost my belief in God, Kit. It died with my father."

"But—"

Rogers stopped her by putting his hand on hers. "Let us not speak of it," he said quietly. Then he corked the whiskey bottle. "I won't drink in your presence again."

Kit, her heart going out to him, nodded.

"And thank you," he said. Then he saw something over her shoulder, and his expression became one of surprise.

"Well, I'll be," he said.

"What is it?" Kit said.

"Mr. Heath Sloate just sat down to dine."

Kit whirled around. At the other end of the room she saw the unmistakable profile of Heath Sloate across the table from . . . Aunt Freddy! Kit's breath left her.

"Come on," Rogers said, standing up. "Let's go say hello."

"No, I couldn't!" Kit said. She wanted to see Aunt Freddy, to throw her arms around her, but she knew it would cause the thing Aunt Freddy hated most in the world—a scene. And how could she tolerate even being near Heath Sloate?

Yet Rogers was now helping her up, and she allowed him to. As they approached the table, Aunt Freddy—her mouth dropping open, and then Sloate, his cool demeanor broken by a sudden flash of shock—saw them.

"Why, Heath Sloate," Rogers said, a little too boisterously. "My worthy opponent."

For a long moment no one spoke, the crosscurrents of emotion passing heavily between the parties.

"Hello, Aunt Freddy," Kit said finally.

Aunt Freddy, looking close to fainting, feebly said, "Kit . . . you're looking well." It was not a good attempt. Kit knew her aunt wanted to say more but was being restrained by the man sitting across from her.

"This is your great-aunt?" Rogers said. "The wonderful lady you've told me so much about? Ma'am, my name's Earl Rogers. May I say that your niece is an absolute gem."

"Why, thank . . ." Freddy began, then held back from completing her thought. She looked terribly confused. She began to tremble. "I must go." She stood up from her place and turned toward the lounges.

Kit took her arm. "I'll come with you."

Aunt Freddy turned to her, and her eyes, now filling with tears, betrayed a terrible inner torment. "No," she begged. "I want to be alone." She turned quickly and scurried away. Kit allowed her to go.

"Well," Rogers said, "I seem to have made a mess of it. My apologies, Heath."

"Get out of here," Sloate said through clenched teeth.

Kit felt a fierce anger rising within her. This man had hurt her, yes, but now he was hurting Aunt Freddy, standing between her and Kit. She wanted Aunt Freddy to be happy, but this was too high a cost.

Rogers said, "And so good night. Come, Kit."

"Would you wait for me outside?" Kit said.

Rogers looked surprised at first, but then as if he approved, he silently bowed and departed.

Kit now faced Heath Sloate alone. She could feel her entire body tensing. She fought for control. "You will not marry my aunt," Kit said.

He looked at her, unfazed. "You have nothing to say in the matter."

"I'll stop you."

An ugly smile came to his lips. "And how do you propose to do that? Freddy wants to marry me. I make her happy. And she knows you are not in your right mind."

"How dare you poison her against me!"

"Keep your voice down, you fool, and listen. I will only say this once. You be on a train to the East by the end of the week. Clear out of Los Angeles for good. If you don't, I will crush you."

The baldness of the threat rendered Kit speechless for a

moment. "No," she finally said. "I will stand against you."

"You? My dear, you couldn't stand against a light breeze."

"As God is my witness," she said.

"God? How quaint of you. I presume you haven't read Darwin."

"What are you driving at?"

"I'm reminding you that we are not God's little children, as you suppose. We are beings that survive by being strong. The weak are consumed. And I am telling you I will consume you unless you leave this city." Sloate raised an oyster on a half-shell and sucked it into his mouth.

To keep herself from striking him, Kit hurried out of the restaurant.

That night Kit could not sleep. Sloate's image and words kept playing through her mind. She saw him as he was—intimidating, mocking, scheming. And Aunt Freddy was the object of his plans.

Both anger and fear raged through her. Powerless. That's how she felt. Powerless to do anything now.

Then she remembered a verse of Scripture, as clear as when her father first uttered it to her: *For God hath not given us the spirit of fear; but of power, and of love, and of a sound mind.*

Papa told her that the night before he died, when she was begging him to stay home. No, he told her, his call was to preach the Gospel. Kit told him she was afraid for him when he was away. He opened his Bible and read 2 Timothy 1:7.

Kit, in the shadows of her room, remembered that moment as if it had happened yesterday. She rose and lit an oil lamp on her desk and took her father's Bible down from its place of honor on the bookshelf. She opened to the passage and read it aloud.

The feelings of fear and anger begin to melt away, like snow on a hill under a warm sun. Closing her eyes, she prayed. *I am here because you want me here, Lord. And until you show me otherwise, I will stay and do your will.* She continued to pray and read the Bible, losing herself in her experience with God. When she finally went to bed, sleep came softly, easily, fully.

Chapter Twenty-two

THE NEXT MORNING Kit was eager to get to work on the case. The preliminary hearing was to start at nine. Rogers had told her she would be essential to the proceeding.

After washing, Kit gave careful thought to her attire. She chose a stylish but simple suit. The fashion was new, compliments of her wardrobe from Aunt Freddy and Mrs. Norris. The dressmaker had insisted it was the latest thing out of Paris, and Freddy had thought it a must.

Kit had to admit she liked the outfit. The close-fitting gown swirled around her feet, while a tailored jacket reached just to the calf. The thing Kit liked most about the affair was the lace cravat blouse, which completely concealed her neck. The lace, being rather simple, didn't look overdone or too feminine. It dressed her up in a professional air, yet softened her just a touch. It made her feel she could go to court and actually make a contribution to the case.

Deciding to have breakfast at the café two blocks away on Spring Street, Kit topped her russet hair with a wide-brimmed hat of cocoa silk. She felt confident and powerful. She felt as though she could take on the world.

Kit stepped out into the bustling activity of First Street. She was getting to know the city and the local establishments now. Living in the offices of her employer helped, though she was planning to look for more suitable lodgings soon.

The morning air was fresh and clean, another marvel to her. This city must have the cleanest air in the world, she thought. Quite a contrast to smoky New York! This was truly a paradise, and a person could fill her lungs without fear of coughing.

As she crossed Second Street, she came upon Garibaldi's Cafe, which she had heard Jory and Luther Brown talk about. A nice Italian man—Mr. Garibaldi?—greeted her and showed her to a table by the window. The room smelled of fresh bread and sausages, and Kit remembered she had not eaten a full breakfast since leaving Aunt Freddy's.

She sighed and looked at the simple bill of fare. She ordered eggs and sausage, biscuits with gravy, and, of course, a glass of orange juice. And suddenly Kit felt entirely at home here. Los Angeles. Working in the law. This was her city now, and she would give herself to it.

A young newsie, his arms full of fresh newspaper, waddled by the window. She tapped on it and motioned for him to bring her a paper. She gave the boy a nickel and told him to keep the change. It was the early edition of the *Examiner*, Hearst's paper.

She unfolded it and glanced at the front page. The left side held a boxed advertisement for N. B. Blackstone Co. Dry Goods. The establishment was offering a selection of silk waists for seven dollars. Kit wondered if she would ever be that extravagant. To the right of the ad was the first story, with large type declaring **BODY**

OF MISSING TAXIDERMIST WASHES ASHORE. In slightly smaller type below this: Mr. Edward Abbey Was Victim of Foul Play.

When they catch the perpetrator, Kit mused, I wonder if Earl Rogers will get the case.

She then scanned the front page, her eyes resting on the large headline on the right. When she read it, her body chilled to the bone: EYEWITNESS TO IDENTIFY FOX AS MURDERER. Below: Even Defense Team Has Doubts About Client.

Kit's felt her arms grow numb. She began to read the story, credited to Tom Phelps!

> The trial of Mr. Theodore Fox for the grisly murder of Miss Millie Ryan on the night of August 10 in the crib district has taken a stunning turn. An eyewitness is set to identify the fleeing suspect as Mr. Fox, and the evidence has mounted to such a state that even a member of Mr. Fox's own defense team has expressed doubts about his innocence.
>
> The defense is led by the skilled attorney Mr. Earl Rogers. He is being assisted by Miss Kathleen Shannon, newly arrived from the East, who has earned a degree in law from the University of New York.
>
> During a recent interview with an unnamed source, Miss Shannon declared her uncertainty about the actual innocence of her client. When asked if her client had in reality committed the ghastly deed, Miss Shannon was heard to reply, "It seems that way."

Kit dropped the paper on the table. The room began to swirl around her, like a whirlpool of darkness into which she was going to fall. Only a voice at her side brought her back to the present.

"You breakfast," the Italian waiter was saying. He set before her a plate full of eggs and sausage.

But her appetite was gone. She looked at the waiter, wanting to say something, but no words came out.

"You no like?" he said.

"I'm sorry..." She reached into her pocket and pulled out a dollar, setting it on the table. "Will that be enough?"

The waiter looked surprised. "You no hafta pay now."

"I can't..." She stood and ran to the door.

"You change!" the waiter called out.

She did not stop.

———

Rogers had read the paper before coming in to the office. His face was tight and his eyes full of reproach. "Do you realize what you've done?" he railed at Kit, who sat before him with her hands curled tightly in her lap. Tears were not an option, although she felt herself close to allowing them at several points.

"We will have a devil of a time finding an impartial jury!" he said, pacing up and down his office. "The entire city has passed judgment. Even if he is innocent, we will have to battle just to get a few of the jurors on our side!"

Kit said nothing, her heart dropping in her chest.

"How could you be so naive? Don't ever talk to the press unless you tell them only what you want to tell them! These men are snakes in the grass. They'll print anything!"

"He told me he wouldn't print it," Kit said sheepishly.

"And you believed him?"

"I—"

"No, no, of course you believed him! Why should I be surprised? I was a fool to take you on. The law is no place for a woman."

He paused and ran his fingers through his hair. Kit tried to quiet her trembling hands. This was it then. Her career over before it started. Heath Sloate did not have to crush her. She had crushed herself.

"Well?" he said.

Kit looked up at him, his blue eyes piercing her veil of discomfort. "I'm so sorry, Mr. Rogers."

"Apology accepted. Now make me an argument."

"Argument?"

"I just told you the law is no place for a woman. You're a woman, you want to be a lawyer. Well, lawyers make arguments. Make me one."

Her thoughts bouncing this way and that, Kit realized he was opening a door. If she was to stay on, she would have to push through it. "I have been educated in the law," she said.

"Education is one thing, sense is another."

"I made a mistake. I will not make the same one again."

"That is a matter of trust. Why should I trust you?"

"Because I have not given you any reason to distrust me."

"The courtroom can be a very tough place." Rogers sat on the edge of his desk, a less threatening position as far as Kit was concerned. "Do you have what it takes inside you to withstand whatever may come up?"

God hath not given us the spirit of fear, she thought.

"I do," she said.

"Even though you are of the tender sex?"

Kit paused. "I believe so."

Rogers suddenly smiled. "Then I believe in *you,* Kit Shannon." He took his watch from his vest pocket, glanced at it, snapped it shut. "We have a preliminary hearing to do. Go get ready."

———

Freddy sat in her garden trying hard to console herself with mint tea. She had no idea how Kit was faring, but she knew the girl had been nothing but a burr under Heath Sloate's saddle since her arrival in Los Angeles.

Kit's strength somehow intimidated Heath. Freddy hadn't seen that at first. She'd only seen his concern for the Fairbank name and her own social standing in the city. But as time wore on and his tirades had become more and more fierce, Freddy began to discern something else. Dare she name it? Was it fear?

She had tried to speak to Heath on the matter, but he refused to be seen in such a light.

"I will not give words to what I believe you are asking me, my dear Frederica," he had said, barely containing his anger. "My only concern—my only desire—is that you not be hurt in this sordid affair."

Freddy wanted to believe him, just as she wanted to believe that isolating herself away from Kit was for the best. But it didn't feel like it. She worried about the girl. How was she doing? Did she get enough to eat? Was she all alone, without a friend to talk to? Worse yet, was she keeping the company of that Earl Rogers? Or Theodore Fox?

Fanning herself, Freddy fought to control her jittery nerves and thought perhaps ill-spirits had invaded her home and were even now plaguing her.

"I should call Madame Zindorf," she murmured. Then, remembering Kit's abhorrence of such practices, Freddy shook her head. "Perhaps not."

Oh, she was feeling so confused. The turmoil was enough to wilt a weaker woman. What was she to say to Heath? How could she convince him that Kit wasn't a threat to him? She felt as if there were no one in the world to whom she could turn. No one to hear her fears and worries. No one to offer her comfort that all would be well.

Chapter Twenty-three

THE PRELIMINARY HEARING in the matter of Ted Fox was held in the courtroom of Judge Wiley Ganges.

Rogers had briefed Kit on the way to court. In the preliminary hearing, he explained, the prosecution had to establish two things. First, that a crime occurred. Second, that there is cause to believe the defendant perpetrated the crime. If the prosecution succeeds to the judge's satisfaction, the defendant is bound over for trial.

"The prosecutors will put on only the minimum amount of evidence they need," Rogers told her. "They will keep back most of their evidence. Our job is to find out as much about their case as we can, and to make sure we nail their witnesses down on their stories. That way, when it comes to trial, we will have their testimony in our hands so they can't change it."

He also told her that most preliminary hearings were fairly brief and boring. But there was nothing boring in the tone and look of Judge Ganges when he first laid eyes on Kit.

She had taken the second chair at the counsel table with Earl Rogers. Ganges was a thin man with a beard who looked a little like General William Tecumseh Sherman. Kit had seen a Matthew Brady photograph of the stern general once, and Ganges' expression was identical.

Ganges took his seat on the judge's bench, gaveled everyone in the courtroom to sit, and immediately said, "Who is that woman?"

Kit saw that he was looking directly at her!

Rogers said, "Good morning, Your Honor. May I present my associate, Kathleen Shannon."

Kit stood, her knees knocking underneath her dress.

"I won't have a woman at the table," Ganges said.

"She is my *associate*, Your Honor. She is helping me prepare a defense."

"I don't care if she's helping you shine your shoes, Mr. Rogers. I want her back in the gallery."

"But—"

"Is she a lawyer or a defendant?"

"Neither, sir."

"Then back with her."

Kit felt like crawling under a large rock. Rogers turned to her and said softly, "We'll fight this one later."

Nodding but feeling humiliated, Kit walked back past the rail and took a seat in the front row of the spectator section. That's when she caught Heath Sloate smiling at her.

She closed her eyes and prayed silently for composure. At the sound of someone entering the courtroom, she looked back over her shoulder.

Tom Phelps.

He glanced around and then met her eyes. She glared at him, her Irish temper blowing a storm through her gaze. Phelps quickly looked away and took a seat in the rear.

A side door opened, and Ted Fox was marched in by a deputy sheriff. He looked even worse than when Kit had last seen him. His head was bowed as he was placed in a chair at the end of Rogers' table. He did not look at Kit.

Ganges ordered the preliminary hearing to begin. Sloate began by calling the county coroner, a meek-looking man named Raymond J. Smith. He described the grisly scene of Millie Ryan's murder: throat slashed, blood everywhere. Step-by-step, led by Heath Sloate, the coroner drew a gruesome picture, one any judge would be loathe to overlook.

When Sloate finished, Rogers rose to cross-examine. Kit knew Rogers was an indefatigable student of medical science. When he questioned doctors, he had told her, he wanted to know just as much as they. Now was his chance. Kit was determined to learn all she could from Rogers' performance.

"Good morning, Dr. Smith," Rogers said.

The coroner nodded at him. "Good morning, sir."

Rogers walked slowly toward the witness box, twirling his lorgnette. "You have stated, sir, that the victim died due to loss of blood as the result of a wound to the neck."

"Yes, sir."

"And the wound was made by a knife?"

"In my medical opinion."

"Do you have an opinion as to the size of the blade?"

"Rather large. I would say in the neighborhood of a Bowie knife."

"Any other neighborhood you would like to visit?"

Judge Ganges cleared his throat audibly.

"I withdraw the question," said Rogers. "Now, Doctor, the wound obviously severed the carotid artery, did it not?"

Kit listened closely. The doctor had not mentioned the carotid artery specifically during his direct testimony, and now he looked surprised that a lawyer even knew about this part of the body.

"Why, yes," Smith said. "That is precisely what happened."

Kit noticed Sloate looking warily at Rogers, hanging on his every word.

"Such a cut," Rogers continued, "with such a weapon, would have required a slicing motion from side to side, isn't that correct?"

Smith paused, thought, then said, "Yes, sir."

"In other words, the killer would have had the victim from behind and administered the fatal wound by reaching around in front of her."

"Yes, that is consistent."

"Doctor, do you have an opinion as to the direction of the knife? Did it pass from the victim's left to right, or the other way?"

Sloate stood up before the witness could answer. "I object," he said. "The purpose here is to establish that the victim died by criminal act. That has been established. Mr. Rogers is now conducting a full blown cross-examination."

"If I may," Rogers said to the judge. "My purpose is to see that this investigation was properly handled and to prevent any change of story at midstream."

"Your Honor!" Sloate exploded. He pointed at Rogers. "This man is questioning my integrity!"

"Now, now," Judge Ganges said. "Settle down. I'm going to allow Mr. Rogers a little bit of room, but not much. Go ahead, sir."

Sloate huffed and sat down heavily, folding his arms.

Rogers resumed with the witness. "Your answer then, sir? In what direction did the knife travel across the unfortunate victim's throat?"

Smith squirmed slightly on the stand, and Kit knew at once that Rogers had laid a trap. If Smith did not answer specifically, it would seem to the court—and later, to the jurors—that the coroner had not been careful enough in his investigation. But if he did answer, that would have the consequence of fixing the response permanently on the record. That would give Rogers ample time to analyze things every which way before the trial.

"Well," Smith said, clearing his throat and looking at his notes, "it appears to me that the knife was drawn across the throat from the victim's right side to her left side."

"Are you absolutely sure of that?"

Again, Smith shifted his weight. "Yes, sir."

Added Rogers, "When the carotid artery is severed in this manner, the blood is forced outward in a violent fashion, is it not?"

"Yes, that is the case."

"In medical terms you call that. . . ?" Rogers prompted.

"Excuse me?"

"It is called projection, I believe."

"Oh yes, yes, quite right, yes."

Kit marveled at how easily Earl Rogers could control a witness. She remembered what Melle Stanleyetta Titus had told her in one of her law classes: Cross-examination was the greatest engine for truth known to man. It was under cross-examination that the weaknesses of a story, if any, were exposed. Anyone who thought he could easily skate around Earl Rogers would have a rude awakening on the witness stand.

"No further questions," Rogers said. As he returned to his chair he looked at Kit, and his eyes twinkled.

She heard a voice behind her. "Masterful," it said in a rich baritone.

Turning, she was shocked to see John Barrymore.

"What . . ." she stammered, feeling her face flush.

"It is a pleasure to see you again."

Kit turned back around and told herself to gain control over her racing heart.

Sloate's next witness was a young and rugged-looking police

officer named Terrence O'Toole. He was the officer who discovered the body of Millie Ryan. Sloate led him through the narrative, including his interview of Rita Alonzo, stopping when O'Toole summoned another officer to the scene so he could report to headquarters.

Once more, Rogers stood up to question a witness. Kit saw O'Toole assume a position like a fighter. No doubt he had been warned to be wary of Earl Rogers.

"Officer O'Toole," Rogers said, "how long have you been a police officer?"

"Just short of four years."

"How did you happen to end up on the Los Angeles police force?"

"End up?"

"Yes. How did you get the job?"

"Why, I applied and was accepted."

"Who conducted your interview, if you recall?"

O'Toole looked quickly at Sloate, his combative demeanor suddenly fading a bit. Sloate said, "Your Honor, this is simply irrelevant. Officer O'Toole's background is not the least bit important to this matter."

"Let me decide what is important, Mr. Sloate," Judge Ganges said. "Mr. Rogers, where are you going with this line of questioning?"

"Qualifications, Your Honor," Rogers said. "Officer O'Toole's experience may indeed be an issue, depending on what he did at the scene."

"All right," said the judge. "A few more questions, then move on."

"Thank you. Officer O'Toole, who conducted your interview?"

"Chief Hoover."

"That would be Chief of Police Orel Hoover?"

"Yes."

"That's not usually what the chief does, is it? Interview candidates?"

"I'm sure I don't know, sir."

"But I'm sure you were honored to be so privileged."

O'Toole shrugged his shoulders.

"By the by, Officer, where were you before you attained this position you now hold?"

"I lived in New York City."

"Ah. On the police force there, were you?"

"Briefly."

"How brief?" Rogers questioned.

"A year, maybe a little more."

"And what occasioned your leaving New York for our fair city?"

"Change of scenery."

"Grew tired of New York, did you?"

"I wanted a change. New York was too crowded."

Rogers paused in an attitude of skepticism. Then he said, "Now, you told us about your interview with Rita Alonzo, the eyewitness to this crime."

"Yes."

"How extensive was this interview?"

"Extensive?"

"How long did it last?"

"Oh, I don't know, a goodly time."

"How long, sir?"

"I wasn't looking at a timepiece."

Rogers sighed. "Give us an estimate. Was it more on the order of ten minutes or an hour?"

"I would have to say more like an hour."

"How much more like?"

O'Toole scowled and said, "Very like, Mr. Rogers."

"I see. You did a thorough job."

"Yes, I did."

"And what you told this court on direct examination was everything of importance, isn't that true?"

"True, sir."

"I don't remember you stating that Rita Alonzo saw blood."

"Blood?"

"Yes."

"Well, she was never in the room."

"I mean on the defendant, on his clothes."

A light seemed to go off in O'Toole's eyes, as if he knew he was in the thick of something he had not foreseen. His face contorted slightly as he looked toward Heath Sloate. On that cue, Sloate stood up.

"There was no blood to be seen, Your Honor," Sloate said.

Rogers exploded. "Your Honor! Mr. Sloate is testifying for the witness!"

"Gentlemen," Judge Ganges said, "if you please! Officer O'Toole, answer the question. Did the witness, whatever her name is, mention anything about blood on the defendant?"

"No," O'Toole answered confidently.

John Barrymore whispered to Kit, "Infidel."

Rogers, eyes ablaze, announced, "Nothing further!"

After he had stormed back to his chair, Heath Sloate rose easily. "That concludes the People's case, Your Honor."

Ganges looked at Rogers. "Anything further, Mr. Rogers?"

"No, Your Honor."

"Then I find that there is cause to bind this defendant over for trial on the charge before the court. Gentlemen, I bid you good day."

The judge banged his gavel.

Outside the courtroom, John Barrymore said, "It would be my great pleasure, Miss Shannon, if you would dine with me tonight."

Somehow Kit had known he was going to ask her that, and inside wild horses pulled her in two directions. He was so magnetic she couldn't help being drawn to him, yet she knew his actor's ways did not comport with her own.

She was losing herself in his smile when she heard a voice behind her. "Miss Shannon?"

Turning, she faced Tom Phelps.

Instantly her trance lifted, and she felt her temper rise. "I have nothing to say to you."

"Miss Shannon, please—"

"Nothing!"

"But I—"

Barrymore stepped to Kit's side. "Sir, the young lady has declined your offer to converse."

"And just who are you?" Phelps said.

"Barrymore is my name. And yours?"

"Phelps."

"A reporter," Kit added.

"Newspaperman, eh?" Barrymore said. "I don't much care for your kind."

Phelps sneered. "I don't really care what you think."

Barrymore's right eyebrow rose higher than Kit had ever seen an eyebrow go before. "Sir, you are a scoundrel!"

"My conversation is with Miss Shannon."

"Only if she consents!"

Kit noticed heads turning toward them in the courtroom hallway.

"It's about that story, Miss Shannon," Phelps said.

"Wait!" said Barrymore. He turned to Kit. "Is this the scribe who penned that calumny against you in this morning's rag?"

Kit nodded.

Barrymore glared at Phelps. "Swine!"

Phelps looked absolutely confounded. "What did you say?"

"Cur!"

"Listen—"

"Away before I dispense with you!"

Suddenly Tom Phelps threw his right fist toward John Barrymore's perfect chin. Barrymore ducked, came up, and landed his own fist flush in the face of the stunned reporter.

Tom Phelps went down with an emphatic thud. He was not going to get up any time soon.

A small crowd quickly rushed to the scene of all the excitement. One voice muttered, "Self-defense. I saw the whole thing."

Barrymore looked at Kit and smiled. "I apologize for the roughhouse, Miss Shannon."

"Mr. Barrymore," Kit said, "I will be happy to dine with you tonight."

Chapter Twenty-four

IN THE JUDGE'S CHAMBERS, Heath Sloate watched as Wiley Ganges lit a cigar and issued a puff of smoke. "What's on your mind, Sloate?" he said in a perfunctory manner.

"I want you to preside at this trial," Sloate said.

The judge squinted at him through the smoke. "*You* want me to preside?"

"That's what I said."

"I'm going to assign this to Judge Dana."

"I don't think so."

"You don't—"

"I want you," Sloate cut in.

"Well, what makes you think I give a hoot about what you want?" Ganges put his feet up on his desk. Heath noticed his black boots were dusty.

Sloate paced slowly across the floor. "I was a bit concerned with your actions in court today."

Ganges said nothing.

"Your rulings in favor of Rogers were disturbing. I will, of course, overlook it, this being merely a preliminary hearing. But during the trial I expect you to be much more discerning."

Ganges pulled his feet from the desk and planted them on the floor as he stood up. "Now, you wait one minute!"

"No, you wait, Judge. You wait until I am through with you."

For a moment both men froze. Then Ganges opened a drawer and pulled out a Colt revolver.

"What are you going to do, Judge?" Sloate said calmly. "Shoot me?"

"Get out of my sight," Ganges said.

"When I get through with you, you'll put that barrel in your own mouth."

Ganges hesitated, the gun shaking slightly in his trembling hand.

"Why don't you sit down, Judge? Let's discuss Pearl Morton."

The name had the desired effect. Ganges placed the gun on his desk and slowly sat down.

"That's better," Sloate said. "Now, I am sure you would rather your wife and children not hear anything about Miss Morton and your, shall we say, intimate acquaintance with her?"

The judge was speechless.

Sloate said, "There is no need for them to know anything. So long as certain conditions are met." He paused, then said, "You will preside at the trial. You will give the appearance of fairness, of course. But you will not bar any evidence I wish to introduce. We can expect Rogers to be prepared, as always, with numerous objections to our presentation. I will indicate to you which ones you may sustain and which ones you will overrule. Are we clear so far?"

Ganges, looking suddenly shriveled, said, "How did a rodent like you ever get admitted to practice law?"

The last gasp of the defeated, Sloate thought. "Spare me your pronouncements of moral indignation," he said. "You are a hypocrite."

Ganges paused, then said, "At least I know it."

"My patience is at an end. Are we agreed or not?"

"You know."

"Tell me."

"Agreed."

"Good. And don't worry. You will find yourself helped in many ways because of your good sense here today."

Looking like he was about to spit, Ganges said, "I don't want your help, Sloate."

Heath Sloate smiled. "You'll get it anyway, Judge. I always pay my debts."

"I am hopelessly in love with you," John Barrymore said.

Kit fought to keep her breathing normal. They were sitting in a secluded booth in one of the finest restaurants in the city—at least that's what Kit concluded after looking at the bill of fare. The waiter had no sooner left the table with their order than Barrymore made his pronouncement.

Scouring her mind for words, Kit felt her lips move, but no sound issued forth. Was he joking? And if he wasn't joking, what should her reaction be? This was the handsomest man she had ever seen, and he was drawing her to him like a moth to flame. Did she have the strength to fly away?

As she sought for something suitable to say, Barrymore leaned toward her and, in theatrical tones, said, " 'It seems she hangs upon the cheek of night, like a rich jewel in an Ethiop's ear; beauty too rich for use, for earth too dear.' "

Swallowing, Kit said, "I beg your pardon?"

"Romeo speaks of Juliet," he explained. "Act I, scene 5."

"I . . . see."

"But Juliet had nothing on you, Miss Shannon."

"Mr. Barrymore, I . . . this is so sudden."

"Fleet are the wings of Cupid. He has found me with his arrow, directly." He tapped his hand on his heart. "I am asking only that you allow me the favor of your company on occasion," said Barrymore. "You shall grow to love me as I love you."

"Mr. Barrymore, you hardly know me."

"Call me Jack. And I know you as well as I need to."

"But I hardly know you!"

"Point taken," he said. "I am a thespian, from a family of the theater. My brother, Lionel, is currently wowing them as Shylock on Broadway. Sister Ethel is doing repertory to great acclaim. I am rehearsing Mercutio for the Morosco Theatre Company. Will you come?"

"I—"

"Splendid. After the run of the play I shall be returning to New York. Lionel and I will be performing together. I would like to make a triumphant return to New York, with a wife."

Kit almost choked on the sip of water she had taken.

"Are you all right, my dear?"

The waiter then appeared, carrying a silver ice bucket in one hand and bottle of champagne with two glasses, held by the stems, in the other. He opened the bottle and poured a little for Barrymore, who tasted it and approved. But when the waiter went to fill Kit's glass, she put up her hand. "None for me," she said.

The waiter seemed momentarily confused, then filled Barrymore's glass. Barrymore waved him away.

"No wine?" he said.

"No."

"Please."

"No."

"Just one."

"Mr. Barrymore," Kit said, her thoughts a little clearer. "My father was killed by a drunken man. It has been my choice not to drink spirits of any kind."

"I see." Barrymore's eyebrow went up. "You are a woman of morals, character, charm, and intelligence. Marry me."

A nervous laugh flew from Kit's mouth. "You're playing with me now."

"I have never been more in earnest!"

"Mr. Barrymore—"

"Jack!"

"Jack, you are an impetuous fool."

"You cut me to the quick, but you are correct. I am a fool for love. Tell me, is there a chance?" He grasped her hand.

"Chance?"

"That you should accept my proposal of marriage. Mind you, I cannot abide rejection!"

Kit cleared her throat. "Mr. Barry . . . Jack, the man who shall be my husband will share with me the things I hold most dear."

"Agreed!" Barrymore said. Then he added, "What are they?"

"First and foremost, a love for God."

Barrymore's eyebrow raised as he grunted.

"Second, active dedication to following His will."

The actor was silent.

"Finally, a preference for quiet evenings at home," Kit concluded.

"Enough! I can't stand to hear another word. My world is falling to pieces!"

"Jack?"

"Hmm?"

"I think you will survive."

Barrymore poured himself another glass of champagne and lifted it to her. "Here's to you, Kit Shannon, breaker of men's hearts!"

He looked her in the eye, and Kit wished at that moment he *was* everything she would want in a man. She wondered what one kiss from him would be like, but knew one thing for sure—it would seal her doom!

Chapter Twenty-five

"THEY KNOW SOMETHING!" Orel Hoover shouted.

"Keep your voice down," Sloate ordered. Though they were in Hoover's office, behind closed doors, Sloate worried his voice would carry right through to the rest of the police station.

Hoover, his face beginning to turn a deep shade of pink, lowered his voice only a little. "How did they find Rita Alonzo?"

"I don't know," Sloate said, thinking. "Rogers is resourceful. It was clever of him to send the woman."

"What do we do?"

"I ought to go down there and beat some sense into your *witness.*" Sloate said the last word with contempt.

"She's a good witness. Always has been."

"She had better be now, isn't that right?" He paused to let the veiled threat of disaster wash over the police chief with full effect.

"What are you saying?"

"You know exactly what I'm saying."

Hoover fiddled with the buttons on his shirt. Sloate thought he looked like a man playing himself as a musical instrument. "Do you . . . oh my, do you think?"

"Do I think what, Orel?"

"The cat will come out of the bag?"

"If you keep acting like this, it will. Calm yourself. Do you have the locket?" Sloate asked.

Hoover nodded.

"And who knows about it?"

"Just me, Officer Wendell, you, and of course—"

"We do not mention that name. Ever."

"I understand, Heath," Hoover said.

"You may call me Mr. Sloate."

Chief of Police Orel Hoover said nothing more.

────────

The cab let Kit out in front of the largest mansion on Flower Street. She let herself through the gate, walked up to the front door, and clanked the ornate knocker.

A butler appeared, looking annoyed.

"Is Miss Wynn at home?" she said.

"Whom shall I announce?"

"Kit Shannon."

He looked at her more carefully. "What shall I say this is regarding?"

"A legal matter."

"Ah, you are from Mr. Sloate's office."

What a thought! Quickly she said, "No, I am not associated with Mr. Sloate. I work with Earl Rogers."

The butler's eyes widened. "I . . . if you will wait here in the foyer." He opened the door. Kit entered a large tiled hall with a huge mirror on one wall. The butler disappeared, leaving Kit to regard a large portrait of Elinor Wynn. She was in an evening gown, and her gloved hands rested together on her lap. Her expression was one of studied innocence masking an inherent petulance. Kit thought the artist had captured her perfectly.

"Miss Shannon?"

Elinor Wynn entered the foyer. She was perfectly coifed and gowned in iced-blue silk that matched the color of her eyes. She glided, seeming to float above the ground as she crossed the room. Kit suddenly became aware of her own more modest dress. The navy linen trimmed in sedate black braid was no match for Elinor's elegance.

"Good morning, Miss Wynn," said Kit.

"I must say I am surprised." The look of slight contempt that the artist had managed to obscure in the portrait was now fully evident on Elinor Wynn's face.

"Thank you for seeing me."

"You have something to tell me about Ted?"

"May we sit?"

Elinor paused, then led Kit into a study. It was all done in dark browns and dominated by the mounted head of an elk over the fireplace. "This is father's favorite room," Elinor said. "He hunts, you know."

"I gathered."

She looked directly at Kit for a long moment, then motioned for them to sit. "Father likes to take me along on his hunting trips. We have a wonderful time. Do you shoot, Miss Shannon?"

"No."

"Pity. It is actually quite restful." Elinor pulled a multicolored cord near the wall. Presently the butler entered. "Coffee or tea?" Elinor asked Kit.

Kit thought a moment. Normally she would have requested tea. But now that seemed more like Elinor's world than hers. Coffee was the brew of choice where Kit was working now. "Coffee, please," she said.

"Tea for me, Humphrey," Elinor said.

"Very good," said the butler, and he left.

"Now, what news do you have of Ted?" Elinor said.

"Miss Wynn, as you know, I am part of the defense team for Ted . . . Mr. Fox."

Elinor stiffened slightly. "Yes, I am quite aware."

"In that regard, I wonder if I might ask you a few questions."

"Questions? Whatever about?"

"Your engagement to Mr. Fox, for one thing."

Elinor glared at Kit. "Are you quite mad?"

"I was only seeking to—"

"That I would remain engaged to a murderer!"

"You seem quite certain that he is."

For a moment Elinor seemed frozen, like a pretty statuette in a garden. "What do you . . . of course I . . . how can you question?"

"Under the law, Miss Wynn, an accused is innocent until proven guilty."

"You don't have to lecture me, Miss Shannon."

"I am only saying that until the evidence is persuasive, Mr. Fox should be given the benefit of the presumption. It seems odd . . ."

"What? Out with it!"

"That one who is engaged to a man one day should turn around and condemn him the next."

The coldness that passed between them was broken by the butler bringing in the tea and coffee. The two woman said nothing as he poured for them, then left the room.

Elinor did not reach for her cup. "I am not sure I like the tone of your questions, Miss Shannon."

"You will excuse me, I hope," Kit said. "But you can appreciate how important certain information is to us."

"Why should that be of any concern to me?"

"Wasn't your engagement to Mr. Fox in question before his arrest?"

"What do you mean?"

"Is the question ambiguous to you?"

"The question is impertinent." Elinor let the fullness of her petulant expression manifest itself.

Kit reached for her cup. "Thank you for the coffee, Miss Wynn." Kit hoped Elinor Wynn's social graces, doubtlessly inculcated since birth, would not end the interview when only the first of the refreshments was being imbibed.

Elinor Wynn said, "I shall answer you. It is true that Ted and I were contemplating an end to our engagement. I simply could not abide his fancifulness any longer. All his nonsense about wanting to build a flying machine! Utter and complete folly! He had no interest in furthering his career."

"Was it his desire to break off?"

"No," Elinor said, with what Kit thought was a certain defensiveness. "In fact, he importuned me not to."

"When was the last time you spoke to him?"

"I don't know. Several weeks."

"Exactly, if you can remember."

"Why, I believe . . . what possible need do you have for this information?"

"Everything will help. Please."

Elinor sighed and finally took a sip of tea. "As I said, I can't be sure."

"Can you remember the day? Was it a Monday? A Saturday?"

"I don't keep careful account of such things."

"I would appreciate it if you could carefully consider it."

Looking momentarily cornered and apparently not liking it a bit, Elinor said, "I believe it was . . . yes, a Friday, sometime in July.

It was a hot night, as I remember, and I told him that—"

"Where were you?" Kit cut in.

"At his home, on Custer Avenue."

"Please continue."

"There isn't much to say. I told him it was over between us. He sulked a bit, but then faced reality. And then I left."

"And you have not seen or spoken to him since?"

"That is what I told you."

Kit placed her coffee cup on the table. "I won't trouble you further, Miss Wynn." She stood and said, "Thank you for the coffee."

Shooting to her feet, Elinor said, "What was the meaning of this visit?"

"As I explained to you, for information."

"Surely nothing I have said is of interest to this case."

"Nothing is sure in the law, except the final verdict."

Elinor's face seemed to drain of color. "If my name is mentioned in court, I'll . . . I'll sue you. I'll sue Earl Rogers!"

"That would not be advisable, Miss Wynn."

"And why not?"

"Because you will lose."

Now Elinor's face grew pink. "You are . . ." She seemed to be hunting for just the right word. Kit stood and, surprisingly, felt not the least bit intimidated.

"Brazen!" Elinor finished. "How you can allow yourself to descend into the gutter like this? Don't expect to ever have a place in polite society!"

"You may have my place in polite society," Kit said, "and do with it as you wish."

Kit walked out, past a startled butler, into fresh air.

Chapter Twenty-six

TED FOX APPEARED singularly uninterested in his fate. As Earl Rogers questioned him in the jail, Kit took notes. She noticed that Ted's eyes had a lifeless quality to them, a resignation. Was it because he had nothing to fight with, being guilty? Kit could not figure it out, and the pressure inside her was building almost beyond her ability to bear it.

Rogers seemed frustrated. "Your trial is in three days," he said. "You need to prepare yourself, and help us prepare."

"Why?" Ted intoned. "The trial is your job."

"We have to decide whether to put you on the stand. A jury wants to hear the side of the defendant, though you can't be compelled to testify. If you do take the stand, you cannot give less than your best. Frankly, you don't look ready to do that."

Ted hardly moved. "What's the use? The papers have me all but on the gallows."

"Forget the papers! The jury is our hope, and you have got to give me something to work with. I can blast away all I want at the prosecution's case, but unless we have a plausible story for you, we are hanging on by our fingernails."

"I'm innocent," Ted said without enthusiasm.

Rogers glanced at Kit, as if this were some sort of turning point. "Good," said Rogers. "But that doesn't help us if you get on the stand and sound like Marley's ghost. Prove to me that you're innocent."

"Prove? I didn't think I had to prove my innocence."

"That's in the Constitution, sure. But now I'm talking about the heads of the jurors. What can I tell them?"

"Tell them I didn't do it."

"What can I show them?"

Ted shrugged.

"You don't have an alibi for the night in question, and in fact there is an eyewitness who says she saw you running from the place."

"I know, I know." Ted put his head in his hands.

Kit watched him with an increasing sense of unease. Why was he holding back? Was he hiding something? Why wasn't he more passionately concerned about his innocence, if indeed he was innocent?

"Ted," she heard herself say. Rogers looked at her as if she had jumped, impulsively, into the middle of a busy street.

Undaunted, Kit said, "When was the last time you saw Elinor Wynn?"

The expression on Ted's face turned from passive anguish to scowling concern. "Elinor? What's she got to do with this?"

"I spoke to her," Kit said.

"Why?"

"Because you were engaged to her. She might have had something important to add to this case."

"And did she?"

"That depends."

"On what?"

"On you."

Out of the corner of her eye, Kit saw Earl Rogers nod. She was on the right track, and her mentor approved.

"I saw her last sometime in August," Ted said.

"August?" Kit said. "Are you sure?"

"Quite sure. Why?"

"Elinor insists she last saw you in July."

Ted's gaze darted between Rogers and Kit. "What does it matter when I saw her?"

"One of you isn't telling the truth," Kit said, "and there has to be a reason for it."

At that Ted stood up, his shackles jangling, and turned toward the opposite wall. "Let's just get this trial over and done with!" he said.

"Stop it!" Kit said, standing as well.

Ted turned around, and Kit felt both men staring at her. She forged ahead. "I will not allow you to throw your life away!"

Ted stared at Kit, and she saw in his eyes a small glimmer of a will to fight. "I don't want to throw it away, Kit," he said.

"Then help us."

"How?"

Kit looked at Rogers. He gave her a half smile and nodded at her to continue.

Kit said, "Why would Elinor lie to me about when she saw you last?"

Ted looked at the floor, as if the answer were there in cold cement. "Maybe she doesn't want to be drawn into this. She's that way."

"What way?"

"Afraid of appearances, of status." Ted looked disgusted. "She will stop at nothing to preserve her precious position."

"It doesn't sound," Kit said, "like you are saddened by your broken engagement."

"Saddened? It was a relief."

"According to Elinor, you begged her to remain."

"That's another lie."

"Then why didn't you break off with her sooner?"

Ted opened his mouth, as if the answer was certain, but he stopped himself. "Cowardice," he said.

Kit did not believe him.

Rogers said, "Fox, can you provide us with anyone, absolutely anyone, who can vouch for your whereabouts on the night of August tenth?"

"I've told you all that I can."

"A friend or acquaintance?"

"No one."

"Your mother perhaps?"

Ted's face tightened. "You leave her out of this!"

"A mother pleading for her son's life is a powerful witness."

"No!" Ted slammed his manacled hands on the table. "If you bring her to court, I'll plead guilty! I swear it."

"Fox, listen—"

"That's final! Do you hear me?"

Kit could tell from Rogers' physical reaction that he was not pleased.

"Gather your papers," he told Kit. Then, rising, he said to Ted, "I have never surrendered anyone to the hangman's noose, Fox. But you are almost throwing yourself at it."

Ted did not answer. He said nothing at all as they left.

Outside the jail, Rogers said, "We have a big mountain to

climb—an Everest. I'm going to need all your wits on this one, Kit. Are you with me?"

"Yes, sir," she said, then smiled and added, "Yes, Earl."

"Good. Then go talk to his mother. But keep it to yourself, and tell her she is not to say anything to anyone about the meeting. All we need is for the word to get back to Fox and have him jump in court crying 'Guilty!' "

Chapter Twenty-seven

THE FOX ESTATE was located two miles east of the Los Angeles River. Bill Jory drove Kit there in Rogers' buggy, pulled by an old warhorse Rogers had named Summation.

"When old Summation gets put out to pasture," Jory said as they rode up East Street, "Earl says he's gonna get him one of those horseless buggies. Says those will be a sign of prosperity."

"They may well be," said Kit.

"Nah," Jory said. "Nothing will replace the good old reliable horse. Those noisemakers are just a novelty."

"I wonder."

"You wait. Los Angeles is a horse-and-electric town, not a gas-powered town. The city fathers won't allow too many of those gas buggies on the streets, no how."

I wonder, Kit thought. Los Angeles, as she was coming to know it, was a delicate balance of the somnolent ease of the Southwest and the vigor of a population boomlet from the East and Midwest.

Here the vital spirit of growth mixed with the steady calm of preservation, and no one really seemed to know what the personality of the final, mature city would turn out to be.

One could see from higher elevations the electric lines that crisscrossed the city and gave it power. They wound their way along the streets of downtown, woven from pole to pole, until only single wires on skinny posts stretched out into the fields and trees of undeveloped land.

Indeed, one could almost say there were two cities here. Stand at the corner of First and Broadway on a busy day and it might seem like New York itself, with hordes of people frequenting the stores and offices and dodging the electric trolley cars of the Yellow Line as they crackled down the middle of the streets. But this was only New York in miniature, for one could, in only a few minutes' time, ride beyond the bustle into the sedate climes of country life. Kit remembered the newspaper ad she'd read touting Henry Huntington's county line of "big red cars" that said, "Live in the Country and Work in the City!"

One could conduct business in the morning at the City Hall, and in the afternoon picnic in the untamed hills of Laurel Canyon. On a Saturday the beaches at Santa Monica and Ocean Park were dotted with bathers who frolicked in the Pacific foam.

That was Los Angeles, and Kit thought it offered the best of both worlds. The city could easily accommodate its population of 105,000 in both business and leisure, metropolitan energy and rustic charm. A blending of new and old in semiperfect harmony.

But as she and Jory approached the Fox estate, a subtle sign of an uncertain future waited for them. Even from a distance it had the look of a once prosperous grounds that was now, for want of care, falling on hard times. Kit knew that Mrs. Dorothea Fox was a widow, but she certainly wasn't destitute. Was this a picture of some other form of distress?

Jory pulled to a stop at the edge of the front walkway. "I'll be waiting right here," he said. "I brought a book."

He reached into a leather satchel and pulled out a red bound tome. Kit read the title. *The Call of the Wild* by Jack London.

"About dogs," Jory said.

Kit disembarked and approached the large Victorian-style mansion. Its dull shade of gray must at one time have been pristine, Kit thought. She knocked on the door.

A woman in a nurse's uniform answered. "You are Miss Shannon?" she questioned.

"Yes."

"Please come in."

The nurse showed Kit to a sitting room where a large bed had been placed, out of keeping with the design and decor. In the bed lay an older woman. She had skin like paper and gray hair in braids. Dorothea Fox seemed so delicate a stiff breeze could do her harm.

"Oh, my dear," Mrs. Fox said when she laid eyes on Kit. "Are you from the Women's Club?"

"No," Kit said. "I'm an assistant to Mr. Rogers."

"Rogers? Rogers? Who is that?" Her voice was thin and reedy.

Kit sat in a chair by the bedside. "Earl Rogers is your son's lawyer, Mrs. Fox."

Mrs. Fox's eyes rolled heavenward. "My son! Oh, my son!" She made the sign of the cross on her chest.

Kit looked at the nurse, a gentle-looking woman, who nodded at her as if to say this is what it was like all the time. Kit could understand that her son's arrest would have a heavy toll. But for Dorothea Fox, the effect was almost lethal. She must have been a delicate thing to begin with.

"It cannot be!" Mrs. Fox wailed. "My son could not do such a thing! Do you believe me?"

Did she? Kit's mind reeled with all of the evidence and interviews and doubts. But then something turned over inside her, like the flick of a switch, and she said, "Yes, I believe you."

"Oh! You are an angel." Her scrawny hand reached out and touched Kit's arm.

Kit patted it. "Mrs. Fox, can you help us?"

"Help?"

"Can you tell us about your son's whereabouts on August tenth?"

"August?"

"Yes. August tenth."

The woman's eyes looked left and right, as if seeking some threatening presence in the room. "I don't like August," she whispered. And she crossed herself again.

The nurse shook her head at Kit, indicating it was hopeless. Kit knew it was. In this physical state, Mrs. Fox would not even be considered competent to testify in court. Any information helpful to the defense, if indeed there were any, would have to remain unavailable. Only if there were a recovery of some sort, which looked unlikely, was there any chance.

Kit stood up. "Thank you for your time, Mrs. Fox."

She looked at her, eyes wide. "My boy! Where is my boy?"

"He's being taken care of," Kit said, thinking of the three meals and a cot in the jail cell provided to her son.

"Will he come to see me?"

That was not something Kit could promise. "We will do our best, Mrs. Fox."

"Thank you," said the old woman, smiling feebly. "You are an angel."

The nurse showed Kit out of the house where Jory and the buggy waited. "Anything?" Jory said as they headed back to the city.

"I'm afraid not," Kit said.

"You look troubled."

"Not troubled, but curious."

"About?"

"Mrs. Fox," Kit said, seeing the picture in her mind. "She kept making the sign of the cross."

"Maybe she's scared of dying."

"Maybe, but that's not the curious part."

"What is?" Jory asked, looking at Kit.

"She's not Catholic."

Back at the office, Kit went directly to see Rogers.

"Come in, Kit Shannon," he said theatrically, reminding her somewhat of John Barrymore. He was alone in his office, his desk messy with papers, his normally careful attire disheveled. The tie he almost always kept carefully knotted at his high collar was undone completely.

"What news have you for your employer?" he said.

"I've been to see Ted's mother," she said. Something was wrong. Kit sat apprehensively in a chair.

Rogers said, "And did dear old mom have anything to say?"

"Nothing, I'm afraid. She's mentally unstable right now."

"Aren't we all?" Rogers leaned back in his chair and put his feet up on the desk. He had removed his shoes.

This was so unlike him! What was the matter? And then it hit her. He had been at the bottle. Kit felt her face begin to heat up. And nearly on the eve of trial!

"You look tired," Rogers said. "Why don't you go on down and—"

"I'm not tired in the least," Kit said.

"Then what's with the furrowed brow?"

"I thought we would be discussing the trial."

"What's to discuss? Our case is a dog, and tomorrow I'll put on a dog and pony show."

Show? A man's life was at stake, and here was his lawyer, getting drunk!

"Surely you want to talk about the order of evidence," Kit said. She had been cataloging and organizing her interviews and the testimony.

"Hang the evidence," Rogers said. "I've got it all up here." He tapped his temple.

Yes, he probably did. His mind was amazing, as she had come to appreciate. But how much more liquor could that mind take before it began an inevitable decline? Suddenly the man sitting before her was not just an employer. It was a man who desperately needed to be saved from himself.

"Earl," she said.

Rogers said, "You want to discuss drink, don't you?"

Of course he knew. He could read people like a book. That was part of his genius. He went on. "You, my wife, my little daughter. You all seem to have my best interests at heart."

"We do."

"Leave my heart to me, will you? I get tired of the attention."

"No one wants to see you get sick."

"Do I look sick to you?"

Not outwardly, Kit thought. But that was not the problem. "I have heard," she said, "of a cure that is effective."

"You mean a sanitarium? You want to plug me in one of those stables?"

"I do not know the record of the medical places. That is not the cure I have in mind."

"Out with it, then," Rogers said.

"My father used to tell me that he only saw one cure for demon rum, and that was the Gospel."

Rogers glared at her.

Kit pressed on. "And he saw his share of men enslaved to drink. The only thing that worked, as far as he knew, was having a man's life changed through the power of God."

"You are taking your father's place now? You want to save my soul?"

"That's God's desire."

Suddenly his voice became low. "Don't mention God."

"Then Adela . . ."

At the sound of his daughter's name, Rogers' face grew darker. "Enough!" he shouted.

Kit's heart jumped. "I'm sorry if I—"

"Get out!"

Backing toward the door, Kit said, "Please, I didn't mean—"

"Go on! I'm sorry I ever laid eyes on you! Get out, do you hear me? Get out!"

With each word Kit felt like she was taking a fist to the chest. She turned quickly and ran out the door, down the hallway past a startled Bill Jory, and into her room. She burned with a combination of anger and hurt. If this was what her association with Rogers was to be like, how could she continue? If he was going to drink like this with a man's life on the line and defend himself by throwing hateful words at her, she could not see a way to stay on. She would not be a punching bag for a sodden drunk!

She felt her Irish temper rising. And she remembered Papa's words from long past. *Don't let the sun go down on your anger,* he had said. *And don't let your anger blot out the sun.*

"Okay, Papa," she whispered. She sat on her bed and closed her eyes. And then it struck that she had not done something she should have done all along. Not once had she prayed for Earl Rogers. Oh, she had been quick to point out his weakness to him. But had she ever taken him before God?

Ashamed at her oversight, Kit began to pray for her employer—for his deliverance from alcohol, for his ability to defend Ted Fox. She asked for wisdom concerning what to say to him when she saw him next.

And then she went to her desk and pulled out a blank piece of paper. She took up her pen and wrote, in bold strokes in the center, the following: *I can do all things through Christ which strengtheneth me.* Someday, she thought, when the time is right, she would hand him that simple but powerful verse, one that she had relied upon since she had been thirteen years old and alone.

There was a gentle knock at her door. Kit rose and answered it. Rogers, who had combed his hair and straightened his tie, stood sheepishly before her.

"I've never been one to be at a loss for words," he said, "but I find them hard to come by now. All I can say is, will you forgive me for what I said?"

Kit felt a warmth engulf her. "Of course."

"I wouldn't blame you if you walked out."

"What about the drinking?"

"It helps me keep the shadows away, Kit. I . . ."

"I cannot stay if you continue." Her resolve surprised her, but down deep she felt this was exactly what she should say.

His face was stoic for a moment, then slowly a smile appeared. "When Adela grows up, I hope she is like you. All right. No more drink until the trial is over. Fair enough?"

It was only a first step, but at least it was a step in the right direction. "Fair enough," said Kit.

"Now," said Rogers, "don't we have some work to do?"

Chapter Twenty-eight

ON SUNDAY MORNING Kit attended church on Hill Street near Sixth. It was a grand, brick edifice Kit had admired from afar. Indeed, there were many church buildings in the city which, on the outside at least, solidified what the *Los Angeles Daily Times* claimed was a "City of Churches." In a recent editorial, the paper noted that several Protestant denominations had constructed houses of worship within the last decade.

That was good news, Kit thought. This city's moral direction would be influenced most by the religious influence of its churches. Her father had always believed that the preaching of the Word was the only thing that could save a soul or move a community.

So it was with some consternation that Kit listened to the sermon by Dr. Edward N. Lazarus.

He was a man in his early forties, Kit guessed, and cut an impressive figure. He had a mellifluous voice and confident air. But his words were altogether another matter.

His sermon was a veiled attack on the Bible as the inspired Word of God. According to Dr. Lazarus, the Germans had shown that the Bible was a collection of merely human writings, full of errors and contradictions, and was to be viewed with a skeptical eye. What mattered was not the words so much as the spirit of the writings. And the spirit of it was "social justice," something that the ancient Jews "knew little of, considering the way they treated their neighbors."

Kit shifted uncomfortably on the hard, wooden pew. What on earth was he saying?

"God, you see, is a Force or Spirit," said Dr. Lazarus, "who is so much more than the mere written word. If we would only work in cooperation with that spirit, a new age of social cooperation would come into glorious flower! There would be no more war. Conflict of any kind would cease. President Roosevelt would no longer need to carry his big stick. And we would all speak softly to one another."

Kit looked around at the congregation. They seemed stiff and unmoving, though attentive.

"And so I say, let us cease to keep our noses stuck in an ancient book and raise our eyes to our fellow man. Let us roll up our sleeves and begin to work for a grand and glorious future."

By the end of the service Kit could not wait to get out. She sought to slip by quickly but was detained at the front door by the minister as he greeted his flock. It almost seemed as if he had been waiting for her.

"I don't believe we have met," he said.

Kit nodded politely. "We have not. I am a visitor."

"So glad to have you, Miss . . ."

"Shannon."

"Shannon, yes. Did you enjoy the service?" Dr. Lazarus asked.

"I . . . the service offered food for thought."

"You enjoyed the sermon, then?"

Suddenly these words popped into her mind: *The truth, the whole truth, and nothing but the truth, so help me God!*

To the minister she said, "I happen to believe the Bible is without error, sir."

Lazarus seemed slightly taken aback. Other parishioners waiting to speak with him turned their attentions toward Kit. She was suddenly a sideshow.

"That is, of course, a belief many of us held in childhood," Dr. Lazarus said, recovering. "But there comes a time to put away childish things."

Should she simply leave? Kit wondered. She was planning to meet Corazón in the park. But something in the clergyman's tone set her off.

"Is it childish to believe God Almighty?" Kit asked. "Or to insist that one knows better than his heavenly Father?"

Now a look of seriousness flashed into Lazarus' eyes. He quickly looked at the small crowd gathered around them. Kit got the sense that several listeners were intent on the discussion because they themselves doubted their pastor's sentiments.

"Miss Shannon, I have a doctorate from one of the finest seminaries in the country. I think I know whereof I speak."

"My seminary is the Word of God, and in it God speaks. And God does not mislead us."

Lazarus suddenly seemed aware that he was being put on the spot and was not at all pleased. "My dear Miss Shannon, the Bible is simply another book, a great book, but God does not speak through the errors of man."

A spark went off inside Kit's head. It grew into a small flame of remembrance. She saw her papa again, Bible in hand. How he loved the Word of God! And how its power was demonstrated in his ministry. "There are no errors in the Bible, sir," Kit said. "If there were, Christianity would be dead."

Something like a stunned silence hung in the air around them.

"That is simply not true," Dr. Lazarus said. "If you come visit me, I shall endeavor to show you that—"

"If the Bible is not trustworthy, then we shouldn't know what to believe."

"Well, I don't think—"

"And if we shouldn't know what to believe, we cannot be sure that Jesus died for the sins of all mankind."

Lazarus said nothing, but his eyes began to widen.

"And if Jesus did not die for our sins and rise again, then Christianity is of no more worth than yesterday's garbage."

Kit heard an older man to her side mutter "Amen."

"Well!" Lazarus said quickly. "As you can see, I have many people to greet." He cocked his head toward the small crowd.

Catching her breath, Kit nodded and turned toward the street. She heard a woman say, "Impertinent!" But the older man to her side said, "Come back and visit us again!"

That was a sentiment that Dr. Lazarus, at least by his facial expression, did not share.

As Kit walked away she wondered if she would indeed come back. What would she do or say? All she knew was that if such thoughts were going to be preached in the city, her optimism about its future would have to be revised. And she felt like somehow she must do something to buck that trend. But that would have to wait for another day. She had a murder trial to concentrate on.

The day was warm and beautiful, and Kit forgot about the sermon enough to enjoy the walk to the little park at Fifth and Hill where she and Corazón had agreed to meet.

Corazón was waiting for her with a picnic spread—ground cloth, plates, silverware—already prepared. Kit embraced her.

"We will have the English lesson?" Corazón said.

"Of course!" said Kit. "But after we eat. I'm famished."

"Famish?"

"Tengo mucha hambre," Kit said.

"Ah, *que bueno!* You are learning!"

"I have a good teacher. What have you brought today?"

Corazón opened a large basket and pulled out what looked like light brown leaves. On closer inspection Kit saw they were biscuit-sized items, but what they could possibly be she did not know.

"Tamales," Corazón said. "From my mother."

Kit smiled at her friend's generosity. Of all the people she had met in Los Angeles, none was kinder than Corazón. Kit took her hand and said, "I want to pray for this meal you have brought us."

Corazón nodded and closed her eyes. Kit thanked God for the food and for the friendship she had come to cherish so much.

And then she took up a tamale. It was warm to the touch. She held it up to her nose and smelled. A scent of spices, peppery but not unpleasant, greeted her. She noticed Corazón watching her, smiling, as if waiting for her to take a bite.

She did. It was like biting into thick paper. The leaves were tasteless and rough.

Corazón laughed. "No, no," she said. *"Mira."* She gently took the tamale from Kit and unwrapped the leaves, revealing something made of what looked like corn meal.

Kit blushed and smiled. "Oops," she said.

Corazón handed Kit a fork and she took a bite of the strange food. A taste like no other burst into her mouth. Spicy hot but moist and flavorful, with something meaty inside, too. It was wonderful.

"You like?" said Corazón.

"Very much." She took another bite, a hearty one this time. And she ate three of the tamales Corazón provided. They also enjoyed sweet Mexican bread and oranges for dessert.

In the middle of the feast, Kit asked about Aunt Freddy. Corazón's face showed marked concern. "I do not like what Mr. Sloate do to her."

"What is it?" Kit asked, imagining the worst.

"Only how he treat her. Madam one time get mad at him when he talk of you. She say he is too hard upon you. Then Mr. Sloate, he get mad back."

Kit shook her head. "Poor Aunt Freddy."

"Madam say she will do as he say, but when he leave she cry. I think she want to see you."

"Oh, Corazón, I want to see her, too. But the time has to be right. Sloate has power over her, and I have to be careful. If I strike too soon things could backfire. If only Aunt Freddy would come and watch the trial."

"No, Mr. Sloate not let her."

"Let her? Is he a zookeeper or something?" Kit let out an exasperated breath. "We have to get her out!"

"How?"

Kit thought a moment, then took Corazón's hand. "How would you like to play carrier pigeon?"

"Like the bird?"

"Yes, a bird with a message."

Corazón's eyes lit up as if she were part of a grand, mischievous conspiracy. "Tell me, then, where do I fly?"

Chapter Twenty-nine

THE MURDER TRIAL of Ted Fox began on a dark Monday morning.

The skies above Los Angeles were thick with nimbus clouds, and an unseasonably cool wind filled the September air. As Kit walked with Earl Rogers toward the courthouse, she felt gooseflesh on her arms. She wondered at once if it was the temperature of the air or the popular climate of the city, which was decidedly against them.

For a week now, in newspapers and conversations, the Fox trial had dominated social discourse. A battle of titans, some called it. Heath Sloate against Earl Rogers. The seasoned master versus the flashy upstart. And a vicious murderer the city had seemingly already convicted.

Indeed, as Rogers and Kit approached the courthouse on Temple Street, the crowd on the sidewalk grew thicker and more verbal.

"This is the one you lose, Rogers!" a man shouted at him.

Rogers flashed his eyes in the man's direction but kept walking onward.

"Take your tricks and go home!" shouted someone else. Again Rogers ignored it.

At the stone courthouse steps a small army of reporters rushed at them, surrounding Rogers and throwing overlapping questions at him.

"Gentlemen," Rogers said. "I have no comment for you now. The trial will speak for itself."

A man with a cigarette in his teeth turned to Kit. "How about you, Miss Shannon? Anything to say?"

"No comment," Kit said.

"Come on, lady," the reporter pleaded. "I'm on your side!"

A likely story, Kit thought. She followed Rogers up the steps, then felt an arm on hers. It was Tom Phelps.

"Miss Shannon."

"Unhand me, please."

"I have to talk to you."

"We have nothing to say." She yanked her arm away and hurried up the stairs.

The lobby was crowded, noisy, and full of smoke. It was almost as if they were entering a theater for a performance, with the audience trying to get a glance at the star players.

Rogers led Kit directly to the courtroom. All of the seats were taken, save for a few reserved for the press. Two consternated sheriff's deputies tried to keep the peace. Rogers marched directly past the swinging gate of the rail, and Kit followed.

Heath Sloate stood near the jury box. He glanced their way, animosity pouring out of his look.

Kit began pulling out folders from her leather briefcase, the one Rogers had given her just that morning. It was a beautiful gift—a calfskin Gladstone, with "K. S." in gold lettering just below the latch. "For the start of a great career," Rogers had said.

Indeed this was the start. Her first trial, even though she was a mere apprentice and, if the judge kept true to form, a spectator. But she would be an interested spectator, and an active one.

Once the folders were out and on the table, Kit heard the familiar voice of Heath Sloate. "Mr. Rogers," he said with a sniff, ignoring Kit. He was wearing a dark three-piece suit, almost the opposite in color to Rogers' lighter, vested apparel.

"What is it, Mr. Sloate?" Rogers said.

"All of Los Angeles, it seems, is here today."

"It looks like it."

"The newspapers are well represented. This is bigger than Barnum and Bailey."

Rogers slapped a pad of paper on the table. "What is it you want?"

Sloate answered calmly. "Reports of this trial will be read as far away as New York, perhaps even Europe. It's sensational. Might make a reputation . . . or ruin one."

Rogers waited.

"Therefore," Sloate said, "it would be to our mutual benefit to fashion a way for both of us to come out, shall we say, smelling like a rose?"

"You want to make some sort of deal, don't you?"

A deal with the devil! Kit thought.

"Let's call it an understanding," Sloate said. "You have a client who is considered one of the great monsters of our time. He could likely be considered our city's very own Jack the Ripper. The populace, and I daresay the judge, will not be satisfied with anything but the noose."

"Sounds like you've got him convicted, Sloate."

"That, sir, is only a matter of time. And your reputation as a trial magician would be forever tarnished. On the other hand, if your client were to change his plea to guilty and accept responsibility for his actions, I would recommend to the judge that he be sent to prison for life. Then you can continue to claim you have never lost a man to the gallows, while I can bask in an efficient victory. Both of us will win."

Rogers squinted. "You think my client is guilty."

"Of course he is. We both know that."

"Do we?" Rogers turned to Kit. "How about it, Kit? You ready to throw in the towel?"

"What has she got to do with this?" Sloate said. "This is a matter between gentlemen."

Rogers spun around to face Sloate fully. "If I saw another gentleman here, I would agree. As it is, we will take our chances. No deal, Sloate."

"You're a fool," he said. Then he looked at Kit with an expression that said, *You and I are not finished either.* He returned to his table.

Kit joined Bill Jory in the gallery. She noticed the chief of police, Orel Hoover, in attendance. Truly, the entire city's attention was concentrated here.

Ted was brought in by a deputy sheriff. For the trial he was allowed to dress in a good suit of clothes. He still had a look of resignation about him, however.

So this was the real thing now. Kit closed her eyes and silently prayed for justice to be done. The strongest evidence against Ted, the testimony of Rita Alonzo, was questionable in her mind. And she knew Rogers would take care of it. She and Rogers had gone over the strategy for days.

Judge Ganges entered, sat, and banged his gavel. "Case of the People of the State of California against Theodore Fox," he said. "Everybody ready?"

"Ready, Your Honor," Sloate said.

"Ready," said Rogers.

"Then let's pick a jury."

For the next four hours Earl Rogers and Heath Sloate took turns questioning potential jurors. They sifted through the men in the box, moving them in and out like chess pieces. There was a lot of posturing, too, as Heath Sloate would state that he was looking only for men "who honored the truth, and want to see justice done." It was so pompous, yet every time he said something like it most of the men in the jury box would nod.

Rogers, for his part, asked whether the prospective jurors believed that all men are innocent until proven guilty. He asked if they understood the meaning of "beyond a reasonable doubt." On a couple of occasions, Judge Ganges gaveled Rogers into silence and said that *he* would be the one to explain the law to the jurors, and not the lawyers.

Not once did the judge interrupt Heath Sloate.

Finally, around one o'clock, the two lawyers agreed on their jury. The judge called for a lunch recess, with opening statements to begin in an hour.

As Kit helped Rogers gather his papers she asked, "How did it go?"

"You saw it, didn't you?" He did not seem pleased.

"It seemed as well as could be expected."

"It wasn't. Ganges is clearly favoring Sloate."

Kit nodded. "That was clear."

"The word on Ganges is that he leans toward the prosecution. I just never expected him to bend over backward. Kit?"

"Yes?"

"We need to watch our back. Something here stinks."

————

Frederica Stamper Fairbank could not stop pacing. Agitation coursed through every sinew of her being. *This house! I cannot stay in this house one more moment! I must go to the trial!*

But then she pulled out the note from the pocket of her dress and read its contents for the twentieth time since she'd received it the day before:

> *My dear Freddy:*
>
> *The trial begins tomorrow, and my strong advice and desire is that you spare yourself the perturbation that would attend your presence there. Suffice to say that I shall keep you abreast of activities concerning your niece and the trial itself. I feel, however, that your attendance would only make things worse for all concerned. In advance I thank you for your understanding, and beg to remain,*
>
>

Your loving,

H. S.
>

Understanding! She had less of it now than ever. Not only was he asking her to stay out of her own niece's affairs, he was suggesting that she miss the social scandal of the year, if not the young century!

Deep down, though, she knew it was because of Kit. Oh, her Kit! Too long they had been separated! She wanted to be near her—not showing she approved of her station, of course—no, that would never do—but to look to see how she might be saved. Saved from this awful profession with which she was involved.

Oh, but Heath! He was firm in his resolve that she should not communicate with Kit. He knew what was best, after all. Didn't he?

With a deep sigh she looked out the window of the morning room, seeing in the distance the red and copper roof of the courthouse. What must be happening in there? She was aflame with curiosity!

She turned as Corazón entered with a tray of coffee. Freddy smoothed her dress and inhaled deeply, so as not to appear anxious in front of the servant.

"Thank you, Corazón," Freddy said. "You may just place it there." She nodded her head toward the coffee table.

Corazón dutifully placed the tray down, then poured coffee into the fine china cup. She added a spoonful of sugar and a touch of cream, stirring the contents.

She continued stirring. "That's just fine," Freddy said.

Corazón stirred more.

"I said that's fine." What was the matter with the girl?

Placing the spoon carefully on the saucer, Corazón stood straight and faced Freddy.

"Yes, thank you," Freddy said. "That will be all."

Corazón did not move. She looked at her hands.

"Well, what is it?" said Freddy.

"I was thought . . ." The maid's voice trailed off as she continued looking down.

"You were thought? Come, come, girl—speak plainly!"

Corazón raised her head. "I was *thinking*," she said, "that madam might be going to town today?"

"Is that a question?"

"Yes, I think."

"What business is it of yours? Really!"

Corazón seemed rebuked but did not move to leave.

"Now, now, there is something on your mind," Freddy said. "Tell me what it is."

"I was thinking you would go to the court."

"Were you? Why?"

"Because of Miss Kathleen."

"Here, now! Have you become a social secretary? What have Kit's affairs to do with you?"

"It was for you I am thinking."

Freddy paused, astonished. Never had Corazón spoken to her in this fashion. "Exactly what were you thinking about me?"

"That it would be good for you to see her, I think. That she want to see you."

Freddy sat in a large chair, suddenly feeling a bit winded. "How do you know this?"

"I have spoken to her."

"When?"

"Sometimes I do." Corazón looked as if she had just been caught stealing silverware. "We talk sometimes. She teaches me better English and I teach her Spanish."

"You mean all the time she has been gone from this house, you have maintained contact? What has she told you?"

"That her wish is that she would see you again, I think. She always ask about you. She thinks about you always. She loves you very much."

Freddy put a hand to her heart. "Did she really say that?"

"Sí, madam."

Tears came to Freddy's eyes. She reached for her coffee, but her hand trembled as she lifted the cup. She put it back down for fear of spilling. She did not order Corazón from the room. Instead, she took up Heath Sloate's note and glanced at it again.

Should she go? Really?

But what about Heath? What about his directions? What would he think?

Heath. Kit. Go. Stay. Her mind was in a frenzy! She paced back and forth in the room, Corazón watching silently.

She stopped at the fireplace and looked at the portrait above it. Jasper Fairbank, his right hand grasping the lapel of his suit, looked confidently outward. What would Jasper have said?

"The oil won't come to you. You've got to go to the oil!"
"Order my carriage!" Freddy said suddenly.
"Truly?" said a startled Corzón.
"Yes, yes. Be quick about it. I'm going to the oil!"

Chapter Thirty

ROGERS AND KIT took their lunch back at the office, with Jory and Luther Brown. As they wolfed down sandwiches and coffee, Rogers told her about opening statements.

"It is essential," Rogers said, "to tell them a story. Jurors are not like us. We lawyers can think about a thing inextricably attached to something else, without thinking of the thing it is attached to."

Jory and Brown laughed, nodding their heads.

"But jurors," Rogers said, "are real people. They want to know what happened. Who did what to whom and why. The prosecutor gets the first word. Many defense lawyers will waive their opening until the start of their case-in-chief. That's disaster! Then the story will be the prosecutor's alone. The images in the jurors' minds will be what he wants them to hear. No! We must tell our story as soon as possible."

Rogers paused for a bite of sandwich. Kit took in every word, hoping that someday she would be telling the story of some unfortunate accused, moving the jurors in their hearts and minds the way Rogers did.

"Now," Rogers said to Kit, "when I'm telling Ted's story, I want you to watch the jury. Watch their eyes, their movements. Try to get a sense of what they are thinking. It's no exact science, this jury business. But I'll want your opinion. Understood?"

"Yes, sir," Kit said.

"Good. Now, whom do you think Sloate will call first?"

Kit thought about it, running through possibilities in her mind.

"Remember," Rogers said, "it's a story. Who would be the logical person?"

"The police officer," Kit said. "O'Toole."

"Right. He can give an account that is dramatic. Now, how shall I handle his cross-examination?"

Kit said, "Use the letter."

"Of course," said Rogers. Two days ago Kit had received a letter from Melle Stanleyetta Titus, her former law professor. Kit had written her at Rogers' instruction after the preliminary hearing. It concerned the New York career of Officer O'Toole.

"Then we're ready," Rogers said. "Except for one thing."

Kit looked at him.

"You're in good with God, it seems," he said. "Ask Him for some help. I think our client is innocent, but we're going to need all the help we can to show it to this jury."

It was a stunning request. He was asking her to pray! It was only a short jump from that to praying for himself. Kit quickly repaired to her room to do as Rogers asked.

Oh, God, give us understanding in this case, Kit prayed. *Let the truth win out. Let justice be done. Help Ted to tell the truth—no matter what it is—let him reveal what needs to be said in order to prove himself innocent.*

Yes, she thought, *I believe he's innocent!*

But there was some veil over the truth that she just could not see through. God could, and she asked Him to tear the veil, just as He had done to the temple curtain when Jesus took away the sins of the world.

"Reveal what is hidden," she whispered. "Let your will be done as the truth is told."

———————

"Gentlemen of the jury," Heath Sloate said to the men in the box, "this is a case of brutal murder. An unfortunate young woman, forced into a life of utter despair, was violently attacked and killed in the most unforgiving way before she had a chance to repent of her ways! And that man—" Sloate turned and pointed a bony finger at Ted Fox—"is the killer. Gentlemen, it will be your duty to see that justice is done."

Kit watched the faces of the jurors, as she had been instructed. They seemed to hang on to every word from Sloate's lips. Most of them appeared to scowl at Ted when Sloate pointed.

The gallery was packed. Kit saw Tom Phelps seated on the opposite side, along with a few other scribblers. Behind him was John Barrymore, who had winked and nodded at Kit.

"Now," Sloate continued to the jury, "you are going to hear compelling evidence that will show that the defendant viciously cut the throat of this young woman, an animal tearing the life out of an innocent. There, behind the facade of a gentleman, sits a black-hearted villain!"

At this, Earl Rogers stood up. "Your Honor, this is not an opening statement, it is a melodrama. I would ask that the court admonish Mr. Sloate to stick to facts, not theatrics."

"I protest!" Sloate cried to the judge.

"Your Honor knows the law," Rogers said. "The opening

statement is not the closing argument. Mr. Sloate's bad playwriting has no place in a courtroom."

As Sloate's face reddened, the judge banged his gavel. "That's enough, Mr. Rogers. I do know the law, thank you. And I'll be the one to run this courtroom. Sit down and let Mr. Sloate continue."

Rogers bowed slightly to the judge, in a way that indicated submission to a bad ruling, and sat. Kit knew the law on this, and knew Rogers was right. Why had Judge Ganges so cavalierly dismissed the objection?

Sloate's opening statement was more of the same, long on inflammatory language and short on specifics. Kit continued to study the jury. The performance was having an impact. Rogers did not object again.

In the middle of his oration, Sloate stopped when a commotion arose in the back of the courtroom.

"Unhand me!" a familiar voice shouted. All heads turned. Kit almost fell off her chair at the sight of Aunt Freddy bustling in just ahead of a befuddled deputy sheriff.

"This is a court of law!" Ganges shouted.

Aunt Freddy seemed oblivious. She looked around for a chair, but every one was occupied. A man stood up and gave Freddy his chair. She harumphed at the deputy and sat down.

"I will have no outbursts from the gallery," said Ganges. Kit suppressed a smile. She wondered how long it would be before Aunt Freddy said something else. But she was here. She had come. Maybe there was hope.

Sloate seemed the most upset—a mixture of anger and embarrassment—but he managed to finish his address to the jury without further interruptions.

When Sloate sat down it was Earl Rogers' turn.

"Gentlemen," he said. "What you have just heard is fiction. And bad fiction, dime-novel fiction, the sort of story your mothers would have tanned your hide over."

Wasting no time, Sloate shouted, "Objection!"

Rogers stopped and shot an angry look at his adversary. That same look was directed at the judge when Ganges said, "Sustained!"

"What!" Rogers bellowed.

"Your statement is inappropriate," the judge said. "It will be for the jury to decide what is fiction and what is fact. Confine yourself to the latter."

Watching the jurors, Kit wondered if they realized what a bias had just been shown. Judge Ganges had rebuked Earl Rogers for the very thing Heath Sloate had done!

Now what would Rogers do? It almost seemed like Sloate and Ganges had orchestrated all this to throw Rogers off his stride in the opening statement.

Pausing, Rogers scanned the faces of the jurors, and then the gallery. Without a word he took two steps toward Heath Sloate and just stood there, hovering, his face doing the talking. It said, *So the fix is in, eh?*

"Mr. Rogers?" Judge Ganges said.

"Yes, Your Honor?" said Rogers with a labored politeness.

"Are you going to continue with your opening statement?"

"Ah." He turned back toward the jury. "Gentlemen, you have just heard the judge tell you that you will be the ones to separate fact from fiction. You have just sworn that you will keep an open mind until all the evidence is in, and then you will make your decision based on facts and law. Well, I trust you will do your sworn duty. If you promise me you'll do that, I'll go sit down and we can begin this trial. Deal?"

Even as Sloate stood up to object, the jurors, as one, were nodding their heads. "Your Honor!" Sloate moaned.

"You can relax, Heath," Rogers said, striding toward his chair.

"The curtain is up. You can start your act now."

Some in the audience laughed, the loudest coming from John Barrymore. Kit would have recognized it anywhere.

"Call your first witness," said the judge.

It was, indeed, Officer Terrence O'Toole, the policeman who had found the body. After taking the oath, Sloate established his credentials, then had him address the night of the murder.

"Tell the jury where you were at approximately eleven o'clock the night of August ten," Sloate asked.

"I was walking my beat," O'Toole answered. "Alameda Street."

"You know the street well?"

"Sure I do."

"What is the character of the street?" Sloate questioned.

"It's not one of the better parts of town."

"Can you explain?"

"A lot of crime, sir."

"What sort of crime?"

"Prostitution, mostly."

"How would you characterize the prostitutes who work on Alameda Street?"

"Characterize?"

"Yes. What sort of women are they?"

Earl Rogers said, "I object, Your Honor. This officer has not been called to render an opinion on the social profile of prostitutes. What possible relevance is there to the facts of this case?"

"Overruled," growled Judge Ganges.

Rogers sat down, this time with a vigor that betrayed his annoyance.

Sloate waited a moment before resuming. "You may answer the question, Officer O'Toole."

"Well, the women down there on Alameda Street are down on

their luck, mostly. They have no other way to make a livin', or that's what they think anyway."

"Are they violent women?"

"No, sir, you couldn't say that, sir."

"Are they stronger women?"

"Sir?" O'Toole asked.

"Physically stronger than other members of their sex?"

"No, I would not venture to say so."

"But for their profession, are they as vulnerable as any other woman?"

"Yes, sir."

"Especially at the hands of a strong man with murder on his mind?"

This time, Rogers objected from his chair. "That is a speech, Your Honor, not a question!"

The judge took a moment to scowl at Rogers. "I will advise you to stop interrupting the questioning, Mr. Rogers. Your objection is overruled."

Kit could see the back of Rogers' neck as it turned a dark shade of red. Then she heard Rogers' voice, packed with barely concealed anger. "I inform this court that I will object to questions that I find improper, and I will insist that Your Honor's rulings are clear on the record."

The entire courtroom hushed at what was a gauntlet thrown. Kit felt her heartbeat intensify. Was such a thing done? Saying such things to a judge? Couldn't he . . .

"Do you wish to be held in contempt of this court?" Judge Ganges said. "If that's your intention, Mr. Rogers, I can see my way clear to accommodate you."

"I am not trying to show contempt for this court," said Rogers. Then he turned, and under his breath, so only the first row of spectators could hear, he said, "I'm doing my best to conceal it."

A wave of laughter. Judge Ganges pounded his gavel on the bench. "I'm warning you, Mr. Rogers!"

"I will withdraw my obviously worthless objection, Your Honor." He sat.

Resuming once more, Sloate asked Officer O'Toole to explain how he came to the murder scene.

"I heard one of the ladies screaming," O'Toole said. "So I made my way toward where I heard it. And there was one of them, one of the ladies, name of Rita, and she said, 'Something terrible has happened.'"

"And how did you respond?"

"I asked her where, and she pointed across Alameda Street to one of the cribs on the other side."

"What did you do next?" Sloate continued.

"I walked over to the door, which was open a bit, and I pushed it open some more and went inside. And that's when I seen her."

"Whom did you see?"

"The poor girl, Millie Ryan."

"Did you know this girl?"

"I knew her by sight, not by name. I learned that later."

"Describe the scene for the gentlemen of the jury." Sloate indicated the jury box with a wave of his hand.

O'Toole turned to the jury and said, "It was very bloody. There was a pool of blood around her head and neck, and bloody footprints from the body to the door."

"These footprints, were they Millie Ryan's?"

"No, sir. They were too big for that."

"What did you do next?"

"I went to a box and called headquarters. Then I stood outside and made sure no one went into the room."

"Did you talk to this Rita?"

"Yes, I did. I asked her to tell me what she saw that night."

"And what did she say?"

"Objection!" said Earl Rogers. "That would be hearsay, Your Honor. We are entitled to cross-examine anyone who speaks to the issues, in order that the jury might make the determination of the truth or falsity of the testimony. Mr. Sloate knows that, and so do you."

The judge looked ready to overrule again, but then he paused. Kit studied his face, for this was one objection that was so firmly grounded in the law even this judge could not ignore it. Or could he?

"Mr. Sloate," Judge Ganges said, "do you intend to call this woman, this Rita?"

"I have not made that decision, Your Honor," said Sloate, looking slightly surprised.

"Well, you're gonna have to," said the judge. "If she's available, call her as a witness. I am going to sustain the objection."

It was difficult to tell who was the more surprised, Heath Sloate or Earl Rogers. After a moment, Sloate asked his final question. "How would you characterize the killing of this poor young woman, Officer O'Toole?"

As if his answer had been fully rehearsed, O'Toole said, "A horrible act of depravity."

"Take the witness," Sloate said to Rogers.

The courtroom seemed to lean forward as one in anticipation of Rogers' questioning.

Rogers removed the gold lorgnette from his vest and held the glasses to his face. He looked at O'Toole for a long time. The policeman began to shift around in the witness box.

Finally Rogers said, "A horrible act of depravity, eh?"

O'Toole's eyes darted between Rogers and Sloate. "Yes, sir."

"When was the last time you used the word *depravity*, sir?"

"I . . . I don't know."

"Is it a word you use often?"

"It's just a word."

"Words have meaning, sir. Words are used to convey thought. This word, *depravity*, has some heft to it. I just wondered if you used that word before this trial began."

"I beg your pardon?"

"Or was it fed to you by the prosecutor?"

Sloate leaped to his feet. "I object! The insinuation!"

"Insinuation is not a grounds for objection," Rogers said calmly. "Surely the witness can answer for himself."

Kit remembered something Rogers had told her. *Sometimes the question is as powerful as the answer.*

"You have stepped over the line," Ganges said. "Mr. Sloate's reputation is well known."

"That's why I asked the question," said Rogers.

Howls of laughter from the courtroom. Kit looked across at John Barrymore, who was enjoying himself enormously. Aunt Freddy, in the back, seemed nonplussed. She caught Kit's eye, then looked down.

"Let us move on," Rogers said. "Officer O'Toole, how long have you been a police officer in Los Angeles?"

"About four years."

"And before that?"

"I served on the force in New York City, I'm proud to say."

"Yes, it's a famous police force, isn't it?"

"Sure it is, sir."

"Why did you leave it?"

"Sir?"

"Why did you leave the New York City police force, where you so proudly served?"

O'Toole shifted in his seat. "I . . . saw that there were opportunities here."

"Just thought you might try something new, eh?"

"Something like that, yes."

"It couldn't be that you had a reason to leave New York, could it?"

"Reason?"

"Other than what you've told us." Rogers waved his arm at the men in the jury box, as if he were one of them, too.

"No, sir," O'Toole said firmly. "I just wanted to try me hand out here."

"I see," said Rogers. He turned and walked to his table, where he picked up a letter that had been folded neatly under a law book. Kit knew which letter it was.

Rogers opened the letter and looked at it a moment. Then to Officer O'Toole he said, "Isn't it true, Officer O'Toole, that you were drummed out of the New York City force for taking money from prostitutes for protection?"

The color drained from O'Toole's face. His chin dropped.

Sloate quickly objected. "I demand to know the basis for this scurrilous charge!"

Rogers said, "Your Honor, I have a letter here from Mrs. Melle Stanleyetta Titus, of the University of New York Law School. She has referenced the date and page of the *New York Times* where this item appeared. Shall I read it to the court?"

"No," Sloate said. "This is not admissible evidence! We have no way to test the veracity of this letter."

"That's quite true," Judge Ganges quickly agreed.

"Your Honor," Rogers said, "I do not wish to introduce this letter into evidence. I was merely answering the query of my esteemed colleague, Mr. Sloate. This is the basis upon which I am asking Officer O'Toole the question. He can answer with a simple yes or no as to whether the charge is true."

For a moment no one said anything. The judge seemed to be

considering what to do, as if all this was new ground for him.

"Very well," the judge said finally. "Answer yes or no and we will continue."

Kit watched O'Toole's face. He had been given time to think. The judge had apparently given him a way out. Only one answer was necessary to get him out of the uncomfortable situation. "No," he said. "That charge is not true."

But the truth of it seemed written across O'Toole's face. Kit looked at the jurors, as Rogers had instructed her to do, and tried to determine what they thought. Their faces were impassive.

Then with a voice dripping with contempt, Earl Rogers said, "I have no further use of this witness."

From the looks of it, things had not gone well for Heath Sloate. But the trial had only just begun.

Chapter Thirty-one

SLOATE'S NEXT WITNESS was the county coroner, Raymond J. Smith. Sloate led him quickly through the same testimony the medical expert had given at the preliminary hearing. This time, Kit noted, Smith lingered longer over the details of the wound. Sloate must have told him to make it as grisly as possible.

Rogers wasted no time in getting to the point of his cross-examination. He held in his hand a sheaf of papers.

"Dr. Smith," he said, "do you recall my questioning you during the preliminary hearing?"

"Yes, sir."

Rogers looked at one of the pages in his hand. "And at that time, do you remember my asking you about the direction of the knife across the throat of the victim?"

"Yes."

"And did you not say that the direction was from the victim's right side to her left side?"

"I believe I said that, yes."

"You believe? It's here in the transcript. Shall I show it to you?"

"No, sir. That is what I said."

"I see. Your Honor, I would at this time like to give the jury a demonstration of the doctor's testimony."

Before the judge could say anything, Rogers turned to Kit and motioned for her to come forward. As Kit rose, feeling the gaze of everyone in the courtroom, she heard Judge Ganges say, "Mr. Rogers, just what are you proposing?"

"Surely Your Honor wishes the jurors to be clear on what actually happened?"

"Of course, I . . ."

"Thank you, Your Honor."

Kit was now standing next to Earl Rogers. She looked toward the back of the courtroom and saw Aunt Freddy fanning herself vigorously.

Rogers reached into his briefcase and pulled out a large hunting knife. Several spectators gasped.

"I have here a knife similar to the one the coroner has said was used to kill Millie Ryan." He held it up for all to see.

"Your Honor," Heath Sloate said, "must we continue with this?"

Judge Ganges looked at the jurors with a furrowed expression. "I think the jury would be helped by this, Mr. Sloate." He nodded at Rogers to continue.

Rogers took Kit by the arm and placed her in front of him, so she was facing the jury. Her pulse was pounding to the point she thought the whole courtroom must be able to hear it.

"Now," said Rogers, "to be consistent with the testimony of the doctor, the wound to Millie Ryan must have been administered this way."

Kit felt Rogers' right hand reach around her, across her chest, until he could grab her left arm. Then he reached with his left hand, which held the knife, so the blade was poised in front of Kit. "Don't move," he whispered to her.

He made a quick cutting motion, from Kit's right to her left, just in front of her neck.

A woman in the first row screamed. The jurors looked at Kit, mesmerized. Her knees wobbled slightly.

"So," Rogers said, releasing Kit, "the wound would have been administered by a man who is left-handed!"

Dr. Smith did not look flustered. "Or," he added, "from the front by a man who is right-handed."

Rogers nodded, then said to Kit, "Thank you, my dear."

Kit resumed her seat, but not before she saw Barrymore give her silent applause. Aunt Freddy had her eyes closed.

To the witness Rogers said, "If this wound were administered from the front, the killer would have been covered with the victim's blood, isn't that true?"

"Not necessarily."

Rogers seemed surprised by this answer. He took up the transcript pages again and turned to one. "Didn't I ask you at the preliminary hearing about the projection of the blood?"

"I recall that, yes."

Rogers read from the page. "And didn't I ask, 'When the carotid artery is severed in this manner, the blood is projected outward in a violent fashion.' Do you recall that?"

"Yes."

"And did you answer 'Yes, sir'?"

"I believe I did," Smith said.

"Thank you. Now about this violent projection of blood—"

He was interrupted by Heath Sloate. "Your Honor, the witness has not been allowed to answer fully."

Rogers turned on him. "The witness most certainly did answer!"

"All right, all right," said the judge. "You want to add anything, Doctor?"

"Yes," said Smith.

"I protest!" Rogers said.

"I'm asking the questions now," said the judge. "You go ahead, Doctor."

Smith looked calm as he spoke. "There are some instances when the issue of blood would not be violent from a wound like this," he said. "Certain conditions of blood flow and the like. There is no one way these things happen."

The judge looked satisfied. So did Sloate. Rogers did not. He said, "You didn't qualify your answer at the preliminary hearing, did you, Doctor?"

"I've had a chance to think about it."

"Then you weren't thinking at the preliminary hearing?"

"Objection," said Sloate.

"Sustained," said the judge.

"No more questions," said Rogers.

Heath Sloate, looking a bit stunned, stood up. "Your Honor, the prosecution requests a recess until tomorrow morning."

Rogers snapped, "But we're just getting started here!"

Judge Ganges banged his gavel. "We'll be in recess until tomorrow morning at nine o'clock." And as quickly as that he was off the bench.

Was this an attempt by the judge to get Sloate off the hook? It seemed to Kit that Rogers had done a masterful job on cross-examination. Sloate would need time to think, all right.

Kit then stood and was immediately set upon by two people—Barrymore and Phelps. Was this to be a repeat of the earlier scene? Would a fight break out here in court?

"Please, Miss Shannon," Phelps said, casting a wary eye at Barrymore.

"Brigand!" Barrymore said.

"Please, one minute of your time!" Phelps said.

"Nay!" said Barrymore.

"In Christian charity!" Phelps said.

Kit almost smiled. Phelps was clearly desperate to talk to her, and he had pulled out his biggest gun, an appeal to her faith! Now she was curious. What harm would a minute do?

"One minute—no more," she said. "I have to help Mr. Rogers."

Phelps's face showed ample signs of relief. Barrymore's, however, was less sanguine. His eyebrow was raised almost to the top of his head.

"If you need me," Barrymore said to Kit, "I shall be at the ready." And with a disdainful glance at Phelps, he left the room.

"I want you to know something," Phelps said.

"I'm listening."

"That story that came out about you and the case and all the intimate details—I didn't write that."

"It had your name on it."

"But I did not write the story."

"Do you really expect me to believe that?" Kit studied his face, as she would have a juror or witness.

"No," Phelps said. "I don't. But at least let me tell you what happened."

Kit folded her arms and waited.

"I did make notes about our meeting that day with Pearl Morton and about this case. And I was intending to write the story. I was angry."

"Why?"

"You know why. I did not like getting the brush-off. Call it male vanity."

"Go on."

"But I couldn't write it. I didn't feel it was right. You thought we were off the record, and as a reporter, I had to respect that," Tom concluded.

"Then how did the story appear?"

"A kid in the office by the name of Bloomfield, a cub reporter who wants to be famous, heard me talking about it, and he transcribed my notes. He turned the story in with my name on it! When it came out I hit the roof. I throttled him. He begged me not to tell. Had this sob story about an invalid mother. Well, I just let it go. But the story was out."

"Anything else?" she said.

"Will you accept my apology?"

"All right."

"Will you let me make it up to you?"

"There is no need. I must go."

"Please!"

"Well," Kit said, "maybe I can think of something." She turned and left him.

Kit returned to Rogers and helped gather up notes and files, placing them in her briefcase. He told her to head back to the office, where he would meet up with her later.

Outside the courthouse the weather had turned dark and cold. Kit started down the steps when she looked left and saw, at the far end of the portico, the figure of Heath Sloate leaning over the trembling form of her great aunt.

Kit's blood stirred at the sight. Unable to ignore them and Sloate's likely manipulation of her aunt, she hurried toward them. As soon as she got there, Kit could see that Aunt Freddy's eyes were red with tears. Those same eyes widened as she saw her niece. The look made Heath Sloate whirl around to Kit. His eyes burned with a hatred more intense than she had ever seen.

"What are you doing to my aunt?" Kit said quickly.

"This is no business of yours!" he said.

"Aunt Freddy, are you all right?"

"Oh, dear!" said Aunt Freddy.

"Leave now!" Sloate said.

"I will not!" said Kit. "This is not court, and you do not have a judge to hide behind. I will not let you hurt my aunt anymore."

There was a chilled silence that hung between them. And then, as suddenly as lightning, Heath Sloate slapped Kit across the cheek.

Kit put her hand to her face. She was too stunned to say anything.

Sloate glared at her. "How dare you insult me! Leave us!"

Kit looked at Aunt Freddy. Her poor face seemed a battlefield of contrary emotions. For an instant Kit feared for her aunt's heart.

Then, suddenly, as if a general had amassed his chaotic troops and formed them into a resolute line, Aunt Freddy's face turned hard.

"No," she said to Heath Sloate. "*You* leave us."

If thunder had clapped at that moment, Kit would not have been more shocked. Nor, apparently, would Sloate have been. His mouth fell open, and his upper lip began to curl. "What are you saying?"

"I don't ever want to see you again," Freddy said.

"But, Freddy . . ."

"Bosh! You may call me Mrs. Fairbank!"

"And what of our arrangement? What of the park you wish to see arranged in your departed husband's honor?" His voice was honey smooth as he seemed to regain his confidence.

"Jasper would jump in his grave if he knew it came at the price of turning against family. It would be a memorial of shame, should I turn away from my niece in order to get it."

"Then what about us?" he said.

Freddy hesitated then. Kit could feel the struggle inside her aunt.

"No," Freddy said finally. "There is no more us."

Sloate looked at Kit, and in his eyes she saw a certain panic, as if all his carefully laid plans had been blown apart. He quickly recovered and bore in on Kit.

"You. You are the cause of all this." His voice rang with pure hatred. "You have been nothing but trouble ever since you came here." He looked at Freddy. "And you, you silly old woman! Why I wasted my time on you is beyond me. By the time I finish with you, you won't be able to show your face anywhere in town. You have crossed the wrong man."

He spun around, and Kit suppressed the urge to stick her foot out and trip him down the steps.

"Oh, dear," Aunt Freddy said, her hand on her chest.

Kit, without a moment's hesitation, put her arm around her aunt and said without any qualm, "You leave everything to me."

"But Heath! He will do what he says! We must get Madame Zindorf to tell us—"

"No! You listen to me." Kit took Aunt Freddy's shoulders in her hands and looked her in the eye. "God is who we will depend on. Not Madame Whosit and no magic spells. Do you understand? The Lord is our light and our salvation; whom shall we fear? Sloate can't hurt you anymore. God will be our strength. Agreed?"

Aunt Freddy nodded her head meekly. "All right," she whispered.

"Good."

"But Heath . . . what will you do?"

"I don't know," Kit said. "Yet."

Chapter Thirty-two

THE NEXT MORNING, Heath Sloate called Rita Alonzo to the stand. She seemed nervous, but with Sloate's gentle prodding, she walked through what Kit knew was a well-rehearsed story.

The jurors looked as if they had no qualms that Rita herself was a prostitute. Who else would they expect to have seen things in that neighborhood?

But Kit and Rogers were prepared for cross-examination.

"Miss Alonzo," said Rogers, treating the witness with gentle tones, "you testified that you saw my client, Mr. Fox, running from the room of the victim."

Rita looked warily at Rogers. "Yes, that is what I say."

"You also told this jury that you saw no blood on the clothes of my client."

"No. No blood."

"You are sure about that?"

"Sure, yes."

"As sure as you are that it was my client that you saw?"

Rita Alonzo nodded, but appeared to be leery of Rogers and where he was leading her.

Rogers maintained his deferential tone of voice. "By the way, Miss Alonzo, you said that you saw all this from your own doorway, is that correct?"

"Yes, I do."

"Across Alameda Street."

"That is right."

"How far is that view, Miss Alonzo?"

"How far?"

"Yes, if you know."

Rita shook her head, as if thinking. Then she pointed to the back of the courtroom. "Here to there," she said.

"I see. So we can say that someone standing in the far corner of this courtroom would be approximately the same distance as my client was from you that night?"

Rita shrugged her shoulders.

"Is that right, Miss Alonzo?"

"Yes, right, yes." She cast a quick look at the jurors.

"Your Honor, if I may," said Rogers.

"May what?" said Judge Ganges.

Turning to the gallery, Rogers nodded his head. John Barrymore stood and walked to the far corner.

"My colleague, Mr. John Barrymore, is now standing approximately the same distance from Miss Alonzo as she alleges my client was on the night she says she saw him."

Barrymore smiled, causing one woman in attendance to sigh loudly, and waved to the jury.

"Will the court accept that?" said Rogers.

Ganges looked toward Sloate, then quickly back at Rogers. "What is your point?"

"I'm getting to that." Rogers nodded at Kit and, as planned, she walked to the large courtroom window and pulled the slatted blinds shut. Before the judge could say anything, Rogers signaled the bailiff, who turned off the lone electric light illuminating the room.

The courtroom was now in virtual darkness.

"Miss Alonzo!" Rogers said loudly. "Can you see my colleague now?"

"Objection!" Sloate's voice.

But the damage was done. There was no way the jury could ignore what was in front of their eyes.

"Give me the light back right now!" the judge bellowed. Kit quickly opened the blinds and the bailiff switched on the light. "Mr. Rogers, that was outrageous."

"But, Your Honor, I merely wanted to re-create the scene for the jurors. It was the dead of night on Alameda Street when the witness says she could see my client. The jury is entitled to see for themselves."

As Kit sat down she watched Judge Ganges closely. Rogers had cleverly placed him between the proverbial rock and hard place. The judge could admonish the jury to disregard what they had just seen, but that would be futile. There was no way they would be able to disgorge the vivid memory. Yet if he left it alone, the image would have tremendous impact—and the judge was clearly not there to help Earl Rogers.

Then the solution came. Judge Ganges looked at Rita Alonzo and said, "Miss Alonzo, how were you able to see the defendant that night? Wasn't it dark?"

The witness sat up straight. "No. The moon was full. Very bright light. Not like in this room!"

Satisfied, the judge nodded and said, "You may resume, Mr. Rogers, but no more tricks."

Earl Rogers paused to let his consternation be known. Having the judge accuse him of trickery was tantamount to telling the jury that he was trying to deceive them. Kit had no idea what the jurors might be thinking now.

To Rita Alonzo, Rogers said, "There are no streetlamps on Alameda, are there, Miss Alonzo?"

"No, but the moon."

"Yes, we have heard about the moon."

"Very bright."

"So you have said." Rogers turned and walked to the rail. Kit handed him the booklet she had been holding all the while.

As everyone in the courtroom watched him, Rogers slowly thumbed through the booklet until he reached a certain page. "If I may, Your Honor. I have here a copy of *Farmer's Almanac*. I'm sure Your Honor will take judicial notice of its authority."

Judge Ganges scowled.

"What relevance?" Sloate said.

"Good question," said the judge.

"Only this," said Rogers. "On August ten of this year, the moon was only in its first quarter!"

A wave of muttering voices passed through the courtroom. Kit felt the effect, and it thrilled her. As a girl she had read Abraham Lincoln's famous cross-examination of Charles Allen. Allen had testified he saw Lincoln's client commit murder by the light of a full moon. But Lincoln had produced an almanac, proving the moon was nowhere close to full. If it was good enough for Abe Lincoln . . .

Heath Sloate barked, "Your Honor, this is outrageous. Mr. Rogers has testified! He is not a witness. I demand that his remarks be stricken from the record."

"But I ask," Rogers said, "that the *Farmer's Almanac* be entered into evidence!"

Judge Ganges banged the gavel for order. Then he pointed the gavel at Rogers, making it look like a weapon. "I have warned you, Mr. Rogers! I have warned you repeatedly! I am going to hold you in contempt of court!"

Rogers did not back down. "And I shall appeal."

"That is your privilege," said the judge. Then he looked to the jury. "Gentlemen, you will disregard what counsel for the defense has said here. His remarks about the almanac are ordered stricken from the record, and you will not take anything he has said into consideration when you deliberate. And counsel's motion to move the almanac into evidence is denied. The court levies a fine of one hundred dollars on Mr. Rogers for contempt."

The judge paused to catch his breath. "Now, do you have any more questions for this witness?"

Keeping composed, Rogers said, "Yes. Who told you to lie under oath?"

"Objection!" cried Sloate.

"Two hundred dollars, Mr. Rogers," said the judge. "Now sit down, sir!"

Rogers returned to his chair.

"May this witness be excused?" Judge Ganges asked.

"Just one more thing," Sloate said, standing. As he did, Kit got the terrible feeling that Sloate had something up his sleeve.

"Miss Alonzo," he said. "Did you know the victim, Millie Ryan, well?"

"Oh yes," she said. "She was my friend."

"Did she wear any distinctive jewelry?"

Without hesitation, Rita said, "Yes. She wore, how you say, a locket?"

"Can you describe this locket?"

"It was very pretty. Gold. With a cross on it."

"A cross?"

"Yes."

"If you saw this locket, would you be able to recognize it?"

"Oh yes. It was very pretty, as I say. She would let me look at it always."

Sloate walked to the witness stand, reached into the pocket of his coat, and pulled out a gold locket on a chain. He laid it on the rail in front of Rita Alonzo. "Is this the locket?"

Rita picked it up. "Yes! This is the one!"

"Thank you," said Sloate. "You may step down."

Kit saw Rogers turn toward Ted, then look at her as if to say, "What do you know about this?" Kit shook her head. It was Millie's necklace! She remembered seeing it when she had talked to Millie at the jail.

Her eyes rose to meet Ted's blank expression. Kit was unable to hide the disappointment that she knew must be evident on her face. Without a word, Ted dropped his head as if signaling defeat.

What did it all mean? What did Sloate have up his sleeve?

She could tell from the look on Rogers' face that he also had no idea.

Chapter Thirty-three

"THE PROSECUTION CALLS Chief of Police Orel Hoover," Sloate said.

From the back of the courtroom, the stolid chief sauntered down the aisle, came through the swinging gate, and stood in front of the witness stand. The court clerk approached with a Bible. Hoover placed his left hand on the book, raised his right, and swore to tell the truth, the whole truth, and nothing but the truth, "so help me God."

What was this? Kit and Rogers never had any idea that the Chief of Police himself would be a witness. What could he possibly offer that was relevant? He was an administrator, not a witness. Anything he might say that recounted conversations would be hearsay, inadmissible evidence. Then again, the way Judge Ganges was going, anything might happen.

Rogers leaned forward in his chair, his intense concentration on the witness.

Sloate began with Hoover's qualifications and years of service. And then he asked him if he had been to the scene of the crime.

"I was the first to arrive after the report came in," said Hoover.

"Did you conduct an investigation of the scene?" asked Sloate.

"I did."

"What, if anything, did you find?"

"A young woman's body and lots of blood."

"What did you do next?"

"I ordered the officer with me to keep people out of the room and then called the coroner's office."

"All routine, is that correct?"

"Correct, sir."

Sloate paced in front of the jury box as he asked the next few questions. "You ordered the arrest of the defendant, did you not?"

"I did, yes."

"On what basis?"

"The description supplied by the witness Rita Alonzo."

"Now, after the arrest, what did you do relating to the investigation?"

"I secured a search warrant for the defendant's residence."

This was news to Kit, and obviously to Rogers, who was sitting up rigidly.

"And did you lead the search?"

"I did."

"Were there any other officers with you?"

"Yes. Two others."

"What, if anything, did you find?"

Before he stated it, Kit knew the answer. It all fit so neatly.

"A gold locket," said Chief of Police Orel Hoover.

Now there was no restraining the noise in the courtroom. All around Kit, voices chattered and mumbled and made outright exclamations of surprise. A man behind her said, "He's as good as hanged."

Her heart sinking like a rock, Kit could find no voice inside herself to disagree.

Sloate's nail was not fully in the coffin. He took up the locket that Rita Alonzo had identified and showed it to Hoover. "Is this the locket you found at the residence of the defendant, Theodore Fox?"

Barely looking at it, Hoover said, "It is."

"Nothing further," Sloate said triumphantly. He returned to his chair, the locket dangling from his fingers. The jury seemed mesmerized by the gilded pendant.

"Take the witness, Mr. Rogers," Judge Ganges said.

What would he do? He and Kit had not prepared anything for Hoover. It was an intentional deceit by the prosecution which, Kit knew, had no obligation to reveal whom it would call. It was the defense's job to anticipate who would be on the stand.

If ever there was a moment for Earl Rogers to demonstrate his courtroom wizardry, this was it.

Lorgnette in hand, Rogers gave Hoover a long, long look. There was no hiding his derision. This would not be a gentle cross-examination.

"Chief Hoover," Rogers began at last, "it is quite unusual for a Chief of Police to take an active role in an investigation, is it not?"

"Not so unusual," the Chief said. "I have done it before."

"When was the last time?"

"Let's see . . . maybe a few months ago."

"What case?"

"I can't recall at the moment."

"We'll give you more time. Think about it," Rogers urged.

Hoover scowled. "I cannot recall."

"You cannot recall, yet you are sure it was only a few months ago."

"Yes, sir."

"How many months is a few?"

"I . . . four, five."

"Your office would have records of this alleged investigation, would it not?"

Heath Sloate said, "Objection. Relevance."

"Sustained," said the judge.

"All right," said Earl Rogers. "You have political ambitions, don't you?"

"Objection!" Sloate cried.

"Of what relevance is this, Mr. Rogers?" Judge Ganges said.

Rogers turned to the judge. "Credibility, Your Honor. I believe this testimony is politically motivated, and I demand the chance to show it."

Judge Ganges stroked his chin and looked at the witness. Kit watched closely. Hoover glanced at the judge with an expression that seemed to say "I can handle it." He may even have nodded his head.

"I'll allow just a few more questions," said Judge Ganges. "Then you will move on, Mr. Rogers."

"Thank you, Judge." Rogers looked at Hoover. "You may answer."

"I have no more or fewer political ambitions than the next man. I do my job to the best of my ability, and if I think I can serve the people of this city or state in some further capacity, I will surely consider it."

The answer seemed to sit well with the jury. Kit saw a couple of the jurors nod.

"You are married?" said Rogers.

"I'm a widower," Hoover said.

"You have a son, don't you?"

"Yes."

"Where is he?"

"He's been sent back East."

"Sent?"

"I mean, he's gone back there."

"Why is that?"

"For his education. College."

"So you have no family here in the city?"

"No, sir."

Judge Ganges interrupted. "That's enough, Mr. Rogers. Change your line of questioning."

"I just have one more question, Your Honor. Chief Hoover, isn't it true that, to enhance your political reputation, you have injected yourself into this case and made yourself into some sort of hero?"

Immediately, Hoover's expression turned to outrage. His cheeks reddened. Even as Sloate stood up to object, Hoover spat his answer. "That is a lie! I have an unblemished record as a police officer, and I resent your insinuation!"

"No further questions," said Earl Rogers. As he turned to sit down Kit thought she saw, for the first time since the start of trial, a look of fear in his eyes.

As Hoover left the stand, Heath Sloate stood up and announced, "The prosecution rests."

Ganges said, "We will break for lunch and reconvene at one o'clock, at which time the defense will begin its case."

"Your Honor!" Rogers said.

"What is it?"

"In view of . . . in view of everything, the defense would request a longer recess."

"Mr. Rogers, I am mindful of the time this jury is putting in."

"I am only asking for a few hours."

"Mr. Sloate, have you any objection?"

With feigned courtesy, Sloate said, "Not in the least, Your Honor."

"Well, all right, then," said the judge. "Back here at three o'clock to begin. Gentlemen of the jury, enjoy a long, leisurely lunch."

He banged his gavel with a foreboding solemnity.

Chapter Thirty-four

BACK IN CHAMBERS, Judge Wiley Ganges pointed a finger at Heath Sloate. "This is going too far!"

"Calm yourself," Sloate said, his voice grating to the judge's ears. Ganges felt himself reaching a breaking point. How had he ever allowed a poisonous snake like Heath Sloate to get the better of him? How?

This was not what he thought being a judge would come to. A jurist with strings attached, made to dance by some unprincipled puppet master.

Yet whom could he blame but himself? He had succumbed to the temptations of the flesh, though to this point he had managed to hide it from his own family.

"You know I will protect you in every way," said Sloate.

"That is small comfort, Sloate."

"I am a man of my word. You will have only to make the ruling I have proposed."

"But you are winning!"

"Maybe. But Rogers has a way with a jury. I cannot afford to take that chance."

Ganges slapped his fist on the desk. "What you are doing flies in the face of everything this system of justice holds dear!"

Sloate seemed singularly unmoved. "You just continue to follow my lead," he said, "and all will be well."

"How do you account for the locket?"

Kit faced Ted in the tiny cell in the back of the courtroom. They were alone now, the deputy having locked her inside with her client. While Rogers was presumably gathering everyone back at the office, Kit was determined to get to the bottom of Hoover's stunning testimony. Either the Chief of Police of Los Angeles was lying, or Ted Fox was not innocent after all.

Ted, looking tired, said, "I can't account for it."

"Try," Kit said firmly.

He looked at her with sunken eyes. "How?"

"Did you take it?"

"No. I never saw it before."

"Then how did it get into your house?"

"I have no idea."

Kit looked into his eyes. "Was it planted there?"

"It must have been."

"By whom? The police?"

"Who else?"

Kit let out an angry breath. "Ted, where were you on the night of August tenth?"

"I've already told you."

"I don't believe you."

"You now accuse me of lying?"

"Yes."

Ted's face reflected astonishment and, in a subtle way, respect. But he did not answer.

Kit's mind was now racing, looking for pieces to fit together. And then, somewhere in the back, a picture started to form.

"You're protecting someone," she said. "And I think I know who it is."

Ted's eyes told her she was right. He looked at her silently, waiting.

"Your mother."

Ted looked at the floor. "How did you find out?"

"I didn't. You just told me."

Ted looked up, surprised.

"I had my suspicions. When I went to see your mother, she kept making the sign of the cross. But you're not Catholic. Why would your mother do such a thing? Because she was taken to the Catholic asylum in San Fernando."

Ted took a deep breath, looking as if he were going to protest. But then he slowly nodded his head. "When the police found her, wandering the street, she was in such a state they took her there. They thought she was just some crazy woman from shanty town. I had to go get her."

"You didn't want anyone to find out," Kit said.

"All she has left is her social standing in this city, and I don't want that taken away from her. Ever since my father died, when I was nine, she has sacrificed for me. I know what people like Heath Sloate can do to her."

"Sloate?"

"He sold a piece of worthless land to her. You remember that day we drove out to the bluff? That land is ours. Ten years ago my mother entered into an agreement with Sloate, without my knowing about it. I didn't find out about this until last year. I confronted

329

Sloate, but he said there was nothing I could do. He said if I tried he would see to it that my mother's reputation, everything she has meant to this community, would be ruined. You remember the night I was arrested?"

"How could I forget?"

"I asked you about being of sound mind."

"Yes!"

"That wasn't about me. It was about mother. I wanted to know if that contract would be good if she entered it under duress from Sloate."

Kit frowned. "But why were you running from the police?"

A half smile toyed with Ted's face. "I threatened Sloate that day. Told him I was going to break his neck if he didn't take that land back. Not a smart thing to do, I suppose."

Kit could not disagree. That was playing into Sloate's hands. "Go on."

"That night a cop wagon pulled up to my house. So I took off."

Shaking her head, Kit said, "Flight is always construed by the police as a sign of guilt."

"Now you tell me. I thought they were arresting me for the threat to Sloate, not for the murder that occurred the night before. I think he set me up!"

Of course! But how were they ever going to show it? How could they if Ted remained resigned?

Suddenly she said, "Are you just going to let Sloate run you to the gallows? What do you think *that* will do to your mother?"

Ted put his head in his hands.

"You can't just give up," Kit said.

"Why not?"

"It's your life!"

"What life? We are particles of matter stitched together. Darwin taught us that."

Kit's hands balled into fists. "Darwin! Is Darwin God?"

"No," said Ted. "But Darwin has shown us there is no God."

"Then Darwin is a fool! And so is anybody else who believes that twaddle! You are not just particles, Mr. Fox. You are a man. You are a living soul. You have a purpose."

"What purpose would that be, Miss Shannon?"

"Do you remember that night we met? At my aunt's home?"

"Ah yes, the social event of the season."

"You told me something then. You said that you were going to fly someday."

"That seems far away."

"Tell me why you want to fly."

"I don't anymore."

"Then tell me why you once did."

For a moment Ted seemed to stare off into the past. "I remember, when I was a boy, when we were in England. My father took me to the cliffs at Dover. It was a clear, clean day. And as I looked out over the channel there, I remember a gull floated—just floated—by us. He was so close I could almost touch him. He didn't flap his wings at all, just rose on the breeze, as if . . ."

Pausing, Ted looked as if he were reliving the moment, free of this holding cell, free of everything.

". . . as if to say to me, 'Come on! Why don't you join me?' And right there I felt something in me. I still don't know what it was, but it was so real."

"Did you ever consider that it might have been the voice of God?"

Ted looked at her with a certain incredulity, but said nothing.

"God is seen in His creation," Kit said. "The heavens declare His glory. We cannot help but respond. Perhaps it was God who told you to take man into the skies, like the gulls."

Suddenly Ted did something Kit had not seen him do for

weeks. He smiled. And his eyes, tired though they were, danced. "And don't you have more than a bit of the divine spark in you, Kit Shannon. In your tongue, at least."

For a moment Kit forgot about everything else. Here again was the man she had met that night. But just as quickly the reality of the situation came crashing back. "You are going to have to take the stand and tell the jury exactly what happened," Kit said.

"No, Kit. I won't do it. I can't."

Kit shook her head. If he would not take the stand in his own defense, there was nothing she—or Earl Rogers—could do. But could she just stand idly by while he let himself get convicted? There had to be some way.

And then, suddenly, like some bright light flashing into a dark room, an answer came.

"I must go," she said.

"Where?" Ted said.

Kit called for the guard.

———

Earl Rogers sat in the dark corner, in a booth away from the crowd. He wanted a drink. Wanted it bad. The locket had done it. Sloate had the upper hand now. Rogers could sense, even without talking to Kit, that the jury had been duly impressed.

The locket! It smelled to high heaven, but there it was.

He looked at his sandwich for the third time without picking it up. His stomach tightened, his nerves shredded. Pinpricks of goose-flesh popped out on his arms. What was happening to him? Had he finally come to the end of the line, the great courtroom lawyer, about to lose to the worst of all possible opponents, Heath Sloate?

No! Always he had found a way. He would now.

Wouldn't he?

"Mr. Rogers?"

His head snapped up. A young man smiled at him. Rogers was in no mood for conversation. "I'm having my lunch."

"I can see that," the man said. He stuck out his hand. "Bloomfield's my name. I write for the *Examiner*. And I have to tell you, Mr. Rogers, I think you're going to do it."

"Do what?"

"Win. Mind if I sit?"

Rogers hesitated, then nodded his head toward the opposite bench.

"I'm covering the trial," Bloomfield said.

"I thought your paper had Tom Phelps on the case."

"There's a little friendly competition. That's why I'm here. I was hoping to get an exclusive story from you. And to offer you a bit of help."

"Help?"

"I know something. Something about Sloate. Maybe something I shouldn't know, but I know. Interested?"

Rogers eyed the reporter. "I'm listening."

"Let me buy you a beer."

"No, I—"

"I insist. Waiter!"

The kid already had his hand up, and the prospect of one glass of cold beer was one Earl Rogers found inviting. Most inviting. He did not protest further.

Chapter Thirty-five

THE CABBIE WAS ACCOMMODATING, racing to get her to San Fernando as quickly as possible. But would it be time enough? Would Rogers think her as crazy as the inmates she would soon see?

The Mission at San Fernando was an adobe structure, white against the dirt of the farmland. Inside the walls of the courtyard, Kit could see trees with gnarled branches and a few dark-skinned mission Indians engaged in various labors.

Just beyond the church, with its crowning cornice topped by a cross, lay a somewhat larger, though flatter, building. On the facing wall Kit saw a row of small windows, each with black bars like a jail cell.

The asylum.

"Wait here," she ordered the driver.

Kit hopped out and approached the forbidding wooden doors

at the front of the building. She tried to open them. Locked. She knocked.

No response. Behind her, a crow made a cawing sound. She turned and saw the bird sitting on a branch in dead tree.

Kit knocked on the door again. This time she heard a latch, and the door opened.

A *padre* wearing a brown robe cinched at the waist with a rope stood in the dark doorway. His eyes squinted at the sun. "What is it, daughter?" he said.

"Father, my name is Kit Shannon. I wish to speak with Thomas Ryan."

"Eh?"

"He is in your employ, I believe."

"I know Thomas, but I do not know you." The priest's florid face was rigidly set. He did not move from the door.

"If you please, Father, I am here on a matter of business."

"We care nothing of business here, daughter. This is a place of refuge for the infirm. For them, business is of no concern."

"My business is with Mr. Ryan." Kit felt her growing impatience bubbling to the surface.

"Mr. Ryan is occupied."

"Please."

"I am sorry." The priest began to close the door. Kit put her hand on it. This seemed to surprise the padre even more than her presence.

"You are a Franciscan," she said.

The priest, eyes wide now, nodded.

"Was it not St. Francis who prayed to the Lord to be an instrument of his peace? That where there is despair, he would sow hope?"

"Why, yes."

"That is why I am here, Father. As an instrument of the Lord's mercy. Please believe me when I tell you this is so."

The priest paused, studying her face. Then he opened the door for her.

Inside, the spare chamber was dark. A wooden table with a lone candle sat in the corner.

"You may wait here," said the priest. He grabbed a large ring of keys from the table and unlocked a door behind it.

"Father?"

"Yes?"

"May I go with you?"

The priest paused and regarded her closely. "What is behind this door would disturb you."

"Please."

"Very well," said the priest. He motioned for Kit to follow him. "But stay close to me."

They entered a long hallway. It smelled like a stable, only worse. Kit noticed straw along the floor, but not fresh straw. There were doors with barred windows along the corridor. A low moan came from somewhere, like a wounded animal. But it was not an animal. It was a human being. Kit looked at the priest. He seemed not to hear it.

Then a scream sounded! At Kit's right, a hand stuck out through the bars of one of the doors. The fingers, inches from her hair, were gnarled, clawlike. She gasped in horror and stumbled back.

"Watch it there!" the priest said, moving Kit to a more central position in the corridor. Then, with his keys, he rapped the knuckles of the extended hand. Another scream, and the hand withdrew.

"Come," he ordered.

Kit followed, aware now of every sound, every movement, but not looking behind the doors. The images in her mind were frightful enough.

Finally, at the end of the corridor, the priest unlocked another door. Through this Kit passed into a large room. She gasped.

The room was filled with human misery. Some bodies, seemingly lifeless, lay curled on the floor, while others moved in purposeless circles. Various sounds emanated from the mass, incoherent and despondent. Kit saw two inmates secured to the walls by leather straps.

A number of priests walked about, occasionally stopping to pray or speak with one of the unfortunates. There were some men in white clothes who carried buckets and brushes and were cleaning here and there. Another man with a pail of water and ladle was giving a drink to one of the restrained men.

Kit recognized the water-bearer as Thomas Ryan.

"Thomas," the priest called.

Ryan looked at them. His mouth dropped open when he recognized Kit. "Miss Shannon!"

"Hello, Thomas."

He came to her and took her hand. "I never expected."

"May we talk?" Kit said.

To the priest, Ryan said, "May we go outside, Father?"

"Ten minutes," said the priest.

"Thank you." Ryan motioned for Kit to follow. He led her out a side door to a small courtyard on the side of the building. "Do you bring news of the trial?" Ryan said.

"Some," said Kit.

"I have not been able to come." Ryan looked at the ground. "You are helping to defend this man?"

"Yes."

"Is he the one who killed my girl?"

"No."

Ryan brought his eyes up to Kit. "Then who?"

"Thomas, that's why I've come. I need your help."

"Me?"

"I need to ask you some questions, and I haven't much time. Will you help me?"

He smiled. "I would do anything for you, Miss Shannon."

"Thank you, Thomas."

And then she began the most important interview of her life.

Chapter Thirty-six

KIT ENTERED THE COURTROOM at five minutes past three. Her body was buzzing. She had to talk to Rogers before the trial commenced.

She saw familiar faces, including John Barrymore, in the gallery. And Aunt Freddy was there, this time with Corazón by her side! When Corazón smiled at her, Kit felt a sense of calm wash over her. But it left quickly when she discovered that Earl Rogers was not in the courtroom.

She saw Judge Ganges talking to Heath Sloate at the bench. Next to Sloate stood a policeman. Something had happened.

Kit moved down the aisle and through the gate. Ted was at the counsel table. "Where's Earl?" she whispered.

"He hasn't come yet," Ted said.

"What is going on at the bench?"

"I don't know. This police officer came in, and he and Sloate have been talking to the judge."

Kit rushed to the bench. Even before she got there, the judge's face exploded with consternation. "Young woman!" he said.

"Where is Mr. Rogers?" she said.

"You get back to the gallery now!"

"This is a conference in open court," she said. "And the defense has a right to be part of it!" Kit felt Sloate's eyes boring in on her from the side.

"I will have you cited!" Ganges said.

"Wait," said Sloate calmly. "We might as well inform Miss Shannon as something of a representative of the defense."

Ganges said, "Well, all right then."

"Go ahead, Judge," said Sloate.

With barely concealed disdain, Ganges looked at Kit and said, "Your employer was picked up in the gutter, dead drunk."

An invisible hand grabbed Kit by the throat.

"This officer," Ganges said, "reported it. Rogers was so far gone they took him to a hospital. Well, that's conduct I won't stand for. If he has such contempt for the law I, as a representative of the law, have the power to remove him from the case."

Kit fought to keep control. "What are you saying?"

"What I am saying, young woman, is that Earl Rogers is no longer the attorney for the defendant. Mr. Sloate and I are discussing a new trial and who might be assigned to do it."

Kit looked at Sloate, at the judge, then back at Sloate. There was now no question in her mind. These two had conspired. They had been conspiring all along. Yet the brunt of her anger was at Earl Rogers. Drunk! How could he do this to Ted? To her? How could he have been so uncaring?

"Now you will remove yourself from the floor," Judge Ganges said.

"Your Honor," Kit said, not moving. The judge flashed his eyes her way. "I would beg the court to allow us time for Mr. Rogers to recover."

After a quick glance at Sloate, Ganges said, "Denied. And you are not to speak to me further! Now go before I have you removed."

Kit turned back to the counsel table. Ted looked at her, pleading with his eyes for her to tell him what was happening.

Then she remembered the letter. The one Rogers had given her when she first went to the county jail. She had saved it, and it was in her briefcase now. She opened the briefcase and took it out, not knowing if it would do any good.

But she could not walk away. Ted's life was hanging in the balance. Without Rogers to defend him, he was as good as dead.

Suddenly Kit was aware of the silence in the place. She looked up from the letter and saw what seemed like all of Los Angeles looking back at her. There were Barrymore and Phelps and Chief Hoover and Aunt Freddy. There was a deputy sheriff, standing at the door, and faces looking in through the door's windows.

And there she was, Kit Shannon, knowing this moment could not be lost. For what she had was something that could not wait.

"Your Honor," she said. "The defense wishes to present its case!"

Now the hush in the courtroom was broken by the low rumble of voices. Kit felt the paper shaking in her hand. Her knees were shaking more. What had she just said?

"What did you say?" said Judge Ganges.

Kit approached the bench, each step laborious. But she did not stop. She handed the letter to Ganges, who snatched it. "What is this?" he said.

"That is the appointment of an agent by Earl Rogers. You will see my name written there."

Judge Wiley Ganges was struck speechless. His eyes kept

looking at the letter up and down. And then he looked at Kit. And while it wasn't explicit, Kit was sure she saw something in Ganges' eyes, something like a spark of admiration for the audacity of her move.

"Let me see that," said Sloate, snatching the letter from the judge.

"Miss Shannon," the judge said to her, his voice softer now. "I cannot allow this."

"But you can," Kit said. And now her mind switched into high gear. She knew she would have to do what Rogers had told her just a few days before—make an argument.

In a flash she remembered something her beloved professor, Mrs. Titus, had told her once in her class in Constitutional law. *"Come, Miss Shannon, make a noise like a lawyer!"*

Now was time to make noise. And the Constitution was the vehicle. Under Mrs. Titus, Kit had come to love and revere this nation's foundational document, especially the first ten amendments known as the Bill of Rights. She had memorized them and the cases interpreting them.

"The Sixth Amendment, Your Honor," Kit said. "In all criminal prosecutions the accused shall enjoy the right to the assistance of counsel for his defense."

"I am aware of the Bill of Rights, Miss Shannon."

"And the accused shall have the right to choose his own counsel."

Judge Ganges appeared to be listening. Kit quickly added, "Mr. Fox has chosen Mr. Rogers, and Mr. Rogers has chosen me to be his agent, and therefore, Your Honor, under the United States Constitution I must be allowed to continue the defense in this case!"

Now Judge Ganges broke into a wide grin. Kit was breathing so hard she thought she might faint. Ganges looked at Sloate and said, "That's a pretty good argument."

Sloate glared at the judge, then at Kit. "You're a very clever girl," Sloate said with disdain. "Too clever by half."

In the face of Sloate's insults, Kit, astonishingly, felt herself growing stronger. "It's not cleverness I am concerned with, Mr. Sloate. It's the Constitution."

"Mr. Sloate," the judge said, "I'm inclined to agree with her."

"You must be joking."

To Kit, Judge Ganges said, "I must warn you, though, that it would be folly for you to try this, Miss Shannon. You are fresh off the turnip cart. Mr. Sloate is a skilled and experienced advocate."

It was true. Kit hesitated. But she did not back down. "I am well aware of Mr. Sloate's . . . attributes. I wish to continue."

"Mr. Sloate?" Ganges said.

"Let her," Heath Sloate said. "I will enjoy watching this woman fall on her face. But before I accede to it, I want it on the record that the client agrees, and that he waives his right to appeal based on this farce."

Judge Ganges called to a deputy. "Bring the defendant up here."

Now the courtroom was so noisy Ganges had to gavel for order. Ted appeared at the bench with a deputy sheriff at his arm.

The judge said, "Your lawyer is incapacitated by drink, and I want him replaced. Miss Shannon, who is not a member of the bar, has nevertheless secured an appointment of authority and wishes to go forward with evidence. If you accept this, Mr. Fox, you will waive your right to appeal this decision. That means if you're convicted, you can't go to a higher court and say you didn't have adequate counsel. Now, you do not have to accept this, and it is my firm advice that you do not. You need an experienced lawyer to represent you, sir. Rest assured you will be assigned good counsel, son."

Ted looked amazed. "You?" he said to Kit.

Kit nodded.

He looked at her intently. "May I speak to my lawyer?" Ted asked the judge.

"She is not your lawyer," Judge Ganges said. "At least not yet. And if you follow my advice she won't be. I'll give you two minutes." Ganges took out his pocket watch.

Kit and Ted went to the side of the bench. "What is going on?" he asked her.

"I have something," she said. "A witness."

Ted's eyes widened.

"If I don't present him now, I'm afraid they'll find out who he is. They'll be able to stop him."

"Then put him on."

"But Ted, the judge is right. I'm not experienced. I'm not even a member of the bar. You can wait for another lawyer to be assigned to you."

"I don't want another lawyer. They'll fix it."

"But—"

He put his hand up. "I trust you. If you think the moment is now, then I want you to do it."

And then he smiled.

Kit felt a surge of assurance. No, she was not experienced, but she knew the case as well as Earl Rogers. If she could just make it through this day, just get her witness on, she could find Rogers, get him back on his feet, keep him sober—and then he could finish the case. She had one witness waiting. She could do it. With God's help, she could do it.

"All right," she said. "Let's tell the judge."

They walked back to Ganges and Sloate. "I am quite satisfied," Ted said. "Miss Shannon may represent me."

"Well, I'll be," Judge Ganges said. With a thin flicker of a smile he said to Kit, "All right, Miss Shannon. It is so ordered. Your client has chosen to go ahead with you, and he has waived his right to appeal. I feel like saying may God have mercy on your soul."

"I won't mind if you do," Kit said.

"Let's get on with it," said Heath Sloate.

The judge banged his gavel. "Bring in the jury!"

As a bailiff repaired to the jury room, Kit rushed to the rail and motioned to Luther Brown.

"Earl's been hospitalized," she said.

"What!"

"Drunk! Go find him."

Luther looked as stunned as she felt. "I'll do it, Miss Shannon." And he rushed from the courtroom.

Then Kit motioned to Aunt Freddy and Corazón. Her aunt came bounding up, knocking at least one man out of her way, followed by the maid.

"What on earth?" Aunt Freddy said.

"Listen," Kit said. "What was it you told me Uncle Jasper liked to say? Jump first and grow wings later?"

Confused, Aunt Freddy said, "Yes. Exactly."

"Well, I've jumped."

Aunt Freddy shook her head. Kit took Aunt Freddy's hand, and then Corazón's. "And I want you both to pray for God to send me wings."

Corazón smiled widely and said, "Sí. I will pray like you show me how."

"But I," Aunt Freddy said, "I don't know . . . how to pray."

"No time like the present to learn!" Kit said. She turned to watch the jurors entering the courtroom.

When the twelve men had filled the box, the judge addressed them. "Gentlemen, due to a certain . . . set of circumstances, the defense will now commence its case under the direction of Miss

Shannon. Accord her all of the attention you would to any other lawyer."

Kit nodded toward the jurors, who looked upon her as if she were some exotic exhibit at the zoo.

"Call your first witness," said the judge.

This was it. Kit turned toward the back of the courtroom and made a motion toward the door. "The defense calls Thomas Ryan."

He came through the door, looking nervous. He walked down the aisle to Kit, who showed him where to stand. He was sworn in and sat in the witness box. As Kit turned to question him, she saw Heath Sloate watching her like a coiled snake. She would have to proceed carefully.

"Mr. Ryan," Kit began, "you are the father of Millie Ryan?"

"Yes, ma'am."

"What is your employment?"

"I work at the asylum in San Fernando."

"In what capacity?"

"Any capacity that's needed, ma'am."

"Does that include the registration of inmates?"

"Yes, sometimes."

"Were you working there on August the tenth of this year?"

"Yes, ma'am."

"Can you tell us if anyone was admitted on that day or evening?"

Sloate interrupted. "Objection, Your Honor! I demand to know what relevance this witness has to the proceedings."

"If I may be allowed to question the witness," Kit said, "the relevance will be shown. Just as Mr. Sloate did with his witnesses during the prosecution's case."

Clearing his throat, Ganges said, "Well, I will allow you a few more questions."

"Your Honor!" Sloat said.

"A few more questions, I said." Judge Ganges shot Sloate a look of rebuke. Sloate sat down with a stunned look on his face.

"All right, Miss Shannon. But please get to the point."

"Thank you, Your Honor." Kit turned back to the witness: "Was anyone admitted to the asylum on August tenth?"

"There were two, ma'am."

Kit paused and looked at Ted. His eyes were steady but pleading. She went on. "Can you describe the two who were admitted?"

"Yes, ma'am. One was a woman, an older woman. The other was a man of about twenty-five or six, near as I could tell."

"This man, what time was he admitted, if you recall?"

"Oh, I was roused from my quarters very late. Early, really."

"You mean in the early morning hours of August the eleventh?"

"Yes, ma'am."

"Can you describe this young man to us?"

"He looked like a gentleman, but he was agitated, violent. His hands were manacled when he was brought in. His right hand was withered. He couldn't do anything with it."

"Meaning that anything he did would have to be done left-handed?"

"Yes."

"Did this young man have a name?"

"I only heard him called Billy."

"Who called him that?"

"The people that brung him."

"How many people was that?"

"Three men. Policemen."

Kit sensed a small stirring in the gallery. She paused. "After that, Mr. Ryan, what happened to this Billy?"

"He was placed in one of the cells."

"Explain what those are."

"The cells are for the most dangerous inmates. They can be

dangerous to others or to themselves, so they have to be watched close."

"Did you ever refer to this young man as anything but Billy?"

"No, ma'am."

"Did you ever find out his full name?"

"Yes, ma'am. This afternoon."

"And what—"

A voice from the gallery shouted, "Stop!" Kit turned and saw exactly whom she had expected. Orel Hoover's face was red, his forehead gleaming with sweat.

"Leave him alone!" Hoover shouted. He pointed at Kit. "You jackal!"

A startled Judge Ganges almost lost his gavel as he hit the bench. "Order!" he said.

Hoover was undeterred. "Yes, it was my own son who was brought there. He is a sick boy, a good boy whose mind was taken away. Must you drag his poor soul into this? Your Honor, will you let this woman besmirch our good name? She is only trying to hide the truth about her own client! My son is an innocent—"

"Chief Hoover," Judge Ganges said softly.

"He is a good boy, a good boy. Why? Why?" And then Hoover choked on his words. Tears began to stream down his face.

"I will see the lawyers at the bench," Ganges ordered.

Kit's body was shaking as if she had a wild animal by the tail. What had just happened was an explosion, but was it enough? Would the judge allow her further questions?

Heath Sloate did not even wait for the judge to speak. "This is slander," he said. "I want this testimony stricken from the record and Miss Shannon held in contempt."

"For what?" Kit said. "Your Honor, Mr. Sloate is attempting to stop relevant testimony, testimony that could cast more than a reasonable doubt on his case."

"You presume to tell me what I am doing?" Sloate spat. He turned to the judge. "I demand that you stop this."

"You demand?" Judge Ganges said. It was a weak response, and Kit thought she saw a flash of resignation in the judge's eyes. He looked at Kit. "Miss Shannon, the Chief of Police is an honored member of this community. You are attempting to suggest that his son is a murderer."

"And what if he is?" Kit said.

"He is not on trial here," said Ganges. "Unless you can offer me evidence that conclusively ties him to the crime here at issue, I cannot allow you to proceed. You know the rules of evidence?"

"I've studied them."

Sloate snorted disdainfully.

The judge said to Kit, "Do you have any evidence to suggest that Chief Hoover's son is possibly the true killer?"

Kit thought. "The fact that he is left-handed by physical necessity, Your Honor. And the testimony of the coroner that is consistent with a left-handed slashing wound from behind."

"Nonsense," said Sloate. "The evidence is inconclusive on that issue. We have no way of knowing what hand the killer used. Miss Shannon is grasping at straws."

Judge Ganges curled one end of his mustache with the thumb and forefinger of his right hand. Kit watched him curl the hairs as if she were hypnotized. The case—Ted's life—was hanging by those slender whiskers.

"I am sorry, Miss Shannon," Judge Ganges said. "I cannot allow you to ask any more questions of this witness on this issue."

"But—"

"No, Miss Shannon."

"What about the contempt?" Sloate said.

"I will not hold her in contempt," Ganges snapped at Sloate. "She's been admonished. That's enough."

Sloate glared at the judge in a way that seemed itself to be in contempt. The judge glared back.

Judge Ganges then turned to the jury. "Gentlemen, the testimony that you have just heard was improper, and is not to be considered by you in any way during your deliberations. And I order the reporter not to record the testimony."

Not enough, Kit thought. *I did not give them enough.* She was sure the real killer was in the asylum, that it was the son of the police chief. But now that testimony had been taken away.

"Do you have further questions on any other matters, Miss Shannon?"

Kit felt the case draining away like sand in her fingers. Should she have Thomas Ryan testify about Ted's mother? It seemed the only way to establish even the possibility of an alibi.

But Ted, what would his reaction be? If he cried out in the courtroom, that could mean the end of the case. The jury would likely read guilt in his protest.

Her head felt light. She looked across the courtroom at Heath Sloate, who had a smug smile on his face. Then she looked out into the gallery, at the sea of faces. For a brief moment all the faces blended together.

Then she saw one that stood out. And she knew immediately what she would do.

"The defense calls Elinor Wynn," Kit said.

Even from where she stood, Kit saw Elinor's face drain of color. The socialite looked right, then left, as if searching for a life preserver after falling off a ship.

"Elinor Wynn," the bailiff intoned.

As if pulled up by invisible strings, Elinor Wynn stood. She did not walk forward immediately, but waited, as if expecting someone to save her.

Heath Sloate said, "What possible relevance is this witness, Your Honor?"

Kit did not hesitate. "If Mr. Sloate will allow me, it will become apparent."

"But I will not allow . . ." Sloate cut himself off.

"Come to the bench!" Ganges said.

Once there, Sloate spoke immediately. "This is a clear attempt to confuse the jury."

"How do you know without her asking a question?" Ganges said.

"You must not allow this witness!"

Kit said nothing. She sensed a power struggle here, and her instincts told her to let it play out.

Judge Ganges said, "I am still the judge here, Mr. Sloate. I will make the decisions about what evidence is admissible."

Sloate scowled. "Aren't you forgetting something?"

Ganges paused. "What I have forgotten, Mr. Sloate, is that I swore a duty to the cause of justice a long time ago."

Kit wondered what he meant by that, and why it should be coming up now. She saw Sloate glance quickly at her, as if he were about to say something, but stopped himself because of her presence.

"Miss Shannon," Ganges said, "I'll allow a few questions. But I want to see the relevance quickly."

"Yes, Your Honor."

"Miss Wynn, take the stand."

Slowly Elinor walked forward. Trying to keep her face impassive under her large, wide-brimmed hat, she did not glance at Kit until she was sworn and seated.

Kit approached the witness. She felt remarkably calm, surprising herself. She should have been almost faint with nervousness, but she wasn't. It was as if she were meant for this moment and was fitting into it like a hand in a glove. She remembered Rogers telling her that she could size people up. Something told her Elinor was the key.

She remembered the day she had gone to see her. The butler thought she had come from Sloate's office. That meant a connection between her and Sloate, but just how much or what relevance it had she was not sure.

All she knew was that she had only a few questions with which to find out.

"Miss Wynn," said Kit, "you know my client well, do you not?"

"I know him, yes." Elinor said.

"You were, in fact, engaged to be married."

"Yes, that is true."

"What happened to the engagement?"

"I broke it off."

Kit nodded. "You loved Ted Fox, did you not?"

After a pause, Elinor said, "Yes, of course."

"Then why did you break off the engagement?"

"Well, I . . . I did not feel that Mr. Fox was willing to do the things a proper husband should do."

"Such as?"

"Such as earn a decent wage so as to take care of his family."

"Is that the only reason?"

Seemingly caught off guard, Elinor stammered her next words. "What other reasons are there? People fall out of love. It happens."

"Or perhaps they fall in love with another?"

"What are you insinuating?"

"Miss Wynn," said Kit, "did you in fact break off your engagement to Ted Fox because of your involvement with another man?"

"Objection!" Sloate was on his feet, storming to the middle of the courtroom.

Judge Ganges paused, his face scrunched in thought. Kit looked at Elinor and saw that her face was twitching and her eyes... Once, as a girl, Kit had seen the eyes of a doe caught in a net as hunters closed in around it. Those were the eyes Elinor Wynn had now. Kit was closing in, she knew, but how far would the judge allow her to go?

"Miss Shannon," said Judge Ganges finally, "is this line of questioning relevant? Because if it is not, I must stop it now."

"Your Honor, if you will allow me just a few more questions, I will show the relevance."

"I object!" said Sloate.

"Overruled!" Ganges said with a firmness that surprised Kit.

For a long moment Heath Sloate stood there, unmoving. It was as if he were trying to will the judge to change his order.

"Resume your seat," said the judge. "You may continue, Miss Shannon."

After Sloate stonily sat down, Kit turned back to the witness and took another leap without wings. "Miss Wynn, how well do you know the prosecuting attorney?"

Elinor Wynn's expression could not have been more telling. The exact nature of her relationship with Sloate was a mystery, but knowing Sloate, Kit was sure it was something indecent. And deeper mysteries were bubbling to the surface of Elinor Wynn's face.

"Your Honor!" Sloate pleaded. "That is an improper question!"

"I believe the witness can answer it," said the judge.

"Would you like me to repeat the question?" Kit asked.

Eyes beginning to dart, Elinor said, "Yes."

"I asked you how well you know the prosecuting attorney."

"I have known him socially. He is a prominent member of our community."

"Has he ever been to your house?"

"Of course. I have had many people of importance at my social gatherings."

"Has he ever come to your house alone?"

"Objection!" Sloate was on his feet and two steps toward Kit. "The insinuation is outrageous!" He pointed a bony finger at Kit. "This woman is dragging our great system of justice through the mud!"

The sight of Sloate's finger was almost more than Kit could stand. "Your Honor," she said, "it is Mr. Sloate who needs a hose!"

The courtroom burst into laughter. Even a few of the jurors laughed, some hiding their mouths with their hands. Sloate himself seemed shocked to the core, but he quickly said, "Do you see the disrespect, Your Honor?"

Judge Ganges put up his hand. "Now, now. Let us all settle down. What are you driving at, Miss Shannon?"

Kit was not entirely sure, but there was, in the far reaches of her mind, a picture forming. It was not yet clear, but it had order and logic to it. And if she was right, it explained everything about this case. Absolutely everything.

"I want to ask this witness about her relationship with the prosecutor, Mr. Sloate."

"No, Your Honor," Sloate protested. "That is strictly out of bounds."

"Why, Mr. Sloate?" the judge said.

"Because . . ." Sloate looked as if he were searching for the answer. "Well, it is just improper."

"That's not good enough," said Judge Ganges. "Go ahead, Miss Shannon."

"Miss Wynn," said Kit, "isn't it a fact that Mr. Fox is the one who broke the engagement?"

"Why . . . no."

"And isn't it a fact that you were so outraged that you sought advice from Mr. Heath Sloate on what you might do to exact revenge?"

"No!"

But the answer was yes. Kit saw it in Elinor's eyes. But could the jury see it?

Now was the time to switch subjects. Kit sensed it. Her mind flashed to what Rogers had told her about cross-examining the lying witness, about misdirecting her until the right moment, then suddenly changing course. It was a matter of instinct, he'd said. Well, that is what she was depending on now. In a distant region of her mind she uttered a silent prayer, then faced Elinor Wynn once more.

"Miss Wynn, do you remember my coming to see you two days ago?"

Elinor Wynn tried to square her shoulders. "I most certainly do, and I did not like your manner one bit."

A few people laughed in the audience. Kit could not tell to whom it was directed—the imperious Elinor Wynn or herself, an object of social scorn.

"Besides my manner," Kit said, "do you recall that I asked you to tell me the last time you saw Mr. Fox face-to-face?"

"I recall that, yes."

"And what did you tell me?"

"I told you it was sometime in July."

"Was it?"

"Yes. That is what I told you."

"Miss Wynn, do you know what perjury is?"

"Of course . . . I do."

"You swore an oath to tell the truth, did you not?"

Elinor Wynn nodded her head affirmatively.

"And do you know there are criminal penalties for perjury, for lying under oath?"

"Yes."

"Then you still have a chance."

"Chance?"

"In fact, Miss Wynn, you saw my client on the evening of August eleventh, didn't you?"

The startled look on Elinor's face was almost as clear as an audible response.

"Didn't you, Miss Wynn?"

"I . . ."

"Didn't you go to the home of Ted Fox on the evening of August eleventh?"

"No."

"The day after the murder of Millie Ryan?"

"I don't know about Millie Ryan."

"Miss Wynn, isn't it true that on the night of August eleventh you went to Ted Fox's house and secretly placed a locket there?"

"Objection!" Sloate said.

"Who put you up to it, Miss Wynn?" Kit said quickly.

"Objection!" Sloate cried again. "Your Honor, stop this immediately!"

"Let the witness answer!" Kit said.

"No," Sloate said. "You must call a halt to these proceedings immediately!"

Judge Ganges banged for silence in the courtroom. It took almost a full minute for the noise to subside. In that span Kit felt suspended in the air, as if by some invisible rope. The rope was on a limb that thrust out over a cliff. Everything would depend on what the judge did next. She studied his face and saw deep rumination there. What was he thinking?

Finally, stroking his mustache, Judge Ganges' eyes turned toward Heath Sloate. "I will allow Miss Shannon to continue."

"No!" Sloate said. "The prosecution objects!"

"Overruled!"

Feeling all the eyes in the courtroom trained on her, Kit slowly walked to the counsel table. She reached into her briefcase and pulled out a single file folder. She opened it and scanned the page that was inserted there. Then she looked up at Elinor Wynn.

"This is your last chance to answer truthfully, Miss Wynn. There are others who will be questioned about this, under oath." Kit raised the file folder for all to see, especially Elinor Wynn. "Did you or did you not place Millie Ryan's locket in Ted Fox's house?"

Elinor began to shudder. And then the dam burst. Tears streamed out of her eyes as she muttered, "Yes, yes, yes."

Kit did not hesitate. "Who put you up to it, Miss Wynn?"

"If the court please!" Sloate shouted.

"Who, Miss Wynn?"

The brim of Elinor's hat shook with her sobs. She lifted a quivering finger and pointed at the prosecutor. "Heath Sloate."

The courtroom erupted in a chaos of voices.

Chapter Thirty-seven

EARL ROGERS SLAPPED HIS HAND to his head, which felt as though it was filled with anvils. On each anvil a sadistic blacksmith was pounding, pounding. He heard himself groan.

He had no idea where he was. He knew he was on his back in a bed of some kind, in a white room that smelled of antiseptic. But beyond that he was lost.

The trial! Vague inklings of reality came to him now. The trial was on, yet he was here. What had happened?

Had somebody jumped him? Smashed him over the head? Tried to kill him? Maybe...

No. He had been in a restaurant... a drink! A reporter had offered him a drink, and he had taken it. He must have taken many more, too. He'd gone over the edge.

Moaning, he put his hands over his eyes. What would happen

to him now? To his reputation? And what would happen to his client? To Kit?

He tried to sit up, but the blacksmiths hit their anvils with even greater force. He moaned again.

Then he heard a voice. A woman's voice. "Now, don't you try moving just yet, Mr. Rogers."

He strived to focus and saw a white-smocked nurse standing over him, her severe features a warning in and of themselves. "Where am I?" he managed to say.

"Sisters' Hospital."

"Who brought me here?"

"I am sure I don't know."

"What day is it?"

"Now see here, you rest."

"But my trial!" He attempted to raise himself, but was met with two strong, resistant hands.

"You are a very sick man, Mr. Rogers," the severe nurse said. "You are not going anywhere. And may I say that your consumption of alcohol is doing you no earthly good."

And a moralist! Rogers closed his eyes, resigned to his imprisonment. And like any inmate in a penitentiary, he would be forced to confront his guilt. The bottle! It had mocked him, knocked him down to a place where he might never recover. No doubt there were already stories circulating. The papers would be full of it. The great Earl Rogers defeated, not by any prosecuting attorney, but by John Barleycorn!

He thought of Kit, imagined her look of disappointment. The imagined visage cut him like a knife. His thoughts turned to God. His father's God, Kit's God—did He have any deliverance left for him?

"Please," said Rogers, his head beginning to reclaim some notion of clarity. "I must get out of here."

The nurse had no sympathy. "You have to rest, Mr. Rogers, there's no two ways—"

He heard a commotion outside his door. A familiar voice shouted, "We have to see him!" Luther Brown's voice!

This was met by a woman's voice saying, "He is not to be disturbed!"

Then Rogers saw Luther step into the room, his right arm held by a desperate nurse. "Earl!" he said.

"See here!" said the desperate nurse.

Rogers forced himself up on one elbow. "Let him in!" he shouted.

"But, Mr. Rogers—" the nurse by his bed started to say.

"Hang it all, just let him in!"

At least his voice was coming back. The force of it brought everyone to a standstill. Luther Brown jerked his arm away and made a motion. Then into the room came Kit Shannon and Bill Jory.

"Kit!" Rogers said. "Bill! What's happening?"

"Please," the desperate nurse said. "Everyone must leave."

"No!" said Rogers. "I want these people here!"

"Then I'll go get a doctor!"

"Good," said Rogers. "And take her with you!" He jerked a thumb at the nurse by his bed. With a loud *harrumph* the desperate nurse left, followed quickly by the other.

"Tell me what is going on," Rogers said.

"It's over," Jory said.

"What is?"

"The trial!" Jory said. "Ganges dismissed the charges! And he ordered the arrest of Heath Sloate!"

"Arrest? Sloate?" Rogers rubbed his head. "What on earth happened in that courtroom?"

Jory told him. He recounted everything in dramatic detail,

spinning it like a yarn that would be told for years to come. "Elinor Wynn is spilling her insides to the police right now. And you should have heard old Sloate squeal when they took him away," Jory said. "Like a stuck pig, he was. But old Ganges, I don't know, he seemed pretty happy about it."

Rogers shook his head in amazement. "Kit," he said, "how did you find Hoover's son?"

Kit stepped forward and told him of her trip to the asylum. "I went to talk to Thomas Ryan about Ted's mother," she said. "I was almost attacked by an immate with a disfigured hand. As I spoke to Thomas, that kept playing in my mind. It was a right hand. I asked Thomas who it was. He knew him only as Billy."

"Short for William," Rogers said. "William Hoover."

"I met him briefly at a party at my aunt's," Kit said. "I remember it was curious how he kept his hands in his pockets. Now we know why."

"But tell me," Rogers said, "how did you figure Elinor Wynn as the one who planted the locket?"

"Process of elimination," Kit said. "The police went to search Ted's house in a group, and it would have been difficult to sustain a group conspiracy, especially if Earl Rogers was the one asking the questions. That left only someone who had access to Ted's house. His mother is bedridden. Only Elinor Wynn comes to mind. Added to that, she lied about when she had last seen Ted. And you know the rules of evidence—a witness who is willfully false in one material part of her testimony is to be distrusted in others."

Rogers nodded. "Good, Kit. Very good. Now, what I really want to know is what was on that piece of paper you waved in front of Elinor Wynn when you asked about planting the locket."

"Yes, me too," said Jory. "Whatever it was, a list of witnesses or some sworn statement, it did the trick."

"I . . ." Kit said.

"Come clean," urged Rogers.

Kit cleared her throat. "Just something I had written once."

"What was it?"

"A verse from the Bible. 'I can do all things through Christ which strengtheneth me.'"

Rogers shook his head incredulously.

"I had intended to give it to you one day," Kit explained. "But at the time it was the only thing I could find to hold in my hands."

"Because you wanted Elinor Wynn to be thinking about what you had."

Kit smiled sheepishly.

"Ah, Kit Shannon! If you weren't a woman, I would swear you were me!"

Everyone in the room laughed.

"I want that paper," Rogers said. "I have a feeling it will be famous someday." As he looked into Kit's eyes, Rogers endured a throb of remorse. "Kit," he said, holding up his hand to her. "I'm sorry."

"No," she said, taking his hand. "You don't have anything to be sorry for."

"But I do. I got stinking drunk."

"No, you had a drink."

He shook his head, uncomprehending.

Kit looked to the door. "Bring him in, Tom."

A moment later Tom Phelps walked into the room. In his fist he held the collar of a young man who looked dazed, like someone had pummeled him angrily. Rogers recognized him. It was that reporter from the restaurant!

"Evening, Mr. Rogers," said Phelps.

"What's going on?" Rogers said.

"This is Hector Bloomfield," Phelps said. "Tell him, Hector."

The young man hesitated. Phelps slapped his ear.

"Ow!" Bloomfield cried. "Okay, okay. I slipped something in your beer."

"You what?"

Phelps said, "Chloral hydrate, Mr. Rogers. Knocks you out like a jug of hard liquor. Now, why would someone do such a thing?"

"Don't tell me," Rogers said. "Heath Sloate was behind it."

Bloomfield hung motionless, like meat on a hook. Phelps slapped his ear again. Then Bloomfield nodded sheepishly.

"And he's ready to tell the whole story," Phelps added. "Aren't you, Hector?"

This time the young man nodded without prodding.

"You're gonna be okay, boss," Bill Jory said. "But Heath Sloate is in a heap of trouble."

"Unless he gets a good defense lawyer," Earl Rogers said. Then he added, "Can anybody think of one?"

Everyone, with the exception of Hector Bloomfield, erupted into laughter.

Chapter Thirty-eight

"MISS SHANNON," said Judge Wiley Ganges, "can you tell me what a Writ of Error Coram Nobis is?"

"Yes, Your Honor," Kit said. She was sitting in Judge Ganges' chambers. Earl Rogers sat next to her but said not a word. "A Writ of Error Coram Nobis is a common law writ, to correct a judgment in the same court in which it was entered, upon the ground of error of fact."

Ganges smiled. His eyes twinkled. "Quite correct, Miss Shannon. How about Res Ipsa Loquitur?"

"A rebuttable presumption that the defendant was negligent, based upon proof that the instrumentality causing injury was in the defendant's exclusive control, and such accident is one that does not ordinarily happen in the absence of negligence."

"Right again. And what is the lawyer's responsibility in our system of justice?"

"To represent the client with competence, loyalty, and zeal, but always with an obligation to the law, justice, honesty, and the avoidance of obstructive conduct."

Ganges looked at Rogers. "I couldn't have said it better myself." Rogers smiled.

"All right, then, Miss Shannon. This concludes my bar examination. You passed. Please stand up and raise your right hand."

Kit stood and raised her hand proudly.

The judge said, "Kathleen Shannon, having satisfactorily passed my examination on your fitness for the bar, and having been sponsored by a member in good standing and, may I add, having impressed the skeptic right out of me, I am now going to swear you in as a full member of the California bar. Do you, Miss Shannon, solemnly swear to uphold the Constitutions of the United States and the State of California and to honor the standards of the legal profession, so help you God?"

"I do," Kit said. "So help me God."

"Congratulations, counsel," Ganges said, extending his hand.

"Thank you," she said.

She turned to Earl Rogers and embraced him. "And thank *you*," she said.

"Come on," Rogers said. "There's something I want to show you."

It was a clear, brilliant day in Los Angeles. Rogers took them by carriage down Spring Street, turning right on First and coming to a stop in front of his office. "I'll be sad to see you go," he said.

"What?"

"I'm afraid you'll be leaving my office."

Kit's heart jumped. "But why?" She turned then and saw Aunt Freddy and Corazón coming down the steps of the building.

"Well, it's about time!" Aunt Freddy huffed.

Kit stepped out of the carriage. "What are you doing here?"

"Why, to see the product of my patronage, of course."

Corazón smiled broadly, as if hiding a precious secret.

"Will someone please tell me what is going on?" Kit said.

"Look," Corazón said, pointing upward.

Kit raised her eyes to the second-story window at the corner of the building. There, in gold lettering, it said:

Kathleen Shannon
Attorney-at-Law

"But . . ." Kit said, a hundred questions flooding her mind.

"But nothing," Aunt Freddy said. "I will pay for this office until you can. In return, I want your personal legal services. For free." She paused and fanned her face with her hand. "I cannot believe I am saying this."

Tears of gratitude leaped into Kit's eyes. She threw her arms around her aunt and pulled her close. "Oh, thank you!"

"Now, now," said Aunt Freddy. "Don't thank me yet. I still cling to the hope that you may change your mind and decide to abandon this flight of fancy."

"Don't you worry, Aunt Freddy. I know there's much I need to learn in order to be socially acceptable, and you will teach me! But I can also practice law, which means everything to me—with exception to my love for you."

"Mercy," Freddy said, looking momentarily flustered. "A good reputation is hard earned and easily lost, Jasper used to say. But in spite of everything, I must say you did a good job in that courtroom. Oh, dear!"

"I don't mean to break into this wonderful reunion," Earl Rogers said. "But what do you say we go take a look upstairs?"

It was a small office but clean and bright. The sun shining through the window cast the letters of her name—now backward shadows—on the floor. A walnut desk and chair sat near the window. Bookshelves, waiting to be filled, lined the walls.

"It's beautiful," Kit said.

"It needs curtains," Aunt Freddy said. "Perhaps a heavy damask, something with a print, I think." She sized the window up as if planning it all in her mind.

Kit sat down behind the desk, totally amazed at all that surrounded her. Her gaze then settled on the top of her desk and a framed photograph.

"Oh!" she gasped and carefully took up the picture. Touching the dark wooden frame, she forced back the tears that threatened to spill. "Where did you get this?"

Freddy put her hand on Kit's shoulder. "I contacted your cousin Victoria. Through no small feat we were able to lay our hands on this, and I felt it should be a part of your new life—just as they were a part of your old life."

Kit stared at the photograph of her mother and father. The photograph, taken on her parents' wedding day, was probably the only picture in existence of the couple. Money and time had never been spared for such frivolous things.

She looked at the radiant face of her mother. So young, and so much like herself. Kit was nearly stunned by the easily recognizable expression. Her father, strikingly handsome and self-assured, stood by her mother's side—just as he had in life.

"There are no words . . ." Kit said, dabbing her tears with the back of her sleeve. Aunt Freddy handed Kit a handkerchief and gently patted her shoulder.

Corazón, who had managed to blend quietly into the background, moved forward to place a small piece of framed embroidery work atop Kit's desk. "When I work on my English letters and writing, Sally help me to make this for you. This is my thank-you."

Kit picked up the piece and smiled. " 'The truth shall set you free,' " she read aloud, then turned it to display it for everyone to see. Her gaze met Corazon's, and tears shone brightly in the younger woman's eyes. "Thank you," Kit whispered, knowing she was desperately close to crying again. "Thank you all."

Freddy tapped her parasol on the floor. "It's time we gave Kit a moment to herself. Come, Corazón. Kit, we shall have dinner at the house promptly at six! And you . . ." Aunt Freddy turned imperiously to Earl Rogers. Her next words seemed to be uttered with some effort. "I shall expect you and your family as well."

Rogers smiled widely and bowed. "It shall be my great pleasure to dine with one of the most beautiful flowers in the garden of Los Angeles."

Freddy's face flushed and fought against the smile that suddenly appeared. "Why, you *are* a devil, aren't you? Until six, then!" And with a mighty swoosh of her dress and train, and with Corazón following, Aunt Freddy left the office.

Earl Rogers said, "I will refer cases to you, of course, but I would still like to have your association on occasion."

Kit smiled. "Yes, Earl. So long as I believe the client is innocent."

"But together we can win *any* case."

"I believe that justice is what should win."

"Ah, Kit. You're still a little wet behind the ears, you know."

"I know."

"Even though, for the moment, you may be the most famous person in the city."

"That will pass."

"Don't be so sure. And I can still teach you a thing or two."

"I know I have much to learn from you, Earl."

"Then what is the most important thing I've taught you?"

Kit pondered a moment.

Rogers said, "Get the money first!"

Shaking her head, Kit said, "I hope that will not be my downfall."

Rogers laughed. "I'll try to be there to catch you." He bowed and exited.

For a long time Kit sat gazing out the window at First Street, at the bustling parade of pedestrians below. She remembered what Tom Phelps had said as they were about to arrive in Los Angeles. *". . . the City of Angels isn't as refined as your eastern hubbubs. We still have one boot in the Wild West."*

Kit nodded as she noted the mixture of carriages and people and even one sputtering automobile on the street. Spit-and-polish businessmen shared the street with rough-and-tumble cowboys. The new met the old in Los Angeles.

"The other boot is kicking at the new century," she murmured aloud, leaning her forehead against the glass. She whispered a prayer of thanksgiving, asking God once again to help her bring glory and honor to His name through the practice of law.

She heard a quick knock as her door opened. In walked Ted Fox.

He was a completely different man from the one who had so recently been sitting, resigned to fate, in a dank jail cell. His suit was crisp, his face clean-shaven under a white skimmer, and the sparkle was back in his sapphire-blue eyes.

"I'm seeking a good lawyer," he said, smiling.

Kit smiled in return, and her feelings took her back to that night they met, when Ted Fox had seemed ready to climb into the sky. "And if you found one," said Kit, "what would you need of . . . her?"

"I would need a yes."

"To what?"

"To an invitation to lunch. With me."

"Is this a purely professional offer?"

"Not quite. Something of the personal, too."

"How personal?"

His face grew serious for a moment. "I would like to thank the most amazing woman I know. And I would like her to tell me more about the voice of God."

A warmth enveloped Kit, like the embrace of a gentle summer's day. It was a warmth of belonging. All of this was so right. Los Angeles was her city now, her home. The people here were her people.

And Ted Fox?

Kit looked down at her bare desktop and said, "It appears my calendar is open."

Author's Note

COURTROOMS AT THE TURN of the last century were a wide open affair. The strict rules of evidence we have today were still in the process of being developed. The lawyer who knew the rules that did exist, and who could argue from their rationales, was an advocate many steps ahead of an opponent who was less diligent.

Trials were studies in resourceful combat. One of the most potent weapons of warfare, of course, is surprise. The same held true for courtroom battles. Today's rules of discovery—wherein the parties to a lawsuit must exchange their evidence and information *before* trial—were virtually unknown in 1903. Either side could wait to present its full evidence until the actual trial. Thus, the surprise witness was not an uncommon occurrence. That's why the best trial lawyers were those who could think quickly on their feet in court, anticipate what the other side might try to present to the jury, and who were ready with their own "bombshells."

Many things that are common in today's courtrooms, such as demonstrative evidence (models and exhibits created to visually show the jury aspects of a case), were in their infancy at the turn of the century. During the 1800s, trials were often viewed as contests in oratory. The lawyer who could turn a phrase, who could mesmerize a jury with a speech—this was the lawyer who often won.

But as the modern era began, innovations started to appear in courtrooms, just as they were flowering in industry and the arts. The idea of showing a jury a deceased's actual intestines would have been inconceivable in 1850. When Earl Rogers, an actual Los Angeles trial lawyer, did so, it was hailed as a great step forward in the art of trying cases.

Rogers also understood that a trial—especially a criminal trial where a man's fate was hanging in the balance—is a drama. To the jury it is not a study in law. It is a story, with good and evil in ceaseless conflict. The best trial lawyers learned to view the facts from the perspective of the common man. Today many trial lawyers enroll in drama and storytelling courses to hone their abilities in this area.

Another major leap Earl Rogers took was the study of human nature. Today we are familiar with so-called "jury consultants" who compile mountains of data about individuals in an attempt to predict their biases. Rogers undertook the study of people using simple observation and common sense. He systematized his observations and was extraordinarily successful at it.

Needless to say, in the early 1900s women were a rarity in the legal profession. And women trial lawyers were virtually non-existent. Only a few women were admitted to the California bar in the early 1900s. Not one was a full-time trial lawyer. This is where the saga of Kit Shannon begins.

A Lone-Star Romance
from
JUDITH PELLA

Judith Pella is the author of several acclaimed historical series including THE RUSSIANS with Michael Phillips and RIBBONS WEST with Tracie Peterson. Now she moves to the frontier land of Texas with a riveting tale that blends together the lives of the courageous pioneers with a poignant, graceful romance about a woman redeemed from a life of shame. You will not soon forget these heart-tugging stories.

Texas Angel

When Elise Toussaint Hearne's dangerous secret is revealed, she and her infant daughter are disowned and soon forced to make the journey to frontier Rio Grande as slaves. There she meets Benjamin Sinclair, a New England evangelist determined to convert the lawless Texans with a strong dose of retribution. Elise, who discovers God through a borrowed New Testament, shows Benjamin that God may have a better way to draw the people of Texas to himself.

Softcover; $10.99 ISBN 0-7642-2278-3

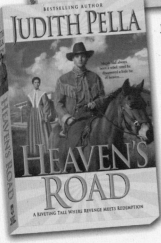

Heaven's Road

From fighting the Mexican army to battling his own father, Micah Sinclair is overcome by bitterness. Faced with nearly certain death, Sinclair is amazed to escape with his life and soon finds himself changing in the face of one woman's unconditional love. Lucie looks to the good in his heart and loves him despite all that needs altering in his life. Will her love be enough? In *Heaven's Road*, it's not only the rugged frontier that needs taming.

Softcover; $10.99 ISBN 0-7642-2279-1

BETHANYHOUSE

11400 Hampshire Ave. S.
Minneapolis, MN 55438
1-800-328-6109
www.bethanyhouse.com

Available from your nearest Christian bookstore (800) 991-7747 or from Bethany House Publishers